PENGUIN TWENTIETH-CENTURY CLASSICS

FIREFLIES

Shiva Naipaul was born in 1945 in Port of Spain, Trinidad. He was educated at Queen's Royal College and St Mary's College in Trinidad and at University College, Oxford. He married in 1967 and had one son. His books include *Fireflies* (1970), which won the Jock Campbell New Statesman Award, the John Llewellyn Rhys Memorial Prize and the Winifred Holtby Prize; *The Chip-Chip Gatherers* (1973), which won a Whitbread Literary Award; *North of South* (1978), the story of his remarkable journey through Africa; *Black and White* (1980); *A Hot Country* (1983); and *Beyond the Dragon's Mouth: Stories and Pieces* (1984). Many of his books are published in Penguin Twentieth-Century Classics, including *A Man of Mystery and Other Stories* (1995), a selection of stories taken from *Beyond the Dragon's Mouth*. Shiva Naipaul died in 1985 aged only forty. David Holloway in the *Daily Telegraph* wrote, 'We have lost one of the most talented and wide-ranging writers of his generation.'

Shiva Naipaul

Fireflies

Penguin Books

PENGUIN BOOKS

Published by the Penguin Group
Penguin Books Ltd, 27 Wrights Lane, London W8 5TZ, England
Penguin Books USA Inc., 375 Hudson Street, New York, New York 10014, USA
Penguin Books Australia Ltd, Ringwood, Victoria, Australia
Penguin Books Canada Ltd, 10 Alcorn Avenue, Toronto, Ontario, Canada M4V 3B2
Penguin Books (NZ) Ltd, 182–190 Wairau Road, Auckland 10, New Zealand

Penguin Books Ltd, Registered Offices: Harmondsworth, Middlesex, England

First published in Great Britain by André Deutsch 1970
First published in the USA by
Alfred A. Knopf, Inc. 1971
Published in Penguin Books in Great Britain in
a simultaneous edition 1970 and in the USA 1984

Printed in England by Clays Ltd, St Ives plc
Set in Linotype Times

To my mother

Part One

Chapter One

1

For Baby, the marriage was a bad one, but it never entered her head that she might complain or refuse to marry Ram. As a girl, she was automatically of less importance; as an indirect descendant (the elder Mrs Khoja was her great-aunt), she hardly mattered. Fortunately, in her eyes what others might have considered an injustice, she considered a law of life. Her pride did not centre on her own person, but resided in the greatness of the Khojas. Thus she accepted without demur the plans of others and married into a family about which she neither knew nor cared.

Ram Lutchman was not a particularly good-looking man, having a tendency to fat. He had a light-complexioned skin, a round face with heavy-lidded eyes and thick, sensual lips which, even when he was not speaking, remained slightly parted. He had married at twenty-three. His parents had arranged the match and he had met his wife only twice before the wedding-day. The Lutchmans considered it a coup. The Khojas were the acknowledged leaders of the Hindu community in Trinidad. They owned several thousand acres of land, an impressive array of jewellery and two big houses, one in Port-of-Spain, the other in the country. To gain even a minor footing there was an achievement and the older Mr Lutchman was well pleased with the arrangements he had made for his son. He was a selfish man and saw the union largely in terms of the advantages he hoped to derive from it. In subsequent years he fawned, flattered and attempted to propitiate first the elder Mrs Khoja and then, when she had been reduced by the infirmities of old age, her son and heir, Govind. With the elder Mrs Khoja he had had no success at all, but he had been slightly more fortunate with her son. Govind Khoja gave him advice about farming (this despite the fact he knew virtually nothing about it) and once went so far as to joke about the political situation with him. The elder Mr Lutchman was grateful for these small favours, regretting only that his wife was not alive to share them with him. He treasured these intimacies until his death.

His son Ram did not complain. For him, marriage to a Khoja meant an opportunity for him to raise his head above the anonymities of Doon Town, an anonymity that had brought the Lutchmans to the verge of social extinction. Ram drove buses for the Central Trinidad Bus Company, whose chief depot and headquarters was in Doon Town. He had left school at sixteen, an education that had lasted longer than that of any of his contemporaries, and was able to read tolerably well, recite the capitals of scores of countries, and possessed an elementary knowledge of the geography and history of the British Isles. Thus his talents surpassed those normally required by the employees of the Central Trinidad Bus Company.

Doon Town, the scene of these adventures, was in fact neither town nor village. It was sufficiently close to Port-of-Spain to make its status ambiguous. Those wishing to swell the population of the capital tended to treat it as a suburb, but in practice it was treated as a separate entity. Doon Town was the catchment area for several villages spread around it. It was surrounded on three sides by the foothills of the Northern Range and to the east by sugar-cane fields and a refinery where most of the inhabitants worked. The elder Mr Lutchman eked out a living by several methods. Primarily, he considered himself a taxi-driver, operating a shuttle service between Doon Town and the outlying villages, but during the harvest he abandoned his taxi and hired himself out to the sugar company that controlled Doon Town's fortunes. In addition to all of this, he cultivated a vegetable plot, the one surviving heirloom of his father's struggles. The cucumbers, tomatoes and watermelons it produced he sold from a stall in Doon Town during the appropriate seasons. His son, vaguely disapproving of these activities, held aloof and refused any share in the work.

The Lutchmans lived near what was called the 'junction', from which roads flowed away in four directions. There was a constant roar of traffic which stopped only late at night and lent Doon Town an air of excitement and busy industry which it did not deserve. Directly opposite were the stalls of the water-melon sellers. While the fruit was in season these were piled to the roof with mounds of deep-green water-melons, some cut down the middle and put in glass cases to exhibit their pink, fleshy insides and shining black seeds. When the season was over, the empty stalls were used by the idlers of the area as a free and convenient shelter from the rain and sun. Gathering early in the morning, they would remain there all day, drinking and gambling, surrounded by hordes of younger boys eager to join the coterie.

One outstanding feature of Doon Town was the number of rum-shops owned by Indians and Chinese. These places were easily recognizable by their overhanging eaves and swing doors. At any time of day, the confirmed drunkards, many of them old Indian men and women, were to be seen sprawled on the pavement nearby, emaciated, dressed in rags, their starved bodies covered with dust and festering sores. They slept on the bare pavement, curled up against the walls of the rum-shops, the meagre bundle of their possessions serving as pillows.

But it was at night that Doon Town really blossomed. It was not safe to be out alone on the streets then. Stabbings were the one constant feature of life. Along the dark alleys leading off the main street, the prostitutes plied their trade. On the main street itself, stalls lit by flambeaux, yellow flames bending before the wind, lined the pavements, selling oysters with pepper-sauce, oranges and black-pudding, their smells mingling with that of the corn being roasted in coal-pots and boiled in oil-tins. Fat, picture-postcard Negresses, wearing panama hats and fanning the flames with bits of rolled-up newspaper, called out their wares and solicited the passers-by. Around the entrances to the town's two cinemas struggling crowds gathered and from the rum-shops came the incessant, tuneless maunderings of the drunks. And the traffic never stopped. Everything seemed to conspire to produce the illusion of frenzy.

It was in surroundings like these, then, that Ram grew up and came to manhood and to which he was eventually to bring the young girl from the Khoja household. He tasted all the joys Doon Town could offer, visiting the rum-shops, the water-melon stalls and the prostitutes in the back alleys. But Doon Town, after all, could only offer so much to a young man who had imbibed the geography and history of the British Isles and who could recite the capitals of so many countries. It was not enough.

The girl he was to marry did not inspire him. Baby was five years younger than he, dark-skinned, with large black eyes and oiled hair falling in plaits down the length of her back. Her nose was the best part of her. It was well-chiselled and aquiline and lent to her face an air of nobility which it would otherwise have lacked. When Ram thought of her, he tried to think only of her nose.

2

The Khojas were vigilant in defence of their traditions. They had long regarded themselves as the natural leaders of the Hindu community. There was some justification for this quite apart from their wealth, since there were other Indian families just as rich, if not richer. But, in the eyes of the Khojas, they had abdicated, lapsed into betrayal of the faith. Many of them had been converted to Christianity and, abandoning the land as a form of investment, a concept sufficiently advanced to be meaningless to the mass of Khojas, had gone into the professions, becoming doctors and lawyers, marrying English wives, living in lavish houses in the city and speaking only English.

The Khojas had triumphed by default, renowned not for their achievements, but for their deliberate backwardness and their eccentricities. In the face of desertion they continued to pride themselves on their orthodoxy, their dubious Brahmin forebears and the store of religious lore that had gained asylum in their bosoms. There was not a single doctor or lawyer amongst them, for the Khojas, having remained oblivious of the professions, regarded any such ambition as heresy, and were content to contemplate and gloat over the thousands of acres of badly cultivated land they owned. In his darkened sitting-room, Govind Khoja meditated not solely on abstract philosophic principles, but also on those endless fields of sickly sugar-cane waving in the wind.

The elder Mr Khoja had emigrated from India as an indentured labourer. He was an indistinct, almost mythical figure, about whom very little was known for certain, though the Khojas tried to pretend otherwise. As depicted to his descendants, he bordered on saintliness. He had been kind, thrifty, virile and ambitious, a paragon of the secular virtues. This, despite their other-worldly pretensions, did not strike the Khojas as being in any way odd. For them, religiosity and wealth were inextricably intertwined. In themselves, they combined the most solid, though usually hopelessly misguided, commercial instincts with an equally solid concern for affairs of the soul. The equations that resulted were models of clarity. The rich were automatically good; the poor must look after their souls. This nurturing of the impoverished soul had also been simplified. Everyone could grasp it. One should eat with one's hands and not use knives and forks; one should say 'pranam' instead of 'good morning' or 'good-bye'; one should not eat beef or pork; children should be beaten regularly and brutally; one ought not to be ashamed to use liberal dosages of coconut oil on the hair and skin. Such, at any rate, were some of the strictures that poverty imposed. In addition, of course, the poor must marry as need and convenience dictated. An ill-conceived, unhappy marriage was nectar to the undisciplined soul. Thus, with an unruffled conscience, could the young girl with the fine nose be consigned to the tendernesses of an alien family.

The elder Mr Khoja, suffering from homesickness, died aboard ship on his way back to India, and the power passed to his wife. She was a stern mistress, guardian not of the soul but of the family's fortunes. Her regard for the latter was mystical, epitomised not so much in land, but in jewellery. She collected assiduously, even selling some of her land to finance certain deals. By the time blindness put a stop to this the legends had already begun to gather. The elder Mrs Khoja was a woman of intense but fleeting enthusiasms. Nevertheless, they all had an underlying unity of purpose: to conserve what she had, and if possible to accumulate more wealth. Unhappily, being a woman of limited intelligence and vision, her passion rapidly degenerated into a simple, unvarnished miserliness. She decided, for example, to grow and mill her own rice and sell the surplus at a vast profit. She bought an expensive milling machine and set aside a special room in the house, called the 'threshing room'. But, she did not know how to grow rice and steadfastly refused to employ anyone who did. 'You think I going to waste my money like that?' she exclaimed. 'You don't know the kind of woman I is if you think that.' And so, the crops were small and of poor quality and no one would pay the prices she asked. The idea was quietly dropped and the milling machine left to rust: she had refused to sell it for less than the original cost.

As the years passed her miserliness and suspicions that people were trying to rob her assumed the proportions of a disease. She withdrew her money and jewels from the bank and, true to the classic type of her disease, secreted her wealth in double-locked boxes which she hid carefully about the house. At about this time too, she started searching out husbands for her six daughters. Her reasons were underpinned by a severe logic: husbands must take full charge of their wives and be responsible for their upkeep. The support of six daughters made tangible inroads on her finances and she was determined to free herself of this burden. Young men were not lacking. Dazzled by the Khoja name and wealth, parents flocked to the house offering up their sons. The elder Mrs Khoja held court in the kitchen and listened calmly to their pleadings. Thus, one by one, she got rid of her five older daughters. Saraswatee, the youngest alone remained. Hers was the nearest to a love match. The young man himself came to court her. Mrs Khoja was appalled. Love was not a luxury the poor could afford, but the young man was insistent and in the end Mrs Khoja gave in, consoling herself with the reflection that now there were no extra mouths to feed – except her great-niece Baby. And the elder Mrs Khoja had plans other than marriage for her: Baby would remain in the house to look after her in her old age. She had developed cataracts and knew that sooner or later she was going to go blind. But an accident intervened and changed all this. Indrani, her eldest daughter, was widowed in the second year of her marriage. For the elder Mrs Khoja, it was a blessing in disguise. She reclaimed her daughter and Baby was put up for sale. The buyers flocked to the house again. The negotiations were brief and to the point. Within two months Baby and Ram Lutchman were married.

The elder Mrs Khoja, much younger than her husband, continued to outlive him in the strange wooden house he had built in the country, looked after by Indrani. Once every year she came to Port-of-Spain to visit her son (she had given him the town house when he had married), travelling by bus and accompanied by her daughter carrying a box of evil-smelling medicines, the mark of her trade and devotion. When blindness finally descended, the active leadership of the clan passed to Govind.

3

From the beginning, then, it was not an affair of the heart that had brought the young Mrs Lutchman and her husband together. Ram bought a tiny, semi-detached house in Doon Town, not far from the junction. He had refused to live with his parents. 'She's my wife,' he told his father, 'and I not going to let she stay in this house and work for you.'

'But what do you think a daughter-in-law make for, Ram?'

'That's what you should be asking yourself. Not me. All that business about daughter-in-law slaving away too old-fashioned for my liking.'

'I think I educate you too much,' his father replied a little sadly. 'Like you fall in love with she or something?'

Mr Lutchman overrated his son's modernity. Ram had not fallen in love with his wife, nor was it simply concern for her well-being that led him to buy the house. The facts belied that.

It seemed, even living apart from his parents, an unpropitious beginning. The house was situated on the Eastern Main Road, one of the four roads sweeping away from the junction, and the traffic never stopped. The rooms were small and bare and the dividing wall was little more than a paper-thin partition. They could hear everything their neighbours said, chiefly the shouts and curses the husband flung at his wife, the almost nightly beatings and their children crying endlessly. There was no running water in the house and to get to the nearest stand-pipe Baby had to walk a quarter of a mile, a bucket dangling from her waist. She was horrified.

It was not that she was accustomed to luxury. On the contrary. The house in which she had grown up was no better furnished, but it was large and protective and the atmosphere communal. In these tiny rooms, she was suddenly alone, cast adrift with an unsympathetic husband whom she suspected of relishing her predicament. The obscenities of the man next door frightened her and every night she listened, alarmed and half-fascinated, to the sounds of their love-making. Their own marriage had not been consummated, Ram still seeking the favours to be found in the back alleys of Doon Town. He had shown no desire for her, and she, on her part, was relieved and thankful.

She lay on the bed, her husband beside her. The curtains had not been drawn and the street-lamp cut grotesque patterns on the walls. The lights from the cars raced across the ceiling. Next door the bed-springs creaked.

'You thinking about what they doing, eh? Now you know why people like them does have so many children.' He laughed. She said nothing.

'Like you going dumb or what, woman? Say something out loud. They not going to bite you. Let them hear you. Let them know who your family is.'

'Ssh, Ram.'

'"Ssh, Ram". What's all this "ssh Ram" business, eh?' He raised his voice, chuckling at the same time. Mrs Lutchman had become accustomed to talking in whispers, afraid that the neighbours might overhear what she said.

The creaking of the bed-springs next door had stopped. Mrs Lutchman studied the shifting patterns of light on the ceiling and listened.

'Time for us to make a noise now, eh?' Ram's voice was deliberately loud. 'After all, we married so we allowed to do that sort of thing now, you know.'

'No Ram. Not yet. Let's wait a little.'

He heaved restlessly, then suddenly he erupted at the top of his voice. 'Listen, woman, because I don't want to have to say this again. From now on you going to do what I tell you to do, when I tell you to do, you hear! None of this blasted nonsense any more. You going to do as I say.'

They had been married a month and that night their bed-springs creaked for the first time.

4

A pattern of life established itself. During the day, Mrs Lutchman did the washing and cleaned and looked after the house. She no longer dreaded walking the quarter of a mile to the stand-pipe and had even accustomed herself to the obscenities and other noises that emanated from behind the thin partition. In time she became acquainted with the woman, a pallid, scraggy creature weakened by her string of pregnancies, and her brood of dirty children. Once every year at Christmas time, she, like the sisters, went to spend a week with the elder Mrs Khoja in the country. This was a joyous time for her and she looked forward to it with ill-concealed delight. Her husband was offended and they had had several quarrels about it. He himself did not go.

Their lives were separate, crossing only at the points of elementary physical duties: the preparation of food, the washing and ironing of his clothes, the questions that sought necessary information ('You coming home for dinner tonight, Ram?'), and, occasionally, a hurried, formal love-making. Ram continued to work with the Central Trinidad Bus Company who, in recognition of his services, promoted him to the rank of inspector. He was away from the house for extended periods, spending the evenings touring the rum-shops and roaming the back alleys of Doon Town with his friends. Chief among these was Naresh, the husband of the harried woman next door, with whom he extended his explorations to the seedier districts of Port-of-Spain, tasting the more varied offerings of the capital. Together they visited the night-clubs that infested the area near the docks, the Chinese restaurants and Naresh's creole mistress who accommodated them both. But Port-of-Spain proved to be merely a slightly magnified version of Doon Town, and Ram fell victim to the same disenchantment. Naresh was disappointed and promised him a further acreage of delicious flesh. They went to more expensive night-clubs, but even there the women were no different; only the prices were higher. All flesh was the same – irresistible, but unable to assuage and smother the lingering dissatisfaction and restlessness. Ram drank heavily and he and Naresh would return late at night, shouting and singing and swearing, Naresh to burden his wife yet further, Ram to collapse in silent exhaustion beside the girl with the fine nose and sleep disturbedly through what remained of the night. Mrs Lutchman treated her husband as she would have done an employer. She did what was expected of her and no more. And then, there was always the reprieve at Christmas time when the family gathered round the old woman at the house in the country.

5

In the fifth year of her marriage Mrs Lutchman became pregnant. She returned, as was the custom, to the house of her girlhood to have the child and stayed there until the baby was a month old.

Mr Lutchman took no pleasure in his son, even though he bore a greater resemblance to him than he did to his mother. The child was named Bhaskar, the name suggested by Govind Khoja. Bhaskar had inherited all the facial features of his father, but his skin was as dark as his mother's. He was not a pretty baby.

Mr Lutchman's treatment of his wife took a turn for the worse after Bhaskar's birth, and it was not long after her confinement that he beat her for the first time. Naresh was encouraged. 'That's the way, Ram. Blows and babies. That's the way to keep them in order. You should have give she about four baby by now. She wouldn't have had no time to make trouble then. But it never too late to learn.'

The day following this beating, Mrs Lutchman left the house and went to stay with Gowra, a distant cousin. Gowra urged her to leave him for good. 'He's my husband for better or worse,' Mrs Lutchman said. 'I can't do a thing like that. Who will look after him?'

'He could look after himself,' Gowra replied.

'I know that man better than you, Gowra. He can't even iron a shirt much less look after himself. No. I got to go back and look after him.'

And a week later she was back. She found her husband taciturn and he did not ask her where she had gone or what she had done. He went through cycles of violence and calm, drunkenness and abstinence, brutality and concern. He claimed he missed driving buses and requested a return to his old job. The company was generous. They agreed and continued to pay him an inspector's salary. Ram drove his buses recklessly and the company, after reasoning with him, threatened to sack him. He made a valiant effort to reform and for some weeks drove his buses with greater discretion. One night in an outburst of sentiment he took Bhaskar on his knee, playing and talking with him and crying.

'What a no-good, worthless father you must think you have, my boy. Not a true father at all. I know you wouldn't understand what it is I saying, but all the same I want you to know that I does suffer a lot for all the bad things I does do. So when you grow up and come to be a big man, you mustn't be like your mother always complaining to her family about me.'

'I never say one word to my family against you, Ram. If you must know, we does hardly ever talk about you.' Mrs Lutchman was sitting on a chair near the window, combing her hair and staring at the cars roaring past.

'Shut up, woman. I not talking to you. I talking to Bhaskar.' Bhaskar gazed up at his father, his eyes blank and uncomprehending. He too began to cry. Mr Lutchman patted him affectionately. 'I don't blame you for crying, son. You could abuse me however much you want. That is your right as my son. I don't blame you any more than I blame your mother.'

'Ram . . .'

'Shut up, woman. I not talking to you. I talking to Bhaskar.'

Mrs Lutchman went on combing her hair, though more slowly.

'No. I don't blame you at all, Bhaskar, for hating me, your worthless father. I deserve everything that coming to me. Everything.' Bhaskar struggled to set himself free, appealing to his mother for assistance.

'Don't say things like that, Ram. You frightening the child. He can't understand what you trying to tell him.'

Mr Lutchman sighed and released Bhaskar, who slid to the floor and crawled quickly across to his mother. She opened her arms to receive him, and lifting him high, she kissed him several times.

The next night Mr Lutchman was drunk again and beat them both. Mrs Lutchman left the house with Bhaskar and went to stay with Gowra. The following day he went to fetch her. She returned quietly. Soon, it became customary for them to achieve their reconciliations in this way. Ultimately, her desertions lost their substance, a ritual without any force either for her husband or herself. When she realized this, she stopped doing it and took up permanent residence.

When Mr Lutchman crashed one of the company's buses they sacked him. For a week he remained at home, morose and silent.

'I feel like going down to the station and breaking all their blasted office windows for them. They make me feel as if I kill Christ just because I run one of their stupid buses into a lamp-post. It was a real sonofabitch lamp-post anyway.'

'Don't be a fool, Ram. They go throw you into jail if you go and break they windows. And what you go do then, eh? Tell me. It don't have no glass to break inside a jail, you know. Is solid iron bars they have inside of there.'

'You keep out of this, woman. None of this is your business. I surprise you haven't gone round to your family as yet to tell them what I do.' He spat contemptuously on the floor, rubbing it in with his boot.

'My family wouldn't be interested in that. They have more important things to think about.'

'Like what? Sitting on their backside and scratching?'

'I wouldn't have you speak of my family in that way, Ram. As far as I can see is you, not them, who sitting on they backside and scratching. What I want to know is this. What are we going to do about money? We can't live on fresh air alone, you know. You got a child to look after.'

Mr Lutchman was sitting at the table near the window. He sat hunched, his head resting on his palms, gazing at the oilcloth. Not answering his wife, he raised his head and looked out at the street. Outside, the never-ending stream of cars went by. There was an oil-lamp on the table and, picking it up, he passed his hands slowly over the sooted glass, exploring its contours. After a while he said softly and, it seemed, with great reluctance, 'You think your family could help?'

'What you take them for? A bank?'

He started up angrily, then as abruptly subsided and sinking back into the chair, put his head back on his palms. His wife softened.

'I didn't mean to say that. But I think we should try to make do without asking them.' She knew that help from the elder Mrs Khoja was out of the question. She cast around in her mind for a useful suggestion. The first glimmerings of an idea began to take shape. It was an attractive thought. Mrs Lutchman frowned and bit her lips and coughed. Her husband watched her curiously. At last she said, with a lame effort at spontaneity, 'Maybe I could sell a few provisions and things. Is a nice location when you think about it. It near the junction and everything.'

'What you know about that kind of thing?'

'I don't see it have much to know.'

Mrs Lutchman came from a family imbued with the entrepreneurial spirit. At one time or another, they had all succumbed and gone into 'business', usually with the same uniformly unhappy results. The urge, however, had survived these setbacks since the Khojas were rarely given to self-analysis. Mrs Lutchman, giving it serious thought for the first time, discovered in herself a hitherto unsuspected passion, an almost instinctive need to sell vegetables which went beyond the bounds of mere necessity. She entertained visions of herself – they rose effortlessly – lost among piles of tomatoes, cabbages, potatoes, watercress, with a scale of tarnished copper to one side and near it an old biscuit tin, the blue label half-obliterated, filled with 'change'. Her visions were precise. Profit and loss were not the prime considerations. Indeed, she hardly considered that aspect of the matter. Her love of commerce was pure, unadulterated.

Mr Lutchman was not happy. 'Do you realize that you going

to make a big fool of we if you go and do a thing like that?'

'How is that? What so foolish about selling a few vegetables? You just have to look beyond your nose and see how much people does go in for it. Take your father for instance. What about all them water-melon and thing he does sell?'

Mr Lutchman lost his temper. 'You want to become a laughingstock? Listen and watch. This is what you go have to do.' He began prancing around her, his palms cupped as if he were holding something, his voice rising to falsetto. 'Cabbages! Cabbages! Ten cent a pound. Look at these full, ripe cabbages! Come and get your cabbages here!'

She watched him, laughing. 'That's a good idea. I don't know why I hadn't thought of it. Since you doing nothing these days you could come and dance on the road for me. We sure to make a profit then with you shaking your backside.'

Mr Lutchman's sense of humour was stretched to breaking point. 'I telling you, woman. Watch your step with me. You want people to laugh at me? I have a position to keep, you know. "Hey", my friends go say, "I see your wife selling provision these days out on the Eastern Main Road." How do you think I go look in their eyes, eh? Eh? "Oh yes," I go have to say, "my wife always wanted to be a market woman." '

Mrs Lutchman flinched, more from fear of being struck than embarrassment, Ram having successfully worked himself up into a rage. Nevertheless, her self-possession was intact. 'You know something, Ram? For a man who used to drive a bus you have a lot of false pride.' She spoke with a dry calmness, a token of her serenity and conviction. 'You have a lot of false pride,' she repeated. Mr Lutchman made as if to grab the collar of her blouse. She cowered and he let his hands fall and left the room muttering to himself and shaking his head. Outside, she heard him calling for Naresh.

Ignoring her husband's disapproval, Mrs Lutchman threw herself with energy into her preparations and her fervour overriding her natural scruples, she made the journey to Port-of-Spain to see Govind Khoja.

6

Govind Khoja was in his middle thirties. He had been married when still in his teens to Sumintra, the daughter of a well-known jeweller. This marriage, from the elder Mrs Khoja's point of view, had two inestimable advantages. The jeweller was rich and he did all her work free of charge. Unfortunately, Sumintra had proved incapable of bearing live children. The elder Mrs Khoja took her daughter-in-law to see the family pundit. He 'smoked' her and chanted prayers. 'It should be all right now,' he said. When the second child, despite these assurances, also died, she reproached the pundit. He suggested she bring her son to him as well. 'It could be the evil spirit get hold of he and not she,' he explained. 'I have seen that kinda thing happen before.' Accordingly, Mr Khoja went and he too was smoked and had prayers said. The third child also died, its mother within a hair's breadth of departing with it. 'It's a strange thing. I just don't understand it,' the pundit apologized. 'Perhaps you better take she to see a doctor.' 'You not the pundit your father used to be,' the elder Mrs Khoja retorted. The pundit was resigned. 'Some of us naturally better than others,' he said. The elder Mrs Khoja did not trust doctors, but the pundit having failed her, she had no choice. The doctor drew a diagram of the physical complexities involved. It was not encouraging and he advised them to give up all hopes of ever having any children. The elder Mrs Khoja was not convinced, but in the end she surrendered to the doctor's authority. However, she never managed to entirely free herself from the suspicion that her daughter-in-law was being deliberately awkward. The pundit was banished to obscurity. Without the patronage of the Khojas his chances of being a success were reduced to virtually nothing.

The office of patriarch suited Mr Khoja well. He was a tall, good-looking, powerfully built man, marred only by the sickly yellowness of his complexion. From childhood, he had been accustomed to receive the respect and adulation of his sisters, a respect and adulation which were maintained and perhaps even augmented after they grew up and were married. Certainly, while their mother was alive, the sisters admitted no diminution in the tribute that was due to the active head of the clan.

He performed his duties punctiliously and was invariably present at the birth, marriage or death of any member of the clan. He kept a record of the birthdays of all his nephews and nieces who, between the ages of one and twenty, each received from him one dollar. On their twenty-first birthday they were given one dollar and fifty cents and struck off the list. At marriages he gave a water-jug and six glasses (he ordered them in bulk and kept them in a large crate under his bed) and when there was a death in the family he made arrangements with the undertakers and paid half the cost of the coffin. This last service was in constant demand. The husbands of the Khoja sisters had a high mortality rate.

All of this he did with a ritualistic relish. Lately, he had developed political ambitions and had taken to giving speeches at prize-giving ceremonies which got his name into the *Trinidad Chronicle* often. 'Khoja makes appeal for common-sense and understanding.' Such were the headlines he received. Nevertheless, he refused to join any of the already established political parties. 'Swindlers and crooks,' he said. 'They have no true social conscience.' He decided to bide his time. 'When the time is ripe I shall come forward and I shall say what I have to say and do what I have to do. When my task is complete I shall leave it to someone else to carry on my work. But this is not the time. Patience is a virtue.' Thus he had described his position to his disciples. His wife was filled with awe and impatiently awaited the fruition of that mysterious process whereby her husband would depart the darkened sitting-room and emerge transformed, a fully-fledged saviour of the island.

Some of Mrs Lutchman's ardour cooled when she stood outside the imposing wrought iron gates of the house in Woodlands. A car, stripped of its engine, was parked in front of the house next door. Mrs Lutchman jangled the bell. A mongrel dog came leaping down the front steps and snarled at her through the bars of the gate. It was fat and well-fed, the pride of its master. Mrs Lutchman respectfully observed its threatenings. A pale woman in a sari appeared at the top of the steps.

'Stop that racket, Shadow. Your master will get annoyed.' Her voice was frail, like weak tea, and plaintive. She gestured fussily and lifting her sari with a conscious delicacy came trailing down the steps.

'Oh Baby!' she exclaimed in mock surprise, pretending she had only just seen Mrs Lutchman. 'I didn't see you standing there.' 'Baby' was the family's name for Mrs Lutchman. Her real name was Vimla, but she had been called 'Baby' from the day she was born and the name had stuck: 'You see what a wicked child he is.' Mrs Khoja pointed at the dog, nuzzling at the hem of her sari. 'What do you think your father would say, eh? Threatening to bite people all the time. You know,' she turned to Mrs Lutchman, 'he bite the little boy next door the other day. Not that it didn't serve him right, mind you. You see how they does buy all kinds of old junk and park it on the street? Wicked child.' She patted Shadow and pulled his ears playfully. Mrs Lutchman smiled sympathetically at Mrs Khoja and at the dog scrambling at her feet. Mrs Khoja opened the gate and she stepped inside. 'You come to see Govind?' Mrs Khoja, adjusting her sari, led the way through a low door on the ground floor. She wore a pair of solid gold bracelets that hung loosely on her left wrist.

'Yes. I have a little business I want to talk over with him.'

Mrs Khoja nodded. She was used to people seeking her husband's advice. Delegations of tenants from the estates came seeking advice and favours every week. 'He's been very busy these last few days. I can't tell you how all the tenants does keep coming here and pestering him. And on top of all that worry Govind working on one of these prize-giving speeches for the Technical College. You know how he does overwork himself. He's a perfectionist in everything he do.'

Again Mrs Lutchman smiled sympathetically. 'I won't take up too much of his time.'

Mrs Khoja giggled. 'Oh, I wasn't meaning you, Baby. You know he would only be too glad to help.'

They walked through the bare concrete room with peeling pillars to the back yard and climbed up the ragged wooden steps to what was called the pantry. The house had its own peculiar smell, a compound of calm and repose, dust, and

Huntley and Palmers biscuits. Mrs Lutchman grew more subdued.

'Have a seat, Baby. I'll go and see what he's doing.' Mrs Khoja disappeared through thick curtains into the darkened sitting-room, the inner sanctum, her husband believing that a murky gloom was conducive to meditation. The kitchen led off the 'pantry'. Mrs Lutchman saw through the open door a vast shuddering fridge, the largest then available. The stove, too, next to it, was extensive. The Khojas furnished on a lavish scale.

Mrs Lutchman did not sit down. She wandered over on tiptoe to a window that looked out onto the back yard, arid and stony, used only for drying clothes. The 'servants' room', a separate outbuilding, never actually used by servants, was shuttered. Blackie, the Khojas' Negro maid, sat on the steps fanning herself. The dog lay panting in its shadow. She saw into the neighbours' yards. In the yard next door a little boy with a bandaged foot was tossing a ball into the air and catching it.

'Baby,' Mrs Khoja whispered, 'you could go in now.'

Mr Khoja was sitting in an armchair, his eyes closed, his glasses resting on a book on his lap. A reading light, tall and with a huge shade fringed with tassels, tinted his saffron skin an even deeper shade of yellow. Mrs Lutchman hesitated, staring at the liquid reflections in the glass-covered bookshelves lining the walls. At length, Mr Khoja shook himself, and opening his eyes, blinked sleepily at her.

'Ah, Vimla. It's you. Sorry, sorry. I was just dozing off.' Mr Khoja, rubbing his eyes, smiled. He alone among all the Khojas addressed her by her proper name. But this he did not because he thought it right or respectful, but simply because he considered it one of the prerogatives of his status. It implied a certain formality and distance between them.

'Sumintra was telling me you was tired.' She, on the other hand, never addressed Mr Khoja by name.

'Sumintra does worry too much about me. A man's worth lies in his work, not so? Some of us have to work with our hands and some of us have to work with our heads. A Chinese philosopher said that a long time ago. You know which one is me.' Mr Khoja laughed softly.

'That's what I always say myself. We all cut out to do different things.'

Mr Khoja put on his glasses, his face lit by a sardonic smile. He sat up. 'Well, what can I do for you?'

'I want your advice about something. Me and Ram was thinking of opening up a little provision business. Just where we are is a good location. As you know, it on a main road . . .'

'What happen? He giving up working for the bus company?'

Mrs Lutchman laughed, but said nothing.

'He give up the job?' Mr Khoja persisted.

'He didn't like the people he was working with.' Mr Khoja frowned. Mrs Lutchman hurried on. 'As you know, we does live on the Eastern Main Road. A really nice location for a little stall, but before you can begin doing something like that you need some . . .' She paused, contemplating the reflections in the bookcases. The creases on Mr Khoja's forehead multiplied.

'You need some capital.'

'Eh?'

'Money. You need money to do a thing like that.'

Mrs Lutchman looked resignedly round the room. 'Yes,' she said simply, 'you need money to do a thing like that.'

They studied each other.

Mr Khoja had his aberrations. He lent her fifty dollars. 'Giving advice is an expensive business these days. Pay me back when you get rich.'

Mrs Lutchman nodded. 'It can't fail,' she said. 'The location too good for that to happen.'

Waving his hand genially, Mr Khoja dismissed her. He had done his good deed.

7

Esperanza Provisions was not the success Mrs Lutchman had hoped. At first, everything was much as she expected. She bought a cart which she painted bright green with the name of the enterprise in bold red letters. The fruit and vegetables were replicas of the imaginary ones she had been carrying around with her for some weeks; the scale was made of copper and it was varnished; and although the biscuit tin had a red, not a blue label, she quickly accommodated herself.

Mr Lutchman, however, had not accommodated himself and for some time had done nothing but glower silently at his wife. She ignored him. She set up her stall on the Eastern Main Road. Unfortunately, it was on the wrong side of the road, on the farther side of the junction where there were no stalls. Competition for space on the side nearer the junction was intense and Mrs Lutchman had failed to find a place. She was not daunted.

She got up at five o'clock in the morning, arranged and sorted the items, and wheeled the cart as the sun was rising across the road to the area of pavement she had marked out for herself. There, she fixed a straw hat on her head, seated herself on a stool and waited for customers. They came in a trickle and bought little: one mango, one orange, one banana at a time. She took her lunch with her, mainly roti and curried potatoes, which she ate with an instinctive and delicate enjoyment, taking large mouthfuls which she chewed slowly, gazing with her rounded, placid eyes at the lines of cars that went by and did not stop.

The sun spoilt the fruit and vegetables. The bananas developed soft black patches, the tomatoes looked dry and crinkled and the cabbages and watercress were limp and faded. The scale grew almost too hot to touch and the biscuit tin was nearly empty. On the fifth day of her vigil, the police ordered her to move. They said she was blocking the pavements and they had received several complaints from residents, a type of activity scarcely ever heard of in Doon Town. There was an argument which ended in a policeman wheeling the cart back across the road, where he parked it on the side street running past the house. Mrs Lutchman followed, straw hat in hand, while her husband watched developments from the window. For a week she languished in the side street, tending her stall of decayed and rotting fruit, eating her roti and curried potatoes and adjusting the straw hat, now quite drained of colour. But release was not far away and took an unexpected turn.

One afternoon Mr Lutchman came running up to her. 'Come, come,' he shouted, 'leave all this nonsense. We got to go and see my father.'

'Why? What happen?'

'You asking too much question. He get a heart attack this morning. Come, leave all this nonsense.'

Mrs Lutchman got up and hurriedly wheeled the cart into the yard. She was grateful for this intercession and for the confusion caused by her father-in-law's illness, as a result of which Esperanza Provisions was allowed to perish without further heartbreak.

That same night her father-in-law died. Mr Lutchman, grief-stricken, wept, paid for an announcement on the radio and made arrangements for the funeral. He drank heavily at the wake. At one point he called Bhaskar, took him on his knee and exhibited him to his friends.

'This,' he said, 'is my only boy.'

The men seated around him murmured sympathetically.

'He's such a nice, well-behaved boy,' Naresh added. 'To think he so young and he gone and lose his grandfather already. Come let me hold him a bit, Ram.'

Even Mr Lutchman was surprised by Naresh's sudden display of affection for Bhaskar. He passed the child to him. Bhaskar started to cry.

'He want to stay with his father, Naresh. Leave the poor little boy with his father.' Funereal growls circulated among the group. Naresh, relieved, let Bhaskar slide from his knee. He sighed and drank some more rum, licking his lips.

Mr Lutchman took Bhaskar on his knee again. 'Only two years old,' he said. 'You know, I haven't been as good a father as I should have been to this boy. Too much worries does affect a man, not so?' With a melancholy smile Mr Lutchman riffled his hands through Bhaskar's hair. The group nodded in agreement.

'Still, he take after you in his features,' one of the men tried to console him. 'He could have been a lot uglier. You should see my last child. You go bawl to see how ugly he is. Take after his mother, lock, stock and barrel.'

After this speech the group was silent.

'But you can't expect people to understand that is worries that does make a man so,' Mr Lutchman continued, breaking the silence. There was another murmur of sympathy. Mr Lutchman gazed at the floor and at the circle of mud-stained boots. One of the men handed him a glass of rum. He took it without looking up.

'The old man leave anything?' Naresh asked.

Mr Lutchman still staring at the floor did not answer for some sime. Bhaskar fought his way off his knee and went whimpering in search of his mother. 'He had more put away than I thought,' he answered at last.

The group bent forward expectantly. 'How much would you say at a rough guess?'

Mr Lutchman meditated on the boots. 'I'm not sure how much exactly, but I would say about five thou.'

Naresh whistled. 'But what was the old man keeping all that money for?' He looked questioningly at the coffin on the other side of the room. Mr Lutchman, taking his cue from Naresh, got up and walked unsteadily across the room to the coffin. He studied the dead man's face through the glass and came back.

'He was a clever fellow, my father. Cleverer than you think. I never see a man who was more careful with he money.'

'You could afford to move out of that place you living in now,' Naresh suggested. 'Buy a house in Port-of-Spain,' Naresh winked at him and, laughing, added, 'You wouldn't have to go so far every night then.'

Mr Lutchman frowned. 'We go see about that when the time come,' he replied, with more than a hint of irritation in his voice. Then, observing how crestfallen Naresh seemed, said soothingly. 'In the meantime we may as well drink this rum up.'

Mr and Mrs Khoja came on the day of the funeral. Mr Khoja was something of a connoisseur in these matters and he cast a disapproving eye at the arrangements that had been made. They brought a wreath. Mr Lutchman cried again when they arrived and led Mr Khoja up to the coffin.

'Who you get this coffin from?' Mr Khoja demanded.

'Mootoo Brothers. People say they is the best for this sort of business.'

'You must never believe what people say. I don't trust Mootoo Brothers one inch. Next time you have need for a coffin come and see me. I know a lot of people in the undertaking world.'

Mr Lutchman said he would.

'Don't forget,' Mr Khoja warned him.

'I promise. I had a feeling there was something fishy about Mootoo Brothers.'

Mr Khoja smiled knowingly. 'You may have a feeling. But I have evidence. Evidence.' He gazed sternly at Mr Lutchman. 'You mustn't take it so hard.' Mr Khoja lowered his voice. 'There is a time to sow, a time to reap and . . .' he looked round as if in search of an audience, '. . . and yes, I'm afraid so, a time to die.' His eyes wandered over the coffin.

'It's a comforting thought,' Mr Lutchman said, 'and you put it so nice too.'

Mr Khoja was embarrassed. 'How is the provision business?'

Mr Lutchman's expression hardened. 'You must ask Baby about that.'

'It not making a profit?' He remembered the fifty dollars he had 'lent' her.

Mr Lutchman appeared to derive comfort from the examination of his father's corpse. It lent profundity to what he said. 'You could say so,' he replied. He spoke to the dead man rather than to Mr Khoja, who also began to speak to the corpse.

'You have any plans?'

'You know one doesn't like to say these kinda things in front of the dead – it does sound ungrateful and hardhearted – but is a fact all the same that the old man leave me enough to think of putting down something on a house in a place like Port-of-Spain.' His shoulders heaved anew. 'It's an awful kinda way to talk in front of the dead. He body ain't even cold yet and hear me talking about money.' He searched in his pockets and brought out a dirty handkerchief with which he dried his eyes and blew his nose.

'There, there.' Mr Khoja patted him on the shoulder. 'The living have got to go on living, you know. The dead don't expect you to mourn for them for the rest of your life. They want you to go on living and working and enjoying yourself.' He spoke with confidence. Mr Lutchman gradually recovered his spirits. The corpse gazed serenely at them. 'If you want I could help you find a job in Port-of-Spain. Mind you,' he went on, having instantly regretted his offer, 'I can't promise you anything definite. In fact the more I think about it . . .'

'I would be very grateful if you could do that for me,' Ram interrupted hastily, seizing his opportunity. 'Pa was always wanting me to buy a house and live there. He used to say to me, "Ram, when you grown up and get married and I is an old man . . ."' The tears welled once more in his eyes.

'He was a good man, your father,' Mr Khoja said mournfully. 'He wanted what was best for you.' He glanced despairingly at the corpse.

'A man couldn't have wanted a better father,' Mr Lutchman confessed, 'and he would have die a truly happy man knowing that you was going to help me.'

'I know, I know,' Mr Khoja said sadly.

8

Mr Lutchman mourned for a week. He wore a black suit and tie, a white shirt and a hat with a black band. He bathed regularly and was sober and attentive to his child and wife. She tried to console him.

'You taking it too hard, Ram. You go get yourself sick if you go on moping about the place like that.'

'A man only have one father in this world, you know. He was a great man in his own way, my father.' And an even more sorrowful expression settled on his face.

'Yes, I know all that. But what about we? What about that job Govind promise to find for you? You haven't done nothing about that as yet.'

'You think I not aware of that? My father only just dead and here you is pushing and tugging me. Do this, do that. A man only have one father in this world.' He drifted off into reverie.

'Just think, Ram, what we could do if we go to live in Port-of-Spain. Govind could find you a nice little job there and on top of that I could run a little business, a little provision shop like I used to have . . .'

'What's that you saying about a provision shop?' His sorrow vanished, reverence for the dead giving way to animosity for the living. 'You always wanting to run a business, be a market woman. People like you does never learn. People could kick you till you all black and blue and you go turn around and say, "Thank you for kicking me black and blue, Madame. Feel free to do that any time you want." It's a kind of disease your family have, always rushing in and out of business and making a mess of everything. There's old Khoja, for instance, thinking that he know all it have to know about coffin.'

It was his wife's turn to lose her temper. 'Eh! But hear him talk and about my family to boot! As if your family could do any more than kiss the big toe or little finger of mine. Tell me who it is you begging to find you a job, eh?'

'Christ! You people really think old Khoja is a god or something. Abusing me about my own father's coffin. Well I never! Well, I go tell you another thing right here and now, woman. He have to pee the same as the rest of we.'

Mrs Lutchman flared. 'You better watch out how you speak about HIM, you hear! He is ten times the man you is or ever will be. His little finger worth more than . . .'

'Do you want to know what you and he and all the rest of you could do with that little finger of his you always talking about?'

Her nostrils widened. 'What, Mr Bus Driver? Tell me!'

Mr Lutchman laughed and abandoned the unfinished gesture he was describing in the air with his finger. Despite his bluster, he had an exaggerated respect, founded largely on superstition, for Mr Khoja. His blasphemies always hovered tantalisingly on the brink, but never quite went over. Mrs Lutchman was aware of this and she used it skilfully. 'Before you abuse my family, tell me about all the wonderful things yours do. Come on, Mr Bus Driver, tell me.' She watched him, arms akimbo. Mr Lutchman noticed again how fine her nose was. He was defensive.

'I never make any great claims for my family. Is you who have the "great family", not me. But the really sad thing is to hear you talk as if you was heir to the fortune or something. But you know what you go get when the time come?'

Mrs Lutchman watched him calmly. Her animal serenity stimulated his rage. 'You won't get his little finger or big toe!' he screamed suddenly.

'I don't love my family for their money and I not jealous of those who have more than me, which is more than I can say for some people. At least my brother is a thinker. You see all them book he does be reading? Tell me what your father do?'

Mr Lutchman's sense of humour was weakening. His eyes narrowed.

'Since you don't want to answer I go tell you what he used to do. A taxi-driver. Driving people round Doon Town for six cents a time. And what did this man's educated son do? He went up in the world, not so? He didn't drive a taxi. Oh no! He had too much ambition. A taxi was too small for him. He . . .' She spluttered into uncontrollable waves of laughter. Her husband gazed intently at her. '. . . he had to drive a bus!'

The next moment he was upon her, smothering her screams and laughter. One resounding slap after another fell on her cheek. Her laughter crumbled away and she struggled to release herself. He pushed her away finally, and she staggered back, massaging her cheeks. Her eyes were red, but she was not crying. The barest ghost of a smile flickered round the edges of her lips. Mr Lutchman was standing by the table near the window. Picking up the oil-lamp, he flung it violently against the partition. It shattered and Bhaskar, attracted by the explosion, came running into the room. A small crowd had gathered on the pavement. Naresh appeared in the doorway, staring at the bits of glass glinting on the floor.

'That's a warning.' Mr Lutchman waved his finger in front of his wife's face and stumbled heavily out of the room, pushing Bhaskar aside. Naresh nodded with grim satisfaction at Mrs Lutchman and followed him out.

'That's the way to treat them,' he said. 'A few more beatings like that and she go know she place.'

They were walking towards the bright lights and crowds of the junction. Mr Lutchman stopped and turned to look at Naresh. 'Why don't you keep your mouth shut, eh?'

'Watch how you talk to me, Ram. I is not your wife, you know. So don't try to put anything on me, you hear. You no different from the rest of we.'

Mr Lutchman studied Naresh's face. His eyes were dull and unsmiling. 'Why don't you leave me alone, eh?'

'So that's how you treating me after all the things I do for you?'

'What you do for me that I have to be grateful?'

'Like you forget all them club and thing? You can't wipe all that away, you know, Ram.'

Mr Lutchman, his lips slightly parted, scowled. 'Why don't you leave me alone, eh?'

Naresh shrugged. 'Sure. Sure. Don't think I'm going to force myself on you.' He started to walk away. Then he stopped and shouted, 'You not different from the rest of we, Ram. Remember that.'

Mr Lutchman ignored the taunt and hurried on in the direction of the rum-shops.

After her husband had left, Mrs Lutchman swept and cleared away the broken glass. She put Bhaskar back to bed and then went and sat at the table by the window. She remained there a long time, tracing patterns on the oilcloth and staring at the never-ending stream of cars.

The atmosphere necessary for mourning and reflection having been shattered, Mr Lutchman went a week later to Woodlands to see Mr Khoja. He was received in the darkened sitting-room.

'Well, I think I can do something for you after all,' Mr Khoja informed him. 'I know someone in the Education Department – we went to school together – he's a big shot in the Ministry now and deals with the examinations and all that sort of thing. I told him about you and he believes he can make a place for you. How do you feel about it?'

Mr Lutchman, not having been invited to sit down, was standing before him, turning and crumpling his hat in his hands. 'That sounds nice. It sounds real nice.'

Mr Khoja smiled. He was casually dressed in a loose cotton shirt, a pair of baggy trousers and felt slippers. 'But you must remember that it is a proper job. This man is doing you a favour out of friendship for me – I helped him out one time when he was in trouble – and you've got to be responsible and interested. Plenty of people would pawn their souls to get a job like that. You can't go . . .' he fingered the collar of his shirt, 'you can't go crashing buses there. I heard about that, incidentally.' He giggled as Mrs Khoja might have done.

'Who tell you about that? It was only a small accident. It was a little lamp-post, that's all.'

'Yes, yes. But you can't go through life hitting lamp-posts, big or small. A lamp-post is a lamp-post. Don't you agree?'

Mr Lutchman laughed. 'It don't have no buses to crash in the Ministry, or lamp-post either.'

Mr Khoja seemed doubtful. 'I was talking metaphorically. But as long as you understand that it's not a joy-ride, that's the main thing.' Mr Khoja settled himself more comfortably in his armchair. 'You must develop a religious attitude to your work, Ram. People, members of my family especially, always seem to forget the repercussions their bad behaviour might have on me. In the end the public will always turn around and say, "Oh, don't you know he is such and such a relation to Mr Khoja." My name will be mud in the Ministry in no time at all.' Mr Khoja spread his arms wide. 'You see the kind of thing I mean?'

'Yes, yes. I know how hard it must be for you.' He squirmed guiltily before his benefactor, punishing his hat more severely, and Mr Khoja, drumming his fingers on the arm of the chair, gazed with mute satisfaction at the penitent.

9

It did not take Mr Lutchman a long time to find a house. Its situation pleased him. His office was not far away and although the charms of the Queen's Park Savannah were lost on him, he was pleased to claim proximity to it. But what above all appealed to him was its undeniably urban character. At last he was living in the city. Mrs Lutchman too liked the house. Her only regret was that it did not have a verandah. She had had visions of herself rocking there in the cool of the evening. 'Still,' she had reasoned, 'you can't have everything.' But the commercial possibilities of the area seemed promising. This, however, she kept to herself.

The house was square and box-like. It was surrounded by a low concrete fence, behind which narrow rosebeds had once run the gauntlet between the neighbouring houses. There were pretensions of having a lawn at the front, but all of this was now completely given over to clusters of rank weed. One of the neighbours had planted a bread-fruit tree close to the fence and its spreading branches nuzzled and scraped against the roof of the house. Mrs Lutchman promised herself to have something done about that.

The construction of the house itself was simple. All its rooms were rectangular and box-like. Downstairs was a sitting-room and kitchen. Upstairs, there were three bedrooms including one very large one. It had electricity and running water.

They hired a large open truck to transport their goods and arrived on a Sunday afternoon. The neighbours leaned out of their windows and watched. Mrs Lutchman, surrounded by beds, mattresses and chairs and shielding her eyes from the sun, scrutinized the uninspiring front of the house: the cream-painted walls reflecting the heat and the glare; the rectangular windows punched at regular intervals in the masonry; the front door with its panes of frosted glass. Already she could see lace curtains bellying gently in the wind from the doors and windows.

There were other advantages as well. The Khojas living in Woodlands were within twenty minutes' walk from the house and she was well placed to visit and receive visits from the members of her family. Moreover, she was pleased that her husband had found a respectable job. And on top of all this she was expecting another child. She turned away from contemplation of the house and looked at the Savannah and olive-complexioned hills lit by the sun. She smiled. She was content.

Chapter Two

1

The Lutchmans lived in a part of the city where the houses, tall and narrow, jostled each other in a competition for space. Their front gardens and fences faced onto narrow pavements and there was a steady flow of traffic along the hemmed-in streets. It was a decrepit area of boarding houses, cinemas, gambling clubs and, as the police and more prosperous residents joyfully suspected, brothels. The Queen's Park Savannah girdling its northern limits provided an element of grandeur. Scattered around it were the houses of the rich (some of them already converted into government offices), the botanical gardens and zoo, hotels patronised by American tourists, the Archbishop's residence and one of the best schools on the island. The streets, running parallel to one another, each had a glimpse of the park and the low range of hills rising beyond it. Southwards, it faded to a region of petrol stations, small shops, gambling clubs and cinemas. Caught between two worlds, there were conflicting ideas as to its status. On the one hand it could be said, 'It near the Savannah. Two minutes' walk and you there.' On the other, 'It too noisy. It have all kinds of clubs and things there.' Both were right; but the latter was more justified. Somehow, the charms of the Savannah ended abruptly immediately one crossed the road and entered the checkerboard of narrow streets.

Mr Lutchman's job at the Ministry of Education provided enough money for his family to live in relative ease. Their second child, another son, had been named Romesh. The name, as with Bhaskar, had been suggested by Mr Khoja, who also gave Mrs Lutchman a dollar on the day he was born. She was grateful for the gift and opened an account at the Post Office on Romesh's behalf into which she put the annual dollar donated by Mr Khoja on each subsequent birthday. These gifts enraged Mr Lutchman. Unlike his wife, the smallness of the sum was not clouded over by the sanctity of Mr Khoja's blessing. 'A dollar! One miserly dollar!' he complained. 'Who do he take we for? Beggars?' And his wife would invariably reply, 'It's not the size of the gift that matter. It's the thought behind it.' 'And it's a damn miserly thought too,' he would retort. Formerly, an argument like this would most likely have ended in blows, but these exchanges were conducted resignedly, almost, one might say, in a spirit of give and take. For the Lutchmans, both husband and wife, had changed.

Mr Lutchman took his job seriously. He drank far less than he used to and only visited the prostitutes occasionally. No one was sure exactly what his duties at the Ministry were. Questioned on this, it was more than probable he would reply, 'It's confidential work. I can't talk about it.' This impressed his wife and she began to refer in mysterious terms to 'Ram's work at the Ministry', with that special emphasis on 'work' which left her audience wondering. Almost the first thing he did after moving into the new house was to buy himself two suits, one fawn-coloured, the other grey streaked with black. They were made from a cheap light material that flapped in the wind – 'fliers' the cloth was called locally – a quality of the material enhanced by Mr Lutchman's fondness for wide trouser-legs.

During the first three years he travelled by bus to the office, leaving home at eight in the morning and returning at six, the evening paper tucked under his arm. Then he announced he was going to buy a second-hand car. Mrs Lutchman was delighted. She was essentially a visionary, and pictured in minute details the excursions the family would make to the beach and the country, herself in front beside her husband, the children sprawled in the back. She made a tour of the neighbourhood in search of someone who wanted to sell a car. She was unsuccessful and in the end Mr Lutchman bought a Morris Minor from a second-hand dealer. There was no room in the yard to build a garage and the car had to be parked on the road. The day the car arrived Mrs Lutchman spent a long time examining it.

'You sure the brakes safe, Ram?'

'The man say so.'

'And the clutch and gear-box?'

'Eh! To hear you talk people would think you was a mechanic.'

'Well, you know how these people does lie.'

However, they did not quarrel and later that evening Mr Lutchman took his family for a drive around the Queen's Park Savannah. Unfortunately, they did not go for drives as often as Mrs Lutchman would have liked. Ram said he was too tired. Nevertheless, he did take them occasionally to scenic spots. Belvedere Hill was his favourite. They went there after dinner and parked on the parapet overlooking the city. From there, it was possible to see almost the entire city spread out below them, a neat grid of twinkling lights. Mr Lutchman's chief interest lay in trying to identify and name streets and areas. 'Look,' he would tell his wife, 'there's Frederick Street and there's Henry Street and there's George Street, and over there is Laventille. You see them?' And Mrs Lutchman, who did not see them, would say, 'Yes, I see.' She was more interested in what was going on in the other cars parked nearby. It was a popular lovers' haunt and occasionally she would nudge her husband. 'Look over there, Ram. Just look at them. No shame at all.' This annoyed him. 'Shut up, woman, and mind your own business.' Nevertheless, he glanced furtively at the other cars from time to time.

Surprisingly, though, Mr Lutchman was not unduly obsessed by the car. He washed and polished it on Sundays and had it regularly serviced, but his concern did not extend beyond that. This passivity in her husband disturbed Mrs Lutchman. His bouts of violence and drunkenness had given way to a kind of perpetual restlessness and generalized dissatisfaction. When he returned from work in the evenings he hardly talked to her. He bathed, had dinner and went to bed. During the weekends, when he did not work, he wandered through the house wrapped in an unapproachable taciturnity, searching the hinges on the doors and windows for the first signs of rust and making minor alterations to the arrangement of the furniture in the sitting-room. The rest of the time he spent stretched on an armchair, gazing at the ceiling, smoking.

He betrayed little interest in 'improving' the house, sharing none of his wife's enthusiasms for new curtains or the repainting which she intended to do one day. The negative passion that had characterized the first days of their marriage, even that had languished. She tried to talk to him about it.

'You don't take no pride in your house at all, Ram. You does leave all the work to me.'

'What do you expect me to do? Make it into Buckingham Palace?'

'I don't expect you to do anything like that. Just show a little interest. That's all I'm asking. It wouldn't kill you to do that, would it?'

'Just leave me alone, woman. I can't take any more of this nagging day and night.'

'Who nagging you?'

'Just leave me alone, I tell you.'

And so she left him alone. Their lives, as before, followed separate paths, but circumstances were no longer the same. The gatherings at Christmas time at the old house in the country were now a thing of the past. The elder Mrs Khoja, blind and totally senile, had come to depend entirely on the ministrations of Indrani, and Indrani, faithful and devoted slave, discouraged visitors. Thus the gatherings had stopped and the centre of the clan's activities shifted to the house in Woodlands. Mr Khoja had instituted an annual cattha, an elaborate religious festivity patterned on those his mother had organized in her more vigorous days, and the celebrations lasting for a week had gradually taken the place of the Christmas gatherings. She saw less of the sisters. One by one their husbands had died and, released from the duties imposed by marriage, several of them had plunged into the world of commerce, running small shops and groceries. Mrs Lutchman watched them enviously from a distance, her own commercial instincts held in check by the longevity of her husband. Her diversions were simple. She feuded endlessly with the owners of the bread-fruit tree. Mrs Lutchman hated that tree. The owners steadfastly refused to give her any of the fruit and she had to clear away all the over-ripe, rotten ones, very soft and yellow, that fell off the tree and littered the yard. To make matters even worse, the roots undermined the fence and she was convinced that one day it would collapse. She had threatened more than once to pour poison on its roots, but she had not yet had the courage to carry out her threat. Thus the tree lived on and in spite of the 'significant' remarks she made about it to the neighbours, she had, all the same, to collect its debris unceasingly. But, during the course of these middle years, some of her dreams did come true. The windows and doors were hung with lace curtains that bellied gently in the wind, and she repainted the sitting-room and bedrooms. However, her ambition to do the same to the outside walls was not realized. Mr Lutchman made the occasional contribution. He bought a bowl-shaped lightshade for the sitting-room in which scores of small insects were trapped and died. Another of his contributions was a 'cabinet', a simple cupboard with glass doors, where Mrs Lutchman kept and displayed her more precious items of table-ware. These were the more dramatic changes. There were others, more gradual, but equally sure. Mrs Lutchman grew fatter, but her nose, which Ram had ceased to notice, remained as fine as it ever had been. Romesh too was growing up. He had accumulated eight dollars in the Post Office Savings Bank and already Bhaskar was preparing for his entrance examination to secondary school. He was taking 'private lessons' from one of the teachers at his school and each day Mrs Lutchman gave him an extra penny to spend as an encouragement. Bhaskar worked hard and on the night before the examination Mrs Lutchman had a pundit come to the house and say a good-luck prayer. She awaited the results anxiously. He passed, but not brilliantly. She hid her disappointment and bought him crisp new khaki trousers and blue shirts and sewed the school's badge on the pockets. On the first day, she accompanied him to the school gates and kissed him. Bhaskar squirmed away and walked slowly into the school yard. She watched him go, dressed in his smart, new uniform and clutching his smart, new books tightly, then turned and walked quickly away.

It was at about this time, shortly after Bhaskar had entered his new school, that Mr Lutchman met Doreen James.

2

Doreen had met Mr Lutchman quite by accident one day when she had gone to visit the Minister of Education to ask official recognition and help for the treatise on Trinidad Indians she was planning to write. She was not successful, but as she was leaving his office (not particularly distressed by the refusal), the Minister called after her laughing and said, 'I've got a man working here who should be able to tell you all you want to know about the Indians. I think he married one of the Khojas. You ever hear of them?' Doreen had, having only recently read a report on one of Mr Khoja's speeches on education, delivered at a prize-giving ceremony. The report had been heavily tinged with sarcasm. The suggestion appealed to her.

Thus it was she saw Mr Lutchman for the first time, seated at his desk in a room which he shared with three fellow clerks. His shirt open at the collar, his tie thrown casually over his left shoulder, his lips, as usual, slightly parted, he was bent industriously over a report pencilling his remarks in the margin.

'Mr Lutchman?'

He did not answer immediately, but continued to scribble in the margins, frowning as he wrote. He had taken great pains cultivating this special office manner. 'Yes. Can I help you?'

'I don't want to disturb you. It's more in the nature of a personal . . .' Doreen, searching for the correct word, studied the fan revolving slowly from the ceiling. The clerks looked up from their desks, interested. 'Well, it's a favour I want to ask you really. The Minister suggested . . .' Again Doreen paused. Her voice had faint traces of an American accent.

'The Minister! Go ahead.' Mr Lutchman stopped writing and tilting backwards in his chair, twiddled the pencil between his fingers. The clerks stared.

'Perhaps I could see you when you finish work today,' she suggested, put out by her reception and the undisguised interest of the other clerks.

'Certainly, Miss. But . . .', borrowing the word, impressed by its elegance, '. . . *perhaps* you could inform me . . .'

Doreen lowered her voice. The clerks returned to their

reports. 'Well, you see, I am planning to write a book on Trinidad Indians. I'm an anthropologist.' She paused and looked questioningly at him to see if he understood.

'Yes, yes. I know what that is. Go on.' Mr Lutchman waved the pencil impatiently. He brought the chair forward and leaned his elbows on the edge of the desk.

'The Minister was saying that you would be able to help me, that you knew a lot about the Khojas.'

Mr Lutchman was forthcoming, always proud, when at a suitable distance, to talk of his connexions. 'I married one of them, so I suppose I know as much as anybody.'

'That's what the Minister told me. As part of my work I was wondering if you could . . .'

'Help you. I understand what you mean.' He drummed with his pencil.

'I could always come to your home if that would be more convenient.'

'No, no. That's all right. Come and meet me after work. We could talk about it then.' He glanced at the report spread open in front of him. 'But now you must excuse me. I have so much to get through today.'

After she had gone Mr Lutchman turned to one of the clerks and said, 'You know what anthropology is, Wilkie?'

'Search me, Lutch. Search me,' Wilkie replied, smiling broadly at him.

They met that afternoon in a snack bar, famed for its ice-cream sundaes, a favourite haunt of bank-clerks and their girl-friends. Mr Lutchman, acquainted only with the less reputable clubs, had never been there before. He felt as though he were trepassing. Doreen arrived late. She came in carrying a brief-case.

Doreen was tall and thin, with a fair, watery complexion that matched her large, watery eyes and a sharp, wedge-shaped nose that was too big for her face. She was a bony, angular, awkwardly put together woman. One got the impression that she had been constructed in a hurry from ill-assorted pieces. Her dress, falling in limp folds from her waist, covered her knees. Her legs were unshaved and she wore a pair of low-heeled shoes. Doreen James, as Mr Lutchman could see at a glance, was not fashionable. Her bosom alone proclaimed her an object of possible desire. It was absurdly feminine in contrast to the overwhelming masculinity of the rest of her, and Mr Lutchman, to divert himself, tried to think only of her breasts.

She walked quickly across the room to his table. He stood up: Mr Lutchman had learned much in his years with the Civil Service. Doreen threw the brief-case on the floor and herself onto the chair he had drawn up for her. She passed her hands through the long tangle of her hair and smiled at him. She sighed and scrutinised the faces of the other customers nearby. Mr Lutchman noted her ease and self-possession and especially the candour with which she examined their fellow customers.

'Have you ordered?' she asked.

Mr Lutchman shook his head.

Doreen, raising her hand, snapped her fingers twice. Two waitresses, got up in 'cute', allegedly ethnic dress set off by gay, useless aprons, were chatting, leaning against the counter. They ignored her. Doreen snapped her fingers a third time. One of the waitresses looked up sullenly and came over to them with an exaggeratedly sinuous walk. She stared at Doreen, notebook poised, licking her red lips.

'What will you have?' Doreen asked him. 'A sundae? It's their spécialité.' She laughed. The waitress was openly hostile.

'A sundae sounds fine,' Mr Lutchman said softly, looking from Doreen to the waitress.

'Two sundaes,' Doreen snapped. 'With lots of nuts.'

The waitress scribbled in her notebook and walked sinuously back to the counter to deliver the order.

Doreen settled herself more comfortably into her chair and resting her chin on her palms gazed at Mr Lutchman. 'I can't tell you how pleased I am to have met someone like you with inside information,' she said. 'I've been planning to write this book for a long time.' She laughed happily. 'It's all going to come straight back from the horse's mouth, as they say.'

The waitress returned with their sundaes, setting the bowls carelessly before them. As she was leaving, she said. 'I was forgetting,' and dropped two paper napkins in front of them, one of which slipped off the table and fell on the floor. The waitress, paying no attention, wriggled back to the counter and took up her station. Mr Lutchman tested his sundae.

'I hope your wife wouldn't get angry to know you out with another woman.' Doreen giggled and started to eat her sundae.

'Wife!' Mr Lutchman murmured, wiping his chin for no good reason with the napkin. He was obeying a sudden prompting which had something to do with the unaccustomed atmosphere of the place, the sullen waitress with the red lips and sinuous walk and the girlish giggles of the woman opposite him. 'That's the first thing you must know. The Khojas don't get married for love.'

The smile faded from Doreen's face. She licked gingerly at the ice-cream on her spoon, serious, apparently concerned at this unexpected declaration, but like her meeting with the Minister earlier that day, not overly distressed by the turn of events.

'You mean it was an arranged marriage?' She stared intently at him, dangling the spoon in front of her lips.

'What else? True, Mr Khoja give me his blessing and a jug and some glasses as well and, true, he does give my children a dollar on their birthday. I must be grateful for all that.' Mr Lutchman wondered at himself.

Doreen's large eyes dilated. 'It must have been terrible for you. To think in this day and age customs like that can still survive. It's like reading Fraser.' That seemed to please her.

'Who's he?'

'Oh, don't you know? He's a very famous anthropologist. My hero, as a matter of fact.' She nibbled at the ice-cream. 'That damn waitress made sure they didn't put enough nuts in it. I love nuts. Adore them. Do you?'

Mr Lutchman shrugged his shoulders. 'I can take it or leave it.'

'I'm sorry. I'm being frivolous and there you are all upset and angry with me for talking about Fraser and how much I like nuts. Do you think it would help talking to me about it?'

'So you can put it in your book?' The prospect that this might be so did not displease him, but a show of anger was, he suspected, more appropriate to the mood he was trying to invent.

Doreen frowned, pushing the bowl of ice-cream away. 'To hell with my book. You are much more interesting and important.' She wrung her hands. 'I feel so helpless, but all the same I would like to talk to you about it. Be your friend and try to help.'

'I thought you was planning to write this book for such a long time?'

'Oh, I'll do it some other time,' Doreen replied vaguely. 'It's a long time yet before I die. But you are flesh and blood. That's so much more interesting.' She giggled.

'What could you do?' Mr Lutchman stared disconsolately at her. 'All that happen a long time ago and I'll only make you unhappy talking about it. What would be the point in that, eh? I can't spend the rest of my life crying on your shoulder.' He was amazed at his own disingenuousness.

'Oh, so you feel I'm all light and sweetness, do you? Men always think that their suffering alone is important. That's the height of selfishness.'

'You don't look to me as if you ever suffer.'

Doreen scowled. She pointed her spoon at him. 'Well, you listen to this and then tell me what you think. I would like to find out if after all that I'm going to tell you you will still say I haven't suffered and suffered a lot in my time.'

Mr Lutchman leaned forward interestedly.

Her love life, a maze of confusion and misunderstanding, provided a suitable theme. She enumerated and described the unhappinesses, the seven abortive engagements through which she had been (admittedly the last three were purely a matter of form), and the several looser liaisons that dotted the past years of her life, in each case isolating and dramatizing her sorrow before serving it up to her listener. Unrequited love and the suffering that entailed were, it seemed, her *spécialité*. Mr Lutchman listened in incredulous silence.

The melodramatic possibilities inherent in the situation had struck Doreen forcibly from the moment she entered the air-conditioned bar with its tables hidden in dark corners, thick velvet curtains covering the windows and dimmed overhead lighting. An affair with a married man was an exciting prospect (she too had been affected by the red-lipped waitress) and during the last few minutes she had been consciously exploring and elaborating the fantasy. Already she could taste the fruits of an enterprise that lay still in the future. She was aware of the fundamental deception, but, swept along by the tide of feeling and artifice she detected in Mr Lutchman, she surrendered to the temptation and gave free rein to her fantasy.

'And so,' she concluded, 'I've made many men and myself unhappy. Would you say now that I haven't suffered?'

Mr Lutchman played with his ice-cream. Around him, the bank-clerks and their girl-friends twittered, their faces obscured in the half-light. He did not answer her question.

Doreen laughed. 'I have surprised you, haven't I? But, you know, I still haven't learned my lesson. Don't you think it would be boring if I did? The flesh is weak and I know that sooner or later another man will come along and tempt me and – I'm ashamed to say it, but it's no good hiding the truth – I know, all the same, that old and not too good-looking as I am, I'll give in and the whole thing will start all over again.'

Mr Lutchman tried to avoid looking at her. 'I think I'll have a beer,' he said.

'That's a good idea. My throat is getting dry with all this talking. I haven't talked to anyone like this for ages.' She laughed and snapped her fingers at the waitress. 'Who was supposed to be helping who?'

The red-lipped waitress came over and took their order. She glanced contemptuously at Doreen's dress. She scribbled in her notebook and meandered slowly back to the bar. They both watched her.

'I've always wondered what's so wrong with adultery,' Doreen murmured, not taking her eyes off the waitress. Mr Lutchman started. They looked at each other and laughed. 'For instance, studying anthropology shows you how many different kinds of things different people believe in. In some societies, in the South Seas for instance, they encourage people to commit adultery, even incest for that matter . . .'

'Excuse me.' The waitress hovered over them, aloof and voluptuous. She took away their ice-cream bowls and dropped two beer-mats on the table, on which she rested the glasses. Doreen was embarrassed and waited for her to go. When she had gone, she said, 'Do you believe in God?' Doreen sipped the beer, making a face as she did so. Mr Lutchman belched and rubbed his stomach.

'I never really think about it.'

'Well, I don't. Don't look so shocked. At the university where I studied I could have counted the number of people who believed in God on the tips of my fingers. Cross my heart!' Doreen crossed her heart hurriedly and went on. 'But the point I wanted to make was this. If you don't believe in God, what does it matter what you do? People should be more realistic about things like adultery. There's no earthly reason why a woman should not go to bed with any man she wants to and vice versa. Vice versa. That's a good one.' She laughed, choking on her beer.

'What? What's that you laughing at?'

'Vice versa. You know. Vice.' She fell into another fit of coughing.

Mr Lutchman smiled weakly and drank some more beer.

Mr Lutchman was genuinely, but not unpleasantly, shocked. 'I don't think you really believe all those things you saying. Would you go . . . well, you know what I mean. Would you do that sort of thing with someone like me, for instance?'

'And why not? Why should you be an exception to the rule? You are a healthy man. I am a healthy woman. Why shouldn't we do what we want? In fact you are in a stronger position than most people when I think about it. Yours was not a love match. You yourself said so. So you would be more justified than most.'

Mr Lutchman shook his head. Doreen patted his wrist. 'Don't look so worried. I was only using you as an example.'

Mr Lutchman was a little disappointed by this. He laughed. 'Thank God for that.'

'You go and think about it anyway. Who knows? You might end up agreeing with me.' She winked at him. He brightened, but only for an instant.

He drove back home depressed by the conversation he had encouraged and the desires it had stirred in him.

3

The tale Mr Lutchman had listened to was a strange one. Doreen James lived alone in the house which she had inherited from her mother, a former headmistress and pillar of the Presbyterian community. Mrs James, despite her responsible position, was in many ways an unconventional woman. For one thing, she had taken a great interest in the sexual education of her pupils and had agitated unsuccessfully for many years to have her school turned into a co-educational establishment. As it was, she had doctors and midwives come to the school to lecture and actively encouraged her pupils to 'bring their problems' to her. Doreen had grown up in this liberal atmosphere. Mrs James joked with her daughter and had discussed with her such matters as chastity and promiscuity. Even her religion she did not regard as entirely sacrosanct. But there were lines to be drawn, points beyond which she would not allow herself or others to go. In the end, when all was said and done, Mrs James did believe in God and the virtues of chastity. However, Doreen's logic was more rigorous and she had decided, from a relatively early age, to suspend all belief in both the existence of God and the virtues of chastity until more positive evidence was forthcoming.

Doreen went to her mother's school, not highly regarded either academically or socially. One reason for this was that no other school would have her and even the less demanding qualifications of the Calvin Girls' College would have proved beyond her but for her mother's intervention. Doreen was exempted from the Entrance Examination. 'I have seen too many worthy people fail those examinations and have their careers destroyed,' she said to her friends and critics. 'I have seen Doreen grow up. That's worth more than a hundred entrance examinations.'

A few people were upset by this rather summary procedure, but on the whole, no one complained. Perhaps just as well, for Doreen's scholastic performance at the school was totally devoid of distinction. Apart from her sporting successes (Doreen played hockey for the school team) there was only one noteworthy incident during the six years she spent there: the undisguised affair she had with a master from a nearby boys' school. Mrs James was not worried and excused her daughter on the grounds that it was all part of growing up. But there was another, larger reason why she was not particularly worried by her daughter's behaviour. Mrs James had good contacts at an American university, a little known institution in the Mid-West, and Doreen, less as a result of academic than biological maturity, gained admission and flew to the United States to 'study'. The event was mentioned in the social column of the *Trinidad Chronicle*, although neither the newspaper nor her mother were inclined to specify what exactly it was she had gone to 'study' for three years. This was not unusual. Almost everyone on the island with sufficient money went abroad at one point or another with the avowed purpose of 'studying', or its more eloquently phrased equivalent, 'furthering one's education', tucked vaguely at the back of their minds.

Doreen blossomed at the little known Mid-Western institution. There, certain unsuspected abilities were brought to light for the first time. Among other things, it transpired she was a first-class debater, speaking with a delivery so passionate that it left her opponents stunned. Her debates were reported in the student newspaper, clippings from which she proudly posted to her mother. Eventually, she was elected president of the debating society and the photographs of her inauguration were published in the *Trinidad Chronicle*, above an article headed, 'Local Girl Hits Jackpot in U.S.'.

But all of this, while heartening and of some interest, failed to reveal that other, more peculiar, talent for which, later on, she was primarily to be remembered.

Obscured in this flood of passionate oratory was Doreen's much less publicized talent for affairs of the heart and the singular ability she had acquired for contracting into and out of a series of engagements. The first announcement was duly transmitted by her mother to the gossip columnist of the *Trinidad Chronicle*. Two weeks later, without any coherent explanation, Doreen wrote to say it was 'off'. Mrs James retracted her statement to the newspaper. Six months later Doreen announced another engagement and again Mrs James reported the event to the *Trinidad Chronicle*. This one lasted longer, but eventually another letter, similarly worded to the first, arrived. This time, Mrs James went in person to see the writer of the column and apologized. In the last three years she spent furthering her education Doreen was engaged to be married four times, but her mother neglected to inform the *Trinidad Chronicle* of the last two.

Then, in her last year, Doreen underwent something of a transformation. No new engagements were announced. Instead, she wrote ecstatic letters to her mother about her consuming passion for anthropology. For a while, she talked of writing a treatise on the Pueblo Indians, and although nothing came of that, the ardour of her new-found love continued to burn brightly and she returned home, unmarried, and pursued by a library of books, her enthusiasm for 'folk-ways' unabated.

Nevertheless, she had not entirely given up hope of marrying eventually, and potential suitors, usually doctors freshly returned from abroad, were invited to the house for dinner. Many of these were men considerably younger than Doreen who, after that first dinner, never saw them again. Soon, it became an established custom, a joke among her friends and the returning doctors. This did not prevent her from entering into another three engagements. 'Once every year at Christmas,' it was said. The first of these was in fact to one of the freshly returned doctors; the other two, old friends from the university who had come to Trinidad on a short visit. It was the price they had to pay for staying in the house.

Doreen went through the required motions with decreasing zest and the last three affairs were little more than a matter of form. She had never been good-looking and now age was creeping up on her, obscuring the vivacity and underlining the uglinesses. Her mother's death formed the watershed and provided her with the excuse she had been waiting for. Doreen retreated into a kind of deliberate unfashionableness. She sat at home and played the piano, read the books on anthropology, tended the garden and thought vaguely but without enthusiasm of the lover who might match her tastes, and dreamed of the treatise she was going to write one day. In such a manner then did she soothe her wounded vanity and attempt to regain some at least of the passion that had characterized her youth.

4

Desperately though he tried not to think about it, what Doreen had said and half-suggested preyed on Mr Lutchman's mind and further coloured his view of his wife, his children and his house. His restlessness and dissatisfaction, which his bouts of dissipation, now grown irregular, had never been able to relieve, had at last gained a point of reference; a possible, if at bottom unreal, avenue of release. He rehearsed the arguments in his mind. 'What's so bad about having a regular woman after all? Once I look after my wife and children, what would anybody have to complain about? After all, it's not as if I murdering them. Baby didn't marry me for love. Doreen was just speaking common sense.' And he looked at his wife and was irritated by her increasing fatness. His irritation expressed itself in prolonged bouts of moodiness and silence, and his confinement in the house gradually grew more irksome to him. There were fundamental differences between having a mistress and spending furtive half-hours with prostitutes. The latter formed part of his restlessness and dissatisfaction, feeding upon and in turn being fed by it. The unvarnished flesh, he had discovered a long time ago, could only multiply but not assuage desire and Doreen seemed to promise more than simply the flesh. Those South Sea Islanders who encouraged adultery and even incest had begun to claim a larger and larger share of his thoughts. Yet Mr Lutchman knew that his torment had little to do with intellectual doubt. Ultimately, he could never meaningfully question the code on which he had been raised and the arguments he rehearsed unceasingly in his mind failed to carry conviction. His distress resolved itself in a struggle between his desire, which was not purely of the flesh, and his situation, which was not capable of satisfying the demands of the flesh.

The freedom that Doreen seemed to be offering him was at the same time appalling and irresistible. He was flattered that, simply as a physical object, she should be prepared to find him interesting, and he met her several times after their first meeting in the little snack bar, where they were served by the red-lipped waitress and had ice-cream sundaes and drank iced beer. Doreen suggested that he visit her. 'I have a whole big house all to myself,' she said. 'You could come and relax there.' Mr Lutchman temporized. He did not wish to make a fool of himself, not as yet anyway. This indecision irritated Doreen, impatient for her fantasy to get under way. 'You know something? For all your talk, you are still under the thumb of that Khoja family as much as you ever were. Deep down you're afraid of what they will say. Don't tell me.'

'It's not that,' Mr Lutchman replied. 'You don't understand.'

'Well, what is it then?'

He stared morosely at her and said nothing. That evening he went home more depressed than ever.

'I have an idea, Doreen,' he said the next time they met in the snack bar. 'Why don't we go for a drive one of these days? I have a car after all.'

'You're just saying that to avoid the real issue.'

'I need time to think about it.' He looked at her imploringly.

'Let's make a bargain then. If I go for a drive with you you must promise to make up your mind.'

'I promise.'

Late the following afternoon, about a month after they had met, Mr Lutchman and Doreen went for a drive along the North Coast Road to Maracas Bay. The road, carved out of the mountainside and clinging precariously to the steep, forested slopes, twisted and curved through the hills of the Northern Range, affording occasional glimpses of Port-of-Spain harbour and the more distant grey of the Gulf of Paria, visible through breaks in the mountains.

The road was hemmed in on one side by the sheer walls of rock, cut away like slices of cake and rising high above them to jungle. On the other, the slopes, not of rock but of brown earth, fell swiftly to the valleys below, where there were citrus plantations, odd geometrical intrusions into an otherwise untidy landscape. Further on, the road floated high above the sea, a green and crinkled disc, its surface overspread by a thin, hovering haze, and sometimes, the wall of rock on the other side giving way, there was revealed, like another more threatening sea, the successive waves of ridge and valley, very blue and thickly coated with jungle.

The road descended abruptly and with a sudden view of the

beach, to Maracas Bay. The beach was deserted. A line of coconut trees ringed the yellow curve of sand, but behind the coconuts the ground was swampy and there was a small lagoon. The waves rose high and solid, before tumbling green and foaming in a steady, heavy roar.

Doreen wore a bikini. Mr Lutchman was slightly shocked and greatly relieved there were no other people present. She swam (but only in swimming pools, she informed him), and, in addition, the waves being large and rough, she was content to paddle in the shallower water. Mr Lutchman, shielding himself behind the open car doors much to Doreen's amusement, changed into a pair of maroon swimming trunks with wide legs which reached down almost to his knees.

He was a good swimmer and went out beyond the breakers, his arms plunging in and out of the water in swift, solid movements, his swimming trunks ballooning behind him, like the hindquarters of some strange sea animal. Doreen, impressed by his skill and agility, watched his bobbing head appearing and disappearing between the troughs as he struck out, seemingly, towards the open sea beyond the headlands that imprisoned the bay. Then he turned and describing an arc swam back towards her, just as strongly, but breathing heavily.

They crawled out of the water and threw themselves face downwards on the sand. Doreen, her hair wet and clinging to her cheeks in thick strands, exclaimed with admiration, 'What a swimmer you are, Ram!' Mr Lutchman, tired by his efforts, laughed heavily and scooping up handfuls of wet sand plastered it along Doreen's back. Doreen giggled and squirmed and carved their names in the sand with her fingers. Mr Lutchman closed his eyes and listened to the sounds of the water rolling past his ears, feeling as he had done on those days, when still a boy, he had run away from school and spent the afternoon exploring the back alleys of Doon Town and loitering by the water-melon stalls. For a long time they lay like that near the water's edge, the sun shining on and burning their backs, the wavelets washing over them in cooling runs. Then, together, they counted one, two, three and leaping off the sand they raced back into the water to wash the sand off their bodies. They dried themselves, Doreen changing immodestly into her dress and Mr Lutchman, averting his eyes, struggling in the shelter of the car door.

On their way back, Doreen suggested they stop and watch the sunset. They parked on the edge of a steep cliff. Below them, a wild, tree-covered slope tumbled far down to some rocks, black and jagged, about whose base the waves curled in frills of foam. Purple clouds brushed the rim of the wrinkling sea. It was like a picture book. The scene affected Mr Lutchman, but not because of its beauty. It was too obvious and, if anything, it embarrassed him. He thought, instead, of the Khojas and the jug and six glasses they had given him on his wedding day; the darkened sitting-room of the house in Woodlands and he, Ram Lutchman, crumpling his hat in his hands; his fat wife with her lust for commerce and their two children. All of that seemed very far away just then, unreal and incongruous. But, then, like those trick drawings which one moment appear in the guise of a human head, and in the succeeding moment melt into another shape, so now, what was distant and near, real and unreal, constantly changed places, and thus in the following moment his wife and family would loom large before him and the beautiful sunset recede into the incongruous and unreal. The two neutralized each other and he was left stranded, suspended between two worlds.

'Come and see me tonight and have a drink.' Doreen's voice broke into his fluctuating thoughts like a wedge. 'I don't honestly see what's holding you back.' She gazed searchingly at his face, half smiling and trying not to.

'Come and have a drink.' Echoes of the elegance he had long dreamed of floated free in that statement, counterpart to the shifting realities of the moment. Suddenly, he was struck by the absurdity of his knowing a woman like this, who half an hour before had slipped shamelessly into her dress and who regaled him with tales of adultery and incest on South Sea Islands. 'You made me a promise. Don't forget that.'

'I will think about it,' Mr Lutchman replied.

He returned home late. Mrs Lutchman served him his food in silence. He watched her bent over the stove heating the food, the curve of her back and her slightly tousled hair telling him of her resignation, her patience, her unquestioning duty to wait on him and see that he had all he needed. Romesh came in and sat down next to him, throwing an exercise book and pencil on the table, asking his father to help him work out a 'sum'.

'Leave your father alone, boy. Go upstairs and ask Bhaskar.'

Romesh made a mute appeal with his eyes, but Mr Lutchman ignored him. 'You hear what your mother say, boy. Go and ask Bhaskar. Don't let she have to speak twice to you.' Romesh, pouting, left the kitchen and stamped upstairs.

'I am going to cut his little tail one day,' Mrs Lutchman said. 'You want some roti with your food?'

Mr Lutchman stared dully at the food heaped on his plate. He passed his hands through his matted hair, stiff and wiry from the seawater. 'I go eat it with a piece of bread. Don't bother yourself.' He began to eat.

'Is no bother. I could do it in a jiffy for you if you like.'

'I say it all right.' His voice grated.

Mrs Lutchman studied him. 'Like you went to bathe in the sea? You looking all sun burn.'

'I went to Maracas after work.'

'By yourself?'

'With a friend.'

'Somebody from the office?'

Mr Lutchman chewed slowly on his food. 'No.'

'Who it is you went with then?'

Mr Lutchman slammed his fist on the table. The plate rattled. He stared at his wife. 'You is some kind of judge or magistrate or something?' he shouted. 'Why you have to ask me all this question for, eh? You think I is a child like Romesh?'

'I ask you a simple question, Ram. You don't have to tell me if you don't want to.' She spoke softly, not looking at him.

'Well, I will tell you since you so curious. I went with a woman. You hear that? I went with a woman. You want me to repeat it for you?'

'No. I hear you the first time, Ram.' She smoothed the front of her dress. She took down a cake of soap from one of the shelves. 'I have a lot of washing to do yet,' she said.

'In the dark?' he asked almost gently.

She laughed. 'If I not careful you won't have any clean shirt to wear to the office tomorrow.'

'My shirts clean enough. You don't have to make a martyr of yourself.'

'Who say I making a martyr of myself?'

'Why else you want to be washing when it dark for then? Put back the soap.'

'Is me you go abuse when you don't have any clean shirt to wear.'

'I say put back the soap on the shelf.' He raised his voice. 'I don't like martyrs.' He got up and walked across to her. 'Give me the soap.'

'I tell you I got a lot of washing to do. I don't have time to go gallivanting . . .'

He slapped her. 'Give me the soap. You not made to be a martyr.'

Mrs Lutchman felt her cheek. 'Why don't you slap me some more, eh? I not big enough to hit you back. Why don't you kick and beat me up, eh?' She presented her other cheek to him. 'Come on. Give it to me good and proper.'

'I not going to make you a martyr.' He returned to the table and stared at the uneaten food. Mrs Lutchman went through the door into the back yard. He heard the tap drumming into the tub. He picked up the plate and stared at it. Then suddenly he hurled it against the wall. The food splattered across the floor and the enamel plate clattered and rolled under the table. The tap was still running into the tub. Mrs Lutchman began to sing.

Mr Lutchman went into the sitting-room and lay down on the sofa. He watched an insect struggling to escape from the bowl-shaped lightshade. Scores of dead insects darkened its base. The trapped insect whirred its wings desperately, struggling up the sides of the bowl but always slipping back and never quite able to reach the rim. Its journeys up the side became steadily shorter and the wings whirred with decreasing effect and conviction. Now and again it made a spurt with something of its former energy, but with less and less frequency. Finally, it surrendered and with its wings spread out crawled lethargically over the heap of already dead and charred insects. Soon, that too ceased and with a final defiant flap of its wings, it settled down, ceasing altogether to move, and died.

Mr Lutchman shuddered and got up and turned off the light. He returned to the sofa and lay down as before. Closing his eyes, he pictured once again the look of the sea as it had been that afternoon, the narrow road winding through the mountains and the hills and valleys folding away towards the east; he explored again the texture of the wet sand and the feel of the sun beating down on his back; he saw Doreen slipping into her dress and recalled the glimpse of her nakedness which, in spite of himself, he had caught; the waves roared in his ears and the sky was very pink, and then the sea too became pink and fussed around a group of black, ragged rocks many miles away. 'Come and have a drink.' The phrase echoed, losing itself in the pink sky and sea. He opened his eyes.

The street light shone into the room, falling in an elongated triangle across the floor. He got up and switched on the light and staggered back to the sofa, yawning. Really, he would be quite content to remain where he was and not have to go anywhere, content to let his wife wash his shirts and cook his food. But, he had slapped her and to that extent he had committed himself to an adventure of a different kind. Perhaps he should apologize, take a drive instead with his wife and children to the Belvedere Hill and name the streets of the city. She would nudge him and draw his attention to the public affections of the other couples. He lingered over the image. Desire stirred, clouding the judgement and crippling the will. He would go to Doreen, 'for a drink'. He knew that. Mrs Lutchman was still washing. He went upstairs to his bedroom and combed his hair and hurried noiselessly down to the car.

Doreen was waiting for him, sitting in the verandah drinking a glass of orange juice. 'So you finally made up your mind, I see.' She laughed, leaning over the verandah rail, her arms extended in welcome, as he walked quickly up the path towards her.

5

This declaration did not lead to an open rupture. It merely normalized, as it were, the official seal to an already existing situation. Mr Lutchman was away from the house for long periods. Sometimes, he was not at home for several days on end. What was happening seemed the most natural thing in the world. If Mrs Lutchman suffered, she did so in silence. She accepted her situation with an heroic resolution, visiting her relatives in town and country, cleaning the house and taking care of the children. When she thought of the other woman, she experienced neither bitterness nor jealousy, but found she could contemplate the image drawn in her mind with something approaching indifference. At first, this surprised her, but she was reluctant to probe further and in time grew completely accustomed to that other presence which seemed to have a much greater claim on her husband. Any considerations of love or affection she would have considered an irrelevance. Her marriage, as she well knew, had had very little to do with either of these things. It was one of the laws of life, a purely formal arrangement which was entered into at a suitable age, demanding duty, not love. And the performance of duty was not affected by betrayal. What was there to be betrayed? Betrayal could apply only if there had been love and affection and their marriage, so far, had been devoid of either of these. As it never occurred to her before not to marry Ram, so now it never occurred to her that she might leave her husband. To do that would have been to imply that she had sought something positive from her marriage. That belonged to another set of ideas quite alien to the Khojas. Thus, her husband's infidelities could not destroy her.

Yet, as time passed, she was increasingly sad. Mrs Lutchman was not a thinker. Like the rest of the Khojas she was constitutionally incapable of thought. She could only feel, suspect, divine. She demanded from life not the cold certainties of reason, but an emotional coherence and consistency which had been provided by the Khojas. Thus, to her husband, she could be soullessly dutiful because her soul lay elsewhere. What reason might have told her in half an hour, her soul took years to perceive. Now, however, it had a dim perception of the initial stresses and strains that were already at work flinging out from the centre the insignificant family cells that, taken together, had formed the might of the Khojas. True, this had been going on for a long time, but only now did its significance begin to dawn on her. The bonds were weakening and, as a result, the emotional coherence was beginning to suffer. The evidence was to hand. Why else would she be living in this house? Why else would the house in the country be out of bounds? Woodlands was not and could never be an adequate substitute. Mr Khoja still wielded his spiritual authority unchallenged, but that could not last forever. The third generation was going to prove infinitely less tractable. Almost anything would shatter the harmony when the time came. And then, what? That contingency had to be prepared for. It would demand qualities of another order, and she could not be certain whether she possessed them. At the first twinges of panic she turned to look at her children.

Physically, they both resembled their father. Bhaskar was short and dark, with a round pudgy face, his mother's large, liquid eyes and a tendency to fatness. There was nothing remarkable about him. As a child, he had done or said nothing that was extraordinary, nothing that in later years one might wish to remember or retail. He was obedient, attached to his mother's physical presence and, as she was never tired of saying, 'a good boy'. His intelligence was average. The masters at his secondary school sent respectable reports of him, more concerned with his behaviour in class than academic distinction. Of that there was no sign. Mrs Lutchman could not hide from herself her disappointment at Bhaskar's dull and pedestrian progress.

Romesh, younger, fairer, was decidedly more handsome and lively than his brother. In him, Mrs Lutchman discerned not only a physical, but a spiritual affinity to his father. He was given to violent rages and fits of hysterical weeping. One of these in particular she could never forget.

One day Romesh and Bhaskar were playing together in the back yard. Romesh was about six years old at the time. He picked up a pebble and tossing it into the air caught it on his forehead and headed it away. 'See if you can do that,' he said to Bhaskar. Bhaskar refused the pebble. 'No, no, I'll get cut.' 'Come on,' Romesh insisted, 'I'll throw it up in the air. I'll do it again and show you.' Romesh tossed the pebble up and headed it away a second time. 'You see how easy it is?' Bhaskar shook his head. 'Look at me doing it, you sissy. Look at me!' Romesh shouted. He tossed and headed the pebble away in a growing frenzy. A spot of blood appeared on his forehead. 'Look at me! Look at me!' Romesh crying, flung himself on the ground. Bhaskar watched him, fascinated. Romesh dried his eyes, but left the spot of blood untouched. He looked up at Bhaskar. 'Don't you ever ask me to play with you again. You hear?' He got up, dusted himself and went inside. Mrs Lutchman, who had watched it all from the kitchen window, had dismissed the incident. But she had underestimated her younger son. Romesh had stuck to his childish promise, preferring instead the company of the children on the street.

Officially, he was a bad boy, having refused on one occasion to say 'pranam' to Mr Khoja. Mrs Khoja had suggested he was suffering from 'nerves', a complaint on which she prided herself. Mrs Lutchman had been greatly flattered by this. It was not often that Mrs Khoja allowed equality to anyone, even in matters like disease. Unfortunately, whatever intelligence he may have been endowed with was more or less perpetually obscurd by the smoke-screen of 'nerves' in which he moved; but the belief in his cleverness persisted and sometimes Mrs Lutchman was tempted to think she was nurturing a genius.

Nevertheless, she was not guilty of favouritism. She boasted that she loved both her children equally. This was true, although in her relationship with Bhaskar there was lurking a pained tenderness, a sorrow she was unable to define, which distressed her. Looking at them anew in the light cast by her husband's desertion and those other dimmer perceptions, she began to develop definite ambitions for them. Bhaskar would be a doctor; Romesh, perhaps a lawyer. But of him she was not so sure. His unpredictability, his 'nerves', betokened the unexpected, and she mentally accepted this reservation in the plans she was beginning to nurse for them.

Chapter Three

1

For some time, Mrs Lutchman had been viewing the coming Khoja cattha with mounting excitement. This gathering of the clan at the house in Woodlands had of late assumed in her mind a significance which she had never bothered to bestow on it before, or even realized had existed. She had come to regard it as an inevitable part of the year's activities. Now, unaware that it had happened, she had isolated and invested it with an aura that hinted more of a recapturing of vanished joys and landscapes than a simple coming together of the family. She was going there to recreate something, to try to keep hold of all the strings that kept her world in motion and incise on her memory the colours, the smells, the features of faces, the discomforts – all the elements that, taken together, had made an intelligible whole. For the first time she tried to avoid thinking about what was to come after it. She had become conscious that the past was indeed past and that the present and future were going to be very different.

She would have liked to have gone there a week beforehand as the other sisters had done, but Mr Lutchman would not let her.

'Who you expect to cook my food when you gone gallivanting about the place, eh?'

'But I thought you had enough friends to feed you and look after you in my absence. You never complain before.'

He seemed sulky, a new thing. 'You is my wife. Khoja have enough people to look after him already.'

She abandoned the retort that rose to her lips. The appeal to duty was irresistible and the thought that she was denying herself actually afforded her a bleak pleasure. She delayed her departure for two days.

The annual cattha caused little change in the normal tenor of the Khojas' life. If anything, the silence of the inner sanctum intensified. The Khojas, husband and wife, had insulated themselves from all the bustling activity and noise downstairs. Here were two rigidly defined worlds whose paths scarcely ever crossed. Now and again, the Khojas would descend to the lower regions to ascertain that all was as it should be, but these visitations were brief, their chief effect being to strike fear into the hearts of those lesser mortals. The one disturbance to their routine was the arrival of the elder Mrs Khoja, accompanied by Indrani. She arrived a week before the cattha and was installed in a room to the back of the house, where she received the respects of the family. Apart from this, the course of life in the inner sanctum continued unchanged.

After the excitement caused by his mother's arrival, Mr Khoja resumed his meditations. He wandered through the darkened sitting-room gazing at the titles of the faded books that thronged the shelves, arranged with care by his wife. The books were arranged according to topic. Mrs Khoja had made the odd mistake. Mr Khoja noticed one of them now. In the history section she had included Wells' *History of Mr Polly*. He frowned and taking it out inserted it in the section labelled 'Literature – English'. The 'Religion – Hinduism' section was the most well stocked. It included such titles as *The Kingdom of God is Within You, The Spirit is Infinite,* and *Yoga as a Source of Truth*. Remembering that he had read them all, Mr Khoja grunted with satisfaction. The odour of an astringent medicine flowed into the room, mixing with the smells of the books and the polished mahogany furniture. Mr Khoja liked the combination. It underlined the atmosphere of retreat and sanctity pervading the room. He was in many ways a sensualist, needing constantly to be surrounded by the tangible reminders of his learning, his goodness, his importance. He studied the furniture, the books, the carpet. They were all suitably heavy and imposing. Again he grunted with satisfaction.

Mr Khoja went into his bedroom. His wife was reclining on the bed dressed in a frilly night-dress. She was staring out of the window at the fluttering leaves of the coconut tree that grew in the yard of the house opposite. Mrs Khoja had not been feeling well recently: she had had another of her attacks of 'nerves'. He asked her how she was. 'Tired.' She smiled tenderly at him. Her hair fell loosely on her pale shoulders and her face shone as if it had been recently oiled.

'You go on resting then. I'll look after what needs to be done.'

She nodded. 'You mustn't tire yourself, Govind. I already tell Blackie what she have to do.'

They enjoyed talking like this to each other, pretending that their work took a lot out of them. In fact, Mrs Khoja did very little. She merely supervised Blackie, the one servant they employed.

Mr Khoja had inherited Blackie from his mother. She cooked, did the washing and swept the house. She slept in a tiny room downstairs. Blackie appeared to have no relatives or friends. No one ever came to visit her and she went to visit no one. She spent much of the day maundering slowly through the house, tired and toothless, dusting chairs and tables. Mrs Khoja would remark with wonder to her guests, while Blackie, within ear-shot, fussed with the glasses of Coca-Cola. 'Her grandfather used to be a slave, you know.' This never failed to arouse them from their torpor and Blackie became the object of much curiosity.

The main event in Blackie's calendar was the annual cattha, since it provided her with her one holiday of the year. This happened not because of any deep-felt regard for her, but simply because Negroes could have no place in the festivities. The sisters reserved for themselves the right to work and Blackie gratefully shut herself up in her room, to reappear only when they had all gone.

Mr Khoja sat on the edge of the bed. The room was at the front of the house and he could see the peaks of the Northern Range beyond the lines of rusted roof-tops. There was a breeze and the light lace curtains were licking at the ceiling, sometimes plummeting suddenly when the breeze abated and winding themselves round the supports of the windows. Processions of cloud slipped across the sky revealing long avenues of blue, which silted up gradually only to reappear elsewhere. He liked this room. He delighted in its airiness, its peculiar sweetish odour of powder and perfumes, and the large canopied brass bed, another gift of his mother, hung with tassels, covered by colourful counterpanes and draped at night with a mosquito net. In one corner of the room there was a large cedar-wood dresser with a set of three adjustable mirrors. Spread across it were the soft, fluffy powder-puffs which his wife loved and her dolls standing side by side. They were expensive dolls – one of them was almost two foot tall – which she had been given as a child. Every year she sewed new clothes for them on a machine which otherwise she never bothered to use, specially delighting in their bonnets trimmed with velvet and their frail underwear. She cooed babytalk to them and once – it was after her third miscarriage – she claimed that one of them had fallen ill and nursed it for two days.

Behind the dolls there was a photograph of them on their wedding-day, she young and childish, overwhelmed by her sari, he tall and thin with a clean-shaven face and a pair of delicate gold-rimmed glasses. Mr Khoja gazed at the photograph and then at his wife. How fat she was! His divinity was shaken. To reassure himself he looked round again at the lavish furnishings of the room, trying to avoid seeing the dolls. It was in complete contrast to the darkened sitting-room. Here was spelt out not repose and meditation, but the scenes of domestic bliss. He was more fortunate this time. He did not see the dolls. Mr Khoja relaxed. His divinity was not self-sustaining.

There was a sound of scraping on the door. It was opened and a young dog came bounding in with a happy bark. This was Shadow's successor, named Shadow II. The dynastic idea was Mrs Khoja's. Mrs. Khoja looked at him. Shadow II nuzzled against the bed-sheets. She ruffled his fur. 'Wicked, wicked child,' she murmured. 'I don't know why your father let you come in here.'

'Out, Shadow! Out!' Mr Khoja stamped his foot angrily and Shadow II, tucking his tail between his legs, slunk out of the room.

'You shouldn't be so harsh with him, Govind. He doesn't know what's right and wrong.'

'Chut!' Mr Khoja seemed genuinely irritated by something.

A faint murmur of conversation drifted up from downstairs. 'What about that? You going to leave that there for everyone to see?'

'What you talking about?' His wife looked at him with surprise.

He pointed at a spot on the wall above the head of the bed. It was an illustrated copy of the Psalm 'The Lord is My Shepherd', showing the silhouetted figure of a shepherd boy and his sheep.

'Nobody go come in here to see it.'

'Well . . .' He tried to suppress his agitation, casting another hurried glance at the dolls. He raised himself from the bed and walked over to the window.

'Okay. Keep it. But I don't like to think what people will say if they see that.'

'What could they say, Govind? God is one. He only worshipped in a variety of shapes and forms. You yourself tell me that.'

'But not everybody know that,' Mr Khoja pointed out despairingly.

'That's their fault. Not ours.'

'No matter.' He smiled at her. 'I just a little tired today, that's all.' He went out of the room, closing the door gently behind him.

2

Two days later Mrs Lutchman arrived with Bhaskar and Romesh. Shadow II growled, but without malice, at the newcomers. For the cattha, certain conventions were suspended. Respect for the dog was one of these. Mrs Lutchman was aware of this and she shouted at him. Shadow II turned and raced up the front steps. Mrs Lutchman pushed the gate open with her suitcase and went in. Some children were playing cricket in the garage at the side of the house. They interrupted their game to come up and kiss her on the cheek. 'Hello, Mousie.' They crowded round her.

'Careful you children don't break any windows,' she warned. She was beginning to enjoy herself. The children returned to their game. Romesh wished to join them. 'You stay right where you is, young man.' She pulled him back. Romesh resisted. Mrs Lutchman slapped him and he stared up resentfully at her. They entered through the door on the ground floor. The flight of steps leading from the front gate to the verandah was reserved for visitors of greater importance than the Lutchmans. That was one convention that had not been suspended.

The ground floor was not normally used by the Khojas and bore all the traces of neglect. It had a bare, deeply rutted concrete floor and box-like pillars with peeling plaster supporting the ceiling. It housed a table-tennis board, the dog, and Blackie's bedroom – a windowless hole built around four pillars partitioned from the rest by a flowered screen, Mrs Khoja's idea of homeliness. In wet weather the ground floor was used for drying clothes.

Nephews and nieces and other strange children, some of whom Mrs Lutchman had never seen before, came up to greet her. She looked about her, her eyes sparkling.

'Renouka! But you getting big, girl. I wouldn't know you if I was to see you on the street.' Renouka smiled awkwardly. She was a tall, thin girl, with plaits coming down to the small of her back. Her face, though faintly scarred from chickenpox, bore traces of prettiness.

'How are you, Mousie?' Renouka came up and kissed her. Mrs Lutchman saw the rouge on her cheeks. However, she said nothing about it.

'But hear she talk, eh! Just like a big woman.' Again she glanced at the rouge. The children laughed and Renouka, blushing, retreated in some confusion.

Smells of stale food and the sound of voices raised in argument drifted in from the improvised kitchen in the yard. Someone was singing a bhajan. Mrs Lutchman recognized the voice immediately. Each of the Khoja sisters had their own speciality and Urmila was the recognized singer of the group. Her voice was not particularly pretty. It was thin and high and quavering, but what it lacked in beauty and technique it more than made up for by its staying power. That was its inestimable virtue. Urmila could sing for hours on end and not get hoarse.

There was another typical sound. A child was being beaten, and its piping wail blended with that of the singer's. It was like a duet, so well did the two voices complement each other.

Mrs Lutchman, her two children in tow, pushed her way to the back of the house. Out in the yard, some of the older boys, stripped to the waist, were lifting weights and doing other exercises. Mrs Lutchman peeped into the improvised kitchen.

The 'kitchen' was a square wooden shed, with a high smoke-blackened ceiling of corrugated iron. It was used principally for storing the Khojas' many unwanted items of furniture and the odd planks of timber that Mr Khoja collected from one of the estates. During the cattha, the furniture was removed to the garage and the timber was cut up to make firewood. The floor was of pounded earth and cow-dung. Here the women gathered to gossip, sing and cook. There were about a dozen women squatting there when Mrs Lutchman looked in.

'Baby! So you come at last. We had nearly given you up for lost. You bring your husband with you?'

Mrs Lutchman was beaming. 'He's not feeling too well. You know how it is, Badwatee, so I thought it was better for him to stay at home.'

Shadows simultaneously crossed the dark faces ranged against the walls. Urmila, who had stopped singing when Mrs Lutchman appeared, resumed her song. The remains of the previous night's meal were still visible in the large pots, like cauldrons, occupying the centre of the room. Their rims were coated with traces of rice and dahl and curried vegetables.

'Go and kiss your Mousies. What do you think you doing standing there with your tongue hanging out?' Mrs Lutchman shoved her sons into the room to make the round of the gathered aunts. 'How is Ma?'

The assembly puckered its brows. 'The same,' Darling, another of the sisters, volunteered. She, too, like Mrs Lutchman, had been given a nickname at birth which had stuck with her ever since. 'She was asking about you,' she added after a pause. It was meant to be a 'significant' remark. Mrs Lutchman took the point and stared guiltily at her.

Their duty done, Bhaskar and Romesh returned to their mother. Urmila's song reached a climax, passed through a moment of indecision, then recovered itself and flowed on. She was the darkest of the sisters, with a narrow face and a slim, hawkish nose. She sang with passion, with the slightest suggestion of manic excitement in her sparkling eyes. One or two of the sisters, intent on preserving their energies for the evening's performance, accompanied her with a discreet hum.

'Chulo, children. We must go and see your nanee and mamoo now.' Mrs Lutchman went slowly up the wooden steps, dragging her sons behind her. She was greeted by the familiar sepulchral silence of the upper floor and the smell of Huntley and Palmers biscuits. On this occasions, however, it was combined with the odour of medicines and the scent of wads of cotton wool soaked in bay-rum. She paused outside the door to the elder Mrs Khoja's bedroom, listening. A faint murmur of conversation reached her. The door was not locked and she pushed it open and went in. The conversation ceased abruptly and the blind woman raised her head expectantly.

The elder Mrs Khoja was sitting up in bed, propped against pillows. She wore a white bandage, wound tightly around her head, above and below which straggling, silver-grey strands of hair were visible. Her face was gaunt and severely wrinkled, loose folds of skin lying on her cheek-bones and drooping from her chin. Her neck too was drained of all substance, the blue veins clearly channelled and the dried skin working on her Adam's apple, as if she were chewing her cud.

The guardian daughter sitting on a chair beside the bed smiled at the intruders and motioned them to approach quietly. Then she bent and whispered in the old lady's ear. Only Urmila's song rippled the silence.

'Baby!' Her voice was surprisingly strong. Her eyes swivelled vacantly in the direction of the doorway, probing the figures standing there, her pinched lips moving regularly up and down, hiding the pink toothless gums. 'Come here and kiss me. Did you bring the children with you?'

'Yes, Ma. They are here with me.' Mrs Lutchman went up to the bed and kissed her. She had long been accustomed to consider herself one of the old woman's daughters. As to her true mother, she was distant, remote, part of a legend concocted merely to comfort her. 'Come and kiss your nanee, children.'

Mrs Khoja held her arms out and encircled the two boys. They kissed her, once on each cheek. She dropped her arms and they slid away.

'Come back here, Rom, and tell your nanee what a bad boy you is to your mother.' Romesh returned and she cuddled him. 'And how is Bhaskar getting on at school, Baby?'

'Very well, Ma. He does work hard.'

'Good. Good.' She continued to cuddle Romesh, laughing, his head resting on her bosom. She let him go and slid further down into her pillows. 'Where is Ram?'

'He wasn't feeling too well, Ma.' Mrs Khoja nodded, but whether 'significantly' or not Mrs Lutchman could not tell. 'Soak my head a little.' The box of medicines was on the floor beside the bed. Indrani searched in it for the bottle of bay-rum and uncorked it. Mrs Khoja put out an arm to restrain her. 'No, no, Indrani. Let Baby do it.'

'I could do it, Ma. I accustom to doing it.' Indrani poured some of the bay-rum into her cupped palms.

'No, no. Let Baby do it.' Mrs Khoja kicked her feet fussily under the bedclothes. Mrs Lutchman took the bottle from Indrani's outstretched hand. The face beyond it was silent, unhappy. Mrs Lutchman poured some into her palm and massaged the old woman's head and forehead. 'I always liked the feel of your hands, Baby.'

Mrs Lutchman laughed. She could feel Indrani's gaze pinned on her. 'It's not I who deserve thanks, Ma. Is Indrani you should be thanking. She's the one who does look after you.' She laughed again, this time with greater gaiety. Mrs Khoja was silent. The room was flooded with sunlight.

'That's enough,' Indrani said, taking away the bottle from Mrs Lutchman with a hint of roughness. 'You better go and see Govind now. She does get tired easily these days.' She semed apologetic.

'I not tired.' Mrs Khoja pouted petulantly and turned her head towards the open window.

'You better go all the same,' Indrani repeated softly to Mrs Lutchman.

Mrs Khoja, chewing, sightless, had sunk back on the pillows. Mrs Lutchman withdrew, the eyes of the guardian daughter escorting her to the door. Downstairs in the kitchen, Urmila was still singing.

Mr Khoja was, as usual, reading in the sitting-room. His wife was having her afternoon rest. He looked up abstractedly when Mrs Lutchman and her sons came into the room. 'Ah, Vimla. You are here.' She might have been late for school. He glanced at and through Bhaskar and Romesh who hung back near the door.

'Say pranam to your Mamoo, children.'

Mr Khoja inclined his head to one side and waited for the magic word. The boys mumbled their pranams. 'Yes,' he said, 'wait till you go to Oxford or Cambridge. Then you could greet me however you want to.' He smiled. 'I see you didn't bring Ram with you.'

It was one of Mrs Lutchman's peculiarities that whenever she was confronted by Mr Khoja, artifice tended to give way to literalness, and admission that everything was, in fact, what it seemed to be.

'No,' she said simply, gazing at the reflections in the glass.

'Working hard?'

Mrs Lutchman shrugged. Mr Khoja examined his fingernails. They were pink and even.

'How's everything?' he asked indulgently.

'As well as can be expected in the circumstances, praise God.'

Mr Khoja did not bother to enquire what these circumstances were. He knew his family well enough to realize that, like himself, they spoke much of the time in formulae.

'Yes. It's him we must always fall back on,' he said.

'That's what I always say myself. You've got to thank God for everything.'

Mr Khoja closed his eyes, frowning. It was difficult to go beyond such a theological non sequitur. Urmila finished her song.

'You've been to see Ma?' he asked.

'Yes. I thought she was looking very well.' Mrs Lutchman woke from the reverie into which she had fallen. 'Well, I think I'll go and change my clothes now. There must be lot to do downstairs.'

'I wouldn't be surprised. But try not to make too much noise while you are about it.' They both laughed. He began to read.

'Chulo,' Mrs Lutchman whispered to Bhaskar and Romesh. They tiptoed out of the room.

3

Each day brought its influx of new visitors. Many of these people were only distantly related to the Khojas, but the merest hint of kinship was a passport to the house. In dark corners, strange women nursed babies, while older, mewling infants crawled at their feet; the young girls gossiped and tittered and flirted with their cousins; in the kitchen, the women pooled their labours and sang; in the yard, the older boys exercised and played cards in the 'servants' room'; while behind the flowered screen, Blackie slept, oblivious of the noise and confusion.

The day was well ordered. Breakfast consisted of biscuits soaked in cups of tea, and when that was over the night's confusion of sheets and blankets was cleared away and the floor sprinkled and swept. Lunch was makeshift, and between breakfast and dinner the boys played cricket on the pavement and in the garage, the women gossiped in the kitchen and the younger children were bathed and looked after by their mothers.

At five, preparations for dinner began. Mounds of cabbages, tomatoes and potatoes were washed and sliced and thrown into the cauldrons. The wood fires flamed and the smoke rose, blackening the walls and ceiling and choking the women. Mrs Lutchman was like a creature transformed. She had changed into a suit of soiled, worn clothes: short-sleeved blouse and a skirt reaching down to her ankles, a uniform adopted by all the women there. The raggedness and dirt were deliberate. To be clean and tidy was to open oneself to the charge of dilettantism, of not having one's heart in the work, or being, to use the favourite term of abuse employed by the sisters, too 'modern'. Thus, they were all spectacularly filthy.

Squatting over the boiling cauldrons, stains of sweat showing on their backs and arms, they stirred the pots with long, flat pieces of wood, resembling paddles, singing as they stirred. Half-hidden in the smoke and steam, her face wet, her eyes shining, Mrs Lutchman joined the chorus in a near hoarse voice, her face lit by an expression of simple animal delight.

At six, Mrs Khoja made one of her tours of inspection. Trailing her sari down the steps and wearing soft, delicate slippers, she hovered uneasily near the kitchen door, trying to avoid the clouds of steam rising from the cauldrons. Shantee, one of the sisters who had appropriated to herself the task of keeping Mrs Khoja informed of all that was happening, detached herself from the steaming pots and bustled up to her sister-in-law. They talked earnestly for some minutes, perhaps about the shortage of banana leaves, Shantee melodramatically urgent and always exasperated about something, opening her eyes wide in warning if an intruder chanced to pass too near; Mrs Khoja smiling, thoughtful and troubled in turns. When the conference was over, she surveyed the food in the pots and gingerly pecked at the samples she was offered to taste. It was assumed that what was suited to her taste must necessarily be all right for everyone.

'It have enough salt?' the sister concerned would ask.

Mrs Khoja considered and for want of nothing better to say, might reply, 'It could do with a few spoons more, I think.'

'How much? Two? Three?'

Mrs Khoja was always mathematically exact. 'Two and a quarter,' she would reply firmly.

Later that night, if anyone complained the food was too salty, he was shown no mercy. 'Who you think you is, eh? You think you know better than your mamee, eh?' He was lucky to escape without a beating. 'I don't know where they does get all these modern ideas from!'

But, most of the time, Mrs Khoja approved of what was presented to her. Then she joked lightly with the sisters. 'I haven't seen your children as yet, Darling. They well?'

'Yes, Sumintra. All of we very well, please God. How you feeling yourself these days?'

'Not too bad. But I does still get these headaches from time to time.'

Anxious eyes peered through the steam at her. 'You should drink a little bush-tea. You try that yet?'

'I does try everything once, Urmila, but I find the aspirin does work the best when all is said and done.'

'So everybody does say, but give me a little bush-tea any day. I find it does work wonders with me.'

'Well, I suppose it different with everybody.'

'That's a very true thing you just say.' Mrs Lutchman gazed with admiration at Mrs Khoja. Heads shook in sympathy and, the matter settled, Mrs Khoja returned upstairs to prepare her husband's dinner.

Food was served on trestle tables about fifteen feet long. There were three such tables ranged beside each other. One was reserved for mothers and their babies and the other two for the older cousins, divided according to sex: the Khojas were aware of the possible dangers that could arise from mixed eating. The sisters were always on the watch for the incipient liaisons that tended to develop during that week of long, hot afternoons with little to do.

'Talk,' they said, 'does lead to we all know what.' And they raised their eyebrows 'significantly' at each other. Accordingly, they looked upon with suspicion and discouraged any too open joking among the male and female members of the clan and in time Badwatee took it upon herself to oversee and report on their doings. 'Better be sad than sorry,' she warned.

The food was brought in in large basins, the rice and vegetables still steaming and almost too hot to touch. Each of the sisters came in turn with her basin, the contents of which she ladled onto the banana leaves. Everyone ate with their hands.

Mrs Khoja made her second appearance then, wandering aimlessly among the tables, chatting with the smaller children and occasionally, as a special mark of favour, patting them on the head. After dinner, the banana leaves were thrown into a large box which was put out on the pavement. The tables were dismantled and the hardboard tops were arranged on the floor and spread with sheets to be used later on as beds.

After he had had his separately cooked dinner, Mr Khoja made his descent to the lower regions. Casually dressed, nylon shirt open at the collar and flopping limply outside his trousers, hands clasped behind his back, he threaded his way through the maze of faces, many of which he did not know, amiably contemptuous of everyone. Now and again he would raise his hand in mild salute to someone he wished to grace, but these vague intimations of friendliness only had the effect of leaving the recipient visibly ill at ease.

If he went up to the table-tennis board, where there was usually a game in progress, the players fumbled, lost concentration and finally stopped. Mr Khoja, his arms still clasped behind his back, and pleased by the disruption he had caused, would smile at the discomfited players, at the same time examining the board for signs of damage.

'Don't let me frighten you, children. Go on with your game and forget about me.'

Embarrassed giggles were exchanged between the players. 'You want to have a game, Mamoo?' one of them had eventually to offer. By this time, a crowd would have gathered round the table. Mr Khoja enjoyed an audience. He accepted the proffered racket, also examining that for signs of damage. 'You mustn't beat me too bad in front of all these people. My old muscles are not match for yours.' He flexed his arms playfully and waved his racket genially at his opponent. The crowd laughed.

'It's I who should be worrying, Mamoo. Not you. You have bigger muscles than me,' the young man risked, afraid that his too intimate tone might offend. But an audience always put Mr Khoja in a good mood.

He laughed. 'Take care I don't beat you then, child.' And the crowd, taking their cue from him, laughed again. The game began. Their eyes followed Mr Khoja's every move, applauding his rare successes and moaning at his copious failures. At last, sweating profusely, he would call a halt to the proceedings. 'I getting too old for this kind of thing. Here, somebody take over from me.'

'You does play very well, Mamoo,' his opponent said gallantly.

'I used to be champion of my school one time,' he would reply, with what truth no one ever knew. However, it was not permitted to doubt it. He would surrender the racket and return upstairs, well pleased with himself at this exercise in democracy.

4

No Khoja function was ever considered complete without a beating. Any infringement of the rules (they could be invented on the spur of the moment) could be made the occasion for one of these entertainments, and children who were rarely beaten at home would suddenly find themselves liable. The choice of the victim was, in the normal run of things, capricious. At such times the sisters became unpredictable forces and, a beating once administered, its influence percolated through the clan. Several more victims were hastily assembled, although none could surpass the grandeur of that first beating, whose majesty echoed ever more faintly down the chain until, finally, the urge spent itself in a mother slapping her three-month-old baby. 'That's the first time I ever hit him,' she would announce proudly to the surrounding sisters and back would come the reply, relentless, unforgiving: 'They got to begin learning who's boss some time. Spare the rod and you does spoil the child.' After that, everybody relaxed and the aunts relapsed into a milder, more inoffensive state.

Saraswatee, Renouka's mother, was the youngest of the Khoja sisters. She betrayed her youth in several ways. Her husband was still alive, she was slim, and her dresses ended above her ankles. All of these were sources of embarrassment to her. The sisters tended to treat her as if she were still a child, never listening seriously to what she had to say. As a result, she longed desperately to be old, fat and widowed, if only on those occasions when the family gathered together.

Burdened with these indelible marks of good fortune, Saraswatee was constantly in search of new ways to improve her status. She tried to sing louder than the rest, wear her dresses longer and dirtier, and speak Hindi, which she did not know all that well. Her hair was oiled and plaited and she stirred the pots in the ramshackle kitchen with a desperate fervour that none could criticize. But to no avail. Nothing could hide the delicacy of her figure and movements or camouflage the natural gaiety of her youth. In a word, when among her sisters, Saraswatee was unhappy.

Renouka was her only child. The sisters disapproved of her. She called her father 'Daddy' and, what was even more incomprehensible, he obviously doted on her. In fact, Renouka was already at the Sacred Heart convent which, if not one of the best, was certainly one of the most fashionable girls' schools in Port-of-Spain. She wore a distinctive grey and white uniform with a royal blue tie and carried her lunch (cheese and tomato sandwiches) in a pink plastic container. The sisters feared for her soul.

'You spoiling that child, Saraswatee. I don't see why you have to send she to one of these school in Port-of-Spain. What wrong with all them school in Arima? Instead you have she wearing this short, short uniform, showing she legs for all the world to see.'

'It wasn't me who send she to that school. It was she father. I didn't like the idea at all, but you know if I open my mouth . . .' Saraswatee stirred her pot uneasily. In fact, the complications that might arise from her daughter going to a school in Port-of-Spain had not occurred to her before. The sisters were not impressed. Urmila snorted.

'I see she the other day on Pembroke Street talking to some boys from the college there and, you wouldn't believe this, but the girl almost act as if she didn't know me.'

'She's getting too modern,' Shantee added. 'You shouldn't expect all these modern girls in their high-heel shoes and rouge and lipstick to come up and kiss they mousie on the street.'

'It's all she father fault,' Saraswatee wailed, her head lowered in distress over the steaming cauldon. 'I always tell him he shouldn't have send she to that school. But you know I does count for nothing in my own house.' She spoke of her husband in a way that implied he was not more than a distant acquaintance, an intruder in her life.

'Well, she better watch out for she self, that's all I have to say on this matter,' Urmila said. Nevertheless, she went on, 'I know all them convent girls well. All they interested in is having boy-friend and wanting to become beauty queen. I was reading a case in the paper the other day about one of them who get expel from the convent. She was making a baby.'

'That's all they good for nowadays,' Shantee replied. 'Having boy-friend and making baby.'

'Well, if Renouka come home to me one day and say she making a baby, she not going to leave my house alive, no matter what she father say or don't say. I go skin she.' She looked defiantly at each face in turn. The sisters were tight-lipped and approving. They had never seen her in such a warlike mood before. 'I go skin she alive,' Saraswatee insisted, warming to her theme.

'Thank God,' Mrs Lutchman broke in, 'I only have sons to worry about.'

'Huh! I wouldn't speak too soon, Baby. You just wait till they grow up and begin drinking and gambling and smoking. They too is more trouble than they worth. I don't know which is worse in this modern generation, boys or girls. You go soon see what you have to be thankful for.' Urmila, leaning back, gloated at her. The sisters were out for blood.

'I go skin she if she ever come home to me and say she making a baby. I go skin she.'

The smoke rose in clouds to the ceiling.

Saraswatee's opportunity to skin Renouka came sooner than she expected. Early the following morning, the house was woken up by screams. It seemed that Renouka had locked herself in the servant's room and chopped off her plaits. The news had spread quickly.

'I going to skin that girl alive,' Saraswatee had declared solemnly to her sisters.

Renouka, crying, flitted among the pillars, with her mother, hair flying, in full pursuit.

'Come here, you little bitch. Come here and let me cut some more hair off your head for you. I going to show you how good I does cut hair, you little bitch.'

Renouka dodged behind the table-tennis board.

'So you think you is a woman already, eh! Cutting off your hair to show off. Who you have to show it off to? A boy-friend? You sure you not making a baby as well? I go show you how to make baby.'

'Oh God, Ma, be reasonable.' Renouka, gripping the edge of the table-tennis board, was tensed for further flight. 'What so wrong in cutting my hair? Is my own hair, I not doing anybody any harm.'

Nephews and nieces, wide-eyed and silent, had taken up strategic positions.

'What's wrong? I go show you what's wrong.' Saraswatee moved swiftly around the table and the chase was resumed. 'Somebody get me a belt. I going to belabour she this morning. I going to skin she alive.' Her voice was already going hoarse. One of the aunts offered a belt, commandeered from one of the smaller boys, who was boxed for his troubles.

'Oh God, Ma! What get into you so suddenly?' Saraswatee swished the belt, hitting out wildly in all directions. 'Don't lash me, Ma. I didn't do anybody no harm.'

'You begging? A big woman like you who know how to make baby begging?'

'Who say I making a baby?' Renouka pleaded. 'All these people looking at we, Ma. Don't shame me, please.'

An aunt, the same who had supplied the belt and claimed to know all there was to know about 'convent girls', came up running to assist in the chase. Renouka was cornered. She backed against the flowered screen partitioning Blackie's room.

'Ma, please, please. Be reasonable. What get into you so suddenly?' She crumpled against the screen, sobbing.

'Come here, you little animal. I going to show you how to run away from me.' Saraswatee reached forward and took hold of her daughter's ears and twisting and kneading them between her fingers, she dragged Renouka, choking on her sobs, her face buried in her hands, away from the flowered screen. The sisters lined up in military formation on either side of them and Renouka was frog-marched through the house, out to the yard and across to the servant's room. Mr Khoja, attracted by the noise, made an unscheduled appearance. He headed the procession that followed them across the yard.

Renouka's hair, which had not been swept away, littered the floor. There was a comb, a pair of scissors and a mirror on a chair in the centre of the room. Saraswatee stared at the evidence.

'I feel like making you eat that hair, rubbing your face in it.' She curled and uncurled the belt around her wrist. Renouka collapsed on the chair, her shoulders heaving, her face still buried in her hands. Faces, illuminated by the same uniformly morbid curiosity, crowded in the doorway. Only the sisters and Mr Khoja were allowed inside. 'Somebody cut me a whip,' Saraswatee ordered. 'A belt too good for she.' She threw the belt on the floor. One of the sisters ran off in search of a whip.

Mr Khoja stepped forward. 'What it is get into you, child?'

Renouka shifted uncomfortably on the chair. She had not removed her hands from her face.

'Answer your Mamoo, you little bitch.'

'What, you was ashamed of your plaits or something?' Mr Khoja always abandoned grammar when he spoke to his relatives. 'I suppose it's all your fancy school friends who put all these ideas in your poor head.' He raised his voice. 'I know we too backward for people like you and your friends, being heathens, and that you ashamed of we. I surprise you haven't become a Christian as yet, at the rate you seem to be going.' This classing of himself with the multitudes brought looks of gratitude to the faces of the sisters. Even Saraswatee unbent momentarily, but its ultimate result was merely to redouble her fury against her daughter. 'Being heathen,' Mr Khoja went on, refreshed by the effect of his words, 'we can only behave like heathens. You must pardon us since we don't know better.' The whip arrived, borne above the heads of the crowd by Darling. Saraswatee tested it. Her audience looked on in silence.

'Get up!' she shouted suddenly, flexing the whip.

Renouka did not move.

'Get up, I say, you little bitch!'

Renouka shook her head.

'All right, you good-for-nothing wretch.' Saraswatee spoke softly now, clenching her teeth. She raised her arm. The whip descended with a swish through the air, landing on Renouka's shoulders with a dull thud. Renouka cowered and screamed and leapt off the chair.

'Ah! So you decide to get up after all. What is it make you

change your mind so sudden I wonder?' Saraswatee succumbed to the frenzy that had been threatening to seduce her since the conversation she had had with the sisters the day before. Again and again the whip descended with the same dull thud, now on Renouka's back, now on her shoulders. Renouka, shrieking, darted like a crazed insect around the room, before finally settling in a corner, where she sank slowly to the floor, her arms like wings ineffectually shielding her head. Saraswatee, her features pinched, her nostrils twitching, closed in on her, raining blows.

Mr Khoja decided to intervene. 'That's enough, Saraswatee. You don't want to kill the child.' For a moment she struggled with him, then, reluctantly, she allowed him to take charge of the whip. Breathing hard from her exertions, she gazed at her daughter sprawled on the floor.

'You better thank your Mamoo for being so kind to you, otherwise, as God is my witness, I don't know what I would have do to you today.' The throng of faces stepped back to make way for her. Staring straight ahead, Saraswatee walked quickly across the room, her long skirt swirling about her ankles, and ran down the steps into the yard. She walked quickly, head erect, ignoring the neighbours peeping over the fence.

'It's a good whip, this,' Mr Khoja said after she had gone. He smiled. 'I'll keep it upstairs in case it have to be used again.' He surveyed the children. 'I wonder which of you it will be,' he said meditatively.

'What you staring at with your eyes sticking out of your heads? You two better watch your step or soon it is you who go be feeling the weight of that on your back.' Mrs Lutchman collared her sons and on each of the two faces standing before her she delivered a resounding slap.

5

The next day, the bamboo and tarpaulin for the tent arrived. Mr Khoja had been given permission to use the yard next door (in exchange for paying the cost of a new fence) and the cousins were drafted to demolish the rotting wooden boards. It was easy work and the smaller children gathered round to watch. Romesh, who had acquired something of a reputation for dare-devilry by virtue of the facility he had for bouncing pebbles thrown high into the air off his forehead, was given a hammer and set to work with the rest. At midday Mr Khoja made one of his tours of inspection to see how the work was progressing. He strolled amiably among the workers, his hands clasped behind his back. 'Work. There's nothing like working with the hands,' he said encouragingly. He stopped, frowning, near Romesh. 'Who it is give this child a hammer?' He scrutinized the workers. The hammering stopped, but no one confessed. 'I thought I say that all small children was to remain inside and not come out here. Remember it is I who would be held responsible if one of them cut they foot on a nail or something like that.' The cousins stared stolidly at the ground.

'Come here, child, give me that hammer.' Mr Khoja held out his arms fretfully.

Romesh refused and took a step back.

'What! What's this! Look boy, I not joking. Give me that hammer right this minute.'

Romesh grasped the hammer more tightly and shook his head.

'Oh, so you want to play stubborn. Well, I'll show you how to play stubborn with me.' Mr Khoja bending forward tried to grab the hammer from him, but Romesh refused to let go and continued to back away, pulling Mr Khoja after him. Mr Khoja tugged at the hammer, shouting. This brought out an array of sisters. There was a struggle. Mrs Lutchman came running up and attempted to drag her son away. Romesh let the hammer fall, and Mr Khoja, who was wearing a pair of open-work slippers, howled with pain and backed away, hopping on one foot.

'I'll show you, you little devil, how to drop hammers on people's feet. Somebody go and get that whip I put upstairs. I'm going to teach this savage here a lesson he will never forget.'

Mrs Lutchman, panic-stricken, examined the injured toe. 'It hurting you bad?'

'Don't touch it there. It very painful.' Mr Khoja grimaced and Mrs Lutchman released his foot.

'You better wash it in some iodine. That go stop it from swelling up.'

Saraswatee, her standing among the sisters immeasurably enhanced, arrived with the whip and handed it to Mr Khoja. He danced painfully around Romesh brandishing the whip.

'Now we'll see who is the more stubborn. You or me.'

'Give it to me,' Mrs Lutchman said. 'He had this coming to him a long time. You does be too soft with them. I go do for him good and proper.'

Mr Khoja gave her the whip.

'Come here, Mr Man. I warn you yesterday you was going to feel the weight of this on your back before long.' She looked around the yard. 'Where is Bhaskar? He might like a little taste of this too.' But Bhaskar was nowhere in sight. She was disappointed. 'I go catch up with him, don't worry.' She reverted to the business in hand. 'Hold out your hands, Mr Champion Hammer Thrower.'

Romesh held out his hands. He did not cry, although his lips were set and his face flushed. When it was over, he ran across the yard and disappeared into the darkness of the house. He lay on the bare concrete floor, curled in a corner. For several hours he remained like that, refusing to eat or talk to anyone.

Mr Khoja, cradling his toe, limped up the stairs.

'That boy does suffer from nerves,' Mrs Khoja tried to console him. 'He not responsible for everything he do.'

'Nerves my arse. They are a lot of little savages down there.'

'Govind! You mustn't speak like that. They is your family after all, and although they don't have your education, you must still try and be nice to them.'

'Huh!' Mr Khoja felt his toe. 'What you say is true, I suppose. I too impatient with them really.'

Mrs Khoja puckered her brows. 'You must learn to be more patient with them.' She thought with delight of her own family and how little trouble they were. Aristocrats, they arrived only on the very eve of the cattha and had the privilege of sleeping and eating upstairs. They did not consider themselves part of the multitude.

The beatings having run their course, life regained its former tenor. In two days the tent was finished, roofed with the bulging tarpaulin and floored with rough wooden planks. There was a circle chalked out in the centre for the puja mound. Mr Khoja had rented three hundred folding chairs. These were stacked in tall piles in the garage, their use forbidden, for no good reason, until the night of the cattha.

During the day, the boys played cricket on the pavement, which always attracted a sizeable audience of Negro boys who were allowed to field, sometimes bowl, but never bat. Now and again, Mrs Khoja would come to the front gate and drive them away.

'You boys, go away from here and leave the children alone. You blocking the gate, Shush! Shush!'

Nevertheless, on the last day of the cattha, the most patient Negroes had their reward. They were called in and fed on what remained of the food.

The nightly concerts reached a climax on the eve of the cattha. Preparations for dinner were less thorough than usual, and after the tables had been cleared and dismantled, the women, with Mr Khoja's permission, brought some of the folding chairs from the garage and set them out in a circle inside the tent. The nephews and nieces sat behind them on benches. Urmila led the singing, beating time with her feet on the floor.

'Let we ask Govind to lend we his drum,' one of the sisters suggested. The idea was received with approval and a delegation climbed the steps to see him. He was in the rarely used dining-room having dinner with his wife's relations.

'I'll come down and play it for you,' he offered. 'It's a long time since I had the opportunity to do that.' Mr Khoja was proud of his drumming and his drum. It had long been regarded as one of the family's heirlooms. The drum had been brought to Trinidad by the elder Mr Khoja and, so it was said, had originally been the property of his father. As such, it was treasured and Mr Khoja allowed it to be used only on very special occasions.

He brought it down to the tent after dinner and, squatting on the boards, placed the drum between his legs. He spent a long time adjusting the strings and making trial runs. 'It getting too old. You got to be careful with it,' he explained to the sisters, who were eyeing him impatiently. At last, all was ready. Urmila sang a solo and Mr Khoja drummed gently. The sisters joined in, clapping and stamping their feet. Taking it in turns, each of the sisters performed her favourite song to the clapping and stamping chorus of the rest. Mr Khoja's drumming grew more confident.

'Dance. Dance. Somebody dance.' He waved at the sisters. The cry was taken up by the audience. 'Dance! Dance!' There were disclaimers and refusals and much laughter, but eventually Darling rose and entered the chalked circle. Arranging her dress, she balanced on the tips of her toes and flinging her arms outwards, began to dance. It was an ungainly performance. Darling staggered round the circle twisting and shaking her body, flinging her arms outwards for no apparent reason and rolling her eyes. However, it was done with energy and conviction which more than compensated for its lack of grace.

'Dance! Dance! Let a new person take over,' Mr Khoja shouted. There were renewed disclaimers, refusals, laughter. The tempo of the drumming accelerated. 'Dance! Dance!' Mr Khoja, gaining confidence by the minute, changed the rhythm often, now faster, now slower, now speeding it up again. Urmila stepped boldly into the circle and lifting her skirts, with a flourish, well above her knees, capered about the circle. Her performance was more accomplished than Darling's. Her arms carved sinuous patterns in the air and she tried valiantly to jerk her neck from side to side in time with the drumming. Some of the children joined in and Urmila, the beads of sweat pouring down her face, left the circle, her face buried in a smile.

'Come on, Vimla, your turn now. You haven't dance yet.' Mr Khoja, his shirt soaked in sweat, took it off and threw it across the room. The sisters pushed Mrs Lutchman into the circle and the drumming started up again. Like Urmila, she lifted her skirt above her knees as she danced, her face aglitter with effort. But, she was not a good dancer and at one point stumbled and nearly fell. Then she too, happy and laughing, left the circle.

'Come on, Saraswatee,' Mr Khoja shouted, 'don't hide yourself behind there. It's your turn now.'

'Renouka,' Saraswatee called, her eyes searching along the benches, 'come and dance with me, girl. Come and dance with your mother.'

Reluctantly, Renouka approached her mother from behind the benches. Saraswatee gazed at her, her eyes shining, and extended her arms. She took hold of her hand and led her into the circle. 'Dance! Dance!' Their arms flailing, mother and daughter flung themselves gracelessly about the circle.

There was a flutter among the benches. The drumming died away and Mr Khoja looked enquiringly at the children. They were pointing behind him. Saraswatee and Renouka stopped dancing and left the ring.

Indrani was struggling slowly and with great difficulty down the steps, guiding the feet of the elder Mrs Khoja. Mr Khoja got up and went to help, followed by an anxious throng of sisters.

'It's all right, it's all right,' Indrani was saying. 'Nothing gone wrong. Don't worry. Ma hear the singing and she wanted to come down and be with you. That's all.' She led the old woman to one of the chairs and placed a cushion on it. The elder Mrs Khoja lowered herself onto the chair and with an alert, eager face, swivelled her head and smiled into space.

'Go on playing the drum, Govind, and let Urmila sing for me.'

Mr Khoja squatted on the floor again and began drumming gently. Urmila sang a bhajan, the same song Mrs Lutchman had heard on the day of her arrival. It went on a long time, Urmila's strong, piping voice exhibiting all its native strength and staying-power, wavering through the tent and out over the fence into the neighbouring yards. The sisters chorused softly, clapping their hands. Mrs Khoja, her mouth working endlessly, listened with a vacant smile. When the song was finished, Indrani leaned over and whispered into her mother's ear. The old woman nodded. Urmila came up and kissed her on the cheek.

'It's a long time since I hear that drum play,' Mrs Khoja murmured. Mr Khoja helped in lifting her off the chair and carried her back up the steps. Urmila dried her eyes with the sleeve of her dress. She had been crying.

Mr Khoja returned and took the drum with him. 'That's enough for one evening,' he said. 'It's getting late and we all have more than enough to do tomorrow.'

The crowd on the benches drifted away and prepared for sleep. The chairs were folded and returned to the garage and the sisters one by one went to find their beds.

Mrs Lutchman searched for her sons among the crowd of bodies sprawled on the floor. She found them huddled together in a corner. She sighed, and, taking off her dress, lay down in her petticoat beside them. She was not sleepy; she had an overwhelming desire to talk to someone, though about nothing in particular. The distress she felt was wordless, instinctive, and the sound of voices no true remedy. They could only aggravate what she already felt. Raising her head, she studied the face of her younger son, pouting and insolent even in sleep; and Bhaskar, so much uglier and more tractable than his brother, about whom she could find nothing interesting to say to others. She was tempted to wake him up. But for what? What could he tell her? She wondered how her husband had managed without her. In the last few weeks he had changed, become sulkier; but why, she did not know. Where was he now? With his mistress? She revived the picture of that imagined face. Why should it affect her now? She turned restlessly and closed her eyes, trying to conjure sleep out of the darkness.

6

The important guests arrived the following day, all of them prominent figures in the political and business worlds. They were met at the gate by Mrs Khoja and escorted solemnly up the front steps (the family was banished to the back of the house) to the accompaniment of her soft, insincere laughter. Upstairs, always tacitly out of bounds, was now emphatically so, only Renouka and another female cousin being allowed there in the guise of servants.

Dressed in their expensive, well-cut suits, the guests behaved as they would have done at a cocktail party. They talked and laughed in small groups, drinking cups of tea. Renouka, wearing a blue apron specially provided by Mrs Khoja ('so that the guests won't mix you up with themselves') wandered about the sitting-room with a tea-pot. The other cousin, also wearing an apron, served Huntley and Palmers biscuits.

Mr Khoja was deep in conversation with a cocoa merchant, explaining the intricacies of the Hindu religion, in part an elaborate apology for not having provided drinks. The cocoa merchant listened with evident interest.

'It never ceases to suprise me, Mr Khoja, how sophisticated your religion really is. From what you have just said to me, I can see you have got to be a really deep philosopher in order to be a Hindu.'

Mr Khoja was deprecating. 'That's not really so, Mr Cardoso. It's a matter of level, if you see what I mean. One doctrine for the peasant, one doctrine for a man like me. They don't expect everybody to know what we Brahmins must know. That would be asking too much. It takes years of study and thought. I suppose I know as much about it as any man in Trinidad.'

'I am sure you do,' the cocoa merchant replied, visibly impressed. 'Maybe you know as much as anybody anywhere for that matter. Even in India, come to that.'

'Well . . .' Mr Khoja laughed uncomfortably. 'I wouldn't quite say that.' He changed the subject, the next best thing to admitting that Mr Cardoso had overestimated his abilities. 'Of course, one doesn't really need to have these catthas. I don't know, you might call them Masses. All one needs to approach God is thought.'

'Why do you have them then, Mr Khoja?'

Mr Khoja spread his arms wearily. 'As I was saying, it's a matter of level. Those on a lower level need these things, and it's my duty to see that the rest of my family . . .'

The cocoa merchant was sympathetic. 'At the same time philosophical and primitive, eh?'

Mr Khoja thought it wise to change the subject again. 'You wouldn't believe this, Mr Cardoso, but even aeroplanes were mentioned in our Bible, the Vedas as we call it.'

Mr Cardoso was incredulous. 'You mean they actually mentioned aeroplanes by name, Mr Khoja?'

'Not quite, you must understand. They didn't know about B.O.A.C. and Pan-Am in those days, but they had the idea, if you see what I mean. Man, they even knew about the atom bomb.'

'You make me feel so ignorant, Mr Khoja. Sometimes I do really regret that I wasn't blessed with a brain like yours. All I'm good for is to sell cocoa.'

'That too must take a talent,' Mr Khoja assured him. 'I'm sure if I try to sell cocoa people wouldn't buy a single bean from me.'

'Come, come, Mr Khoja. You could put your mind to anything and be a success.'

Mr Khoja smiled resignedly. 'Well,' he said, 'what to do?'

Mrs Khoja joined them. 'Ah Mr Cardoso. I'm glad you could come.'

'Anything for you, my dear Mrs Khoja.'

'Flattery will get you nowhere.' She giggled.

'Your husband has been telling me all there is to know about Hinduism.'

'Yes. Govind knows a lot about that.' She spoke slowly, trying to put into practice the lessons her husband had given her on grammar and enunciation.

'How is Blackie?' Mr Cardoso asked. 'Has she gone back to the plantation?'

They all laughed. Mr Cardoso looked at Renouka and her cousin talking together. Mrs Khoja followed his gaze. She stamped her foot angrily. 'You can't take your eyes off them for a minute and they up to some mischief. You two girls,' she shouted, stamping her foot, 'I didn't bring you up here to chat, you know. I bring you to work. Go and see what the guests need.'

'Family?' Mr Cardoso continued to stare at the two girls who had wandered off with their trays.

Mrs Khoja did not wish to commit herself. Her husband came to the rescue.

'My nieces,' he replied frankly.

'You can't miss the family resemblance,' Mr Cardoso said. 'The one with the short hair is pretty.'

Mr Khoja was surprised. It was not often that strangers paid attention to members of his family. He had always assumed that they were, in some strange way, invisible and that terms like 'prettiness' could hardly apply to them. He studied Renouka, trying to free his mind of these assumptions and see her as, perhaps, Mr Cardoso saw her.

'You think so? Yes, she's not bad at all when you think of her in that sort of way.'

'How else do you think about her then?' Mr Cardoso looked at him curiously.

'What?' Mr Khoja was taken aback. He laughed. 'Yes, yes. I agree with you. She is pretty.' But he spoke without conviction. The habits of a lifetime could not be set aside that easily.

'Mr Khoja! You are neglecting us!' a man on the opposite side of the room called across to him.

Mr Khoja was relieved. 'Let's go and talk to Mr Alfonso; he's opening up biscuit factories all over the place these days.'

Mr Khoja drifted off and the group broke up.

7

Downstairs, even the relative freedom of the previous days disappeared and was replaced by a new constraint. That day the women were not allowed to sing in the kitchen. 'Some of the guests might not like it,' Mr Khoja told them. Instead, they prepared the food for dinner several hours beforehand, and made the prasad, the offering, that would be distributed after the cattha. Later on, they changed into their best clothes and lost their tempers. Children were slapped and cried and ordered to be quiet; while quarrels, conducted with muted malevolence, broke out fitfully among the cousins.

The folding chairs and benches had, earlier that morning, been set out in rows around the puja mound. Those near the front were reserved for the important guests being entertained upstairs, and were specially dusted and covered with cushions. The boys, banned from playing cricket on the pavement, sat in the garage playing dominoes, ludo and cards, while the Negro youths from the street poked their faces through the bars of the front gate. In the yard, mothers bathed and dressed the younger children; others washed the piles of banana leaves needed for later on in the evening.

At seven o'clock Mr Khoja, followed by his guests, entered the tent. Darling, whose task it was, showed the strangers to their seats. Mrs Khoja fussed uselessly in the background and ordered Badwatee to put an extra two and a half spoons of salt in the rice. The rest of the time she chatted with her relatives, who were trying desperately to behave like tourists. One of them even had a camera slung around his shoulder. As a woman, she had no direct part to play in the cattha, but as the wife of Mr Khoja she was allowed a seat near the front.

A few minutes after Mr Khoja had led his guests into the tent, Indrani arrived with the elder Mrs Khoja and an armchair was brought and placed near the puja mound. The guests rose when she appeared and the children, unnerved by this show of respect, shifted indecisively on their benches. The sisters, themselves surprised by this show of respect, glared suggestively at the children and several of those sitting within easy reach had their ears wrung,'Get up, you little bitch. You want all those people in front to think your mother make you without any manners?' In response to these blandishments, the cousins rose and waited while Indrani and Mr Khoja adjusted the old woman in her chair.

The pundit alone remained seated and took no notice of what was going on, assiduously studying the large, well thumbed books that lay open in front of him, wetting the tip of his index finger each time he turned a page. Mr Khoja was at his most magisterial. He wore a dhoti and draped around his neck a garland of red and yellow flowers. His hair, freshly washed and shining, clung smoothly to his scalp. He took his place at the mound beside the pundit. Darling rushed up and whispered urgently in his ear. Mr Khoja shook his head and she withdrew to the back of the tent, casually slapping one of the children on the way. 'Who you think you looking at?' she asked. The child started to cry and its mother delivered a second slap on its cheek. After that he was quiet.

The cattha began.

It went on a long time. The pundit, his voice quickly settling into a drone, read from the book. At intervals conch horns were blown and bells rung; babies cried, others coughed, some fell asleep, and incense fumes wandered through the tent, a sweet and suffocating presence. The guests with a polite wakefulness followed everything. Sitting at the back of the tent, their faces drawn and serious, the sisters watched the culmination of a week's work, a culmination which, discarding their efforts, regarded them as essentially unimportant. The glory, such as it was, belonged to Mr Khoja and his guests.

At last it was finished. The guests rose and congratulated Mr Khoja. They examined the mound and questioned the pundit. Indrani, assisted by Mr Cardoso, carried the old woman back to her room. Mr Khoja, pleased by the success of his performance, laughed jovially with the guests and escorted them back to the sitting-room, where they were to be fed on proper plates with knives and forks, and provided with white napkins.

Downstairs, the trestle tables were laid with banana leaves, and the woman ladled the hot food from basins onto the wet leaves. On this last night all the suspicions and posturings of the past week were laid aside. Boys and girls were permitted to eat at the same table and even joke with one another if they wished. Families too came closer, and mothers who during the week had abandoned their motherhood for a vaguer, more generalized maternity that recognized no particular child as its own, returned to their sons and daughters, trying to give them the best of what there was, encouraging them to eat to their hearts' content, and kissing and cradling them when they grew annoyed.

Mrs Lutchman sat beside Bhaskar and Romesh.

'You behaving like a real spoil fish tonight, Rom. Eat some more food, otherwise you won't grow up big and healthy like your Mamoo. Come, let me divide it up for you. Eat one bit for Bhaskar, one for your father, one for me, one for your Urmila mousie, and that's a good boy.'

Romesh, however, refused to be drawn.

Dinner was followed by the distribution of the little paper bags of prasad, sprinkled with grated coconut and bits of banana.

'You want another bag, children?' Mrs Lutchman asked. Romesh and Bhaskar nodded. 'All right. I'll ask Urmila mousie to give you one.' And Urmila mousie gave them not one, but two bags of prasad.

After the prasad had been distributed the Negro boys were called in from the street and given the remains of the food. When this had been done the sisters worked until late, folding and taking the chairs back to the garage, tying the banana leaves into bundles and putting them out on the pavement. They went to bed only several hours later, but since many of the visitors had already left with their families there was less competition for space that night.

The next morning they turned their attentions to the kitchen. The floor was sprinkled and swept and the cauldrons washed and taken upstairs to be stored. Blackie, her period of hibernation over, emerged from behind her flowered screen, and took up, as if nothing had happened, where she had left off. There was not much else to be done. Mrs Lutchman, discarding her rags of the previous days, changed into a proper dress and climbed the stairs with her two sons to make her final farewells. The sitting-room bore no trace of the previous evening. Mr Khoja was already back at work, preparing another of his speeches. Mrs Khoja was asleep. The boys said their pranams. This time Mr Khoja made no remarks about Oxford and Cambridge, simply waving them wearily away. The old woman, exhausted by her week away from home, kissed her and the children and sank back on the bed. Indrani interrupted her packing to administer a fresh dose of medicine.

The sisters, all of them like Mrs Lutchman wearing more normal clothes, stood aimlessly in the kitchen talking softly among themselves and staring at the smoke-blackened walls and roof. Mrs Lutchman took her leave of them and, as before, Bhaskar and Romesh kissed the circle of faces, now so much more subdued than on the day of their arrival.

They walked through the empty house, followed by Shadow II, recently released from his confinement. Mrs Lutchman paused outside the gate. She noticed there were now two cars stripped of their engines parked on the road outside the house next door. The sun was bright and yellow and Mrs Lutchman sought the shadows of the fences as she walked, struggling with her suitcase, up the street to the bus-stop.

Chapter Four

1

Mr Lutchman and Doreen went for drives together into the countryside, visiting tiny, out of the way villages, forgotten among the cane fields, where Doreen, still pretending to be engaged on anthropological research, talked with the peasants and took notes. In the south of the island they discovered, behind the main roads and oil refineries, a type of life and landscape whose existence they had never suspected.

The village of Bengal was one such place. It was one of a series of villages strung out along a narrow tarred road that wound its way through the sugar-cane, although near Bengal itself the fields, being more low-lying and swampy, were given over to other, less usual crops like water-melons and cucumbers. The names of the neighbouring villages were similarly derived: Lucknow, Calcutta, Benares. But Bengal was different from the rest and not merely because of the absence of sugar-cane. It was smaller and less prosperous than the rest, its houses, or rather huts, built not in a line facing each other and hugging the curves of the road, but set well back in the fields. The latter stretched flat to the horizon, broken here and there by clumps of trees; but much of it was essentially marsh-land overgrown with tall grasses and scarred by irrigation channels and pools of stagnant water. These, when seen from a distance, reflecting the light and sky, resembled sheets of smooth, grey metal scattered at random over the surface of the plain.

Doreen and Mr Lutchman had come there on one of their rambles. They had driven south from Port-of-Spain to San Fernando and for a short while had followed the coast road beyond San Fernando before turning, at Doreen's prompting, inland. It was already late afternoon and the peasants, groups of men, women and children, were returning home from the fields, hoes and rakes dangling from their shoulders. Some of them rode on the trays of bullock carts and lorries. Several times they had to wait while the carts crawled slowly out of their way and the children sitting in the tray shouted remarks at them and made faces. Others, heedless of the traffic, walked in the middle of the road, crossing to the verge only after repeated soundings of the horn. There, standing in a sullen group in the grass, their sun-blackened faces lit by a mild curiosity, they waited for the car to pass. The road narrowed until finally it was only wide enough for one car, and lorries and tractors coming from the opposite direction had to teeter dangerously on the brinks of the ditches bordering the road on either side. The smells of the country deepened, a mixture of dust and sugar-cane and animal droppings. They passed cattle and buffalo pens, long sheds with black roofs, that stank. Doreen was ecstatic.

'They've got the Pueblo Indians right here,' she exclaimed delightedly, leaning her head out of the window and gazing, her eyes shining with anthropological fervour, at the fields and rolling hills, the poverty of the houses they passed, the raggedness of the children, some of whom crouched naked under stand-pipes washing themselves, the morose faces of the older women leading animals or balancing buckets filled with water on their heads.

Each village centred round its shop, the social centre and place of relaxation, where the men sat out on benches and chairs in the shadow of tall, spreading trees and watched the twilight procession returning from the fields, eyeing the young girls.

'Come here with me, darling!' one of them, a hat drawn low over his face, his eyes red and insolent, had called to Doreen, patting the seat of an empty chair.

Doreen had waved back, laughing. 'Another time, perhaps.'

Mr Lutchman was annoyed. 'You shouldn't pay any attention to them, Doreen. These people dangerous, you know. The men here mean what they say.'

'Don't be stupid, Ram. He was only joking. You could see that.'

'These people don't know what joking is. Take my word. I

bet when we passing back he go still be sitting on that chair waiting for you.'

'You are being ridiculous, Ram. Anyway, what's the harm if he still waiting for me there when we pass back? He might be very lonely and unhappy for all you know.'

Mr Lutchman frowned. It reminded him too much of what he suspected was his own status in Doreen's eyes. Seen thus, from the outside and objectively, he began to understand it for what it was. He brooded. 'Lonely! Unhappy!' He drove a little faster.

'You are jealous of him?' She pouted petulantly, the sun falling on her hair, lighting up her cheeks. He looked at her. Drawing closer, she draped her arm across his shoulders. Mr Lutchman, squirming uncomfortably, removed it.

'You mustn't do that sort of thing here, Doreen. These people not accustomed to seeing that sort of thing. It might give them ideas.' That, however, was not at all what he wanted to say.

'Really, Ram. You behave just as if they were animals.' And, as with Mr Lutchman, that was not at all what she wanted to say.

She moved away and resumed her examination of the countryside. The land here was completely flat. Even the hills had disappeared. Irrigation channels dissected the fields into neat rectangles, the water at this time of day pink, the colour of the clouds banked high and lowering low on the horizon, like ranges of very high mountains. They seemed to promise rain, yet these were not rain clouds. It was a peculiar landscape, different from anything else the island had to offer, with none of that dryness or tropical lushness typical of most other parts, but, strange for Trinidad, suggesting remoteness and large distances. Even the villages seemed to be different, giving the impression of completeness and self-sufficiency, free of the untidiness that characterized those other conglomerations of people (such as the conglomeration Mr Lutchman had sprung from), neither village, nor suburb, nor town.

Bengal was the last of the chain of villages. The road stopped a few hundred yards beyond it, petering out into fields and forest and, beyond that, uncultivated swamp and grass land.

A group of about a dozen huts built at various distances from each other were scattered about the fields. Doreen, the desire to take notes irresistible, suggested a stop and Mr Lutchman parked in the yard in front of the village shop.

It hardly deserved the name. It was a hut only slightly larger than its neighbours. Like them, its outer and inner walls were mud-plastered and the roof was thatched. The walls, cream-coloured and fissured by the sun, bulged in places where poles had been inserted to strengthen them and support the roof. The yard, itself the colour of the walls, was packed hard, swept bare of any vegetation and crossed by a network of minute cracks. The hut seemed to be not the work of man but to have arisen naturally, a protuberance of the soil. There was a small, wiry tree growing in the bush where the fields began. Some chickens, the only sign of life, were roosting in the branches.

Mr Lutchman, leaving Doreen who wished to make some 'sketches', went into the shop. Above the door there were two advertisements, one for soft drinks, another for a medicinal ointment. The atmosphere inside the shop was dry and musty, hinting of abandonment and commercial collapse. It reminded him of Esperanza Provisions in its last, dying days. There were a dozen bottles of soft drinks ranged on a sagging shelf, not the brand advertised above the door, but a substitute, cheaper local concoction called 'Sunny Fizz'. There were no medicinal ointments of any kind.

He rapped loudly on the counter. 'Anybody home?'

The shop was partitioned from the rest of the building by a curtain. 'Coming,' a man's voice rattled, as much an answer as an expression of surprise and inquiry. Sounds of bustle came from behind the curtain accompanied by sighs and much coughing. The curtain bulged and a man of about sixty, his hair thin and white and fluttering, pushed his way into the shop. He examined Mr Lutchman with interest.

'You have any Coca-Cola?'

'Only what you see on the shelf, mister.' He was very short and his wrinkled skin made him look excessively frail. His eyes, however, were bright and he darted curious bird-like glances at Mr Lutchman's clothes and the car parked in the yard.

Mr Lutchman bought and drank a Sunny Fizz. This, he imagined, was how Americans must feel. The man watched him drink.

'Coming from San Fernando?' he asked.

'No. Port-of-Spain.' The Sunny Fizz fizzled with a sickly warmth in his throat.

'Port-of-Spain!' He appeared to consider the implications of this. 'You know St James and Belmont?'

'I don't live too far from there.'

'I used to work in St James when I was a boy, in one of them big stores down there.'

Mr Lutchman in his turn appeared to consider the implications of this, but he said nothing.

'You ever come across a Mr Franco?' the old man asked.

'I don't think so.'

'It was for him I used to work. As office boy, you know. But I suppose he must be dead by now.' The old man shook his head sadly. 'All that man could think about was money. Day and night all he used ever to think about was money. It funny how some people like that. As if they could eat money.' He seemed genuinely grieved.

'That's not a nice way to be,' Mr Lutchman agreed.

'You ever hear about the Khojas?' The old man seemed to think that his question had a logical connexion with what had gone before.

Mr Lutchman was guarded. 'A little.' His touristic fantasy began to wear off.

'A little!' The old man was astounded. 'But what you does do so that you never head about the Khojas?'

'I didn't say I never hear of them. I say I only hear about them a little.'

'They is one of the richest families in this island, man. They own this land.' He pointed at the floor.

'Which land?'

'The land on which this house build for a start.' The old man was beginning to get excited.

Mr Lutchman was silent. Doreen, her sketching finished,

entered the shop, mentally noting what she saw. 'We better be going back,' he suggested. 'It almost dark now and it's a dangerous road.'

'You are too much of a coward, Ram. All this driving in darkness business is a heap of old superstition.' She gazed at the wall and ceiling and the paltry display of goods on the shelves. 'Fascinating. There is no other word for it.' She rested her notebook on the counter.

'What?' The old man looked at her, then at the notebook, puzzled.

'I say it's fascinating,' she repeated.

Uncomprehending, he shook his head at her. Doreen laughed, pleased to discover this example of illiteracy.

'I like your place here. It's very nice.' She raised her voice, assuming that being illiterate he must also be deaf.

'Yes, yes. I glad you like it, but it too quiet for city people like you.'

'No. Not at all,' Doreen shouted. 'I like quiet places. It's beautiful. Very different, you know.'

'I glad you like it.'

'I'm writing a book,' Doreen went on. 'That's why I was doing all that drawing outside just now. I hope you don't mind.'

'Eh?'

'I say I'm writing a book.' Doreen was almost shrieking at him now. 'And I was hoping you didn't mind my drawing your house. Look. I'll show you.'

She opened the notebook and showed him the sketches. 'They are only very rough drawings,' she warned him.

'You does draw very nice.'

'So you don't mind?'

'No. What I have to mind? You does draw very nice. A real artist, eh?' He winked at Mr Lutchman, who ignored him.

'Doreen, I think we ought to . . .'

'Don't be so fussy, Ram. They will think you have no manners at all if you just drive off like that.'

A woman's figure bulged briefly through the curtain. She was carrying a lighted oil-lamp which she rested on the counter. It was dark outside and the frogs had set up a chorus in the fields. The woman stared inquisitively at the strangers. The old man turned to her. She, on the other hand, was truly deaf and he spoke loudly, pointing at Doreen and Mr Lutchman.

'They come all the way from Port-of-Spain.' The woman opened her eyes wide in wonder but remained silent. 'They does live near where Mr Franco used to live. You remember Mr Franco?' She nodded.

'Who is Mr Franco?' Doreen asked. The old man did not answer her. 'I'm writing a book,' Doreen screamed at the woman. She opened her eyes even wider, but still she said nothing. 'I like this place. It's beautiful. I was telling your husband how much I liked it. Look. I made some drawings.' She showed her the sketches. The woman studied them briefly. 'You like them?' The woman stared at her. Doreen gestured expansively. Mr Lutchman hovered in the doorway, staring out at the darkness and the fireflies wheeling in the air, tiny flakes of coloured light.

'You know,' the old man said to his wife, 'they come from Port-of-Spain and they never even hear of the Khojas.'

The woman spoke for the first time. 'How that?' she asked her husband. 'You sure they come from Port-of-Spain?'

'Well, that's what he say. He say he only hear about them a little.'

Mr Lutchman watched the fireflies wheeling through the darkness.

'What's all this?' Doreen stepped closer to the old man. 'Who's never heard of the Khojas?'

The old man pointed at Mr Lutchman. 'Your husband over there. He say he only hear a little about them. Living in Port-of-Spain and never hearing about the Khojas.' He shook his head wonderingly. 'Why, they own all the land you see about you here.'

'Well I never!' Doreen's eyes danced over the room before settling on Mr Lutchman's irresolute back. 'But he is one of them. He married into the family.'

'Eh? What you saying? Like you making joke with me?'

'No. I'm not joking with you. I'm telling you the truth. He's a Khoja. He married one of them.'

The old man looked at his wife, then at Doreen. 'You sure you not joking with we?'

'No, no. I am telling you the truth. Married into the family.'

The old man looked at his wife again. 'I thought there was something about the face,' he said. 'You not his wife? You have a little of the Khoja features about you too.' The old man was worried. He seemed to believe there were Khojas lurking invisibly all around him. He contemplated Mr Lutchman's back.

'Is Khoja who send the both of you here to see what we doing and keep an eye on the place?' He was visibly disturbed.

'Oh no,' Doreen hastened to assure him. 'We just came here for a drive. We didn't even know that the Khojas own all this land.'

The old man was still suspicious. 'They own all the land around here. Mr Khoja does come here himself every month or so to look around. Sharp as a razor that man. Sharp as a razor. Doesn't let you get away with one little thing. The old lady used to do it sheself before she get blind. She was even worse than he. A real terror. You could ask my wife how she used to come here and bawl me out when I do something she didn't like. When last you see she?'

'I have never seen her in my life,' Doreen replied.

'What? How's that? You is a Khoja yourself, not so? The features give you away.'

Doreen laughed. 'You've got it all wrong. I'm not a Khoja at all.'

The old man was puzzled. Doreen enjoyed his confusion.

'You not maried to he?' He jerked his chin at the immobile Mr Lutchman.

'Did he tell you we were married?' Doreen asked interestedly.

'No, no. He didn't say anything like that. I was just wondering. That all.'

Doreen was disappointed. 'We are just friends,' she said. 'He's helping me to write my book.'

The old man nodded. His wife tugged at his sleeve and whispered something in his ear.

'Why don't you stay and have some food with we?' he offered.

The woman stared at her lips.

'But that will be too much trouble for you,' Doreen protested half-heartedly.

The old man rested his hand on her sleeve. 'No trouble,' he said. 'You like chicken?' He winked at her.

Doreen remembered the chickens she had seen roosting in the tree. 'Well, if you insist.'

'I insist.' The old man toyed happily with the unfamiliar word.

'We better be going home, Doreen. We can't let them kill a chicken just for we. Is a waste. They not rich people, you know.' Mr Lutchman, ending his vigil in the doorway, came into the shop.

'You sure you don't mind?' Doreen asked the old man.

'I insist,' the old man chirruped. 'How we go mind a little thing like that? Is not every day we does see one of the Khojas. I does kill a chicken every time Mr Khoja come down here.'

'That's very kind of you.'

Mr Lutchman scowled at her and returned to the doorway to resume his vigil.

'Suresh!' the old man called. A small boy came running into the shop from the room at the back. He stopped abruptly when he saw Doreen and Mr Lutchman and stepped back shyly into the curtain. 'Suresh is my grandson,' the old man explained. 'He does spend he holidays with we. Go and catch a chicken for me, boy. These people come all the way from Port-of-Spain to see we.'

Suresh ran through the shop out into the yard. There was a flutter of wings in the tree and several chickens ran squawking past the door pursued by Suresh.

'What fun!' Doreen went to the door to watch the chase. Mr Lutchman stood impassively by her side staring at the glow of the distant oil refinery near San Fernando.

'You like it?' The woman joined them, gazing at the panic-stricken birds running stupidly in circles. 'Suresh does enjoy catching chickens. Is good exercise for a boy, not so?' She smiled contentedly into the darkness. Suresh had one of the chickens by the tail. It squirmed and cried and flapped its wings. Feathers flew into the air. Suresh, laughing fell on the ground with it, securing his grip inch by inch and crawling behind the alarmed and terrified bird.

'What fun!' Doreen stepped out into the yard.

At last Suresh had the chicken properly in his grasp and, holding it by the neck, walked panting and triumphant to the three figures standing in the doorway and held it up close to Doreen's face. The chicken endeavoured vainly to beat its wings, but Suresh had curled one of his arms around its back. 'Marvellous! Marvellous! You are a very brave boy. I'm sure Ram couldn't do that.' She ruffled his hair. Suresh grinned. Mr Lutchman, his face set, said nothing and avoided looking at the chicken and the triumphant Suresh. Suresh grinned, showing his teeth, very white and even. He left them and disappeared down the side of the hut.

The woman nudged Doreen in the ribs. 'You want to see him kill it?'

'Could I? I would love to. Nature red in tooth and claw. I would love to see him kill it.'

'I don't think you would like that, Miss,' the old man said. 'It have a lot of blood in it.'

'I'm not afraid of a little blood. Nature is cruel. We can't fight against that. Women who faint because they see a little blood are fools. They feel they ought to faint. I'm not like them.' She giggled. 'I'm very bloodthirsty.'

The old man had not understood much of this. He shrugged 'Go and watch him kill it then, if you want to.'

The old woman took Doreen by the hand and led her to the back of the hut where Suresh was stripping the feathers from the chicken's neck. It looked pink and very slender and when it was bare of feathers Suresh twisted his fingers firmly round it and began sawing at it with a large knife. There was a gush of bright red blood, some of which splattered on Suresh's arms. He laughed and with smiling eyes exhibited his dying prize to Doreen. Its blood spurted in a thin red stream. But she was looking not at him. Instead, she was gazing out over the fields at the lights of the neighbouring huts. Voices came floating in on the wind. The frogs kept up their chorus and the mosquitoes whirred, settling on her face and arms. She ran quickly back to the shop, where Mr Lutchman and the old man were talking.

'And so you don't see Mr Khoja much then?' the old man was saying. Mr Lutchman was leaning against the counter. Doreen stood silently by the door, rubbing her face and arms.

The old man shook his head sadly. 'I thought the sight of all that blood would have been too much for you. I don't like it much meself.'

'The blood had nothing to do with it. It was all those damn mosquitoes. The place is crawling with them.'

The old man winked knowingly at Mr Lutchman. 'I know how it is,' he said soothingly.

Her distress pleased Mr Lutchman. 'You look for it,' he said quietly.

'You too cruel. You shouldn't say that kinda thing to she.' The old man went up to Doreen and put his arms around her. 'Come and rest in the back-room. I go make a cup of tea for you. That will make you feel a lot better.' He lifted the lid of the counter and led her through the curtain to the room at the back. Mr Lutchman followed them.

The back room was little more than a shed. The walls and floor were mud-plastered and the only ventilation was a large square hole in the wall, over which a screen had been drawn. In one corner there was a low bed covered with a faded counterpane. Along another wall a simple wooden bench had been placed. The centre of the room was taken up by a plain wooden table on which an oil-lamp, the only light in the room, burned. A hammock, made from jutebags sewn together, was suspended from the rafters. Here, the family relaxed and slept. It was spotlessly clean.

'Come. You lie down on the bed a little bit and I will go and make you a cup of green tea.'

Doreen protested and sat on the hammock instead. She rocked gently, scratching her arms. The old man went into the kitchen, divided from the main room by a wooden partition decorated with out-of-date calendars, gifts from Coca-Cola and

Pepsi-Cola illustrated with pictures of sun-tanned, bright-eyed American girls and their gormless boy-friends.

'So you never heard of the Khojas at all?' Doreen kicked her legs up in the air.

'I didn't say that.'

Doreen laughed, apparently completely recovered. 'What you said comes to the same thing.'

'I knew they would have made a fuss if I said so. I didn't want them to . . .'

'You can't fool me, Ram. You wanted them to think you were some kind of businessman from Port-of-Spain, don't tell me.'

'Tell me more since you know everything,' Mr Lutchman, sitting on the bed, glared resentfully at her.

'You can't get out of it that way.'

'I don't see that I have anything to get out of. What about that chicken, eh? The mosquitoes! For someone as "blood-thirsty" as you, the more mosquitoes that suck your blood the happier you should feel.'

'We weren't talking about that. We were talking about you and the Khojas.'

'What about them? Don't think I haven't noticed that during the past few weeks you have been using them as a stick to beat me over the head with. What you trying to prove by that, eh? Tell me.'

'I'm not the one who is trying to prove something.'

'What you trying to say?'

'Nothing.' Doreen clapped her palms together and stared at him.

Mr Lutchman laughed. 'Incest. Adultery. "I don't see why a woman shouldn't go to bed with any man she wants to." What it is *you* trying to prove?'

'I proved what I was trying to prove.'

'Don't be too sure.' He got up from the bed and walked across the room and lifted the screen that covered the window. Smells of cooking came from the kitchen. The frogs had stopped their croaking. The old man returned with a cup of tea.

'I hope it not too strong for you.'

Doreen took a small sip. 'It's lovely. Just the way I like it.'

Mr Lutchman laughed quietly. Doreen looked at him.

'You want some tea too?' the old man asked, going up to him.

Mr Lutchman withdrew his head from the window. 'No. No.' He sat on the bed again, resting his head against the wall.

'You looking tired,' the old man said. 'Why don't you lie down on the bed a little if you want to?' He started to remove the counterpane.

'Don't bother, Mr Ramgoolam.' Mr Lutchman pushed him away gently. 'I'm fine like I am. The bed is lovely as it is. Just the way I like it, as a matter of fact.' He laughed again, avoiding Doreen's gaze which he could feel fixed on him. 'The food smells really good.'

Mr Ramgoolam was perplexed. 'Nobody could cook a chicken like my wife.'

The chicken was curried and brought in in a large pot. Mrs Ramgoolam ladled the bits onto enamel plates and gave them a roti each. Together with her husband and Suresh she squatted on the ground.

'I am not accustom eating on tables,' she said. 'I don't find the food does taste the same when I do that.' She grinned at them, tearing her roti into halves, and began to eat.

Doreen eyed the plate of food set before her. 'Could I have a spoon or something to eat it with? My hands are a bit dirty.'

Mr Ramgoolam leapt to his feet, embarrassed and apologetic. 'Sorry. Sorry. I should have remembered that. I does forget that not everybody grow up eating with they hands. You want a spoon too, Mr Lutchman?'

Mr Lutchman had not touched his food. He considered the offer. 'No, not for me, Mr Ramgoolam,' he replied with sudden decision, 'I will eat with my hands like the rest of you.' Doreen looked at him and, as before, Mr Lutchman avoided her gaze. He got up from the table. 'In fact, I think I will join the rest of you on the ground as well. I agree with your wife. The food does taste much better that way.'

'You don't have to do that just to please, we, Mr Lutchman. We don't mind you eating on the table.'

'I'm not doing it just to please you, Mr Ramgoolam. I really want to eat on the ground with you. And call me Ram. Forget all this Mr Lutchman business.'

Mr Ramgoolam went into the kitchen and returned with a spoon for Doreen. Mr Lutchman squatted on the ground beside his hosts and following Mrs Ramgoolam, tore his roti into two and dipped it into the gravy. Mrs Ramgoolam, sucking noisily on a bone, grinned delightedly at him. She ate quickly and messily, the gravy running down her fingers.

Doreen, alone at the table, sat straight-backed on her chair, her fingertips lightly touching the edge of the table, head bent slightly forward, staring with expressionless eyes at the steaming chicken. She lifted the spoon and after staring at her distorted reflection, dipped it unenthusiastically into the chicken.

Conversation flourished on the floor. 'So Baby is your wife,' Mr Ramgoolam mused, rearranging his legs into a more comfortable position. 'I used to see she whenever I went to the big house on business. But she was a small girl then. Time does really fly, eh?' He tried unsuccessfully to bring Doreen into the conversation, directing his last remark at her. However, all he received in return for his efforts was a pallid smile. She continued to peck at her food.

'The chicken not nice?'

'It's lovely. Just . . .' She stopped in mid-sentence and rested the spoon at the side of her plate. 'It's very nice. Your wife is a first-rate cook, but I don't normally have a big appetite and you gave me such a lot.'

'Watching your figure, eh! Okay.' Mr Ramgoolam laughed, winking at Mr Lutchman. Mrs Ramgoolam smiled delightedly at everybody, sucking her fingers as she sucked her bones, noisily and with gusto.

Mr Lutchman ate a great deal. 'I have never had a better meal in my life, Mr Ramgoolam. Your chickens must have something really special about them.' They had finished eating and Mr Lutchman was reclining in the hammock massaging his stomach. Suresh and Mrs Ramgoolam had retired to the kitchen. Doreen had eaten less than half the food on her plate. When she had finished, she wiped her hands and mouth with a handkerchief.

'Let we have a little smoke,' Mr Ramgoolam suggested, taking a pipe out of his pocket.

'That's a good idea. Is years now since I last smoke a pipe.'

'I really think we ought to be getting back now, Ram.'

'You just can't leave like that, Doreen. Here you make these kind people go out of their way to catch a chicken and cook it for you, and the moment you finish eat it you want to run away. What they go think if we go and do a thing like that, eh?' Mr Lutchman sucked comfortably on the pipe. 'Tell she how you go feel about that, Mr Ramgoolam. Tell she it wouldn't be a nice thing to do.'

'It wouldn't be nice,' Mr Ramgoolam confirmed.

Doreen frowned. 'I think I'll take a little walk then, if you don't mind. It's getting very close in here with all that tobacco smoke.'

'Yes. That's a good idea, Miss. A walk go do you good.' Mr Ramgoolam nodded emphatically at her. 'It does get nice and cool out here in the evening. When my legs was better I used to go for long walks in the fields . . .'

Doreen did not wait for him to finish. She pushed her way through the curtain.

'Watch out for the mosquitoes,' Mr Lutchman shouted after her.

She did not answer and walked through the shop and out into the yard.

Mr Ramgoolam shook his head. 'Like we vex she or something?'

'Don't bother your head about she, Mr Ramgoolam. She go cool down outside.' Mr Lutchman settled himself comfortably in the hammock.

'You does drink?' Mr Ramgoolam whispered suddenly.

'You have some rum?' Mr Lutchman was equally conspiratorial.

Mr Ramgoolam chuckled happily. 'I does always keep a little bottle handy. You want some?' He winked at Mr Lutchman and went across to the bed. Getting down on his knees, he lifted the counterpane and felt with his hands under the bed, winking at his guest from time to time until he found the bottle. 'I got to hide it from my wife. She hate to see me drinking.

But a man must have something to relax with is what I always say.' The bottle was half-empty. 'I does have a little nip every night,' he explained. 'It does make me sleep like a baby.' He uncorked it and took a drink. He smacked his lips and, closing his eyes, sighed. 'You want a cup or a glass?'

'The bottle good enough for me.' Mr Ramgoolam passed the bottle to Mr Lutchman and he too smacked his lips and sighed. 'Is good rum this,' he said.

2

Doreen sat on the bonnet of the car, now and again swishing her hands through the air to drive the mosquitoes away. The sky was cloudless, very black and splattered with stars. To the north, it was lit by a pink glow, the fires from the oil refinery near San Fernando. A wind blew over the fields, bending the grass before it. She shivered, but the coolness of the air was pleasant and clasping her arms about her, she willed the goosepimples to rise. In the tree, one of the chickens stirred restlessly, disturbing the others.

There was a sound of laughter from the hut. She recognized Mr Lutchman's voice and the less assured wheeze of the old man. She wondered what they were doing, but almost immediately the thought drifted away from her mind and she tried to imagine what Mr Ramgoolam had looked like as a young man taking walks in the fields at night. It seemed a most unlikely thing for him to do. Then that thought too drifted away and in its place came the faces of a succession of lovers. There was none among them she could single out and imagine as a self-contained whole. They appeared dream-like and insubstantial out of the darkness, vanishing as abruptly as they had come, devoid of either coherence or passion. She had never, she realized, loved anyone; had never been able to summon that genuine spurt of passion which might have at least redeemed and lent life to one of those faces. Sitting there, warding off the mosquitoes, she was unable to tell whether the face before her was that of a real person or merely the product of heı own fancy. Her sense of loss was at that moment acute.

Doreen slid off the bonnet. There was another burst of laughter from the hut. She returned to the shop and opened the notebook which she had left lying on the counter, reading the notes and studying the sketches she had made. That too was dull and lifeless. What an absurd person she was! And Mr Lutchman, he too was no less absurd than she. She tore out the pages and crumpling them into a ball she walked back out to the yard and mustering all her strength sent it sailing into the air and out over the field. Then she went back towards the hut.

Another burst of laughter greeted her as she entered the room at the back of the shop. The bottle of rum was nearly empty. Mr Lutchman and Mr Ramgoolam were sitting together in the hammock which was swinging slowly back and forth. Their laughter petered out when she appeared through the curtain. Mr Lutchman stared guiltily at her and straightened himself.

'Me and Mr Ramgoolam was just having a bit of fun. He was talking about how his mother used to beat him when he was small.' Mr Lutchman spluttered afresh into laughter and Mr Ramgoolam buried his face in the sacking. However, he quickly checked himself. 'Seriously, though, you would find it very interesting for your book. There was that time his mother give him six cents to buy butter and you know what the rascal do with the money? He buy sweetie instead and went back home and tell he mother that the butter drop in the canal. And he mother say, "Come and show me which part of the canal it drop in and let me butter your backside for you." And he take she back to the canal and she make him search that canal for three whole hours, telling everybody she see that she was going to butter his backside for him. And the rascal would never confess.'

'It do go down well in your book,' Mr Ramgoolam confirmed, lifting his face from the sacking. 'I had a fever for a whole week afterwards.'

'And you could bet your bottom dollar that he never tell she after that he drop anything in the canal.'

Doreen laughed. 'You've been drinking too much, Ram. You think you'll be able to drive back?'

‘Yes. Don’t bother your head. All that business about drinking and driving is a load of superstition.’

Doreen nodded and said nothing.

Mr Lutchman watched her suspiciously. ‘What’s the matter with you? Not so long ago it was you breathing down my neck when I suggest we go back home.’

‘I’m not complaining. I’m prepared to wait until you are sober.’

‘Why you suddenly adopting that kind of tone for?’ He looked at her. She seemed to be receding from him. His hilarity vanished altogether. ‘All right,’ he said tiredly, ‘we better go home now.’

‘You could stay a bit longer. I don’t mind.’ Her watery eyes smiled placidly at him.

‘No. We’ll go back to Port-of-Spain now. It’s getting late.’

‘As you wish.’

Mr Lutchman started to say something, then changing his mind he turned to Mr Ramgoolam. ‘I go come back to see you another day, old man – with a bottle of rum.’

‘You don’t have to bring any rum with you,’ Mr Ramgoolam replied. ‘But it would be nice if you could come and see we again. Is not everyday we does have people coming to see we.’

‘I’m sorry about not liking your curry,’ Doreen said. ‘But I’m not accustomed to eating such hot food, like Ram is.’

‘Don’t worry about that, Miss. But you too must come and see we again.’

‘That would be a pleasure, but I’m not going to make any promises. It’s out of my way really.’

Mr Lutchman looked at her queerly. His bewilderment faded into depression.

‘Don’t worry, Miss.’ Mr Ramgoolam eyed the empty rum bottle and with a note of true regret in his voice added, ‘I shoulda thought of that.’

Doreen took some dollar notes from her purse. ‘Here. That is to make up for the cost of the rum.’

Mr Ramgoolam waved her away but without any real conviction and Doreen pressed the money into his palm. ‘I shouldn’t be taking anything from you, Miss,’ he murmured. ‘You is a truly kind person, though.’

'Nonsense. Buy yourself some more rum. To remember me by.' For a moment she stared with something akin to sadness around the room. However, she brightened almost immediately. 'Come on, Ram. To Port-of-Spain.'

Mr Ramgoolam followed them out into the yard, still clutching the dollar notes between his fingers. The car would not start. Mr Lutchman cursed. 'It will start, Ram,' Doreen said. 'Don't worry.' Mr Lutchman cursed again. With a cough, the engine stuttered into life and they moved slowly out of the yard.

Mr Lutchman drove carefully. They spoke little. Doreen stared out of the window at the darkened countryside and the succession of villages, now mere clusters of light, through which they had come earlier that afternoon. The man who had hailed her was still sitting under the tree with several other men. He recognized the car and shouted, 'Darling, so you come back to me.' The men roared with laughter. Doreen kept her eyes fixed on the road.

Once on the coast road, Mr Lutchman drove more quickly. They could see the lights of San Fernando in the distance. 'Civilization,' Doreen murmured, more to herself than to her companion.

'What's that you say?'

'Nothing, nothing.'

'You had a good time?'

They looked at each other.

'It was fun,' Doreen said, and turned once more to stare out of the window.

3

It was not long after this excursion that Mr Lutchman's passion for gardening developed. He bought a set of miniature garden tools – a fork, a spade, a rake and a pair of clippers. His interest in gardening seemed to have arisen unpremeditated. It had come upon him suddenly one Sunday morning when, probably for the first time since they had moved into the house, he was taking a stroll through what little yard there was and his attention had been caught by the patchy remains of lawn, a ragged reminder of the previous owner's industry. He looked over the fence and compared it with the healthy green strip he could see in the neighbour's garden. That same day, he set to work, weeding and removing the stumps of the dead plants. He went to the Queen's Park Savannah and uprooted clumps of grass which he brought back and planted at evenly spaced intervals.

'They go jail you if they catch you rooting up they grass like that,' Mrs Lutchman told him.

'Who tell you that? Since when a little blade of grass so valuable?'

'Nobody saying is the blade of grass that valuable, but is public property you taking. I mean, if everybody begin thinking like you, soon it go have no Savannah at all out there. Someone go go up to the race-track one day and say, "I like the look of this rail. I think I go take it back home with me and make a fence with it." What go happen then, eh? Tell me.'

But, in spite of these discouragements and threats, Mr Lutchman persisted. The police did not catch him and with the infusions of new grass the lawn flourished. Success stimulated ambition. He decided to have an anthurium patch on either side of the house and rose-trees to the front, and it was the search for these items that formed the theme of the first excursion on which he took his children after their return from the Khojas.

They went on a Sunday morning, leaving after breakfast. Mr Lutchman, dressed in a pair of short khaki trousers and a thin cotton shirt, was in a good mood. A straw hat sat rakishly on his head.

'We going to come back with more plants than you ever see in your whole life,' he declared to his wife.

She laughed. 'And where you going to plant them? On the pavement?'

'It have more room in this yard than you think, woman. I going to make this place a real Garden of Eden.'

Mrs Lutchman shook her head, laughing quietly. 'I looking forward to that. I always wanted to live in the Garden of Eden.'

She too was happy, although she had not been invited to

accompany them. An aura of domesticity had descended over her husband in recent weeks which had not escaped her notice. She knew that he saw his mistress less frequently and was content to spend most of his spare time at home playing with his set of gardening tools. This excursion did not worry her, but why this should be so, Mrs Lutchman could not say.

They drove to a house on the outskirts of the city. Doreen, whom Mr Lutchman has not seen for several weeks, was sitting on the verandah reading a magazine. She looked up when the car stopped and ran down the steps smiling. Mr Lutchman turned to Bhaskar and Romesh.

'Watch your behaviour in front of this lady, the two of you,' he whispered.

'I haven't seen you for ages, Ram,' Doreen said. She was looking not at him, but at the children, surprised, inquiring. Her voice was light and gay.

'My sons,' Mr Lutchman explained.

Doreen walked up to the car and put her head through the window. 'Hello, children.' Bhaskar stared gloomily at her. Romesh shrank back into the corner of the seat.

'Say good morning to Miss James.'

'Miss James! Call me Doreen, children.'

Mr Lutchman shrugged his shoulders and walked slowly up the path to the verandah. He sat on one of the cane-backed chairs scattered around it and picked up the magazine she had been reading. It was a copy of *Life*. He flicked through the pages, pausing to look at the occasional photograph, and put it down.

Doreen came in with Bhaskar and Romesh. 'It's got some really marvellous pictures in it this week,' she said, leaning over his shoulder, 'and a very interesting article on nudism.'

'Yes, I saw that. You must hide it from the children.'

'For Christ's sake why? There is nothing obscene about the nakedness of the human body.'

'You are being bloodthirsty again, Doreen.' He had lost the desire to imitate that outrageousness which had been Doreen's chief weapon against him. If nothing else, it had been too tiring. Doreen had always been one step ahead and he was not sufficiently inventive. It was all a game and her talent for it never ceased to amaze him. Now, however, that amazement was melting into amusement.

Doreen blushed and lit a cigarette.

'Since when you take up smoking?' he asked.

Doreen ignored the question. 'It's good for children to be aware of these things,' she went on, the blue smoke filtering through her nose, 'otherwise they would find out in lots of more unpleasant ways. How did you find out? Tell me.'

'You know you taught me everything I know, Doreen.'

Doreen laughed gaily. 'You are a case.'

'You would have to show those pictures to the children over my dead body.' He stared stubbornly at the magazine.

'You are a fascist, Ram.'

Mr Lutchman did not know what a fascist was but he was flattered to be called one. It raised his status. 'All right. So I am a fascist.' He grinned, well pleased with himself, and stretched out his legs in front of him.

Doreen studied Romesh hanging over the rail of the verandah. She walked over to him and curved her arms about his waist.

'What's your name?'

'Romesh.'

'And your shy brother sitting over there?'

'Bhaskar.'

Doreen raised her head. 'What pretty names you give your children, Ram.'

'I didn't have anything to do with it.'

'They are nice all the same. Your wife must have good taste.'

'She didn't have anything to do with it either.' Frowning, he picked up the magazine again. 'It was her family who give them those names,' he added after a while.

'You mean the Khojas?'

'No. The Rockefellers.'

Doreen laughed. 'They control everything, don't they? The Khojas, I mean.'

'Everything.' Mr Lutchman turned the pages of the magazine. 'Anyway, I didn't come here to talk about that. I was looking for somewhere to buy plants.'

'Plants?' Doreen detached her arms from Romesh's waist.

'I making a garden.' He spoke as if he were challenging her.

'I thought you didn't have enough room for that.'

'It have enough.' Mr Lutchman scowled. 'I was going to ask you to come and help me choose, but since you seem to know all about the size of my yard . . .'

'I won't go if you insist on behaving like a child.'

Mr Lutchman got up and leaned against the verandah rail, staring at the empty street. 'Me behaving like a child!'

'I have a party to go to this afternoon. A cocktail party.'

Mr Lutchman turned round to look at her. He saw that she was lying. Doreen avoided his glance.

However, he did not contradict her. 'It wouldn't take all that long,' he said.

'Well, once we are back before five,' she replied.

'Don't worry. I wouldn't want you to miss your party.'

'What about lunch?' She slapped Romesh on the shoulder. 'You want a Coca-Cola?'

Romesh nodded. Bhaskar showed signs of animation.

'This way then, children!' she called, 'Tally ho!'

They left after lunch. The roads were empty and Mr Lutchman, silent and tight lipped, drove quickly. In a few minutes they were out of the city and driving along the Churchill–Roosevelt highway. At first, the road was bordered on either side by flooded fields of rice and watercress. Further on, however, the land was drier and uncultivated, the predominant colour changing from green to a reddish brown and covered with flat, monotonous acres of sun-scorched grass broken intermittently by blacker, burnt-out patches, the areas recently ravaged by bush-fires. Ahead, the road wavered and dissolved in the whirling currents of hot air rising from its surface, appearing at times to be inundated by a smooth surface film of water which reflected the trees and grasses growing at the side of the road. There were narrow, tarred roads hidden among the grasses, remnants of American activity during the war, but in their abandonment and desertion seeming much further removed in time.

They left the highway and drove along one of the wider, better preserved lanes for a mile or so before turning off into a stony, deeply rutted track. Ahead of them was a tall, wooden gate, some of its hinges torn away, teetering dangerously from its supporting posts. A large sign proclaimed in peeling, faded letters: 'Gardens and Zoo. Plants for sale. Visitors welcome to look around. Admission: six cents.'

Doreen whistled in disbelief. 'I would hardly recognize the place. Look at how everything is falling down.' She had been here several times before, when still a young girl, with her mother. Mrs James had been extremely proud of her garden. Doreen, however, had neglected it. The place was owned by an ageing English couple, a retired major and his wife, who had decided to settle in Trinidad. In its day, it had become well-known and prosperous, admired especially for its collection of tropical birds and fish.

They drove through the gate. There was a rambling red-brick house with French windows and a low roof from which hung dead and dying plants in baskets. The house was set in an extensive, decaying garden dotted with mango trees of a more select variety than was normally to be found on the island. The lawn was being watered by a gardener.

He waved furiously at them. 'Stop! Stop! Where you think you going?' He dropped the hose and came limping across the lawn as quickly as he could, muttering all the time under his breath. 'You shoulda sound your horn before you come driving in like this. This is a private place, you know.'

Doreen stuck her head through the window. 'Is Samuel still here?' she shouted at him, in that special manner she had come to cultivate with illiterates.

'What you want with Samuel?'

'Does Samuel still work here?' she shrieked.

'How you know Samuel uses to work here?' The gardener wiped his face with the sleeve of his khaki shirt.

'I used to come here when I was small. Samuel used to work here then.'

The gardener examined her face and figure, his eyes lingering over her bosom. 'Samuel dead years now.'

'How sad.'

'Nothing sad about that. Is drink what gone and kill him. It was what take his father as well.' His eyes returned to her bosom, lingering there as before. Doreen withstood this silent scrutiny. At last, the gardener raised his eyes. 'So if is Samuel you want . . .' He made a gesture that implied the utter hopelessness of this or any other quest they might be engaged on.

'It's not Samuel we come to see,' Mr Lutchman interrupted. 'We come to buy some plants from you.'

'What kind of plant?'

'We have to have a look around first before we decide that,' Doreen countered.

'I could tell you how much kind of plant we have here by counting on the tips of my fingers.'

'We would like to look around for ourselves,' Doreen insisted.

'And you want the children to see the animals too, eh?' He brightened and leaned confidentially against the fender. 'Well, I go tell you something, lady and mister. Most of them gone and dead, just like your friend Samuel. All it have now is about two mongoose and agouti and they go dead soon if I not careful.'

'It's plants we come for,' Mr Lutchman was losing his temper.

'I don't think you would find any kind of plant you want here. The drought we having killing them off like flies.'

'You don't sell plants any more?' Doreen stepped out of the car.

'What you want to buy?'

'Look here . . .' Mr Lutchman began to shout.

'Ssh, Ram. Losing your temper will get you nowhere.'

'To hell with you.'

'It depends on what you have,' Doreen said to the gardener. She was being exaggeratedly patient.

'Look, Miss, I telling you . . .'

Mr Lutchman cursed and started the car. Doreen paid no attention to him.

At that moment, a withered old woman appeared on the porch. 'Eustace! What's all this racket about?'

'They come to buy plants, Mistress Beamish,' Eustace shouted back.

'Well, why don't you sell them then? I don't see why you have to make a fuss with everybody who comes here.'

Eustace nodded bitterly and the old woman returned inside the house.

'Okay. Come this way and I go show you.' As they started to move off, he suddenly stopped them. 'Ah. You think you could fool me as easy as that, eh? You was trying to put one over on old Eustace, eh!'

They stared at him, mystified. Eustace tapped his pockets. 'Six cents from each of you,' he said. 'You see the sign yourself. And no half-price for children either.' They paid him. He pocketed the money and went and turned off the hose. 'Got to be careful with the water,' he explained. 'The Works Department nearly murder we the other day for wasting water. The old lady,' he added, without any apparent connection with what he had been saying before, 'the old lady crazy as hell.' Tapping his forehead, he started down the side of the house.

The main part of the garden stretched behind the house, an area of greenhouses and vine-covered trellises. Everything around them bore the traces of decay. Nearly all the glass in the greenhouses had been broken and not replaced, the plants inside gone completely to seed. The vines on the trellises had been left untrained and had spread out in a tangle of untidy trails, competing with the inevitable parasites that had by now virtually overwhelmed them.

They stopped before a bird-cage as big and as well equipped as those in Port-of-Spain Zoo. But here, the lines for perching and the food trays were in a shambles and there were only two ruffled parrots, who stared lugubriously at them for a time before continuing to peck unenthusiastically at each other.

'You know,' Eustace said, pointing at the parrots, 'they is old men now, but they does never stop fighting. They go murder each other one day and then everybody go throw the blame on old Eustace.' He sighed, leading them on to the empty fish tanks overgrown with moss. 'It used to have hundreds of goldfish in there at one time. Then they all catch a sickness and dead overnight. Again the blame fall on old Eustace head. It was me who had to take them out and throw them away. The Sanitation Department nearly murder we for that. The old lady crazy like hell.' He shook his head sadly and led them to the flower-beds.

These were choked with weeds and suffering from a lack of water, which appeared to be reserved for the lawn at the front. All of these things Eustace pointed out and described in the same mournful fashion, not altogether devoid of a certain macabre pride in his role of scavenger and chief executioner.

'You have any orchids remaining?' Mr Lutchman asked.

'Come this way and see,' Eustace said. They entered the enclosure reserved for orchids. Mr Lutchman's eye was caught by a butterfly orchid, yellow and spotted and shaped exactly like a butterfly. It was the only healthy specimen left.

'You like it, Doreen?'

'It's your choice,' she said. 'I personally wouldn't buy it.'

Mr Lutchman bought it.

'I go give it to you at cost price,' Eustace offered. 'It already half dead.'

Encouraged by Eustace's generosity, Mr Lutchman bought half a dozen rose-trees growing in bamboo pods. Eustace hugged all the pods close to his chest, refusing any help.

'This is my job, Mister. I have to make up the bill for you. You go and have a look round the rest of the place.'

Eustace twinkled genially and left him. Doreen had wandered off with Bhaskar. Mr Lutchman listened to her ringing laugh. He walked slowly down a side path with Romesh, his hands buried in his pockets, Doreen's laughter fading behind him. Directly ahead he saw a row of young avocado trees planted, like the roses, in bamboo pods. He was tempted. They were a special kind of avocado, with fruit as creamy and as yellow as butter when ripe. He circled round the bamboo pods. There was no one in sight and not far away was a little gate. He could take it out that way and collect it later when they were driving back. Swooping down suddenly, he snatched up one of the pods.

'That's not nice, Mister. That's not a nice thing to do at all.' Eustace, coming up behind him, tapped him on the shoulder. He shook his head, making small scolding noises. 'You thought I had gone to make the bill, eh? But I too smart to do a thing like that. That's what I does tell all the people who come here, but I does be hiding right behind them bushes there.' He indicated a spot further down the path, chuckling quietly. 'Is not a good example to set to your little boy.' Romesh looked at his father. 'People does always try to pull a thing or two on old Eustace, but, as you see, I too smart for them.' Eustace gazed steadily at him, languorous, indulgent, amused.

'I wasn't going to thief anything. You could ask my son. I was just about to come looking for you as a matter of fact.' Mr Lutchman appealed to Romesh for support. Romesh, biting his lower lip, said nothing.

'I know you was, Mister. I know you was.' Eustace wagged a finger at him. 'Everybody always coming to look for me when I catch them. Is a funny thing. But, you know, it's not good doing that kind of thing too often. One day the police go throw you in jail and when you tell them you was just about to come and look for them, they not like me, you know. They wouldn't believe you. And what you go do then?' Eustace's languor intensified. He seemed to be on the point of falling asleep.

'Look. We could come to a little settlement between the two of we. What you say to that?' Mr Lutchman glanced at Romesh.

'Now you bribing me,' Eustace replied, also glancing at Romesh. 'I doesn't take bribe, Mister, but a little gift for the wife and kiddies, well that's a different matter.' He spoke slowly and very gently.

'How about a dollar?' Mr Lutchman searched in his pockets.

'But what you take me for, Mister?' Eustace became more animated. 'That wasn't a nice thing what you try to do with that plant, you know.'

'Two dollar.'

'Now you talking to me, Mister. Mind you, is not all that much in the circumstances. Say two dollars and fifty cents and we go call that good.'

Mr Lutchman gave him two dollars and fifty cents. 'I don't know what I woulda do if you was the sort of man to take bribe from people. I count myself lucky that I dealing with a man like you.'

'Some people is really terrible that way,' Eustace admitted, folding the notes carefully and stuffing them in his pocket. 'Bring the zabocca with you and come. This time I really going to make up the bill.' Eustace grinned and Mr Lutchman and Romesh followed him back up the path.

Doreen and Bhaskar joined them in what Eustace described as the 'office', a dilapidated shed furnished with a table and chairs and used chiefly for storing tools. Eustace arranged the plants on the table, and, taking a pencil and piece of paper from a cupboard, started to enumerate with laborious care the various items, licking his lips and making up the prices as he went along. He spoke softly to himself. 'One red rose plant,' he sucked on the pencil and rolled his eyes up to the roof, 'one dollar and twenty cent. One zabocca tree,' scratching his head and gazing pensively round the room, but not at Mr Lutchman and Romesh, 'two dollars and fifty cent.' He was a long time adding up, rubbing out mistakes with his finger and checking and counter-checking. At length, he read out the cost, casting a dubious eye at the column of figures and holding out his hand for payment.

'Let me run through that.' Doreen took the sheet of paper away from him brusquely, frowning at the scrawled figures.

'Don't bother, Doreen. I go take his word for it.' Mr Lutchman hastily counted out the money.

Doreen dropped the piece of paper on the table. 'It's your affair if you want to be cheated.'

'Yes, yes. It's my affair.'

'Nobody ever accuse me of cheating them before. I is a honest man doing my work and minding my own business.' Eustace stared morosely at Doreen, but she was already walking across the lawn towards the car with Bhaskar and Romesh. 'What I do that she have to begin accusing me like that?' Eustace demanded. 'Anyway, people not suppose to walk on the grass,' he concluded triumphantly.

'Come. Help me take these plants to the car before I really decide to check the bill.'

'Now you too starting up on me . . .'

'Come. Help me take these plants.'

Eustace got up and obediently gathered to his chest most

of the bamboo pods on the table and followed Mr Lutchman out of the shed.

'I would have you know, Miss, that people not allowed to walk on the grass.' Eustace glowered at Doreen, arranging the plants which could not go in the boot on the back seat.

'And what you going to do about that?' she replied.

Eustace was cowed. 'Everybody does take advantage of me in one way or another.' He sighed and shut the door.

On their way back Doreen said, 'I see you bought a zabocca tree, Ram.'

'Yes. You see right.'

'I didn't know you had enough room in the yard for it.'

Mr Lutchman pressed his lips together and drove a little more quickly.

'What's the time now?' she asked a few minutes later.

'Just gone five.'

'You better hurry up. I still have a lot to do before the party.'

'I was forgetting. Who giving this party?'

'Oh, just a few friends, you know.'

When they arrived at her house, Doreen kissed Bhaskar and Romesh hurriedly and jumped out of the car. 'Goodbye, Ram. I hope the garden is a success.'

Mr Lutchman nodded, tapping on the steering wheel. 'And have a good time at your party,' he said.

Doreen flushed and seemed to hesitate, as if there was something else she wished to say. Instead, she waved abruptly and ran up the path to the verandah and disappeared into the house.

Mrs Lutchman was there to greet them at the front gate. She helped unload the plants. 'A zabocca tree!' she exclaimed. 'And an orchid! Like we really going to have a Garden of Eden here.'

Chapter Five

1

Mr Lutchman took great pains with his garden. The rose trees were his particular favourites and he spent the weekends in the garden, cutting and pruning and grafting. The latter he had learned from a book on roses stolen from the Public Library, and fired by what he had read there, he devoted many hours to carving neat incisions on the stems with a penknife, transplanting them to other trees. Mrs Lutchman was sceptical, convinced that this interference was 'bad' for them.

'You go only end by killing them if you go on cutting them up like that, Ram.'

Mr Lutchman, the penknife poised nervously between his fingers, cursed. 'You making me spoil the damn thing now, woman. Why don't you keep quiet, eh? I read a book all about it so I know what it is I doing. Is the sort of thing you have to do if you want the roses to be nice.'

And the roses were nice. There were red, white, yellow and pink ones. Mr Lutchman gloated. 'What you saying about my killing them off? Come here and look at this one. You ever see a rose as pretty as that in your born days? It healthy as the day is long.' Delicately holding the stem, he sniffed at the petals. He closed his eyes. 'It just like perfume,' he murmured. 'Smell that, woman.'

Mrs Lutchman smelt it and gazed in admiration at her husband. 'It just like perfume,' she agreed.

Mr Lutchman was secretly surprised by his success. Like his wife, he had been half-convinced that grafting was bad and would eventually kill the trees.

The avocado tree, however, worried him. He had planted it in the back yard where there was more room and where also he felt it was less likely to be got at by thieves. 'These trees does spread all over the place,' he explained to his wife, 'and

I don't want the people next door to just tiptoe and pick all the pears off the tree.' Unhappily, it was troublesome from the start, and in a manner for which his optimism had not prepared him.

He had no need to worry about thieves. The tree grew slowly and hesitantly and seemed on several occasions to be on the point of dying. Each time Mr Lutchman, desperate, applied more fertilisers, and the tree, responding to the treatment, would reply with an ephemeral burst of greenery before again subsiding into its former somnolence. Mr Lutchman, losing his temper, would blame his wife. 'Is you who making this blasted tree behave like this,' he shouted at her one day when it was frailer than usual. 'I know you didn't like it from the first time you set eyes on it.'

Mrs Lutchman was patient and reasonable. 'But what you think I would have against the tree, Ram?'

'That is what you have to tell me,' he shouted back at her, eying the thin, yellowing stalk with undisguised bitterness. 'You don't know how much trouble I had to go through getting this blasted, sonafabitch thing.'

'What trouble?'

'Stop contradicting me, woman. I tired of all this contradiction day and night, night and day.' Calming down, his bitterness turned to sorrow. 'I just don't understand it. I went through so much trouble to get it, nearly got thrown in jail in fact, and no sooner I bring it home it start behaving like a blasted donkey. Is more than flesh and blood could take, I tell you.'

'Who nearly throw you in jail? Don't tell me you went rooting up more grass in the Savannah. I was warning you . . .'

'Keep quiet. It have nothing to do with grass.' Bending down, he examined the leaves. He thought of Eustace. 'It go dead soon,' he said.

Mrs Lutchman had come up behind him. 'Maybe it don't like the wind,' she suggested. 'Some plant like that. Why don't you put a few stick around it and make a little fence?'

'Fence my arse,' Mr Lutchman grumbled, pulling roughly at one of the leaves. It came away easily in his hand. 'The sonofabitch bound to go and dead soon,' he said, staring at the leaf. 'Fence or no fence, manure or no manure, it bound to dead soon.'

All the same, he did fashion a windbreak of sorts for it and the tree appeared to be marginally happier as a result, though even so it grew unsteadily and reluctantly. The tree weighed heavily on his mind and Mr Lutchman, overcome by guilt, finally confessed to his wife.

'I think I know why it behaving so,' he said.

'Why?'

'Is because I was trying to thief it.'

Understanding dawned. 'That's the exact reason why,' she said. 'Crime does never pay.'

Thus Mr Lutchman, having come to expect little from the avocado tree, was content to abandon it to its own devices.

2

Mrs Lutchman did not intrude on her husband's gardening activities, though she was sufficiently proud of the roses and the butterfly orchid (which flourished) to boast about them to her family. They received the news coolly, without enthusiasm. Urmila had said 'Huh! I have better things to do with my time than grow roses.' Mrs Lutchman had dismissed it as simple jealousy. She did not tell Ram. What she had done and her judgement of their reaction would have implied a defence of his interests, an intimacy, that would have embarrassed them both, ending, most probably, in him abusing her for 'talking about what is not your business'. The history of their marriage precluded any concessions to such overt acts of concern and affection. At home, she preferred to voice her admiration from a distance and, if possible, obliquely. Thus, the 'Garden of Eden', suitably ironic, was one of her favourite phrases. It was a mask behind which she could disguise her admiration.

This obliqueness formed part of a larger reticence which she had come to practise with regard to her husband. However, it was a reticence that reflected not her former indifference, but something else, resembling affection, which she had begun to feel for him. Unaware how it happened, she now always thought of herself relative to him, his presence inducing in her a sense of order and belongingness. Her husband's bodily presence, the house and garden, Bhaskar and Romesh, these had become the focus of her loyalties.

Mrs Lutchman could detect in her husband's new occupations distorted echoes of his estrangement with Doreen, about which she knew next to nothing and could only guess at. She saw the underlying placidity he had gained from surrender, so that what had emerged from the rupture was not negative, the ending, pure and simple, of an affair, but heralded the emergence of something new in him, an alteration of personality and mood which while not consciously directed towards her, did, having nowhere else to go, flow inevitably in her direction, seeking a new level of adjustment.

Outwardly, there was little to indicate that any change so fundamental had occurred between them. There were the same quarrels, the same physical separateness, the same distinction in their activities. But, this was habit, instinct, an arrangement with which neither of them would have wished to interfere. He could cling only so long to Doreen's absurdities; she, only so long to the Khojas.

What had distressed her at the Khoja cattha was the mood of farewell. She recalled the eyes of the children watching them dance, no different from the expression they might have had at the zoo when confronted by a strange animal. She had noted the unease she had felt when, on that last morning of the cattha, the sisters, dressed in all their finery, had been standing around in the temporary kitchen, as if suspecting they had gone too far, taken part in excesses which they now regretted and hoped to expiate by this display of the other extreme. She had wanted then to return home to her house and husband, knowing that from now on her true place was to be there, inhabiting that house beside him, and therein lay, if not the happiness, the contentment.

3

Like his passion for gardening, Mr Lutchman's interest in photography developed suddenly. A friend at the office had happened to mention casually that he had a camera which he would like to sell. The idea had caught Mr Lutchman's fancy and for a few days it floated alluringly in his mind.

'Look at that sunset,' he exclaimed to his wife one day. 'It would be really nice to take a photo of that, eh?'

Mrs Lutchman was taken aback by the suddenness of this outburst. She glanced briefly at the sky and then at her husband, saying nothing.

'You know what your trouble is, woman? Your trouble is you can't appreciate beautiful things. Look at all them colours. Orange and pink and purple. You ever see anything like that in your born days?'

'You think I blind or something, Ram? I does see the sky every day. What so great about it all of a sudden?'

'Watch what you saying to me, woman. I tired of you always contradicting me. You must have some respect for me and remember I is not a fool. You think I don't know it does have a sunset every day? I was just saying it would be nice to take a photo.' He stared resentfully at her.

'Yes. It would be very nice to take a photo, Ram. But you need to have a camera before you do a thing like that. You just can't shut your eye and say click, you know. Photograph don't drop down out of the sky.'

'I know photograph don't drop down out of the sky. But just have a little patience.'

'Don't go and do anything foolish, Ram.'

The following morning, Mr Lutchman approached his friend at the office. 'How much you asking for that camera you was talking about, Wilkie?'

'I didn't know you was interested in that sort of thing, Lutch.'

'Oh, I been interested in photography for a long time, but what with one thing and the other I never had the opportunity to do much about it. You know how it is. How much you asking?'

'You name a price.'

'Twenty-five dollars?'

Wilkie laughed loudly. 'You know what kind of camera it is I have, boy? Is a high-class German job. Flash-bulbs, light meter, the whole works, man. Twenty-five dollars! I must remember to tell the boys that one.' The 'boys' played a large and mysterious role in Wilkie's life. He referred constantly to them. Mr Lutchman regretted having asked him about the camera. He was afraid of what the 'boys' might say when they heard of his offer, but it was too late now to turn back.

'Okay. Okay. Don't kill yourself. I wasn't to know all that. Tell me how much it is you asking.' He was losing his temper. Wilkie stopped laughing and gazed seriously at him.

'I go be frank with you, Lutch,' he began. 'Listen, man, cameras is technical things. It take me years to learn how to use them properly, and if you don't know nothing about them, you go be just wasting your money if you buy an expensive one.'

'Who say I don't know anything about it? I tell you I was always interested in that sort of thing.'

'All the same,' Wilkie said. 'I would advise you to start off with a cheap one. One of them little fifteen-dollar Japanese jobs for instance.'

'You just trying to put me off. I don't see that handling a camera is all that difficult.'

Wilkie smiled. 'So you think that, eh? Don't say I didn't warn you, Lutch. The price is a hundred dollars.'

'A hundred dollars!'

'But what you think it is, Lutch? That camera cost me two hundred dollars new and it still in perfect condition. Man, is a favour I doing you when I think about it.'

Mr Lutchman, against his better judgement, bought the camera.

'A hundred dollars! And just to take photos of the sunset?'

'What do you mean just take photos of the sunset?' Mr Lutchman turned the camera delicately in his hands. Before him on the table were the several booklets that accompanied it. 'I have a lot of other things you could do with a camera. Think of all them snapshots I could take of you and the children. I always wanted we to have a snapshot album.'

'You read the booklet they give you?' Mrs Lutchman asked.

Mr Lutchman had tried to, but given up in disgust. 'They

useless,' he replied. 'They just have a lot of big word and confusing drawing. I could do without them.'

Mrs Lutchman was doubtful. 'I think you should read them first,' she said.

Mr Lutchman chose to ignore her. 'I sure you would like to have a snapshot album,' he repeated, hoping to shift her attention from the booklets.

'First time I hear of that one. Since when you love we so much?'

'Watch what you saying to me, woman.' He squinted through the shutter. 'Is a really great camera this. Cost two hundred dollars new, you know.'

'Who say? I sure it only cost him about fifty dollars.'

'I warning you . . .' But then, his imagination caught by another glorious possibility, he changed his mind and said instead, 'I could send pictures to the *Trinidad Chronicle*. They does pay good money for that. In no time at all this camera go pay for itself.'

'What you go take picture of? Me washing clothes in the back yard?' she burst out laughing.

For a moment Mr Lutchman doubted and a shadow crossed his face. Then he brightened, struck by a happy recollection. 'You thought I was going to kill them roses, not so? I remember you was running your mouth all over the place when I was doing the grafting. And I going to do the same thing this time. I'll go to the library and borrow a book on photography. That will be a hundred times better than any booklet. Mark my words.'

Buoyed up by this decision, his wife's scorn and the threat of Wilkie's 'boys' ceased to bother him.

He stole a book on photography from the Public Library, refusing to use the camera until he had read it. It was big and impressively illustrated. One photograph in particular delighted him and, cutting it out, he plastered it on one of the walls in their bedroom. It was a picture of a lowering sky, laced with storm clouds, each edged by a bright, meandering ribbon of silver. The caption said: 'Every cloud has a silver lining'. The other photographs, all equally dramatic, showed skies being ripped apart by flurries of lightning and fields of fragile flowers bending before sweeping winds. It was a strange book, curiously violent, and it appealed greatly to Mr Lutchman. 'The man who take these photos is a genius,' he declared to his wife. 'A genius!'

At last he felt ready to tackle what he described as a 'subject'. He bought his first roll of film and drove out into the countryside, searching for clouds with silver linings and fields of flowers bending before the wind. Finding neither of these in sufficient abundance, he photographed instead bullocks rolling in the mud and peasants at work in the fields. He returned home from these expeditions excited and pleased with himself.

'But I thought you was going to take pictures of we,' Mrs Lutchman reproached him.

'More important things must come first,' he replied. 'I going to send these to get develop and you go bawl when you see the kind of photographs I been taking these past few days.'

He awaited the return of the photographs with mounting excitement. Eventually, a little yellow and red packet arrived. Mrs Lutchman and Bhaskar and Romesh gathered excitedly around him.

'Hmm. Like that one didn't come out properly,' she murmured, looking at the first photograph he took out of the packet.

'Shut up, woman, and mind your own business.'

He took out another.

'It very funny, Ram. I wonder why they all come out so black and spotty.'

Mr Lutchman brought his fist down heavily on the table. 'Take the children and go from here,' he shouted. 'I don't want an audience standing up around me and breathing down my neck. Go! Go!'

Mrs Lutchman left the room with Bhaskar and Romesh. When she returned about an hour later, Mr Lutchman was still sitting there, his head buried in his hands and the spoilt photographs scattered over the table. She picked up one and looked it, shaking her head sorrowfully.

'They not so bad, Ram. You could still make out some things in one or two of them.' She collected them into a pile.

'After all, it was only your first try. You couldn't expect to be perfect right away.'

Mr Lutchman moaned softly, moving his head from side to side in his palms. 'Throw them in the dustbin. I don't want to see them again.'

'No need to throw all of them away, Ram. As I was saying, it have some good . . .'

'I say throw them away.' He raised his voice, lifting his head off his palms. Mrs Lutchman took the photographs and dropped them in the dustbin.

'Maybe it was the fault of the people who develop it,' she suggested. 'You can't trust anybody these days. You could never tell, but maybe they spoil them just to spite you. People like that, no getting away from it.' Mrs Lutchman proceeded to elaborate her theory of human nature. 'Take all these children who you does read about winning scholarship and all kinds of thing in the newspaper. One half of that is bribery and the other half is plain cheating. And don't talk about what does happen round election time. Govind was telling me about that the other day. You know what they does do? They does throw all the ballot boxes they don't feel like counting in the river. You can't trust people any more. What I would suggest for you to do is to start developing your own photo. That is the only way you can make sure you getting your money's worth.' Thus, after her own fashion, she sought to comfort him.

Mr Lutchman seemed interested. The idea of developing his own photographs appealed to him. 'I think you right. Is a very sensible thing you just say. I go buy a developing kit. That way no piss'n'tail person will try and make a fool of me.'

Reluctantly, he asked Wilkie's advice.

'Why, Lutch, like you broadening out. How is the camera?'

'It's going fine. I like it. Those Germans are fine craftsmen.'

'A truly great camera that, Lutch. Even now I does miss it sometimes. You taking lots of good pictures with it?'

'Not as much as I would like to. I find the developing too expensive. That's why I thought I would try and develop my own.'

'True. True.' Wilkie stroked his chin, gazing pensively at Mr Lutchman. 'You must bring some of the photographs you take and let me see them, Lutch. If you want, come to think of it, I could develop them for you at a small charge.'

Mr Lutchman laughed. 'I want to learn how to do it myself, Wilkie.'

'Well, bring some of your photographs along to the office one day anyway,' Wilkie insisted, reverting to his pensive expression.

'I don't think they would interest you. Is only snapshots of the family and that kind of thing. More of a personal nature, you understand.'

'I understand, Lutch. I understand.' Wilkie smiled lazily. 'It was only a request. Don't do it if it will embarrass you. So you want to develop your own now, eh?'

'You know much about it?'

Wilkie laughed. It was the kind of question he loved. 'You should ask the boys about that, Lutch. They will tell you how Wilkie does spend all his time lock up in dark room. Is one of my hobbies.' That was another of the things Mr Lutchman disliked about Wilkie: his 'hobbies'. He had scores of them.

'It easy?'

'Nothing's easy in this world, Lutch, as you well know. But is a funny thing you should ask. It so happens I have a spare kit which I could sell you. Mind you, it's not the most sophisticated . . .'

'One has got to be simple at the start.'

Wilkie stared at Mr Lutchman, his face broadening into another of his lazy smiles. 'Quite right. Quite right. It does take a little practice,' he agreed. 'How about ten dollars?'

'Sounds reasonable to me.'

'It's a gift, Lutch. A gift at ten dollars. The boys would think I'm crazy. But for you, well . . .'

Mr Lutchman bought the developing kit.

This time he was less ambitious, confining himself to photographs of the family. But even this had its tribulations.

'All right. The three of you line up against the fence. This is going to be a group study.' Mr Lutchman, the camera dangling from his neck, arranged them in line, stepped back into the road and shook his head disapprovingly. 'Bhaskar, bring your face in the light, boy. Yes, that's it. Now smile. Say cheese.' Strained expressions settled on all three faces. 'Chut. You call that a smile. Say cheese, I tell you.' Mr Lutchman was beginning to lose his temper. 'Watch your step with me, Romesh. You looking as if you going to a blasted funeral. You better say cheese or otherwise it go be your funeral if you not careful. Grin! Grin!' he howled at them. The strained expressions deepened.

They were standing on the pavement in front of the house. A group of the curious gathered to watch. Mr Lutchman was becoming increasingly ruffled. Mrs Lutchman, to ease her discomfort, stared stolidly at the pavement. Someone shouted at her from a passing car. 'Say cheese, darling,' and blew a kiss at her. 'Come here and I go say cheese to you, you sonofabitch,' Mr Lutchman shouted back, shaking his fist at the car. The curious laughed. Mr Lutchman walked up to one of the smaller children. 'Who you think you laughing at, eh?' he bellowed in the child's face. 'I go straighten that smile off your face for you.'

'Mister, you better leave that boy alone,' a muscular Negro on his way to the cinema at the corner growled at him. 'Is not your child.' He squared himself, ready for the fray.

'Okay. Okay,' Mr Lutchman apologized. 'I didn't know what I was doing.'

'Well, you better watch it next time.'

Mr Lutchman nodded and the man, mollified against his wishes, waved his finger threateningly at him and continued down the street, pausing every now and again to make sure he was behaving himself. Mr Lutchman put the camera back in its case. 'Come. We better go back inside.'

The group study went inside, grateful for this reprieve, and had their photographs taken in the sitting-room.

'Well,' Mrs Lutchman said, when the roll of film had been exhausted, 'you sure you know how to develop them?'

'I know all it have to know. Wilkie tell me all about it in the office the other day.'

'You mean to say you still trust Wilkie after all that man

do to you?' Mrs Lutchman, reflecting on her husband's previous failure, had compiled a lengthy mental dossier of Wilkie's crimes.

Mr Lutchman stifled the curses that rose to his lips. 'Come upstairs. You have to help me with this. And you better make sure nobody disturb me for the next two hours or so. This is a tricky business.'

They went up to their bedroom. 'Now it got to be dark, otherwise it won't work,' he explained. As directed, Mrs Lutchman switched off the lights and drew the curtains.

'That dark enough?'

'No good.' He watched her disconsolately. 'You have any suggestions?' Despite appearances, he had a healthy respect for his wife's resourcefulness.

Mrs Lutchman examined the room. 'How about under the bed? It have enough room for you to lie down under there and you could cover your head with a blanket to make really sure.'

'Is a foolish way to have to do it, but I suppose is the only thing. I wouldn't like Wilkie and his boys to see me doing it like that.' He laughed. 'Well, then. We better get all the stuff together.'

Mrs Lutchman brought in the kit and several saucers and basins of water as he had instructed. Mr Lutchman studied the assortment of paraphernalia spread at his feet. He could feel his confidence ebbing away. He got down on his hands and knees and crawled under the bed. Mrs Lutchman handed him the various items one by one. Finally, she helped him drape the blanket over his head. She sprawled on the floor and peeped at the huddled mass, following the vague movements of her husband's arms under the blanket. For the first few minutes all went well. 'I don't see what so difficult in this,' he said. 'Child's play.'

'I tell you you shouldn't believe everything Wilkie tell you,' Mrs Lutchman shouted back encouragingly.

Confidence waxed under the blanket. Mr Lutchman even began to whistle.

'Child's play. I really don't know what Wilkie was talking about.'

'I always say that you could do anything you put your mind to,' Mrs Lutchman echoed.

Then it was that she heard the first splash. Mr Lutchman swore softly. The basins clanged against each other, the movements under the blanket lost their assurance, becoming more abrupt and frenzied. A thin stream of water flowed into the room.

'What happening, Ram?'

'One of the blasted basins fall over.'

'Take your time, man. Don't hurry.'

He uttered a string of curses. 'I getting all wet under here and I can't see a damn thing. Is like a blasted lake now. I hate this sonofabitch thing.'

'Don't lose your temper, man.'

'Oh God! There goes another sonofabitch.' There was a loud splash and a stream of water gushed into Mrs Lutchman's face.

'What you doing under there, man? You wetting up the whole room.'

A steady, muffled roar of anger and distress issued from under the blanket now. There was another splash, followed by a howl of despair, as more water flowed into the room, bringing with it little strips of crumpled paper. The blanket heaved as Mr Lutchman struggled wildly to free himself. 'Take this sonofabitch blanket off me,' he screamed. Mrs Lutchman pulled the blanket away to reveal the drenched, gesticulating figure of her husband. She could make out a confusion of overturned basins and saucers and soaked strips of paper stuck to the floor and littering her husband's body.

'To hell with that piss'n'tail Wilkie', he cried, crawling slowly and painfully out into the room. Crumpling the pieces of paper, he straightened himself and began flinging them violently through the windows. He turned on his wife. 'All this wouldn't have happened if it wasn't for you and your stupid ideas.'

'What you blaming me for? What it is I do that you have to throw the blame on me?'

'Is you who tell me to do my own developing, not so? And who send me under the bed with a blanket?'

Mrs Lutchman did not bother to answer these reproaches. She brought him a towel. 'Go and dry yourself with this before you catch cold,' she said.

After this episode, Mr Lutchman neglected his camera. He did make one or two passing references to it, but only when something had gone wrong and he was feeling depressed. Then he would mutter to himself, 'Is just like that sonofabitch camera.' For the rest he left it severely alone.

Mrs Lutchman, taking charge, put it and the developing kit away in a box lined with cotton wool which she secreted in the wardrobe. She regarded the camera as her first true heirloom and in her mind she rehearsed the scene that would take place when she gave it to Bhaskar. So affected was she by this picture that she cried as she hid the box among her clothes.

4

Mr Lutchman had to discover new ways to amuse himself. He bought some anthurium lilies as he had long planned to do and planted them at the sides of the house, but the excitement generated by these new arrivals was short-lived. There was little more he could do with the garden other than try to maintain it in its present condition; but even this, due to one of those unforeseen setbacks to which he now seemed unusually liable, was proving difficult.

One day, out on one of his rambles in the country, he had chanced upon a spreading weed with round, green leaves, very pretty, that covered the ground evenly like a carpet. He had brought some of it home and shown it to Mrs Lutchman. 'Look at that, woman,' he said, thrusting a handful of the weed close to her face. 'This could make a really nice lawn, don't you think? You should see how pretty it does look when it have a large space to grow over.'

'But is just a weed, Ram. It all right for the country, but not for here.'

'You just wait and see. This idea go spread like wildfire. I don't know why nobody ever think of it before.'

Ignoring his wife's protests, he cleared a patch of lawn and planted it. He was right. It did spread like wildfire and in two months the rest of the lawn was overwhelmed by a soft green blanket of the weed. Unfortunately, in the town its charms were less apparent. Mr Lutchman was puzzled by its behaviour. 'I just don't understand it,' he said. 'Out there in the country it was looking so nice and here it looking . . . is just like that sonofabitch camera.'

'This is the kind of thing that does happen when you stubborn and don't listen to what other people say. You feel you know everything. I hope this teach you a lesson.'

'But you shoulda see how nice it was looking out in the country.'

'That may be so. But here . . . that don't look like a lawn to me at all. It more like a patch of weeds if you ask me.'

'Well, a man can't be right all the time. Everybody, even Churchill, have to make a little mistake now and then. I go root it up.'

'I sure Churchill wouldn't plant a weed like this in he garden. He have more sense than that, you take my word.'

'I go root it up and plant some more grass. Don't worry.'

Easier said than done. The weed was intractable and all Mr Lutchman's efforts to get rid of it failed. It spread to the neighbouring yards.

'The strangest thing happening in we yard, Mr Lutchman,' one of them called over the fence to him, the same the greenness of whose lawn had so impressed him. 'This funny kind of weed suddenly come and it choking all we plants.'

'I know,' Mr Lutchman commiserated. 'It happening to we too. Choking all we plants. I can't think where it come from.'

However, the roses continued to flourish, but Mr Lutchman despaired of ever tasting any of the fruit from the avocado tree. On his occasional inspections he would stand morosely before the windbreak and thinking of all the fruit he was missing, shake his head and say, 'Not in my lifetime. Not in my lifetime.'

Mr Lutchman announced plans to extend the wall at the back. The reasons behind this were obscure, part of an endemic restlessness. He mentioned his dislike of the neighbours staring into the yard and his fear of a thief breaking into the house one night. Neither of these explanations convinced his wife.

'I must say I don't know what kind of thief go decide to do that. He won't find nothing worth his trouble here. Some spoon and enamel cup that's all.'

'You is a truly ungrateful woman. What about the light-shade I buy? And the cabinet? You think they worth nothing?'

'I still don't see why you need to build a wall.'

'And what about the zabocca tree, eh? I does see how them bitches at the back does be staring at it every day.'

Mrs Lutchman laughed. 'Perhaps they might feel sorry for we and bring we another one.'

Mr Lutchman lost his temper. The vagaries of the avocado tree had never really ceased to rankle. 'I always know you didn't like zabocca tree. Right from the start you had something against it, not so?' He approached, peering into her face.

'Don't start with that nonsense all over again, Ram. Be sensible, man.'

Mr Lutchman moved away from her, pacing up and down and staring up at the ceiling, rubbing his chin. He stopped suddenly and looked at her. 'That's it,' he said. 'At long last I understand.'

'Understand what?'

He resumed his pacing, strolling easily about the room. 'I know now why you don't want me to raise that wall. You think you could fool me, eh? But I find out now.' He shook a finger at her.

'Find out what?' She was slightly alarmed.

'So you still pretending. All right, I go tell you.' He paused for dramatic effect. 'I know you have a man,' he said.

Mrs Lutchman, her anxiety gone in an instant, dissolved into uncontrollable laughter. Mr Lutchman struggled to maintain his seriousness. 'All these years you been fooling me and going with another man behind my back. Tell me, he nicer than me?'

'A lot more handsome,' she spluttered, her whole body shaking with laughter. 'He does come here to serenade me every night.' She clasped her arms round her stomach. 'Oh God! I can't remember when last I laugh so much. It killing me.' A tear rolled down her cheeks.

'You want to know why I extending the wall now?'

'Why?' She brushed the tear away with the sleeve of her blouse.

'To stop your man coming in here every night and serenading you. That's why. From now on is I who go be serenading you. You hear that?'

'Very sensible. Very sensible. But since when you does play the guitar?' She buried her head in her arms, engulfed by yet another wave of laughter.

'I does play the guitar very well,' Mr Lutchman replied seriously. 'You wait and you go see how well I does play it.'

Mr Lutchman raised the height of the wall by four feet and along the top, as an added refinement, there were jagged bits of broken bottle, specially chosen by him, protruding from the cement. No longer considering himself liable to explain his action, he carried out the reconstruction with an unwavering determination. Mrs Lutchman, not interfering, watched the gradual blotting out of the house at the back, until only its roof was visible. Mr Lutchman, pleased with himself, contemplated the result.

'Now, if your man try to climb over this wall, he bound to cut he hands and foot. So I would warn him if I was you.' He tapped the brick affectionately and pointing at the slivers of glass glinting in the sun, smiled and said, 'This go teach him a lesson.'

There were few gaps separating these successive flurries of passion. One obsession, either through failure or fulfilment, rapidly gave way to another equally inexplicable, and to each Mr Lutchman brought the same devotion and frenzied marshalling of his energies. Mrs Lutchman could discern no pattern in his behaviour, no links between one obsession and another, and this sometimes worried her. The reconstruction of the wall, which at the time she had treated as a somewhat elaborate joke, had soon ceased to be funny. It had dawned on her that, very possibly, he had begun to half-believe his own fantastic accusations.

His fondness for swimming reasserted itself, but allied with this was a new obsession. He had decided to make 'men' of his sons and teaching them to swim seemed to be one way of doing this. 'Look at Bhaskar,' he said to his wife. 'He don't play cricket, he don't play football. He does behave like a real girl. No. I must make a man of that boy before it too late.'

'He does collect stamps.'

'Stamps! Stamps don't give you muscles. No. We need more brawn not brain around this house.'

'He does study very hard.'

'I don't see him coming first in class. The only prize I ever see him win was for being the best behaved boy in the class. You call that a prize?'

'That's only because the masters does cheat him.'

'Chut, woman! Is because he don't get no exercise, that's why.'

Thus, Bhaskar and Romesh were dragooned into going to the beach, going early one Sunday morning. They drove westwards out of the city at a time when there was virtually no traffic on the roads. The sun had not yet cleared the mountains and there was a lingering chill in the wind that drove the clouds, still carrying hints of an earlier rosiness. The road, built over a mangrove swamp and overlooked by the lower foothills of the Northern Range, was set well back from the sea, which glimmered through the screen of swampy vegetation and the lines of coconut trees growing on banked beds of earth.

The coastal strip here, fringing the Gulf of Paria, was unattractive. There were no beaches in the proper sense of the word, just vague, ill-defined stretches of mud inundated at high tide, and when the water receded (at full moon as much as half a mile) there were revealed the acres of black mud littered with discarded tins and other debris. However, to the north-west, the mountains came closer to the sea and there were a series of small, rock-strewn beaches. One of these was larger and more popular than the rest. Nearby were the bauxite docks and the tall, cylindrical tanks and chutes coated with thick coverings of pink dust. Normally, there would be a ship lying idle at anchor on Sunday mornings.

Mr Lutchman parked the car on the road and they climbed down some concrete steps built into the sides of the cliff and changed into their bathing trunks under a solitary almond tree.

The sea here, known as the Carenage, was noted for its calmness, the waves folding gently against the stones. Mr Lutchman, wearing his maroon swimming trunks, waded circumspectly into the water with Romesh, stepping gingerly over the mossy stones, taking care not to cut himself on the more jagged edges. After a few feet the stones gave way to mud and he plunged into the water with Romesh, showing him how to use his hands and feet. Bhaskar, despite his father's encouragements, had remained on the beach. He had brought a book with him and was pretending to read.

Mr Lutchman called to him. 'Come, come. Put down the book. It don't have nothing to be frightened of. Look at Romesh. You shouldn't let him put you to shame.'

Bhaskar shook his head. 'Next time, Pa. I like just sitting here and reading.'

'Put the book away, boy.' He came out of the water. 'Come with me. I got to make a man of you.' He took the book away from him. 'You could read that another time. Come. Come.'

Bhaskar got up reluctantly and let himself be led into the water.

'Lie flat on my arms and I'll hold you up. Beat your foot and hands like this.' Mr Lutchman demonstrated.

'You go take your hands away and leave me to sink. I know you.'

Mr Lutchman slapped him. 'Don't be foolish, boy. I trying to teach you, not drown you.' He laid out his arms parallel to one another across the water. 'Look at Romesh. You see how easy it is. He not frighten like you. Come on, lie down over my arms and beat your hand and foot like your brother.'

Bhaskar shook his head again. 'I don't feel like it this morning,' he said. 'Next time we come, I promise. I have to finish reading that book by tomorrow, otherwise I would have tried today.' He took a step back from his father.

'You making me angry, boy. Fourteen years old and still a sissy.' He grabbed Bhaskar's arm and attempted to pull him deeper into the water. Bhaskar resisted, flailing frantically. Mr Lutchman slapped him a second time. 'Go away from here,' he shouted. 'Take yourself away from here and go and put your skirt on.'

'I go swim with you next time we come, Pa. But not today. I must get accustom first.' He gazed appealingly at his father. Mr Lutchman pushed him away.

'Go and find your skirt and brassiere,' he said quietly. 'Go on.'

Bhaskar crawled out of the water and went and sat under the almond tree.

On the following Sunday, he paddled hopefully in the shallower water, part of his programme of gradual acclimatization. 'Look, Pa. You see how I learning by myself.'

'Learning my arse. Go and put on your skirt and brassiere.'

Bhaskar complained to his mother. They were all three of them in the sitting-room.

'Why you does always be telling the boy to put on he skirt and bra for, Ram?'

'Because he's a little girl, that's why.' Mr Lutchman winked flirtatiously at his son.

Mrs Lutchman examined Bhaskar with a medical detachment. 'He don't look like one to me.'

'That's because he always hiding under your skirt.'

Bhaskar protested. 'I was learning to swim very well by myself, Ma. You can't expect people to do everything at once.'

'You shouldn't be speaking like that to him then, Ram. You hear what he say. He was learning very well by himself. It's not good to say things like that to him.'

Mr Lutchman turned to Bhaskar. 'Hello, Tarzan.'

Bhaskar prodded his mother. 'That's the kind of thing I mean,' he said. 'He always saying things like that to me.'

'If he don't want to learn to swim with you, that is his business, Ram. He might go drown for all you know, the way you does behave. I don't see how Tarzan come into it.'

'I was learning very well by myself,' Bhaskar insisted.

'Hello, Nelson.'

'You see what I mean, Ma. He wouldn't give me a chance.'

Mr Lutchman cursed. 'You could bet on one thing. I not taking him to the beach with me again. Nelson here go be putting we all in the shade soon.'

'Don't think he go dead because of that,' Mrs Lutchman replied.

Mr Lutchman was as good as his word. After that, he never offered to take Bhaskar again, but the loss was not a great one. His taste for these expeditions to the Carenage dwindled. He preferred, if anything, to go by himself and eventually his desire to make men of his sons disappeared altogether. No new passion coming to fill its place, he returned to the garden, which had been suffering from his neglect, and resumed his war against the proliferating weed.

5

The summons went forth from the house in the country: the elder Mrs Khoja was dying.

The old woman, tended by the distraught Indrani, was brought, at her own request, to Port-of-Spain so that she might die in the house of her son and heir. She arrived in an ambulance and was carried up the front steps on a stretcher, swathed in grey blankets, escorted by the suppressed sobs of Indrani, clutching her box of medicines frantically under her arms.

Within hours, the sisters had been informed and had gathered in a solemn mass at the house in Woodlands. Their mother was put in the back room, the room always reserved for her, and where no one but Mr Khoja and Indrani were admitted.

The occasion permitted a relaxation of the rules and the sisters sat in silent congregation in the darkened sitting-room, keeping vigil and straining their ears to catch the smallest sound that might emerge from what they called the 'sick-room' Mrs Khoja, overwhelmed by events, had retired to her bedroom, where she fussed furtively with her dolls. It was early morning and the sounds from the street – the men sweeping the pavements, the revving engine of the refuse truck, the rattle of the dustbins – were muffled by the closed doors and thick curtains. Their vigil had already lasted a full twenty-four hours, eked out with cups of strong, black coffee served by Blackie. Shantee and Darling had sunk deep back in their chairs, eyes closed but not asleep. Half-filled cups of coffee lay scattered at their feet. Urmila stared straight ahead of her, wide-eyed and unblinking, while Badwatee, sitting next to her, counted the beads of a chaplet. This heresy, however, went unnoticed. Saraswatee's eyes were red and puffed and she kept wiping her lips with a handkerchief. She sat next to Mrs Lutchman, who gazed at the reflections in the glass of the bookcases.

The door to the 'sick-room' opened softly and Mr Khoja's head appeared through the gap. 'One at a time,' he whispered. Saraswatee started to cry. She was ignored. 'Urmila, you better come first.' Urmila got up mechanically, straightening her dress, and with her eyes fixed straight ahead of her, walked stiff-backed into the bedroom. The door closed. She did not remain there long. Two minutes later she re-emerged with that same mechanical rigidity in her gait, in marked contrast with her eyes, which were moist and slightly red. She returned to her chair and sat down without saying a word, though several of the sisters darted enquiring looks at her. One by one they went in, and all like Urmila returned red-eyed and silent to their seats. Mrs Lutchman, not of the blood royal, was the last to go in.

Indrani was bent low over her mother, the box of medicines lying open on a chair beside the bed. There was the familiar over-powering smell of cotton wool soaked in bay-rum. Mr Khoja stood in a corner of the room, staring out of the half-opened window. The sun fell in a rectangular patch across the bed. Mrs Lutchman tiptoed over to the bed. She was crying, drying her tears with the sleeve of her dress. Indrani signalled her to be quiet and passed a damp towel over the old woman's forehead.

'You can touch she hand,' Indrani said, soaking the towel in a basin of water. 'She not unconscious yet.' Mrs Lutchman controlled a fresh wave of tears and touched the old woman's hand, caressing the frail, wrinkled flesh.

'That's enough. You better leave she now and go. We go call you later if anything happen.' Indrani had obviously rehearsed this little speech beforehand. Mrs Lutchman trailed a despairing look at the body stretched out under the blankets and tiptoed out of the room to rejoin the sisters.

They all sat and waited as before, numbed and brooding, fingering their bracelets (Badwatee her chaplet) and gazing at the rows of books locked behind their glass doors and the photographs on the wall. Blackie came in with a tray and collected the coffee cups and went out to the kitchen.

'How is the children?' Saraswatee asked Mrs Lutchman.

'They very well, thank God.'

Urmila shook her bracelets disapprovingly and with a sheepish discomfort the two women fell silent. The door to the bedroom opened again, revealing Mr Khoja's head. 'All of you better come in now.' His head disappeared behind the gap. It was as if they were being called to give evidence in a court of law. There were a few quickly stifled sobs as the sisters filed into the bedroom and stood in a circle around the bed.

The old woman's Adam's apple rose and fell in slow, uneven movements. Spasmodically, she clenched and unclenched her fists. 'Mohun, Mohun,' she called after her dead husband, and the sound rose from her lips and floated thin as a wisp through the window and out of the room. She mumbled incomprehensibly after that, her voice falling softer and softer, until there were only the soundlessly moving lips. Indrani put her ear close to her mother's lips.

'What is it you want to say, Ma? Tell Indrani. She here beside you listening.'

'She spirit travelling already,' Urmila murmured. 'It not going to be long now.'

Indrani rubbed the towel feverishly over the old woman's head. Next door a little boy shouted as he went off to school. It seemed like a signal.

'Oh God, Oh God,' Indrani shrieked suddenly. A wail rose fom the circle of sisters and they pressed forward to the edge of the bed.

'Oh God, Oh God,' Indrani moaned, still rubbing the towel on the old woman's forehead. 'Ma. Ma. Come back to we. Come back to we.' She kissed her mother's cheeks, her shoulders heaving convulsively. Urmila grabbed her arms and attempted to pull her away from the corpse.

'Indrani, your crying won't help she now. She in another world already. She had a good, long life. It was time for she to go and join Pa.'

The sisters wailed.

'Ma. Ma. Why you leave me for? All these years I look after you. What you leaving me to do now? Ma. Ma.' Indrani fell sobbing across the old woman's body, wringing the towel. She resisted Urmila's efforts to drag her away from the bed, but eventually she surrendered and allowed herself to be led out of the room. Mr Khoja stepped forward through an avenue of sisters and knelt down beside the bed. He kissed his mother on the cheek. Then he drew the blanket and covered her face.

'I'll go now and make the arrangements with the funeral home,' he said.

He ordered an ornate open coffin made of white painted wood and decorated with religious symbols, patterned in green and red sequins. For two days, the body lay in the darkened sitting-room and on the third day a procession of cars drove to the banks of the Caroni River, where prayers were said and the body cremated. During the following week, the sisters ate nothing but boiled food. When the period of mourning was finished, the poor of the city were fed in a great feast at the Poor House in St James.

6

For several years, the elder Mrs Khoja had survived mummified, in a state of stagnating decrepitude, relieved only by her annual visit to Woodlands. The passage of time during these last years had wrought little change for better or worse. Physically, she had grown frailer, and spiritually she had grown more dependent on the ministrations of Indrani; but this apart, the doctors from Port-of-Spain came and went (latterly with decreasing frequency), prescribing the same medicines and uttering hopefully the same formulae of advice and phrases of unflagging sympathy. And Indrani, who knew it all by heart, scarcely bothered to listen, choosing instead to follow her own instincts in all matters medical. It appeared to do the old woman little harm.

In time, Indrani had sought to monopolize her mother and employed every stratagem to prevent the doctors coming. She appealed to her religious sentiments. 'All these doctors no good for you, Ma. They don't know what they doing. A pundit just as good, if not better. And if is a pill you want, I have exactly what you need.' She indicated the medicine-box. Indrani appealed as well to her mother's miserly sentiments. 'Think of all that money they charging you, Ma. My heart does bleed when I have to hand them all those dollar notes. They cheating you right, left and centre.'

These approaches, when taken together, were irresistible, and thus Indrani having discouraged all potential rivals (the doctors still came, but their visits were mere formalities; as for the promised pundit, he never materialized) had gradually established her hegemony. It had been a skilful piece of diplomacy. She was unstinting in her care and devotion, a jealous and tyrannical guardian of all that concerned her charge, and ultimately she too entered into and shared the mummified atmosphere of that house where she lived alone with her mother, a martyr to her trade, tending and ministering to the old woman's needs and whims, unheeding of the claims and cares of the rest of the family.

The likelihood of the old woman's death had receded to the point where it was no longer thought of as a plausible event. To her family, it seemed that the elder Mrs Khoja had been created whole as she now was: ageing, blind and the possessor of a vast fortune; a monument fashioned to exist in perpetuity. Her forgotten youth, like that future death itself, was to them a fantastic concoction, a subject fit only for idle speculation. It was this very insubstantiality, this air of a fabulous creature, and further, in later years, her abstraction and divorce from the more mundane concerns of the clan, that had lent her (and it) a certain religious aura, as of something fated and preordained by the gods. She was above reproach, above questioning.

Her mania for collecting jewellery, for example, was not regarded as being susceptible to moral scrutiny. Like herself, the family's wealth was believed to have sprung fully formed out of nothing, a divine dispensation. Her possession of it, and the absurd uses to which she had sometimes put it, never rankled. She was a truly papal figure, and thus the wealth of the clan, as embodied in her, was never, so long as she was alive, considered a commodity material enough to have its exact value assessed. Nor did it occur to them that it might be fought over. It was a holy relic.

Much of this authority had descended, inevitably, to her son. He too was a papal figure, but to his regret, on a substantially reduced scale. He had not sprung, like his parents, fully formed out of nothing. There had been too many witnesses to his childhood, his youth and his manhood; and with the years the number of these witnesses had multiplied. Therefore his divinity, potent though it was while his mother was alive, carried within itself the seeds of a future disintegration. The occasion only was lacking for the proletariat below to rise in rebellion.

With his mother's death, two things happened. His divinity was deprived of its sustenance and the disposition of the inheritance was brought into prominence. Its distribution, at first a matter of simple curiosity, soon became one of vital concern. It was only a question of time before the aunts and nephews and nieces would be thinking in terms of richer and poorer and when that happened, the holy relic would cease to be holy and the flood-gates would be open wide for revolution. Therefore, it was with considerable anxiety that Mr Khoja, shorn of his divinity, watched the bulk of the inheritance fall into his own hands.

7

Each of the sisters, including Mrs Lutchman, received five acres of land and some pieces of jewellery, although Indrani, in recognition of her services and devotion, was given double the amount of land together with the house in the country. Mr Khoja received the rest.

Mr Lutchman was incensed. 'So the old witch never change she colours even at the end,' he said. He examined the pieces of jewellery—a ring, some bracelets and a gold necklace studded with the cheaper stones—which his wife had set out for his inspection on the kitchen table.

'I don't think of it like that,' she replied, disappointed by his response. Mrs Lutchman herself was secretly surprised that she had been treated equally with the sisters. 'Even if I didn't get nothing I would have been happy. And another thing. The woman dead now and you have no right to call she an old witch. She never do any harm to you. You should have a little respect for she memory.'

'I leave that for you and rest of them. I can't remember you having much respect for my father when he did dead.'

'This is not the same thing.'

'What you mean? My father was a human being too, you know. He wasn't no old witch like she.'

Mrs Lutchman could see that he was working himself up to one of his rages. 'Okay, Ram. Have it your way. I know I not perfect and I must have said a lot of things at the time which you didn't like. But that don't mean you have to repeat everything I do word for word.'

This mollified him, but he was reluctant to give up so easily. 'Well, I can't think of any other name to give she. To think of all the things you do for she, working like a slave in that house day and night when you was a child. And what do you get? A few mangy pieces of jewellery and a piece of land in Fyzabad that not big enough for you to even put your foot down on. She leave you rich like Rockefeller, if you ask me.' He laughed.

'I didn't ask you anything. If it wasn't for she I would have been a beggar on the road. My parents die when I was five years old and only she would look after me. And for that I'll always be grateful. I not like you thinking only of how much land she leave to Tom, Dick and Harry.'

'That's the trouble. She leave everything to Tom. And Dick and Harry ain't get nothing at all.'

'I count myself lucky for getting anything at all,' she insisted. 'I never do anything to deserve it.'

'What about the rest of them then? They was she children, not so?'

Mrs Lutchman looked at him, but said nothing. She brushed a few crumbs off the table and, gathering them up in the lap of her dress, walked carefully across the room and emptied it into the sink.

Mr Lutchman was struck by another happy idea. 'What

about Indrani, eh? Sacrificing twenty whole years of she life to keep that old witch alive. And what she get for it? A few more acres of bad land and a breakdown house. Meanwhile, old Khoja sitting on his backside in that house, lording it over everybody, never lifting his little finger to help his mother, is he who gone and get everything.' He gathered up the bits of jewellery into his hands and stared at them. 'I hope Sumintra choke on all them jewels she get.'

'And I hope you choke on everything you just say.' Mrs Lutchman flared her nostrils. 'And I would have you know that all of this isn't any of your damn business, you hear. Who get what and who didn't get what is nobody's concern except for my mother and Govind. So you better keep your mouth out of all this.'

'If he was a man he would give it all to Indrani.'

'Who the hell is you to be talking, eh?' Mrs Lutchman walked up to him, bringing her face close to him. Bhaskar and Romesh, attracted by the noise, came and stood near the door. 'All that land and jewellery that your tongue hanging out after is his and not yours. Try and remember that. Keep saying that to yourself morning, noon and night. It's not yours or anybody else's. If he want to give Indrani something that's up to him and him alone. If he choose not to give she anything that's his right too. You don't have anything to do with all that.'

'If he was a man he would give it all to Indrani,' Mr Lutchman repeated.

'If he was a man. If he was a man. I warning you, Ram ...' She brought her face even closer to his. She caught sight of Bhaskar and Romesh. She stopped short. 'What you little sons of bitches standing there listening to we for, eh? You think is a party you seeing? Well, I going to give the both of you the best party you ever had in your life . . .'

They raced away from the door. 'We didn't do nothing,' Romesh cried.

'I go show you how to listen to big people talk. And don't call for your father either. He not going to help you.'

Mrs Lutchman set off after them. For a while they dodged her successfully around the avocado tree, hoping she would tire and give up, but the sight of that sickly growth seemed only to infuriate her further. Mr Lutchman watched from the kitchen window, applauding her agility.

'That's it, Baby. A little more of that and you go be running the three-minute mile soon.' He laughed.

Bhaskar tripped and fell and in a moment his mother was on top of him. 'All right, Mr Man. I go show you how to run the three-minute mile now.' Romesh, seizing his opportunity, ran into the house and raced upstairs. 'Don't think you going to get away so easy, Mr Romesh,' she shouted after him. 'I go be catching up with you later. But for the moment, is you I going to deal with, Mr Champion Swimmer.' And holding Bhaskar securely by his shirt-tail, she slapped him hard several times, before letting him go. He crumpled on the ground. 'You just like Pa. Taking advantage of me.' Mrs Lutchman, for good measure, slapped him again. 'Say that again, Mr Champion Swimmer.' But Bhaskar would not oblige. Breathing heavily, Mrs Lutchman returned to the kitchen. Mr Lutchman smiled at her: it was his way of expressing his admiration.

Romesh had barricaded himself in the lavatory and agreed to come out only after several entreaties and promises from Mrs Lutchman that he would not be beaten.

'You sure you not going to beat me, Ma?'

'I wouldn't tell you a lie, son. Come and have your food.'

Romesh, keeping well away from his mother, came and had his food. After dinner, Mrs Lutchman called him to her. 'Come here, son, and let your mother pet you.'

Romesh was doubtful. He looked at her suspiciously. 'You trying to trick me. I could see it in the way you trying not to laugh.'

Mrs Lutchman giggled. 'No, no. Is nothing like that at all. I just want to pet you. Come.' She held out her arms. Romesh, still doubtful, consented nevertheless and nestled his head on her bosom.

'Ah-hah! I tell you I was going to catch you.' She locked her arms tightly around him.

'You tricked me. You promise . . .' Romesh squirmed frantically, but his mother's grip was secure.

She smiled pleasantly at him. 'I going to allow myself to break just this one promise,' she said. 'Ram, pass me your belt.' Mr Lutchman unbuckled his belt and handed it to her.

'Hold out your hands, Mr Man.'

Romesh turned to his father. 'Pa . . .'

'Do as your mother say,' Mr Lutchman replied.

Romesh nodded slowly, no longer resisting. It was meant to be a heroic submission, and he looked calmly at both his parents in turn. He held out his hand.

When it was all over Mr Lutchman said, 'That boy seeing too much film if you ask me.'

Later that night, when they were alone in their bedroom, Mr Lutchman, added, 'But you is a real trickster, you know, woman.'

'Look, Ram,' Mrs Lutchman began sharply, 'I don't want you to start up with me now. As you yourself say, he seeing too much film. A beating good for him.'

'I not saying anything to criticize you. I just say you was a real trickster, that's all. There you was promising the boy . . .'

'Well I had it in my mind to beat him a long time ago. I couldn't beat Bhaskar and let him escape scot-free.' She paused and looked at him. He was smiling. 'I know I shouldn't have fooled him like that but . . .'

They both dissolved into laughter.

8

Not only in the Lutchman household had the inheritance caused a stir. There were rumblings of discontent (perhaps less outspoken but no different in intent) in hearts other than Mr Lutchman's, though for the moment it was still subject to the customary submission to all that issued from on high. Every household had its incipient cell of rebellion, its prototype Mr Lutchman, inclined to speak out against the injustice of so unequal a division of the family's wealth. The nephews and nieces, less tied than the aunts to instinctive submission, were at the front of the rising wave of protest, held in check partly by the novelty of the situation, partly by their fastidiousness in not wanting to appear too greedy. No one actually dared to claim a larger share for themselves. They preferred to go into battle camouflaged, waving the cudgels on behalf of someone else, and the universal object of their interested sympathy was Indrani; she who had spent the 'best years' of her life 'slaving' for the old woman and had not been sufficiently rewarded.

Immediately after the cremation, Indrani had removed herself to the house in the country. She had not mourned communally as the other sisters had done, and had adopted none of the outward signs of mourning displayed by the rest of the family. Her clothes were the same as those she had worn when her mother was alive and she did not eat the ritual boiled foods prescribed for the period of mourning.

No one complained about these omissions. It was realized, albeit dimly, that her peculiar relationship with the old woman exempted her from these restrictions. Her fit of weeping and despair in the bedroom was the one conventional expression of grief she had allowed herself. At the cremation, she had stood apart from the sisters, detached and apparently unmoved, gazing with a dispassionate fixity at the flames and clouds of smoke leaping over the coffin.

The nature of her grief puzzled the family, though they were prepared to believe that its intensity, in some way not meant to be understood or probed, far outstripped theirs. So it was that Indrani had stepped without pause or interval from one role into another; destined to be marked out from the rest, a figure of mystery to be respected and when need be propitiated, if not loved. She lived shuttered in the old house, an isolation not disturbed until, unbeknown to her, she was chosen as the object of universal pity.

Chapter Six

1

The Khojas, although fervent Hindus, had traditionally observed without discomfort many of the events on the Christian calendar. Having from early on confused religion with magic, they had come to hold the majority of religions in a superstitious dread, genuinely afraid of the vengeance rival gods might let fall on the clan should they be offended.

Nevertheless, their tolerance had its limits. The one religion they steadfastly refused to have anything to do with was Islam. It was only here that their orthodoxy, whose strictures were normally confined to members of the clan, became aggressive. Everything connected with it was considered obscene, the work of the devil, and if any member of the clan had gone so far as to contemplate marriage with a Muslim, the ensuing scandal would have been no less than if he had wished to marry a Negro. But Christianity, and especially Catholicism, was looked on with a more indulgent eye. During Lent, for example, the children were forbidden to sing calypsoes: it was their version of a 'sacrifice'. And naturally, Easter was celebrated with Easter Eggs.

Christmas was, of course, at the top of the list. The elder Mrs Khoja, not trusting to the efficacy of any one religion taken entirely by itself, had felt that only when Hinduism was combined with Roman Catholicism was she then immune from all disaster. Therefore, she had recited novenas and paid furtive visits to the local Catholic Church. This eclecticism had been inherited in full by her daughter Badwatee, who, refining her mother's instincts, went so far as to flirt with the idea of conversion, until threatened with expulsion from the clan. In the end, she had contented herself with going to Church on Sundays and attending midnight Mass on Christmas Eve.

This, however, was not typical and she had always been regarded as a potential renegade.

Preparations for Christmas started a week in advance, directed by the elder Mrs Khoja. All the furniture was taken out of the house into the yard to be dusted, 'sunned' and polished. New curtains were bought and coloured paper ornaments and streamers hung from the ceiling. On Christmas Eve, giant sponge cakes were baked. On Christmas morning, the children were given cheap whistles and paper hats. (Govind of course was an exception. He received more expensive presents.) Lunch was the big meal of the day. There would be roast or curried chicken and rice, and afterwards a huge pail of ice-cream was churned in the yard under a mango-tree and served in transparent red bowls, otherwise never used, with a slice or two of the sponge cake. With this the celebration reached its climax.

In later years, when he had taken over the active leadership of the clan, Mr Khoja pretended to remain aloof. Despite this, he accepted without complaint the Christmas cards and presents he received from his sisters, although he gave them nothing in return.

'If people want to be stupid and give me presents, that's their affair,' he told his wife.

Ostensibly, he was more of a purist than his mother had been. 'Hindus should only celebrate the Hindu festivals. I don't want people to think me stingy. If someone decide to send me a gift for Davali, I will send them one too. But for Christmas? No sir!'

Mrs Khoja had upset him by her fondness for the psalm 'The Lord is My Shepherd'. He had not suspected that she too possessed this hidden eclectic streak, and it had been the cause of their first quarrel. Mr Khoja himself was largely to blame. The first year of their marriage he had consciously set aside for her 'education'. She could neither read nor write. He had taught her and, as a bonus, discussed religious questions with her. The programme was, on the whole, a successful one, until he divulged his pet theory that 'all gods are one God' to her.

The idea appealed greatly to Mrs Khoja and gave her the

excuse to do something she had always hankered after: to have a copy of 'The Lord is My Shepherd' in her bedroom. Secretly, she searched out a copy and pinned it to the wall above her bed. She was going to 'surprise' her husband and show him what a receptive pupil she had been.

'What you think you doing with that thing, Sumintra?'

'You like it? The picture of the sheep really nice, don't you think?'

'Where you get it from?'

'Badwatee. It was she who give me the idea in the first place.' This was only partly true.

'Badwatee! You mean to say you letting that woman lead you astray after all what I teach you?'

'But you say all god is one God.'

Mr Khoja smiled sourly. 'You don't understand.' He stared lamely around the room.

'But if all god is one God, I don't see . . .'

'So Badwatee teach you to answer me back as well?'

'But Govind . . .'

'Look here, Sumintra. Like you forget I have a position to keep in this family?'

'I could keep it here in the bedroom. Nobody does come in here except you and me and the dog.'

Mr Khoja knew he was trapped. 'All right. Have it your own way. But remember, if you let anybody see that, you will have a lot to answer for.'

Thus, at the very outset, Mr Khoja's pretensions to orthodoxy had suffered a serious blow, but the thought of having to give his family presents at Christmas being just as, if not more painful than his wife's betrayal, he clung anxiously in public to his purism. As it was, no one sent him presents for Davali.

Despite Mr Khoja's official disapproval, Christmas continued to be celebrated. Each cell within the clan had an outer circle of non-Hindu friends with whom presents were exchanged, though with one another there was a definite reticence and a lurking embarrassment whenever the subject was discussed. It was a symptom of the changing times that, following the elder Mrs Khoja's death, the spirit of emancipation showed itself in the increasing seriousness with which Christmas was treated. Saraswatee and Renouka set the tone by being the first to have a Christmas tree, and there were fresh rumours concerning Badwatee's conversion. These Christmas activities of the various cells did not overlap. Each, looking towards itself and its own outer circle of Christian acquaintance, ignored the rest. Ultimately, Christmas served to emphasize their essential separateness and distinctness from each other.

2

Mrs Lutchman looked forward to Christmas, but her desire was drawn not from these later developments, but from her longing to recreate in her own house the atmosphere of those earlier Christmases celebrated in the old house.

She tried to do everything as she remembered it had been done. She took all the chairs out into the back yard, dusted, 'sunned' and polished them. She hung new curtains and in a fit of enthusiasm varnished the steps. The radio, adding its own frenzy, played carols and other Christmas songs incessantly. She had her favourite: 'Silent Night'.

She was down on her knees washing the kitchen floor. Mr Lutchman sat idly on the edge of the table watching her, twirling a knife between his fingers. He had, so far, kept aloof from the preparations. Through the open kitchen window, they could hear the neighbour's radio clearly, playing her favourite carol.

'I can't tell you how much I love that song, Ram. I used to know all the words by heart when I was a child. It does make me feel like crying when I hear it.'

'Sometimes I does think you really stupid, you know, woman. What so great about that song? Is just a lot of stupid words.'

'Oh, Ram. Why you does want to spoil everything for me?'

Mr Lutchman looked at her bent back, symbol of unflagging duty. He relented, dismissing the retort that arose to his lips. 'You right. It not so bad when you think about it. Is a nice song.'

His wife smiled gratefully at him and went on washing the floor.

Some time had passed without Mr Lutchman, to his wife's unbounded relief, developing a new enthusiasm. The pressures, however, had been building up, and only the memory of his failures had kept it under control. Recently Mrs Lutchman had noted with alarm his growing moodiness. Photography had been disastrous; he had lost his taste for swimming; and the garden bored him. He looked round wildly for some new avenue of release. Like all his enthusiasms, this one descended upon him without fuss, the result less of deliberation that of a chance word or phrase. This time, it was Mrs Lutchman who was the unwitting instrument.

'But what's come over you, Ram? Like you feeling sick or something?'

He shook his head. 'Is nothing like that. I just a little restless, that's all.'

Mrs Lutchman considered. 'You know why that is? Because you idle. If you would only help me about the house you wouldn't have time to feel restless. I have so much you could do now to help me, especially as is Christmas.'

Christmas. Something stirred in Mr Lutchman. He looked at his wife. He remembered the varnished steps; the new curtains; 'Silent Night'. Surely there was something in all this for him. The call to action was nagging, irresistible. His imagination blossomed. Christmas. At last, his pent-up energies had found a mode of expression.

'Stop what you doing, woman, and listen to me. I have an idea.'

Mrs Lutchman was alarmed. 'What you mean? What it is you getting so excited about?'

Mr Lutchman raised his hand. Mrs Lutchman fell silent. 'I going to make this a Christmas you will remember for the rest of your life.'

'Don't go and do anything foolish, Ram. I do almost everything it have to do already except bake the cake.'

'Cake! I not talking about cake. You ever thought about getting a Christmas tree?'

'Christmas tree! Like you going mad or what? You think just because Saraswatee and Renouka . . .'

'You forget Saraswatee and Renouka. They don't have nothing to do with this. I going to get we a Christmas tree that six foot tall. You ever see them lights that does bubble? I going to get we some of those as well.'

'Think of the expense, Ram.'

'You leave that to me, woman. And we also going to have a Yule Log. I bet Saraswatee and Renouka not going to have that.'

'What's that?'

'Is a little log with a candle stick in the centre. Is a German thing originally, I believe.'

It was Doreen who had taught him everything he knew about Yule logs and Christmas trees. He stopped speaking and for a while thought about her. Mrs Lutchman laughed.

'Where you learn all these things from, Ram?'

'You think I ignorant like you?'

'Well, once you know what it is you doing and don't put the blame on me when things go wrong, I don't mind.'

'Who say anything going to go wrong? I know what I doing this time. Believe me.'

3

Mr Lutchman had not seen Doreen since the day they had gone to buy flowers. The end of their adventure had come as a tremendous relief to him, although he had never entirely ceased to believe that he had missed something and made a fool of himself. Nevertheless, the decision to see her did not spring from any desire on his part to resurrect that relationship. He was not curious about the life she led apart from him or jealous of any lover she may have had subsequent to him. What distressed him was the unfinished character of the affair, an incompleteness which had left too many problems unresolved. Mr Lutchman's concern centred on himself, on his self-esteem. He wished to be reassured that Doreen did not regard him and the times they had spent together as simply a quaint aberration. His wife too, whose existence he had never really acknowledged to others, he now wished to bring forward, to demonstrate how successfully their lives had been welded together.

Christmas, then, had become for him a summing-up, an opportunity for reassessment, a tacit confession. By these means he might hope to reassert himself and put into a comprehensible perspective a multitude of sins and failures. If he could do that, some of the more ragged edges of his life could be smoothed, the pockets of acute discomfort might disappear and he could contemplate what he had done with a greater serenity. It was largely with this in mind that he decided to invite both Doreen and Wilkie to dinner on Christmas Eve.

Two days before Christmas, Mr Lutchman drove to the house, so familiar to him, on the outskirts of the city. Nothing seemed to have changed. It might have been only yesterday that he had last been there, drinking glasses of iced orange juice and reading old copies of Life magazine while Doreen, dressed in a loose cotton shift, talked idly of her latest theories. Doreen, unalterable as the rest, rocked on the verandah reading a magazine. Only the tinge of apprehension he was beginning to feel warned Mr Lutchman that a silence of almost two years separated him from what at first sight seemed so familiar.

He rattled the gate. Doreen raised her head from the magazine with a glance of irritated inquiry. She did not immediately recognize him.

'Come in if you want something,' she shouted without getting up.

Mr Lutchman pushed the gate open and walked hesitantly up the path.

'My God! It's Ram.' She threw the magazine on the floor and getting up hurriedly, ran down the steps to meet him. 'I had given you up for dead.'

Mr Lutchman, grinning sheepishly, stopped and stared indecisively at her, unsure what he should say. Doreen spread her arms in effusive welcome. 'I never expected you to come and see me again. Come here and let me take a good look at you.' Shielding her eyes from the sun, she walked slowly around him. 'You are getting fatter. All that home cooking must be doing you good.'

'How was the party?'

'Party? I don't . . . Oh that! I see what you are getting at. It was very good. I had a great time there.' She giggled and taking his hand dragged him after her up the steps to the verandah. 'Have a drink.'

Mr Lutchman accepted a bottle of beer. They sat in the sitting-room.

'How is the garden?' Doreen asked.

'It's fine.'

'You get lots of roses?'

'Hundreds.' They both laughed. Mr Lutchman drew patterns on the frosted beer-glass. 'I and the wife was wondering if you would like to come and have dinner with we on Christmas Eve.'

'Why Ram. That would be very nice. I would like to meet your wife. But . . .' She peered closely at him. 'I didn't know you celebrated Christmas.'

Mr Lutchman examined her face to see if she were laughing at him. He decided not. 'It was just an idea we had. The boys would like it too.'

'They must be getting really big by now.'

'Yes. Bhaskar going to be taking he school certificate soon.'

'Bhaskar. Oh yes. He's the quiet one.'

Mr Lutchman sipped his beer. It was pleasant being able to talk so freely about his family, to lift the restraint that before had weighed so heavily on him. He relaxed and gazed without longing at the elegant furnishings: a shining piano and on its lid, a tapering vase filled with flowers; the paintings of tropical landscapes on the walls; the shelves of books.

Mr Lutchman smiled into his glass of beer. 'How's the book?'

Doreen giggled. 'Oh, don't you know? I gave that up a long time ago. I'm leading a quieter life these days.' Her eyes roamed over the paintings. 'I'm not so bloodthirsty as I used to be. I would like to do some teaching one of these days. Yes. I've got some ideas on the subject. I would like to teach them the facts of life before they learn even to read and write.'

'I thought you wasn't so bloodthirsty as you used to be.'

'What? You mean about teaching them the facts of life?' Doreen slapped the arm of the chair and grinned at him.

'So you not interested in the Khojas any more?'

Doreen laughed. 'Of course I am. I'm not that flighty. They still fascinate me although I no longer want to write a book about them. The point is, I just can't write. God knows the number of times I've tried and failed.'

Mr Lutchman nodded. 'What I really wanted to . . .'

'Well, don't take it so calmly,' Doreen interrupted him. 'You should be sympathizing with me. It's a tragedy. But tell me what you wanted to say.'

'What I really wanted to ask you – apart from coming to have dinner with we that is – was whether you could help me find a Christmas tree, a big one, and a . . . a Yule log.'

'A Yule log?'

Again Mr Lutchman suspected that she might be laughing at him. He went on quickly, hoping to smother the ridicule. 'You know. We was talking about it one day when we went out on one of them drives. You was talking about America and how you used to have one there. A little log with a candle stick in the centre.'

Doreen frowned. Mr Lutchman watched her anxiously.

'Oh yes. I remember now. That was a lovely excursion. I haven't been on a trip like that for ages. Since last seeing you, in fact.'

'I myself don't do that sort of thing much these days. Old age getting hold of me.'

'I tell you what, Ram. I think I still have one here which I brought back from the States with me. I had forgotten about it until now. I'll give it to you, a Christmas present from me.'

She got up and went into one of the bedrooms. Mr Lutchman listened to her ruffling through a wardrobe. He was grateful to her for talking about the past, acknowledging its existence without embarrassement. A certain value had been put on the adventure they had had together, thereby denying the absurdity he had feared.

Doreen returned, carrying a small log, its bark thick and impressively incised, with a red candle stuck into it. 'Merry Christmas. All you need is some cotton wool to spread over it so as to look like snow.' She handed it to him.

'A red candle! I must say I never see one of those before.'

'Haven't you? In the States you can get them in all different colours. Red, green, pink. I've even seen a black one.'

Mr Lutchman stared at her in disbelief. 'You does live and learn,' he said. 'Imagine a black candle! But now you must come and help me choose a Christmas tree as well.'

They went, that very afternoon, to one of the large department stores in Port-of-Spain. There were billowing throngs of people on the pavements and the curbs were lined with carts piled high with apples, some wrapped in purple tissue, and pears, yellowing, wrapped in white tissue. Bunches of grapes were buried in boxes of sawdust. Seasonal tunes blared from loudspeakers placed above the shop entrances, interspersed with loud, raucous entreaties to the pedestrians to come in and buy. One shop, however, was more sedate than the rest. There were no loudspeakers above its entrance; instead, the management had contented itself with a twinkling neon sign: 'Bring Christ Back Into Christmas'. It was doing a roaring trade.

The sky was already darkening but the street lights had not yet been switched on and the glow from the rows of lighted shop windows – a jungle of Santa Clauses and sleighs and reindeer, coloured bulbs flashing on and off, glittering, drooping trails of tinsel, piles of mock snow – spread a multicoloured patchwork of light and shadow across the pavements. This blended with the sharp, pungent smell of the fruit carts, enveloping the shoppers shouting and ploughing a passage along the pavement, their parcels bundled aggressively against their bosoms.

Doreen and Mr Lutchman stopped to buy some apples which they ate standing on the roadway, dodging the crawling traffic.

'Christmas is really exciting, eh,' Mr Lutchman exclaimed,

casting rapturous glances about him as he munched on his apple. Doreen, standing close beside him, holding on to his arm, so that they should not be separated in the crowd, agreed.

'I never knew you were such a romantic, Ram.'

'Call me what you will,' Mr Lutchman replied happily. He was pleased to discover a word able to describe his behaviour, even if that word was meaningless to him.

'Balloons! Balloons!' A withered man with pink patches on his skin approached them with a box of balloons. 'How about a balloon for the lady, Mister? Or the children. You mustn't forget the children. After all, Christmas is for children. The Lord Himself was a child once. I have all sizes and all colours, look for yourself and see.' He dangled several balloons before them. 'You ever see balloons so pretty, Miss? And they strong as well. Strong as steel and iron put together. I wouldn't tell you a lie.' He said all this in a gushing, sing-song chant, dancing around them. 'They don't burst as quick as other balloons.' The balloon seller crossed his heart. 'Made in England. That's why. Buy a dozen for the children, Mister.'

'Okay, Mister. I'll take your word for it. Give me a dozen.'

'I wouldn't tell you a lie, sir. I wouldn't tell you a lie.'

Mr Lutchman counted out the change for a dozen and the baloon seller pretended to look elsewhere.

'Marvellous! Marvellous!' Doreen murmured after the balloon seller had left them.

'What so marvellous about that? You see the patches on his skin?'

'What's happened to your romanticism all of a sudden?'

'Nothing. I just don't think there is anything so great about a man selling balloon who have pink patches on his skin.'

'You know something, Ram?'

'What?'

'You are getting ratty in your old age.'

Mr Lutchman shrugged his shoulders. 'Call it what you will,' he said, and laughed.

They examined an array of Christmas trees, real and artificial, in the department store. Mr Lutchman liked the artificial ones better, although he was reluctant to admit it.

'Really, Ram. I don't see what the problem is. I don't see how you could possibly like those when you have right before your eyes the genuine Canadian article. The very same ones people use in the States in fact.'

'I didn't say I didn't like them. All I say was I find these other ones nice too.' He touched the neat, even fibres of an artificial tree and gazed with longing at the shining red berries placed at the tip of each branch. 'We not in the States now,' he added defiantly. 'With those other ones you'll have to buy a different one each year. But this will last me for years and years. I'll never have to think of buying another Christmas tree again.'

'Yes. You are getting ratty. You buy what you want. Buy an artificial one, if you like them so much. They are very nice too.'

'Not if it will look stupid.' He gazed worriedly at her.

'Go ahead. Buy it,' she urged him. She called the saleswoman.

Carrying the tree high above his head, Mr Lutchman fought his way across to another counter, where the decorations were on display. He spent recklessly, thus attempting to make up for the disappointment he feared he had caused Doreen. He bought a set of coloured lights that bubbled, several boxes of glittering balls, 'icicles', 'angel-hair' and strands of tinsel. As a final finishing touch, he bought a star to put at the top of the tree.

'This is going to be a champion Chistmas tree, Doreen. A champion tree.'

'It couldn't help but be,' she replied.

'Just one more thing we've got to do now. Those boys don't read enough. I must buy them some books.'

The department store sold everything. They fought their way across to the book counter which was slightly less crowded. He bought *Coral Island* and *Treasure Island*.

'Nothing like the classics,' he said.

Doreen, who disapproved of his choice (she had wanted something more 'daring'), nodded. 'Nothing like the classics,' she agreed.

4

'So you get your Yule log after all. Well I never.' Mrs Lutchman turned it in her hands. 'What will people think of next, eh?'

'What do you mean "What will people think of next"? That's traditional.'

'And it have a red candle to boot. I never see one of those before.'

'Candles does come in all kinds of colours. Even black.'

'You could have fool me. I must say you does live and . . .'

'Yes, yes. I hear all that before,' Mr Lutchman interrupted. 'You better give it back to me before you drop it.'

Mr Lutchman took it from her and went into the sitting-room where he spent a considerable time experimenting with various positions for it, finally settling for the top of the cabinet.

He took great pains decorating the Christmas tree. At first, the string of bubbling lights would not work. 'I going to kill the bastard who sell me this. I going to wring his neck for him before the year out. You wait and see.'

'Maybe,' Mrs Lutchman suggested timidly, 'the plug not connect up properly.'

'What you know about this kind of thing, woman? Try and bear in mind that is I wearing the trousers around here.'

He fiddled with it for a while longer, taking out and inserting a succession of bulbs, swearing vengeance on a widening circle of the commercial world. 'Is these bloody Japs to blame. Is they who trying to cheat poor people like we. I glad the bastards lose the war. I personally would have kill every single one I lay my hands on. I swear to God.'

'I still think is something wrong with the plug, Ram.'

'I thought I tell you to keep your mouth out of this, woman.' He glowered at her. 'Is I who put the plug on. I is not a fool, you know.'

Not replying to this, she unscrewed the plug and examined it. Mr Lutchman watched her out of the corner of his eye.

'As I thought,' she said. 'You didn't join up the wires properly. Look at how they sticking out all over the place.' She held up the plug and exhibited the unconnected wires.

'Okay. Okay. So you happen to be right this one time. But don't try and play too smart with me. Is not I who make the kiss-me-arse plug.'

Mrs Lutchman connected up the wires. After that the lights worked. Mr Lutchman, soured by his wife's success, threatened to slip into disenchantment and he would have done so but for her flattering admiration for his efforts.

'The tree looking real nice, Ram.'

Mr Lutchman, thinking discretion the better part of valour, was modest. 'You think so?' He forced himself to grimace. 'Yes. I don't suppose it all that bad really.'

Bhaskar and Romesh had been strictly forbidden to interfere. 'If either of you,' their father had warned them at the outset, 'touch these decorations with so much as a little finger, you not going to have a hand or foot intact by the time I finish dealing with you.' Having taken this threat at its face value, Romesh had seized the opportunity to go to the cinema and Bhaskar was content to watch from a distance.

'Now, for the final effect,' Mr Lutchman announced, 'for the truly champion effect, you have to wait till I put on the angel-hair.' Mr Lutchman searched for the box and, behaving as though he were a magician pulling rabbits out of a hat, began draping it lightly over the tree. 'This is to make it look like frost,' he commented.

Mrs Lutchman circumnavigated the tree. 'It pretty, man. It real pretty.'

Encouraged by her steady stream of praise, Mr Lutchman threw caution to the winds, abandoning his previous modesty.

'I bet you the tree Renouka and Saraswatee have have nothing on this one. It must be the best tree on the whole street.'

'Is a champion tree we got here,' Mrs Lutchman confirmed.

Mr Lutchman flushed with pride. He turned to Bhaskar. 'Come and help me with this, son. There is nothing like a little teamwork.'

On Christmas Eve, it rained. Mrs Lutchman, standing at the kitchen window, stared at the slanting lines of rain pouring from the leaden sky. Stamping her foot in vexation, she closed the window and went to find her husband. Mr Lutchman, as Doreen had suggested, was arranging cotton wool on the Yule log to look like snow.

'Ram . . .'

'What now?' He continued to arrange the cotton wool.

'A terrible thing gone and happen.'

He turned to face her, alarmed by her expression. 'What? Tell me. Don't stand there looking like a jumbie.'

'All the blankets and sheets I was drying for tomorrow get soak. Now we won't have anything clean to put on the bed for Christmas.'

Mr Lutchman was angry, but relieved to discover it was nothing worse. 'Something always have to go wrong at the last minute. You should have seen the rain was coming.'

Mrs Lutchman did not attempt to excuse herself. She looked at him helplessly. 'I know. Is all my fault. I don't know what it is get into me.'

He softened and, for the first time since they had been married, he walked up to her and curled an arm affectionately around her shoulder. Mrs Lutchman started to cry.

'I don't know what it is get into me. Like I getting stupid or something.' She wiped her tears away with the sleeve of her dress. Mr Lutchman stared at the sparkling Christmas tree and the cotton-swathed Yule log.

'Don't worry about it, Baby. I just think of a plan.'

'What you going to do?' she asked worriedly.

'You does ask too many questions,' he replied gently. He removed his hand from her shoulder. 'Go and put on some nice clothes. We going for a drive.'

'Where?'

'I tell you you mustn't ask so many questions. Is curiosity what kill the cat, not so? Go and put on a nice dress.'

Mrs Lutchman put on a 'nice' dress and, afraid of annoying her husband, asked no more questions.

'Tell me,' he said, when they were in the car, 'which is the best place for buying blankets and things?'

'Ram . . .'

'Tell me.'

She told him.

It was still raining heavily when they returned to the car laden with new sets of blankets, sheets and a pink counterpane that Mr Lutchman had found specially attractive. They did not go home immediately. Instead, they went to the snack bar famed for its ice-cream sundaes. The bank-clerks and their girl-friends were not present and the place was relatively empty. They were served by the red-lipped waitress. She examined Mrs Lutchman with interest and smiled inwardly as she took their order.

'And we want them with lots of nuts,' Mr Lutchman said.

The waitress nodded and brought them two ice-cream sundaes liberally sprinkled with nuts. When they had finished, Mr Lutchman said, 'You want to hear a few carol?'

'That would be nice.'

They drove through the rain to the Queen's Park Savannah and stopped near the grounds of the Governor's house. The trees there had been decorated with strings of bulbs and under one of them a crèche had been built. A handful of people had gathered around it. Carols played softly. They sat in the car and listened, returning home only after they had heard 'Silent Night'.

'Come on,' Mr Lutchman urged, immediately they were inside the house, 'Go and spread the sheet and blanket on the bed right away.' He hurried her up the stairs and watched from the doorway as she made the bed. 'Don't forget the counterpane.'

'Learn some patience, man. I only have two hands, you know. You can't make a bed just by whistling.' Mrs Lutchman bustled blissfully about the bed, adjusting stray edges and smoothing unsightly wrinkles.

Mr Lutchman studied the finished effect. 'Well, what you think? You like the counterpane I buy for you?'

'It very pretty, Ram. That was a very generous thing what you do.'

'I was getting tired of all them old sheets and blankets in any case.' He walked round the room, his hands clasped contentedly behind his back. Mrs Lutchman stood at the foot of the bed.

'Don't tell me you crying again, woman.' He came quickly

up to her. 'I do this for you. For you.' His arms swept over the counterpane. 'I thought it would make you happy. Instead . . .'

'Don't get angry with me, Ram. I happy. The trouble is I too happy. I just being stupid again. That's all.'

'Give we a smile then.'

Mrs Lutchman smiled at him.

'That's better. We can't have any of this stupid crying. Is Christmas, remember. And we have people coming to see we tonight . . .'

'Ram . . .'

'Wait. Before you say anything I got something to show you.'

He went to the wardrobe and brought back the two books he had bought the day before. 'I buy these for Bhaskar and Romesh. I notice that Romesh especially don't be reading anything at all. Literature is one of the most important things in this world. I don't want them to grow up idlers standing on the street corner whistling at girls.' He showed her the books. 'They is nice books, not so?' Mrs Lutchman nodded. 'They are great books,' her husband went on, as if she had disagreed with him. '*Treasure Island* is a classic. I myself read that when I was a boy. It much better than giving them guns or something like that. I think they should ban toys like that.' This was another of Doreen's theories, that military toys stimulated 'aggression'. Mr Lutchman could not remember the full argument, but he was quite content to repeat its conclusion. Unlike most of her other theories, this one was at least understandable. 'Now, what it was you wanted to tell me?' he asked in an outburst of good-natured accessibility.

Mrs Lutchman gazed uneasily at him. 'I don't know how to put it, Ram.' Her discomfort grew. 'It's all these people you inviting tonight. Miss James and that Wilkie who hate your guts.' Time, far from lessening, had only increased Mrs Lutchman's animosity towards the man whom she had come to regard as the architect of so many of her husband's misfortunes.

'What about it?'

Mrs Lutchman's eyes wandered restlessly over the counterpane. 'Well, you know in the house I was brought up in, nobody ever teach we to eat with knives and forks and I don't want to shame you in front of all your friends . . .'

Mr Lutchman looked steadily at her.

'It might make more sense,' she continued hurriedly, 'if I eat by myself in the kitchen before they come and then that nigger Wilkie won't be able to laugh at you in the office . . .'

'None of that, woman. I don't want to hear you say another word about it. You going to eat with we whether you like it or not.'

'But Ram, be sensible. I go only make a laughing stock out of you.'

Mr Lutchman twisted his face as if he were in pain. 'You going to eat with we. Is not Mr Khoja you dealing with now. Remember that.' He seemed to be trying to convince himself as much as her. 'I tired of all this damn nonsense about knives and forks. If you want to eat with your hand then you will damn well eat with it and I go deal with the sonofabitch who laugh at you. This is my house, you hear. My house. These people are not coming here to judge me or you. They are coming here as my guests. I invite them to come here. They are my guests.' He had forgotten his wife, his words directed at unknown, generalized mockers who had, for a long time, been peopling his silences. He left the room abruptly, slamming the door, and went downstairs to the sitting-room.

5

Mr Lutchman's invitation had surprised Wilkie, although he had accepted it with alacrity.

'The boys won't forgive me for deserting them on Christmas Eve, but thanks for the invite, Lutch. I looking forward to it. Nothing like a real Indian curry is what I does always say.'

'I think you will be disappointed, Wilkie. We don't have curry for Christmas,' Mr Lutchman had answered coldly.

Wilkie was the first to arrive that evening, dressed and looking quite different from the man Mr Lutchman had been accustomed to meet in the office every day. He wore a neat grey suit that was slightly too small for him, a striped shirt with silver cuff-links, his initials carved in bold relief, and a green and yellow striped tie. His shoes, narrowing sharply at the toes, were black and beautifully polished, set off by an embroidered pair of lime-green socks, meant to echo the tie. He smelled of eau de cologne. Mr Lutchman had never realised quite how black Wilkie was, a blackness that the eau de cologne, in a curious sort of way, served to emphasize. Looking at this garish apparition standing self-consciously fashionable on the front steps, Mr Lutchman felt a definite satisfaction at having lured Wilkie away from his natural surroundings and suspected that he had him at a disadvantage.

Wilkie held out his hand to Mr Lutchman, something he had never bothered to do before. 'What a rain we had today, man,' Wilkie declared. 'I thought it was never going to stop.' He grinned broadly, displaying a fine set of flawlessly white teeth and perfuming the region immediately about him with whiffs of Colgate.

'Come in, Wilkie. It's nice to see you. Come in.'

Wilkie stepped gingerly across the threshold, his thighs straining at the seams of his tight trousers. 'Is a really nice house you have here, Lutch. It near the Savannah and everything. One of the boys used to live around here at one time. I always thought it was a foolish thing he do when he up and leave.'

'But now he's all the nearer to you though, Wilkie.'

Wilkie succumbed to a bout of semi-controlled laughter. 'Lutch, Lutch. I must say that's a good one. You should have been one of the boys. They would like the kind of joke you does make.'

Mr Lutchman frowned and led him through to the kitchen. 'Come and meet my wife,' he said. Wilkie shuffled after him (his trousers were really much too tight), gazing with wide-eyed, ingratiating wonder at all he saw in his passage through the house. Mrs Lutchman raised her head sourly from the stove when they entered the kitchen.

'Mr Wilkinson at your service, Ma'am,' Wilkie, without waiting to be introduced, bellowed good-naturedly, leaping precipitately across the room and extending an eager hand.

Mrs Lutchman, confused and taken aback, returned his greeting limply, trying to catch her husband's eye.

'That food smells delicious, Mrs Lutchman. You must be a truly wonderful cook.' He stared at her with shining eyes. 'I have always said to the boys that we Negroes just never learn to cook like you Indians and I'll go on saying it. Smell that aroma!'

Mrs Lutchman laughed deprecatingly while Wilkie strolled around the room with an air of desperate cordiality. He swung suddenly on his heels and turned to face Mr Lutchman. 'You are a lucky man, Lutch, to have a wife who is such a good cook. And such a beautiful house, too. I notice the garden as well. Such roses. I didn't know you was interested in that sort of thing, Lutch. If ever you want any seeds or things like that, just ask me.'

'So you does a little gardening yourself, Mr Wilkinson?' Mrs Lutchman asked.

'One of my hobbies, Ma'am. A man of many parts,' Wilkie giggled.

'You married, Mr Wilkinson?'

'No, Ma'am. No. I haven't had the courage to take the plunge as yet. But for a bachelor I don't do too badly.' Wilkie grinned at her. 'There are one or two people who like darning my socks.' He slapped Mr Lutchman across the shoulder and winked at him. 'See what I mean, Lutch?'

'Do you like baked chicken, Mr Wilkinson?'

Wilkie rolled his eyes to the ceiling. 'Do I like baked chicken? Why, Mrs Lutchman, it's sheer heaven to me. I could eat that sort of thing all the time. I can't wait to sample some of your cooking.' And again Wilkie orbited the perimeter of the kitchen with that same air of desperate cordiality with which he had introduced himself, and despite herself Mrs Lutchman began to unbend a little.

'You work in the same office as my husband, Mr Wilkinson?'

'I have that privilege, Mrs Lutchman.' Wilkie adjusted his trousers, in preparation for another of his orbits.

'He does talk a lot about you,' she said gallantly.

'Does he? I'm truly flattered by that Mrs Lutchman.'

She threw a despairing glance at her husband.

'Let's leave she to get on with the food, Wilkie. Come and let we talk in the other room.'

Wilkie allowed himself to be guided out of the kitchen.

Doreen arrived soon after, bearing presents for Bhaskar and Romesh and a box of chocolates for Mrs Lutchman.

'You shouldn't have done that, Doreen. It's a waste of money.'

'Nonsense, Ram. Anyway, it's rude to say things like that.' She arranged the presents at the foot of the Christmas tree. Doreen stared pleasantly around her. She, unlike Wilkie, was dressed much as usual, in a light cotton frock and low-heeled shoes, except, Mr Lutchman observed, she had shaved her legs. She smiled inquiringly at Wilkie.

'You haven't introduced me to your guest as yet, Ram.'

Wilkie, who had been sitting expectantly on the edge of his chair since Doreen's arrival, now sprung to his feet, like a mechanism triggered into action, and bore down determinedly on her with hand outstretched.

'Mr Wilkinson of the Department of Education at your service, Ma'am.' For an instant he seemed on the point of kissing her hand, then recollecting himself, he pumped it heartily instead. 'I believe we have met before.'

'Have we?' Doreen studied his face carefully. 'I'm sorry, but I don't think I remember when, Mr Wilkinson.'

Wilkie laughed, not in the least put out. 'Not met exactly, if you see what I mean. I saw you the day you came to the office to see the Minister. You came to speak to my friend Lutch as well.'

Doreen blushed. There was an awkward pause during which Wilkie's eyes darted back and forth from her to Mr Lutchman.

'Of course,' she began slowly, pointing at him, 'you were one of the . . .'

'Clerks. Yes . . . I'm sorry. I didn't get your surname.'

'James,' Mr Lutchman glowered at him. 'Miss Doreen James.'

'That's right, Miss James. It was then I first had the pleasure. I was one of those clerks. We can't all have the top jobs in this world. What you say to that, Lutch?'

Mr Lutchman nodded his head in sullen agreement.

'What do you do for a living, Miss James?'

'I'm an anthropologist.'

'Oh yes. I remember Lutch asking me what that was the morning you came to the office.' Wilkie grinned pleasantly at Mr Lutchman. 'Excuse my ignorance, but what . . .'

'It is primarily the study of the way primitive peoples live, Mr Wilkinson.'

Wilkie took it in good part. 'I didn't know you had connexions with that sort of thing, Lutch. You've been hiding things from me.' He wagged a finger playfully at him.

'Is that one of your hobbies as well, Wilkie?' Mr Lutchman turned to Doreen. 'Wilkie here has hundreds of hobbies. Let's see,' he began counting them on his fingers. 'Photography. Film developing. Gardening. Cricket. Football. Tennis. Woodwork. Stamps . . .'

'There you are wrong, Lutch. I have never collected stamps in my life.'

'Do you really do all these things, Mr Wilkinson?'

Wilkie was modest. 'I try to develop myself all round,' he confessed. 'Why, I think I have even managed to influence old Lutch here in my time. How's the photography and developing coming on, old man?'

'We'll talk about that later, Wilkie. I must introduce Doreen to my wife now.'

Wilkie tittered knowingly. 'This should be interesting, I think,' he whispered to Doreen.

'I don't see why, Mr Wilkinson.'

Wilkie, embarrassed, followed penitently behind them.

'I've been longing to meet you, Mrs Lutchman. I feel as though I've known you a long time.'

Mrs Lutchman giggled and turned to her husband for rescue. 'Ram tell me a lot about you too.'

Wilkie, standing in the doorway, tried to appear noncommittal. He had yet to make up the ground lost a few moments ago. 'Mrs Lutchman is a great cook,' he shouted. 'I can't wait to have a taste. Can you, Miss James?'

He was ignored. Mr Lutchman glanced briefly at him and looked away.

'I've brought you a box of chocolates as a Christmas present, Mrs Lutchman. I hope you like them.'

'They's expensive chocolates, Baby. And she buy you a really big box to boot.'

'Really, Ram. You are embarrasing the both of us.'

'Food will be ready soon,' Mrs Lutchman said, 'and the boys should be back from the cinema soon. Why don't you take them to the drawing-room?' She appealed to her husband.

'Let me stay here and help you,' Doreen offered.

'No, no, Miss James. You go and sit with them in the drawing-room. It don't have all that much to do.' She swished them gently out of the kitchen.

'The Christmas tree is terrific, Ram.' Doreen went up close to it. 'I like the lights.'

'Yes, it looking real nice,' Wilkie admitted grudgingly.

Mr Lutchman gazed at the bubbling lights and twinkling decorations. 'It's the angel-hair what make it look so good,' he said.

Wilkie, his earlier ebullience vanished, stared glumly at him.

When Bhaskar and Romesh returned from the cinema, dinner was served at the rarely used dining-table in the sitting-room. Mrs Lutchman had prepared two chickens, which she brought in on separate dishes, together with the loaves of fresh bread she had baked herself. Mr Lutchman helped to lay the table with knives and forks and paper napkins. His wife looked at the formidable array with grim foreboding, as did Wilkie, though he disguised his astonishment better.

They took their seats at the table. Only Doreen seemed to be entirely at her ease. Wilkie stared suspiciously at the knives and forks and paper napkins. Mrs Lutchman, to occupy herself, cut up the two chickens.

'Shall I serve you or will you help yourself?'

Wilkie, to divert attention from himself, fussed needlessly with his cuff-links and Doreen, realizing her responsibility, said cheerfully, 'You serve us, Mrs Lutchman.'

'You mind if I use my hand, Miss James?'

'Not at all. Not at all.'

The strain eased and one by they handed up their plates.

Doreen took up her knife and fork. The rest followed suit. Wilkie grasped his tightly and awkwardly, as if afraid they would squirm out of his grasp. He watched Doreen's expert and easy manipulation. He adjusted his grasp. That was no better. Finally, he rested them on the side of his plate and resumed his examination of his cuff-links. Mrs Lutchman sawed manfully away at her chicken, but she was obviously unhappy and ill at ease. And so were Mr Lutchman and Bhaskar and Romesh. Then Romesh, in a fit of exasperation, threw his knife and fork on the table and picked up the chicken with his fingers. The rest watched him enviously. Wilkie still had not touched his food. He was now adjusting his tie. Doreen, realizing that a fresh responsibility had been laid upon her, discarded her knife and fork.

'Romesh is right,' she declared. 'The only satisfactory way to eat chicken is with your hands.'

'That's what I always say,' Mrs Lutchman agreed, gratefully discarding her knife and fork.

'Damn tie,' Wilkie said, and, as if he had seen his food for the first time, picked up his chicken and started to eat.

'Common sense,' Mr Lutchman echoed, dropping his knife and fork with a clatter on the side of his plate.

At the same time, Bhaskar, unobtrusively and without comment, laid down his. They started to laugh and talk.

'Mr Wilkinson, you are much too quiet,' Doreen said. 'Tell us about your hobbies.'

Wilkie struggled to find a suitable witticism but failed. 'They not very interesting,' he replied sadly and retreated back into his gloom.

The Christmas tree glimmered and glowed and bubbled in the background, throwing weird shadows across the floor and ceiling.

'There's one thing you have forgotten, Ram,' Doreen called across to him.

'What?'

'You didn't light the Yule log.'

'Imagine I forget that.' His confidence by now fully restored, he wiped his mouth and fingers with the napkin (Wilkie immediately did the same and, to emphasize the point, flourished it casually for a few seconds) and went off excitedly to search for a box of matches. The Yule log was lit. Mr Lutchman stepped back to admire it. Doreen and Mrs Lutchman applauded.

'Bravo! Bravo! Don't you think it's a nice Yule log, Mr Wilkinson?'

Wilkie nodded gloomily and pecked without appetite at his chicken. He listened morosely to everything that was said, vainly dredging his mind for some subject on which he could extend himself.

'Have some more chicken.' Mrs Lutchman held up one of the dishes and they all gave themselves a second helping. Wilkie, however, refused.

'Like you lose your appetite, Mr Wilkinson?'

Wilkie smiled unhappily at Mrs Lutchman. 'I was never a big eater.'

'That won't do, Wilkie. You must have more than that.'

'No, no, Lutch. This fine for me.' Wilkie shielded his plate with his hands.

'Not even a potato?'

'No thanks, Lutch.'

'Have some wine then,' Mr Lutchman suggested, disturbed by Wilkie's evident distress. 'I bought a bottle of Gilbey's specially for tonight.' He went across to the cabinet and flourished the bottle. 'A little glass of this will do you wonders,' he said, pouring them both a generous portion.

'Thanks, Lutch old boy. You is a real friend.'

Mrs Lutchman crinkled her nose. 'Ram, you smell something?'

Mr Lutchman sniffed. 'What kind of smell?' His heart sank.

'I not sure. Like as if something burning.'

'Your wife's right, Ram. Something is burning.'

Mr Lutchman stared at them as if they were conspiring against him. He swivelled slowly in his chair. There was only one thing in the room that could catch fire. Wilkie lifted his head, betraying signs of interest. Suddenly Mr Lutchman bounded off his chair and pounced on the Yule log. 'Is this sonofabitch cotton wool that gone and catch fire,' he shouted, holding up the Yule log for all to see. Mrs Lutchman rushed to assist him. Grey threads of smoke curled upwards from the smouldering cotton wool.

'Don't stand holding it there like that,' she shouted, 'go and throw some water on it before it go and burn the whole house down.'

Mr Lutchman ran into the kitchen with the burning log and threw it into the sink, letting the tap run on it. He shredded bits of the sodden cotton and stared at them. 'You is a real sonofabitch,' he said. He returned to the sitting-room swearing softly to himself and sat down heavily on his chair. 'Just like that blasted camera,' he muttered.

'Don't worry, Ram. It's only a small disaster. That sort of thing is always happening to Yule logs. Believe me.' Doreen leaned across the table to comfort him. Mr Lutchman sulked into his plate.

'I don't know why you ever tell me about the blasted thing for.'

Wilkie, rapidly returning to life, laughed. Mr Lutchman regretted the kindnesses he had been showing him. 'I don't see anything so funny in this house burning down, Wilkie.'

'Sorry, Lutch. I didn't mean it that way. But all the same I must tell the boys about this. They go kill theyselves laughing when I tell them.'

'You know what you and your boys could do, Wilkie?'

'Come, come. It was only an accident. Calm yourself, Ram,' Doreen intervened. 'Actually, as Mr Wilkinson said, it was really quite funny. I remember the identical thing happening in the States when I went to spend Christmas with some friends. We even took pictures of what was happening. It was really quite funny.'

They all laughed, Wilkie and Romesh loudest of all. Mr Lutchman turned to his son. 'To bed with you, young man.'

'Why?' Romesh flared. 'Why you picking on me for? Everybody laugh. Not only me.'

'I don't want any of your back answers, boy. You'll do as I say.'

'Ram, let the boy stay. Is Christmas after all.' Mrs Lutchman patted her son.

'Well, see that he keep quiet,' Mr Lutchman muttered.

Wilkie's reanimation was by this time almost complete and he reminded himself of all that lost ground he had yet to make up.

'That reminds me, Lutch. You was going to tell me about all the pictures you take with the camera I sell you.'

Mrs Lutchman frowned at Wilkie. She had, until now, been almost prepared to forgive him most of his sins. 'Mr Wilkinson, I would have you know that my husband could be as good a photographer as you if he decide to put his mind to it. And,' she added darkly, 'especially if people don't try to cheat him.'

Wilkie was offended. 'Ah Mrs Lutchman, I wouldn't have expected a woman like you to say something like that to a man's face.'

'Keep out of this, Baby,' Mr Lutchman implored her. 'This is none of your business.'

'Is very much my own business if somebody decide to insult you in your own house,' Mrs Lutchman retorted, gazing savagely at Wilkie.

'Nobody trying to insult me,' Mr Lutchman protested weakly, envying his wife's boldness. Even Wilkie was playing nervously with his napkin.

But Mrs Lutchman, giving herself up to a righteous indignation, was not to be stopped. 'And I would tell you another thing to your face, Mr Wilkinson. That developing kit you sell him was no damn good either. I don't understand how you could cheat people like that and be so bold-face about it.'

Wilkie laughed, but without a great deal of conviction. 'Well, I never.' He wiped his lips with the napkin. 'All I ask was to have a glimpse of some of the pictures he take.'

'You not worthy enough to see them, Mr Wilkinson.'

'What's all this about a camera?' Doreen asked.

Mr Lutchman, bemused by the turn of events, said nothing. His wife, however, answered, 'Mr Wilkinson here sell him a bogus camera for a hundred dollars and an even more bogus developing kit.'

'None of the pictures ever come out,' Mr Lutchman confessed softly, addressing Doreen.

Wilkie cooed triumphantly. 'So. Like you was fooling me all the time, Lutch? You shouldn't do things like that, man. People does always find out in the end, you know.'

'I think you are damn fool, Mr Wilkinson,' Mrs Lutchman declared. 'And you could tell your boys I say that as well. They don't frighten me, you hear.'

Wilkie got up. 'I didn't come here to be insulted by you or anybody else, Mrs Lutchman.' He flung the napkin down on the table, but it slipped off and fluttered limply to the floor, a disappointing end to a fine gesture.

'Don't tell me that, Mr Wilkinson. Tell yourself. Is you who cause all this unpleasantness to happen. And I would be grateful if you wouldn't throw things about on the floor like that. Is I who have to clean it. Not you.'

Wilkie walked indecisively to the door. Mr Lutchman's confession, coming too early, had rather spoilt his fun, and Mrs Lutchman's uncompromising belligerence was more than he had bargained for. Even the boys could not be regaled with this tale for ever.

'You don't have to go so soon, Wilkie. Stay a little longer and drink some more wine with me.' Mr Lutchman brandished the bottle. Wilkie hesitated. Mr Lutchman, seeing that he was cowed, pursued his advantage. 'Come on, Wilkie. I don't hold anything against you, and anyway I didn't invite you here to quarrel.'

Mrs Lutchman, her hostility unabated, said, 'Let him go if he wants to, Ram.'

'Keep quiet, Baby. You insult the man enough already.'

Mrs Lutchman took this in the spirit in which it had been intended. Her husband was complimenting her. Appeased, she settled back into her chair and resumed her meal.

Mr Lutchman assumed command. 'Don't behave like a little boy, Wilkie.'

'Stay with us, Mr Wilkinson,' Doreen urged, smiling genially at him. 'I really would like to hear about your hobbies.'

Wilkie returned to his chair, stooping on the way to collect his napkin from the floor. He accepted another glass of the proffered wine.

The remainder of the evening passed without incident. Wilkie, though cowed by Mrs Lutchman, was affable and Mr Lutchman crowned the party with success when he said to him, 'I would like a few tips on this photography business, Wilkie. I tired wasting my money and making a fool of myself.' Wilkie obliged and gave him a discreet tour of the pitfalls lying in wait for the amateur, going so far as to tell them of the elementary mistakes he had made when he first took up this particular hobby. They all laughed happily and without malice. Mr Lutchman listened to him intently and asked the correct questions, although he had no intention of ever using the camera again. After dinner, Mrs Lutchman offered them slices of her sponge cake, which they all praised. 'You bake beautiful cakes, Mrs Lutchman.' 'Thank you, Mr Wilkinson,' she replied, nodding stiffly.

At midnight, Bhaskar and Romesh were allowed to open their presents. Doreen had given them large illustrated books on biology (for Bhaskar) and history. Romesh did not hide his disappointment. He glanced cursorily at the pictures and left the book lying on the floor. Bhaskar, however, was effusive in his thanks and sat on a chair thumbing through his assiduously.

Mr Lutchman was more threatening when they unwrapped the books he had given them. 'I am going to give you two weeks to read that book,' he warned Romesh, 'and if by that time you haven't finished it I am going to skin you alive.' Doreen stifled her disapproval. 'You are incorrigible, Ram.'

Like many of the words she used to describe him, Mr Lutchman had no idea what it meant. Still, he was pleased that words existed that could describe him. It was a comforting thought. He laughed and replied, 'Call me what you will.'

6

'That Wilkie finally get what was coming to him.' Mrs Lutchman laughed quietly and watched the lights on the Christmas tree bubble. Mr Lutchman, stretching his legs out before him, closed his eyes and yawned. 'I think we had a good time in the end though,' she added. 'Doreen was very nice. I like she.' Mr Lutchman appeared not to be listening. Mrs Lutchman got up with a sigh and began clearing the table. 'You want me to take off the top light, Ram? You looking very tired to me.' Mr Lutchman, his eyes still closed, shrugged his shoulders, settling down more deeply into his chair. Mrs Lutchman switched off the light and went into the kitchen.

Lit only by the Christmas tree, the shadows grew monstrous in the semi-darkness, playing with greater energy across the walls and ceiling. There was a noisy bustle of cars and people on the street. The cinema on the corner was having a late-night show and groups of young men, singing and swearing, drifted slowly along the pavements. Mr Lutchman, disturbed by the shouts and the lights flashing past the windows, opened his eyes and stared sleepily around him. Wrapping paper littered the floor near the Christmas tree and there were wine stains on the table cloth, which had almost fallen away from the table. The smell of stale food was strong. One or two of the balloons had burst during the course of the evening and most of the others hung limp and flaccid from their strings. 'Sonofabitch,' he muttered, thinking of the balloon seller and his promise. In the kitchen, he heard his wife singing above the rattle of the plates and the running tap. Attracted by the light and noise on the street, he opened the front door and stepped outside. A steady stream of cars and people passed him. 'Happy Christmas, mister!' A man, smelling of rum, swayed heavily past him. The Savannah, empty, was obscured in the darkness, but the line of black hills stood out clearly against the bright sky. He returned inside, bolting the front door.

He straightened the edge of the table-cloth and, picking up the crumpled sheets of Christmas wrapping, went into the kitchen. Mrs Lutchman was still singing her song. Rolling the bits of paper into a ball, he flung them through the window.

'Ram! How you could do a senseless thing like that, eh? Is I who would have to break my back picking it up tomorrow, you know.' Her face creased in annoyance. Mr Lutchman, not answering, sat at the table, head bent. She softened. 'Why don't you go to bed now, Ram? You had a hard day today and yesterday. All this excitement must have tired you more than you think.' He got up obediently and left the kitchen. She listened to his steps, slow and heavy, ascending the stairs.

The neatness he had longed for had proved impossible to achieve after all. True, Doreen had shown a real tenderness towards him. But that was a calculated consideration. It had sprung from her awareness of the gulf, unbridgeable, that separated him from her. The concern she had shown for him was not, in essence, very different from that she might have displayed towards a child whose founderings had aroused her sympathies. It was not he but Doreen, and especially his wife, who had cowed Wilkie. He had done no more than exploit the fruits of their victory. And what kind of victory was that? At the bottom he felt that he and Wilkie were not very different from each other, the 'boys' as much a figment of the imagination as his own interest in photography had been.

Mr Lutchman changed into his pyjamas. He closed the windows and, drawing back the pink counterpane, sat on the edge of the bed and waited for his wife to come.

Chapter Seven

1

Mr Lutchman rushed excitedly through the house, searching for his wife. 'Baby! Baby! Where you gone to, woman? Come, I got something to show you!'

'What you making such a racket for, Ram? I not deaf, you know.'

'Come! Come! You would never guess what gone and happen.'

He dragged her protesting through the kitchen out to the back yard. 'Look! Have a good look at that.'

'I don't see nothing.'

'Use the eyes God give you in your head, woman. Look at the hundreds of flowers.'

'Ram! You right. It flowering. Well! . . .'

The avocado tree had burst into flower, though not in the 'hundreds' Mr Lutchman had claimed for it.

'Well, what you go to say now, eh? You still think I killing it?'

'I never say you was killing it. In fact . . .'

'Thought I didn't know what I was doing, eh! This go teach you to contradict me in the future. Look at all them flowers. Millions! Trillions!'

Mrs Lutchman nodded resignedly.

'If any sonofabitch try to steal any of this I go do for them. What flowers, man! I have never seen the like in my born days.'

The avocado tree bore its first fruit. The pears were soft and yellow and tasted like butter. There were not many fruit on the tree and Mr Lutchman, afraid that they might be stolen (he suspected that the entire neighbourhood had fixed its gaze on his tree) or go bad, hoarded them carefully, wrapping them in layers of newspaper and storing them in a dark cupboard to ripen.

Every morning before going to work, he unwrapped and examined them. 'Not yet,' he would say, 'I only going to eat this thing when it perfect. What a zabocca!' When they were 'perfect', he cut thin, niggardly slices which he distributed with a religious seriousness to his family at breakfast and dinner, trying to observe whether they truly appreciated their good fortune. Presiding over the kitchen table like a high priest, he probed and questioned and criticized.

'Notice how creamy it is, Baby. Taste it slowly. Don't bite it as if it's a piece of bread. See how it does melt in the mouth all by itself.'

'Oh God, Ram. Why can't you let we eat the thing in peace? You go make me choke on it if you go on like that.'

'You people just don't know how to appreciate really good things.' He cut a small piece for himself and ate it slowly. 'This is the best kind of zabocca in the world. Just look at how them two animals mouthing it down.' He pointed his knife at Bhaskar and Romesh. 'Eat it slowly, boys. Let it melt for itself like butter. It not going to run away from you. That way you go taste the full flavour.' He cut himself another even tinier slice and demonstrated. But his family did not share his enthusiasm.

'I don't find it so different from any other zabocca,' Romesh said.

Mr Lutchman jumped up from his chair as if he had been stung, and confronted the heretic. 'What? What's this? You better watch what you saying to me, boy, or I go put my belt over you, you hear.' Romesh flinched. 'Not so different from any other zabocca! I have a good mind to take it away from you and not let you have any more. You is a real little savage.'

'Don't let him bother you, Ram. He is only a child. He don't have your understanding and experience.'

'You keep out of this, woman.' He walked up to Romesh. 'You have a lot of mouth for a small boy. But I never see you read that book I give you for Christmas. Oh no! All you want to do is go to the blasted cinema and come back home and behave like a star-boy. I go show you how to play star-boy with me.'

'Don't let him bother you, Ram. He's only a child. He have a lot to learn yet.'

'Only a child! It does break my heart, I tell you, to hear my own children talk to me like that. If only the little sonofabitch knew how much trouble I had to go through to get the tree in the first place and how after that for years the same sonofabitch tree wouldn't grow, he wouldn't stand up and say to me what he say this morning.'

'You thief the tree. And don't think I didn't see how you was frighten and begin begging the man when he catch you.'

Mr Lutchman grabbed his son by the hair and slapped him. 'Say that again. Let me hear you say that again, you little bitch.'

'Ram, Ram. He's only a child. He don't know what it is he saying.'

'I still think your zabocca is a damn rotten zabocca,' Romesh suddenly screamed, sweeping his plate off the table. 'Is a rotten, rotten zabocca, you hear! And you could murder me, I don't care. I go still stay your zabocca is a damn rotten zabocca. Look at me. I mashing it up under my foot. Look at me, look at me . . .'

'Why, you little . . .' Mr Lutchman's eyes contracted and his face went red. Romesh pulled himself free of his grasp and ran to the door where he stood watching his father, breathing hard. 'Why, you little . . .'

'Ram, Ram, for God's sake.' Mrs Lutchman went up to her husband, and took hold of his arm.

Romesh took a step into the kitchen. 'I not frighten of you, Pa.'

'You little . . .'

'Ram! The child don't know what it is he saying. Come. Take me for a drive. Take me for a drive. He's only a child. Cool down a little. Don't go to work this morning. Let we go and have a bathe in Carenage instead.' She drew him out of the kitchen. Mr Lutchman stared at his son, a look of silent, unutterable bewilderment on his face. Romesh stepped back to let them pass, his eyes fastened on his father. He watched them go. When he heard the car start, he threw himself sobbing on the floor.

The paucity of fruit heightened the value of the avocado tree in Mr Lutchman's eyes and, after a long period of neglect, he intensified his efforts to strengthen and preserve it. This in turn stimulated a renewed interest in the rest of the garden. The weed he had introduced was as intractable as ever, but by waging an unceasing war against it he managed to keep it within the bounds of decency. He brought more plants, including a vine with red, bell-shaped flowers which he trained to grow against the sides of the house. As he had done at the beginning, he spent the week-ends and much of his spare time in the garden, weeding, watering and grafting. Life at the Lutchmans gradually assumed an even, gentler pace.

Mrs Lutchman did her accustomed social round. She attended funerals and weddings with an equal zest and listened anxiously on visits to members of her family to the rising complaints and murmurings about the inheritance. On returning home, she would give a detailed report of all the latest developments to her husband. His appetite whetted by these briefings, he would usually launch into a vigorous tirade against all the 'gang' of 'money-grabbing' Khojas. However, her latest outing had produced one unexpected item of news which she felt was bound to please her husband and take the edge off his invective.

'Govind give Indrani another five acres of land,' she informed him happily. 'I always say that people should wait before they criticize. He didn't have to give she anything, did he?' Looking at him, she was less sure now that they were face to face of the salutary effect she had convinced herself this bit of information would have. He remained silent, contenting himself with a quizzical smile. 'I mean, nobody force him to do it. That come from the own goodness of his heart.' She waited for his approval. It was not forthcoming.

'Is not charity people want, Baby,' he replied quietly. 'Is their rights they fighting for.'

'You wouldn't say that if you hear the way Urmila and Shantee especially does talk. They not fighting for anybody rights. They want all they could lay they hands on. They not interested in anybody else but themselves. Rights!'

'That may be. I don't know about Urmila and Shantee, but it seem to me that they no worse than Govind. Is the old Khoja disease all over again. Too much money and too little brains. You wait and see. They go lose all that money one day because they so stupid.' He smiled at his wife. 'Anyway, I wouldn't be surprised if the only reason old Khoja give Indrani that extra piece of land is because it wasn't good for anything. I know old Khoja better than you think. They don't come much stingier than he. Take my word.' He resumed his examination of the rose-trees.

'How you know the land he give she not good for anything? You see it? That land is good sugar land. I don't know what you expect the poor man to do. Like you want him to give she the shirt off his back? You want him to be a pauper like the rest of we?'

'To hell with it, Baby. As you was saying a long time ago, all this is none of my business. I tired of hearing about all that mess and confusion. Just leave me alone and don't tell me anything more about it.'

Her husband's behaviour puzzled and disappointed her. 'You is a really funny man, Ram. Not so long ago you was blowing your mouth off about it and now you saying that you don't want to hear any more about it. I see now that no matter what Govind do, people still going to abuse him. Is a crying shame the way some people does behave.'

'That's right. Now you have had your little say I don't want to hear any more about it. You understand what it is I saying?' He spoke slowly, as if he were very tired. He took a deep breath.

Mrs Lutchman studied his face. 'You sure you feeling well, man?'

'Yes, yes. Just leave me alone, Baby, and don't bother me with all that gossip. A man need a little peace and quiet at some point in his life. All of we have we own battle to fight. And Urmila and Shantee battle is not my battle.' He looked up at her and smiled again. 'Is not you I vex with, Baby,' he added more gently. He laughed suddenly. 'Is these damn roses.

They getting too old. We need some young blood in this garden. Is more than enough work for one person. I could do with a little help. You could help me. You have any wedding to go this Sunday?'

'Yes. I get invite to one in Chaguanas. I'll take the boys with me so they don't disturb you.'

'They don't disturb me anyway. Romesh does hardly ever be at home. And as for Bhaskar . . . well, he always does be too busy studying, or so he say.' His face clouded. 'You sure you have to go to this wedding?'

She nodded with a simulated weariness. 'They is the sort of people quick off the mark to take offence. Anyway, she's a nice girl and I feel it would be rude if I don't go.'

'Is amazing with the number of funerals you does go to that it have anybody in this world left to get married at all.' They both laughed and he waved her away and returned to his roses.

3

The wedding season was in full spate and almost every weekend Mrs Lutchman went away to a different 'wedding house' with or without Bhaskar and Romesh. It was the time of year when Mr Khoja's stock of jugs and glasses needed constant replenishment. The invitations arrived with the regularity of postcards at Christmas time, all of them extremely ornate with scalloped edges and gilt lettering and at the bottom rounded off with an R.S.V.P. which, if taken literally, would without doubt have given rise to the greatest astonishment and marked one off as an eccentric for life. It was a mere flourish and only a handful of the initiated actually knew what the letters stood for. On these invitations, only the announcement that the daughter of so and so was getting married to the son of so and so was meant to be taken seriously. The invitation to 'luncheon' was, like the invitation to reply stuck at the bottom, a piece of rhetoric. Food was indeed provided, but the air of formality implied on the invitation was deceptive. It was served to almost anyone who happened to be present, legitimately and illegitimately (there was no way of distinguishing the two), and at times separated by several hours from that indicated on the card. Only the very elect might be served punctually; for the organizers of Indian weddings judged their success by the width of failure that separated their promises from the actuality.

The more intense the confusion, the nearer to disaster it had been, the greater the repute it attached to itself. 'I telling you, man,' people would exclaim with pride, 'that wedding was nearly three hours late. For a time I thought the bridegroom wasn't going to turn up at all.' This was a not uncommon occurrence. It was a nightmare that haunted every bride's parents. But, more often than not, the bridegroom did turn up, albeit several hours late, and his father or mother would excuse their lateness by saying, 'You should have seen the confusion over at we place. So much people pushing and shouting, you could hardly breathe.'

Thus weddings with their suggestion of unpredictability were a perennial source of excitement and speculation (the latter chiefly about the dowry), and Mrs Lutchman looked forward to them greatly.

On the Sunday, Mr Lutchman watched his wife get dressed. 'You realize you haven't been home for at least the last four week-ends. I does hardly get a chance to see you at all these days, the way you always hot-footing it somewhere.'

Mrs Lutchman was applying small dabs of perfume behind her ears and examining herself in the mirror. She was wearing a dress of cream satin and the bracelets she had been left by the elder Mrs Khoja.

'You never complain before,' she said, twisting her head to one side to adjust her earrings. 'I thought you used to be glad to have we out of the house so you could have peace and quiet.' She picked up a fluffy pink powder puff, sprinkled some powder on it and passed it lightly over her face, at the same time biting and sucking her lips. She spoke to his reflection in the mirror.

'I bet they wouldn't miss you if you don't go. I sure they don't know half the people they does invite to these weddings.'

'Have it your own way, Mr Know-All. But I have to go anyway. I know the bride too well to do a thing like that.'

Mr Lutchman was scornful. 'Don't give me that one, Baby. I sure you only see she once or twice, if you ever see she at all, that is. If you know she so well, then how come I never meet she?'

'You confusing me, Ram,' Mrs Lutchman replied pettishly, applying a dab of perfume behind her ears.

'You wouldn't consider . . .'

'No, I tell you. How much times do you expect me to repeat that?'

Mr Lutchman nodded slowly and returned downstairs to his plants without another word.

At last they were ready to leave, Mrs. Lutchman, Bhaskar and Romesh.

'So, the little tribe is ready to go. All right. Have a good time.' Mr Lutchman was squatting on the ground, a tattered straw hat fixed at a rakish angle on his head, turning over some anthurium stalks in his hand and shaking his head. He sighed. 'It looks like some of these sonofabitch plants gone and catch some disease. You can't turn your back for one minute and something like this does happen.'

'We won't be as long as last time, Ram. I think we should come back before midnight.'

He looked up at her, tilting the hat further back on his head. 'Why don't you let one of the children stay with me for a change?'

'That's up to them. I don't mind.'

Mr Lutchman called Romesh to him. 'How about staying home with me today, son? You don't want to go to no stupid wedding, do you? Keep your father company for a change. We two could work in the garden all afternoon weeding and watering the plants. You could work with me hand in hand. What you say to that, eh? I'll even let you wear my hat if you want to.' He took off the hat and stuck it playfully on his son's head. Romesh pushed his hand away and the hat fell on the ground.

'I want to go with Ma,' he said, his voice thick.

Mr Lutchman laughed softly and picked up the hat. He twirled it on his fingers for a few seconds before putting it back on his head. He put an arm round his son's waist and drew him nearer. Romesh grudgingly allowed himself to be caressed. 'So, you don't want to stay with your father? You don't want to help him out in what your mother used to call the Garden of Eden?' Romesh was not to be drawn and extracting himself from his father's grasp, retreated to the gate.

'I want to go with Ma,' he repeated.

Mr Lutchman stared at him for some moments without speaking. 'All right, son. I don't want to force you. You do what will make you happy. How about you, Bhaskar? You want to keep your father company?'

Bhaskar was indecisive. He looked from his mother to his father.

Mr Lutchman laughed. 'So you too dying to go to this wedding.'

'I didn't say so, Pa. I was only trying to make up my mind.'

'Don't bother. I could see what you want to do written on your face. Go with your mother.'

Bhaskar cast a despairing glance at his father. 'I . . .'

'Go, go with your mother.' Mr Lutchman pushed him away.

'We won't be long, Ram. I'll try to come back as soon as possible.'

'No hurry, Baby. Have a good time.' He struggled to his feet and escorted them to the gate. Mr Lutchman watched them go down the street, Romesh running ahead and shouting. He suddenly realized that Bhaskar was almost a young man, not a child any more. He walked along, slightly stooping, next to his mother. Mr Lutchman shook his head. 'I must teach that boy to walk properly,' he said. Romesh, racing well ahead of them, was already at the corner, staring up at the cinema posters. 'And I must discourage him from going to the cinema,' he added. Once, halfway down the street, his wife turned round and waved to him. He waved back and waited a little longer before he shut the gate and went inside.

4

Chaguanas lay in the sugar cane country, and during the wedding season it produced, perhaps in all Trinidad, the most abundant crop of marriages. In addition, it produced more than its fair share of murders and near murders. Sugar apart, weddings and funerals were its stock in trade.

The street on which the 'wedding-house' stood, a narrow back lane leading off the main road, was choked with cars and Sunday dressed people, some already drunk, offering sips of rum to all and sundry, and milling about on the pavements and shouting good-naturedly at each other. As soon as they had left the main road, they were greeted by the whining blare of Indian popular music coming from loudspeakers, which, as they neared the house, grew to a deafening pitch.

The wedding house was recognizable, apart from the wall of sound that surrounded it, by the greater density of the crowds spilling out from it. Mrs Lutchman's eyes assumed the sparkle reserved for occasions like these, indicating that she was back in a type of element long familiar to her and reminiscent of the days of her childhood. But this being a social, not a strictly family affair, she smiled pleasantly enough at everyone as she threaded her way through the cars and people, holding Romesh tightly by the hand. For some, she kept a grimmer smile, those who from bitter experience she knew to be charming when sober, but capable of the wildest excesses when drunk. These were the professional trouble-makers and weddings were their favourite hunting grounds. A wedding wrecked by a group of these men was too much even for her more robust taste in these matters.

Casting an experienced eye over the chaos that presented itself to her, she surmised that the bharat – the wedding procession from the groom's house – had not yet arrived. The means she employed to come to this conclusion were instinctive, not intellectual. To an amateur, the difference would have been unintelligible, so great was the prevailing confusion, but Mrs Lutchman had been trained from childhood to distinguish between the minutest intensities of anarchy and confusion. Thus to a professional, such as she undoubtedly was, what was presented to her was evidently not that total chaos which, with the arrival of the bharat, would soon be descending upon the wedding house, but something milder. She hurried on.

The Khoja sisters, when present at a 'function' such as this, where they had no close ties with the family involved, tended to form a cohesive front, moving from room to room in a tightly knit group and commenting, always with a faint hint of disapproval, at the arrangements and people they saw around them. They behaved, in a sense, as a corporate self in defence of that grandeur to which they believed themselves to belong. Mr Khoja, should he be coming, would, on arrival, be pounced upon to be swallowed and digested before being released for the general consumption. In this way, they asserted their rights and prior claim to the affections and attentions of the great man.

Now, however, responding to the change of mood that had overtaken the clan since the death of the elder Mrs Khoja, this corporate self had split, as by binary fission, into two quite separate selves, one of which pounced and one of which did not pounce on the great man immediately he arrived. The former corresponded to that group of sisters, Darling, Saraswatee and Mrs Lutchman, who defended Mr Khoja's right to the bulk of the inheritance; the latter, Urmila, Shantee and Badwatee, to those who disputed that right. Nevertheless, the line separating the two was as yet sufficiently indistinct to permit a certain amount of cross movement, thereby allowing those sisters less sure of themselves the opportunity to bask in the reflected glory thrown by their brother's shadow; or of course, to demonstrate their independence.

Mrs Lutchman was greeted by the usual cries of affection on both sides. 'Baby! So you manage to make it after all. How is that no-good husband of yours?'

'I leave him home doing some gardening. How's the bride?'

Bhaskar and Romesh made the round of the assembled aunts.

'We haven't seen she. She lock sheself up in the bedroom all morning. Modern times, you know.' Urmila darted 'significant' glances at the sisters, pointing at the same time at an unambiguously locked door.

Romesh left the room.

'Where you think you going, young man?' Mrs Lutchman shouted after him.

'To play,' he answered, running out into the road.

'She dressing?' Mrs Lutchman asked.

The sisters did not know. 'You better ask Renouka that. It seem only she have the right to be in there.' Urmila nodded grimly at Mrs Lutchman. Saraswatee sitting straight-backed on her chair, gazed at the floor.

'Young people these days have a mind of their own,' Mrs Lutchman pointed out indulgently. 'I was only asking because I have a gift for she.'

'What you giving she?' Urmila asked.

'A set of brush and comb.'

Urmila twitched her nostrils, a sign of her contempt. 'Well, if you knock on the door, somebody sure to put they hand out and take what you have to give.' She laughed scornfully.

Mrs Lutchman knocked on the door. Urmila's prediction was correct. The door did open and a hand shoot out. Mrs Lutchman surrendered the brush and comb set. The hand withdrew and the door closed.

The sisters were hurt: they had not been admitted into the inner sanctum. Indian brides, on the days immediately preceding their marriage, were transformed into creatures of mystery. It happened to the most commonplace of them. The young girl, previously taken so much for granted, was suddenly surrounded by an indefinable aura that enhanced her attractiveness. She became coquettish, quick-tempered, shy, and, after a fashion, grown-up. On her wedding day, this process reached its climax and only the closest relatives and friends were permitted to enter the bridal bedroom. Nevertheless. the Khoja sisters had always taken it for granted that entry there was one of the prerogatives of their status.

'That was Miss Renouka whose hand you just see,' Urmila said when Mrs Lutchman returned to her seat. 'You should see how fashionable she is these days. High-heel shoes and all. Your daughter is a real film-star now, not so Saraswatee?'

Saraswatee flushed and glanced round helplessly at the sisters. Deprived of her daughter's support, she was at a total loss. Mrs Lutchman noticed that her dress ended well above her ankles. More people came into the room and knocked at the door, and Urmila studied the comings and goings of the disembodied hand with a malicious satisfaction. The bride's mother, an extremely fat and very dark woman, swept into the room, dabbing her cheeks furiously with a handkerchief and engulfed in an odour of cheap scent. It was a bitter moment for the Khoja sisters to see her throw open the door imperiously without knocking and be swallowed up by the darkness in the bedroom.

'She is the ugliest woman I ever see in my whole life,' Shantee whispered. The sisters laughed.

The bride's mother came out from the bedroom almost immediately, now fanning herself with the handkerchief.

'Whew! All this heat and confusion. It going to drive me mad,' she exclaimed, beaming at the sisters. 'There must be a million people here. I sure we won't have enough food and chairs for all of them. Why don't you all go out and sit in the tent? It much cooler there for a start and that way you bound to get a seat. I can't think what is going to happen when the bharat come. Sheer murder if you ask me.' She swept out of the room, flurried but immensely happy.

'I wonder who she think she is.'

'I could tell you what she father is, Darling,' Shantee said. 'A low-caste Madrasi cane-cutter.'

Darling laughed. 'And to think that somebody like she ordering we about. I can't believe my ears. "Go and sit in the tent!" Well, I never!'

The tent, built at the side of the house, was already quite crowded and there was a loud hum of chatter behind the blare of the loudspeakers. Urmila surveyed the scene. 'You wouldn't catch me going out there.'

'Anyway,' Badwatee added, 'we have to wait for Govind.'

Urmila gave her a scathing glance. But she knew that without him, the day's events would have no focus.

Mrs Lutchman walked out to the verandah to search for Romesh. She saw him laughing and chatting in the midst of a group of men she knew to be troublemakers. He had obviously been performing his favourite party trick of bouncing pebbles off his forehead, for one of the men was throwing a quite sizeable pebble into the air and encouraging him to 'head it'.

'I don't like Romesh mixing with those men,' she said.

Urmila's nostrils twitched. 'Young people have a mind of their own,' she replied.

'Romesh! Come here at once!'

He pretended not to hear her.

'Romesh! I warning you!'

He stamped his foot angrily and walked reluctantly towards her.

Mr and Mrs Khoja arrived long after the wedding was supposed to have started. There was a rustle of interest among the guests in the tent when they were spotted, and several people as a mark of respect got up from their seats. The loud-speakers stuttered into silence.

Mr Khoja pushed his way amicably up the front steps and Mrs Khoja, who was wearing one of her gorgeous saris, kept her eyes fixed on the ground to make sure she would not trip or sully the border of her sari. The bride's mother and father flapped through the tent in hot pursuit and the faction of faithful sisters, determined to head them off, rose to their feet as one and hurried out to the verandah where, discarding ceremony, they pounced and almost instantaneously swallowed their brother, as it were, whole.

The rebels, Urmila chief among them, their faces lit by acidulous smiles, gathered in a solemn circle around them. The faithful having had their fill, the pressure relaxed and the regurgitated Mr Khoja was able to detach himself from the smothering embrace. He emerged smiling and slightly out of breath and, gathering his energies, prepared himself for the second wave of assault. The rebels, however, stood their ground, not wanting to seem to make the first move. The bride's parents, nonplussed, looked from one to the other, wondering whether they should step in to fill the breach. They started to move forward. The rebels hesitated and then, with sudden decision, leapt on their brother, swallowed, digested and regurgitated him in a matter of seconds, and then turned him over for the delectation of the low-caste Madrasi cane-cutter's daughter.

'I so glad you could make it.' The cane-cutter's daughter wrapped herself ecstatically around Mr Khoja. Her husband contented himself with shaking the great man's hand.

'How is the bride to be? She nervous? I remember on my own wedding day I was so nervous I could hardly stand.' Mrs Khoja giggled and tickled her husband's elbow affectionately.

'She's a big girl, Mrs Khoja. She cooler than all the rest of we put together, mark my words. You want to see she?' The bride's mother led the way to the bedroom and the sisters, unable to resist the temptation, followed.

Urmila prodded Shantee and scowled when, as before, she threw open the door imperiously and went in without knocking. 'She showing off,' Shantee whispered behind her cupped palms. 'Low-caste Madrasi!'

The bride, standing in front of a full-length mirror, was having her sari adjusted by Renouka.

'Look who it is come to see you, Sona,' her mother said.

Sona flicked her eyebrows in annoyance and peered at the newcomers in the mirror. Recognizing Mr Khoja, she stayed Renouka's hand and ran up tittering to kiss him.

'We bring a little present for you,' Mr Khoja said, signalling to his wife, 'just a jug and a set of six glasses. I think you should find it very useful,' he added, glancing at the multitudes of jugs and glasses that lay scattered on the bed among the other presents – cutlery, towels, sheets, kitchen equipment, brush and comb sets.

Sona squeaked with delight. 'You could never have too much of that kind of thing,' she said, putting the box wrapped in pink paper on the bed.

'Everything does come in useful in the end,' her father commented glumly.

'That's a really pretty sari you wearing, girl. Turn round, let me see.' Sona swivelled on her heels. Mrs Khoja, feeling the material, nodded approvingly. 'Is not you who buy it for she, is it?' she asked Sona's mother. 'Is really fine quality material and such a pretty design too.' Sona's mother was not insulted. Any compliment, even a backhanded one, coming from the Khojas was to be treasured and savoured.

'Yes. Is I who buy it for she.'

'I must say that really surprises me.' Mrs Khoja believed that she had a monopoly of all that was good and expensive on the market. As it was, she could not help feeling that Sona's mother's buying such a sari was an act of presumption. 'I have one just like it,' she continued in the same astonished tone, 'but I must say that I don't really think it tie all that well.' She seemed happier. Renouka, several pins stuck between her teeth, scowled at the floor. 'Is a difficult business, you know. You should have somebody who know about these things.'

Renouka, retreating to a corner of the room, stared sullenly at the sari she had helped tie. 'I don't see what wrong with it,' she said.

Mrs Khoja ignored her. 'Would you like me to help you tie it, Sona?'

Sona was unable to hide her embarrassment. She looked guiltily at Renouka. 'She's been wearing saris for years, Ren,' she said apologetically.

'You can do what you want, Sona. Is your wedding not mine. But I must say I don't see what so wrong with the way I do it.'

Mrs Khoja giggled. 'Really, child. You should be more modest when speaking to your elders and betters. You mean to say you actually want to compare yourself with me?' Mrs Khoja shook her head and laughed. Urmila, standing in the doorway, was enjoying herself immensely. Mrs Khoja called Sona to her. 'Let me tie your sari for you, child. You should at least look nice on your wedding day.' She began unwinding the sari.

Renouka spat the pins on the floor. 'Well, since there is nothing more for me to do here, I may as well go home.' She picked up her handbag which was lying on the bed and strode across the room, pushing the sisters aside. She slammed the door hard. Saraswatee, a look of desperation on her face, ran off in pursuit of her daughter.

'Something should be done about that girl's temper,' Mrs Khoja said.

'She's a convent girl. All of them is film-star and you can't tell film-stars what to do.' Urmila, wagging her head, giggled. Many of the sisters, rebels and faithful alike, chorused agreement.

'Look, this is woman's work, so I better give you a fatherly kiss and go.' Mr Khoja kissed Sona on the cheek and left the room. The sisters filed out after him. They were well pleased with themselves. Revenge had been theirs.

The bharat arrived not long after and the chaos when it did so was total. The tent was much too small to accommodate everybody and scores of the bridegroom's guests – the main victims of the seat shortage – were forced to stand on the road or sit on the bonnets of their cars.

Sitting in a row, near the wooden platform where the wedding ceremony was to take place ('ring-side' as Mr Khoja described it), the Khojas were a phalanx of solid respectability, exclusive and superior to all around them. The sisters chattered quietly among themselves, passing judgement, invariably unflattering, on any of the better-dressed women who were unfortunate enough to catch their eye.

'You see how she paint up she face? Just like if she is a prostitute.'

'For all you know she is one. I have seen she type before. You can't trust them an inch.'

'Look at she,' Ursula said, pointing to another well-dressed woman. 'You see how she weigh down with jewellery, as if she alone own jewellery in the world.'

'And you should see the way she does treat she children. Running about the place in rags, I tell you.'

Thus they entertained themselves until the pundit took his place in the 'ring'. The bridegroom, a pale, good-looking young man, weighed under by the heavy ornamentation draped around his neck and a tightly wound turban, staggered down the aisle between the chairs escorted by his father, who bowed first to the pundit and then to Mr Khoja. Looking lost, bewildered and entirely unhappy, the bridegroom lowered himself carefully onto the cushions provided and gazed sadly at his naked feet.

'They say he was really wild at one time.'

'He father rich though.'

'He used to go around with that Mahabir girl. Don't you remember the big scandal when she father thought she was pregnant?'

'It wouldn't surprise me one bit if she was.'

Sona appeared soon after. She too seemed unhappy and

bewildered when she lowered herself onto the cushions.

'They say it was a love match.'

'Huh! I know what they mean when they say is a love match.'

'You don't have to tell me. All them convent girl showing they leg.'

The wedding had begun. The pundit's voice wavered drearily in the heat and every now and again the bride and groom made circuits of the platform. It went on, like all Hindu ceremonies, a long time. The familiar, wearied somnolence descended on the guests, broken occasionally by drunken shouts and singing from the road.

'What? What? Don't speak so loud. You making people look at we. A message, you say?'

'A message? A message for who? This is not the time and place to be . . . Yes, yes. Well, don't get so excited.'

'Baby! Baby!'

'What?'

'A message for you.'

'What kind of message? Surely it could wait until . . .'

'Something about Ram.'

'What is it, Shantee? Tell me.'

'He not . . . he . . .'

'Tell me.'

'Don't get frighten. Keep calm.'

'Tell me.'

'He get a heart attack. But he not dead. Don't . . .'

The line of Khojas wavered and finally broke. The pundit's chant stopped. People scraped their chairs angrily and glared at them. Mrs Lutchman, supported by Mr Khoja, walked slowly from the tent.

'Somebody run and get some smelling salts,' Mr Khoja ordered.

'I don't want any smelling salts. Where is the children?'

'They with me, Baby,' Mrs Khoja said. 'Don't worry.'

'Take me to him quick.'

Mr Khoja led her quickly through the yard to his car. Mrs Lutchman, dry-eyed and silent, got into the back with Bhaskar and Romesh. 'Quick,' she repeated.

'Don't worry, Vimla. We'll be there in no time at all. Why don't you sit back and relax? You can't do anything until you get there.'

Mrs Lutchman paid no attention. She sat forward on the edge of her seat. 'Take me to him quick. Quick.'

5

Mrs Lutchman climbed the steps slowly, assisted by Mr Khoja. The door to the bedroom was ajar.

'Let me go in alone,' she said.

'You might be . . .'

'I not frighten. I want to be with him. Alone.'

He lifted his arm off her shoulder and pushing the door full open she went inside. All the windows in the room had been opened wide and there was a strange smell, perhaps of some medicine, which she was unable to identify. The curtains bellied in the breeze blowing in from over the Queen's Park Savannah. A woman – the doctor – was standing near the head of the bed, her stethoscope hanging from her neck, her eyes dull and impassive. She signalled Mrs Lutchman to be quiet.

The pink counterpane had been folded back and Mr Lutchman lay stretched on the white undersheet. He was in the same clothes he had worn in the garden earlier that afternoon. Mrs Lutchman pictured him as he was then: the sunburned face gazing up at her and asking her if she would stay; the straw hat tilted rakishly on his head; him placing it playfully on Romesh's head; his melancholy acceptance of their departure; the farewell wave of the hand when they were already halfway down the street.

She looked around her now, searching for the straw hat. She saw it on a chair beside the bed. Her husband's eyes were closed and the light cotton shirt he was wearing shifted restlessly, ruffled by the wind. All the buttons had been undone. She had to look carefully to see if he were still breathing. He was, gently and imperceptibly. As she looked, a thin, white streak of foam trickled from his nostrils and came to rest on his upper lip. The doctor stared intently at it and then, with a swift glance at Mrs Lutchman, she left the room. Mrs Lutchman's gaze strayed from her husband's face. She did not realize the doctor had gone out of the room until she heard her talking softly to Mr Khoja on the landing. For a while, without understanding what was being said, she listened to them whispering. Then she ceased to listen and her eyes returned to her husband's face. She looked again at his chest. The cotton shirt moved restlessly as before, but this time she could detect no other movement. His lips, as always, remained slightly parted. She started to cry.

6

For Mr Khoja, a death in the family meant, above everything else, work. Any grief or sadness the occasion might have aroused was crowded out by that sense of duty which guided him on all such occasions. 'Crying is a luxury I can't afford,' he would say at these times. His interest, then, was primarily organizational and it was with a thinly disguised pride that he now reviewed some of his better funerals as he planned for the task that lay ahead of him.

Immediately Mr Lutchman's death had been officially confirmed by the doctor, he took charge. 'I'll take the two children home with me, Vimla, and let Sumintra look after them until we get some more order around here. We can't have them cluttering up the place.' Mrs Lutchman nodded tearfully. 'And you don't have to worry about anything. I'll put out an announcement on the radio and I'll pay my half of the coffin as usual. You could set your mind at rest on that score.'

He took Bhaskar and Romesh to Woodlands. Mrs Khoja, fearing that Romesh might have an attack of 'nerves', was extremely solicitous. She allowed them into the darkened sitting-room and gave them tea and several slices of cake.

'Poor little boy. Your father gone and dead just when you need him most.' She patted Romesh. He squirmed under her caresses and continued to eat his cake. 'You is a luckier boy, Bhaskar. At least you coming to be a big man now. You'll have to look after your mother soon.' Bhaskar stared seriously at her, but he too continued to eat his cake. 'What you want to be when you grow up?' she inquired cheerfully. 'You want to work for the Government like your father?'

Bhaskar shook his head. 'Nothing like that, Mamee. I going to be a doctor.' His voice was muffled by cake.

'A doctor!' Mrs Khoja giggled. 'But you need money for that, boy, and – brains.'

'I hoping to get a scholarship.'

'Ah yes.' Mrs Khoja seemed not altogether happy. 'What kind of scholarship?'

'One of them Island scholarships.'

'But there's only one or two of those. You got to work very hard and be really bright to get one of them.' Bhaskar continued to eat his cake stolidly. 'Supposing you can't get to be a doctor, what you going to do then?'

Bhaskar pouted sullenly. 'I going to be a doctor,' he said.

'Like you really set your heart on that, boy. I hope you not disappointed. You doesn't always get what you want in this life. But you really never think of doing anything else?'

'No. Since I was small I always wanted to be a doctor.'

'You going to miss your father?'

'He was my father. I must miss him.' Bhaskar, avoiding her eyes, played with the crumbs of cake.

'You learn to swim as yet? Your mother was telling me that he used to . . .'

Bhaskar frowned. 'Ma was exaggerating what happen. I was learning very well by myself.'

'So she was saying. What about you, Rom? You going to miss your father?'

Romesh bent his head low over his plate. He was crying. Mrs Khoja hastened across to him and smothered his face with kisses. 'Poor child. Poor child. Here, eat some more cake, that will make you feel better.' Romesh pushed her hand away. Mrs Khoja took the plate and rested it on the floor. He seemed vexed. 'I'm not crying because of him. I don't feel sorry at all.'

'You mustn't say that, Rom. Maybe you don't feel sad now but that's only because of the shock.' She cradled his head. 'Bhaskar going to be a doctor. What about you, son? What you want to do when you get big?' Romesh sobbed louder.

'Look at the way you crying and you say you not feeling sorry.'

'I tell you I not feeling sad for him,' Romesh screamed at her.

'All right. All right. So you not feeling sorry for your father. But what you crying for then?' He sobbed louder. 'You sure you don't want any more cake?' Romesh shook his head. 'You want to finish it off, Bhaskar? Is a shame to let all that good cake go to waste.' Bhaskar eyed the plate on the floor with interest. He hesitated. 'Have it if you want it,' Mrs Khoja urged, 'otherwise I'll just have to throw it away.'

Bhaskar, abandoning his scruples, leant forward and picked up the plate.

Mr Khoja handled all the arrangements with a business-like efficiency. At six o'clock, what was called the 'ice-box', a crude affair, deep-sided and stained a dark, dull brown, arrived from the funeral home. It was brought into the house by two men, dressed in black suits and wearing hats, the motto of their firm (Courtesy and a Quiet Consideration, But a Part of Our Service) blazoned across their shirt-pockets. They stood mute and inseparable, enveloped in a funeral discretion born of many years' service, while Mr Khoja and Mrs Lutchman discussed what would be the best place for 'the body'. It was finally decided that it should be placed along the wall occupied by the cabinet. Mrs Lutchman removed all her most precious pieces of tableware and carried them upstairs to the bedroom. When this had been done, Mr Khoja signalled to the two men, who jumped forward and with an exaggerated delicacy carried the cabinet into the kitchen. The ice-box was set on trestles and moved into position. Then the men went upstairs with Mr Khoja and Mrs Lutchman to 'prepare the body'.

Mr Lutchman was dressed not in his best clothes (that would come later), but in a pair of blue cotton pyjamas. His face was washed and coated with a dark powder to relieve the unnatural pallor and his hair was neatly parted and combed. This done, 'the body' was brought downstairs to the sitting-room and laid in the ice-box. To Mr Khoja's disgust, it leaked, and a basin was put under it to catch the drips of water coming from the melting ice. 'I ask them to make sure it was a good box,' he fumed. 'If they not careful, next time I'll go to Mootoo Brothers. They don't seem to realize that I'm one of their best customers. You just can't expect people to do anything right these days.'

The mourners began to arrive after dinner. As they came in, they all went one by one up to the coffin and studied, more with curiosity than with sympathy or sorrow, the drawn, tight face, frozen under the circle of glass. Wilkie, when he entered the sitting-room, crossed himself and went into the kitchen to find Mrs Lutchman. She was making coffee. Wilkie was dressed more simply than he had been on Christmas Eve. Gone were the too tight trousers, the ready smile and desperate ebullience of that evening. He was almost dignified.

'I heard it on the radio,' he said. 'I couldn't believe my ears when I hear it. Is a shocking thing.' Mrs Lutchman handed him a cup of coffee. 'I never expect something like that would happen. True, these last few weeks he was always saying how tired he was, but I never thought it was anything serious.'

Mrs Lutchman arranged the cups of coffee on a tray. 'Death can take us any time it want to, Mr Wilkinson. Is nothing we can do about that. As the saying goes, time and tide don't wait for no man.'

Wilkie gazed at her with frightened eyes. 'I want you to know, Mrs Lutchman, that I truly sorry about what happen last time I was here. I truly sorry about all that talk about the camera.' He drank his coffee slowly.

'That's all in the past now, Mr Wilkinson. You don't have to apologize. Ram didn't hold it against you. Anyway, you wasn't to know that this was to happen. Go in the drawing-room and have your coffee.' She smiled at him, and with the tray propped precariously against her stomach, she followed Wilkie out of the kitchen.

Doreen too had heard the announcement on the radio. When she came, she tiptoed up to the coffin and stared for a long time at the frozen face, her hands clasped tightly together and hidden by the folds of the simple white dress she was wearing. Mrs Lutchman joined her.

'He looking so peaceful,' she murmured. 'Is almost as if he is asleep.'

'Yes.'

'You know, it was only this morning . . .'

'Yes, yes. I know. Come and sit and talk to me.' Doreen looked around the room. 'I see that Mr Wilkinson is here. He's looking abnormally subdued.'

'He's not such a bad person really.'

'Where are Bhaskar and Romesh?'

'They should be back soon. They staying with my brother wife for the time.'

'You must introduce me to your brother. I have been wanting to meet him for a long time. Are most of these people here the other members of your family?' Doreen's eyes travelled along the row of sisters. She suppressed a smile. Mrs Lutchman nodded.

The Rebels and the Faithful sat on opposite sides of the room. Neither faction was above demonstrating its loyalty or disaffection twice in the same day, but Mr Khoja having returned home for dinner, they had not been given the chance. Instead, they were forced to content themselves with various ritual assertions of coldness: the raised eyebrow directed at no one in particular, the low, malevolent laugh, the whispers loud enough to carry but not to be deciphered that floated in among the veiled heads. They were, up to a point, enjoying themselves. Having most of them lost their husbands relatively early in their married life, the Khoja sisters had come to regard the possession of a husband as something of an anachronism, which disqualified the victim for membership of the inner circle. Husbands, they felt, were sources of dissension, and thus a death in the family, while technically considered a bereavement, was in practice thought of as one of the more positive steps in the progression to maturity.

Like weddings, death attracted many people whose acquaintance with the family was tenuous. The neighbours came in droves to offer their condolences to Mrs Lutchman. Several of them mistook Urmila for her, probably because she had the most soured expression among those present. Discovering their mistake, they laughed loudly.

'But look at my crosses, eh! Taking you for she. Well I never.'

'And don't forget that's the dead man over there in that big brown box. All the men you see here still alive,' Urmila would reply drily.

'Don't take offence, my dear. Is a mistake anybody could make. You and she is as like as two peas.'

The confusion settled, the stranger looked at the dead man and clicking her tongue mournfully, sat unobtrusively in a corner and talked to no one. 'Who is she?' someone would ask Mrs Lutchman.

'I never set eyes on she in my life. She must live on the street.'

However, no one would turn the intruder out, who therefore continued to 'keep the wake' wrapped in a melancholy contemplation of the walls or ceiling.

The sitting-room was dotted with many such people. Some of them had even cried a little. 'I used to see him going to work every morning in the car,' an extremely fat and rounded Negress said to Mrs Lutchman. 'He used to pass my little house as regular as clockwork. And I always used to say to myself, "He looks like a very nice man." As you know, my dear, there are not many men in this world one can say that about. My own Horace – he pass away many years now – was a terror to behold. I'm not afraid to say that even though he dead. God will protect me. But your husband was a different kind of man. You could have tell that just by looking at him. You could ask my daughter Joan if I didn't used to say that every time I see that little Morris Minor pass the house.' She brushed a tear away from her cheek. 'Joan would have come tonight sheself but she does do domestic work in Santa Cruz and she couldn't get away,' the woman added in explanation. Then, throwing her hands into the air, she uttered a brief wail, after which she was silent for the rest of the evening.

'I never seen that woman in my life,' Mrs Lutchman said to Doreen.

Naresh arrived and ignoring Mrs Lutchman sat down next to Urmila. He had brought a bottle of rum. No sooner had he taken his seat than he uncorked it and poured some into an empty coffee cup. Urmila, her nostrils twitching, watched him.

'You don't waste any time, mister.'

Naresh pointed at the coffin with the bottle. 'We used to be bosom pals in we younger days, Ram and me.'

'Is you who teach him all he bad habits then?'

'I can't tell you all the wickedness we used to get up to. Every night as a rule we used to come to Port-of-Spain and have a really good time in all them clubs and things. Ram was a real high liver in those days. He used to like his fun. that man, although he used to like to pretend all that wasn't really for him. He begin getting too big for he boots after a while . . .'

'You don't have to tell me that.'

'I can't tell you how he used to insult me. So, one night, I let him have it good and proper.' Naresh sipped his rum. He began to mellow and a drunker, softer light shone in his eye. 'Still, he wasn't all that bad, when I think about it. I never really had the opportunity to see him all that much after he move to Port-of-Spain and buy this house.' He screwed up his face in mock agony. 'It seem like only yesterday it was his father who was lying there in that coffin and he was sitting here next to me, just like you is now.' Naresh bowed his head. Urmila fidgeted.

'He give Baby a lot of hell in his time,' she said.

Naresh pretended to be surprised and hurt: 'You shouldn't speak of a dead man like that. I not saying he didn't have his faults, mind you. I myself was telling you how he used to like going to them clubs and things. But he can't answer for himself now. Anyway, tell me what you mean.' He brought his head into a suitable position for listening.

Urmila drew her chair further away. 'He had a woman he was supporting. Just like the rest of you men.'

'Not me. Not me. I admit I used to have my fun, but I never support any woman with my money.'

'Not even your wife, eh?'

'Like you don't like me at all.' Naresh laughed.

Urmila looked at him severely. 'I don't know about you, but your friend lying in that box there was no saint. You mean to say you never hear about it?'

Naresh swung his head lazily. 'Well, I did hear one or two

rumours, but you can't believe everything you hear. Who is the woman?'

'Since you don't know nothing about it, I don't see why I should tell you. I don't want anybody to accuse me of spreading gossip.'

Naresh brought his chair closer. 'Whatever you tell me I will treat in the strictest confidence. It wouldn't go further than these two chairs.'

'Well . . .' Urmila edged her chair closer to his.

'In the strictest confidence,' Naresh swung his head.

'She,' Urmila hissed.

'Who? Who?' Naresh's neck tautened and he darted eager glances around the room.

'That woman with the bosom sticking out from she white dress. The one talking to Baby. Some people have no shame at all.'

Naresh whistled and gazed wonderingly at Doreen. 'Tricky little fella,' he said, gazing at the coffin.

'I think she name is Doreen. Doreen! A real street name that is. Don't stare at she like that. They go think we talking about them. I know I shouldn't have tell you. You have no discretion at all.'

Naresh turned away reluctantly. 'You don't say.' He whistled again. 'What you say she name is?'

'Doreen.'

'You really mean to say that Ram and she . . . and here she is talking to he wife as if nothing happen.'

'I do say.'

'A tricky little woman, eh!' Naresh took a large sip of rum and smacked his lips. 'You would think Baby wouldn't let she enter the house. Look at how they talking together. Just as if they is the best of friends.'

Urmila scowled. 'That's because Baby don't have a mind of she own. I sure that Doreen trying to cook up some wickedness with she now, as if taking away she husband wasn't enough. Planning to take away somebody else husband, if you ask me.'

'You don't say.' The possibility seemed to interest Naresh. He looked again at Doreen.

'Look me in the face,' Urmila ordered. Naresh did as he was bid. 'You think I is the kind of person to make joke?'

'No.' And he meant it.

'Good. You just remember that.'

At that moment, the Khojas, together with Bhaskar and Romesh, came into the room. Urmila's face tightened. She smiled sourly at her brother and Mrs Khoja while the Faithful duly pounced and devoured them. When they had disgorged their brother, she got up and delivered a perfunctory kiss on his cheek. Mrs Khoja she ignored.

'I don't understand how some people could bear to suck up like that.'

'What you say?' Naresh inclined his head hopefully.

'Nothing. Nothing.' Urmila drew her chair away from his, this time with an air of finality. Naresh shrugged his shoulders and, leaning back in his chair, poured some more rum into his coffee cup.

Bhaskar, when he had come into the room, had gone straight to the coffin and scanned with dull, lifeless eyes the basin half-filled with water, the rough brown wood of the coffin and the waxen face staring up at him through the glass, as if they were all parts, equally important, of a whole whose significance escaped him. Romesh averted his eyes and seeing Doreen beckoning to him, ran quickly across the room. She opened her arms to receive him. Mr Khoja was standing aimlessly in the centre of the room.

'That's my brother,' Mrs Lutchman said.

Doreen stared at him. 'I would like to meet him.'

Mrs Lutchman went up to him and whispered in his ear. He turned and looked at Doreen, half-smiling.

Mrs Lutchman introduced them.

'Ram has told me so much about you,' she began.

'Wait a moment, Doreen.' Mrs Lutchman called Romesh to her. 'Go on upstairs, young man. You shouldn't be listening to big people talk.'

Romesh shook his head. 'I frighten.'

'What you frighten of?' Mrs Lutchman caressed him.

Romesh pointed at the coffin.

'But he won't hurt you, son. He was your father. He love you.'

Romesh shook his head. 'I frighten.'

'Let him stay with us, Mrs Lutchman.' Doreen tickled his chin.

Mr Khoja frowned. 'He's only playing on our sympathies. I wouldn't expect an Oxford man to be frightened of things like that.' He chuckled. 'He knows well there is nothing to frighten him upstairs.'

'We'll go and talk to Mr Wilkinson, son. He's sitting all by himself over there.'

'You are going to spoil that child, Vimla.'

But Mrs Lutchman, all the same, guided her son across the room to Wilkie, who smiled sadly at them when he saw them coming.

Mr Khoja was piqued. 'Nobody listens to me. They all feel they know better. But mark my words, they're going to regret it one day. That boy especially. You know he nearly broke my toe once out of sheer spite.'

'I don't believe it.' Doreen gazed at Romesh talking to Wilkie.

'It's true. You mustn't let his innocent face fool you. He dropped a hammer on it deliberately. I still have the scar to prove it.'

'It must have been an accident, I'm sure.'

'Accident! You don't know my family, Miss James.'

Doreen giggled. She surveyed the sisters. 'They seem harmless enough to me.'

'You were telling me about Vimla's husband. What was it he "told" you about me?' Mr Khoja smiled from a great distance.

'Lots of fascinating things. At one time I was planning to write a book on Trinidad Indians.'

Mrs Khoja joined them.

'Vimla's husband has been telling this lady lots of "fascinating" things about us, Sumintra.' Mrs Khoja, realizing that her response was all-important, giggled scornfully. 'What did he say that was so "fascinating", Miss James?'

'He used to tell me all about those religious ceremonies you used to have.'

Mr Khoja exchanged glances with his wife. 'I suppose he explained Hinduism to you?' His eyes twinkled merrily.

'Nothing like that,' Doreen replied more guardedly. 'In fact he said only you knew all about that.'

Mr Khoja relaxed. 'That's an exaggeration, Miss James. Typical of the members of my family. I only dabble, you know.' He looked at his wife and laughed. 'It's a complex religion, Miss James. It needs years of study. I have hardly done more than scratch the surface . . .'

Mrs Khoja, recognizing her cue, stepped in. 'That's not true, Govind. You are being modest.'

'Modesty is not honesty, Mr Khoja.' Doreen grinned pleasantly at him.

'I suppose in my own small way I do know a little about it, Miss James. One tries as one must, but one somehow never manages to achieve the Whole Truth.' He gazed wistfully at Doreen. 'But tell me about yourself, Miss James, Apart from the book, what do you do?'

'Well, I'm not writing the book any more. I can't write.'

'Now it's you who are being modest, Miss James.'

'Call it what . . . no, I'm not being modest. It's the truth. What I'm really thinking of doing is teaching. My mother used to be a teacher.'

'You mean you are the daughter of Mrs James who was head of Calvin College?'

Doreen nodded.

'It's a small world. I gave a lecture there on Rousseau once. So you are thinking of teaching! I myself am very much interested in the theory of education. That explains Rousseau.' He laughed.

'I too have some ideas on the subject,' Doreen replied, warming to her theme. 'I've been heavily influenced by Rousseau myself.'

Mr Khoja beamed at her. 'Have you read his Confessions?'

'Of course I have. It's my Bible. Absolutely fascinating.'

'I think we must be kindred spirits, Miss James . . .'

Mrs Khoja yawned. She left them and went into the kichen

to make herself a cup of coffee. When she returned to the sitting-room her husband was deep in conversation with Doreen.

7

The men from the funeral home arrived at noon the following day. A screen was set up around the ice-box and Mr Lutchman was washed and dressed again, this time in his best grey suit, a crisp white shirt and a black tie. The corpse was sprinkled liberally with perfume and a fresh film of powder applied to the face. He wore no shoes, only a new pair of socks. As an added refinement, Mrs Lutchman put a handkerchief sprinkled with her own perfume into the breast pocket of the suit.

The coffin in which Mr Lutchman was to be cremated was simple and unadorned. It was an open box made from cedar wood, superficially polished to a shining brown, with silver-plated handles, the only ornamentation, attached to the sides. The ice-box was taken away and the remaining pieces of ice thrown into the gutter at the front of the house. The new coffin was placed in the centre of the room and the wreaths which had come were laid out along the length of the dead man's body, hiding in a tangle of fern and carnation the carefully wrought dress and the sliver of handkerchief visible above the breast pocket. It served the additional function of hiding the shoeless feet.

From early afternoon, the house filled up with mourners, the women in black, white or mauve dresses, veils draped over their heads, the men in dark suits and hats. The air in the sitting-room had a heavy sweetness, laden with the reek of cheap perfumes and the mingled scents of flowers. Several of the women, digging into their handbags, produced frail Japanese fans, decorated with birds and flowers, which they flapped incessantly in front of faces masked by thick layers of powder. Everyone complained of the stifling heat.

Groups of men had taken refuge outside and stood chatting idly among themselves on the road and pavement, wiping their necks and faces with handkerchiefs. Naresh formed the centre of a group that had reserved the garden at the front of the house to itself. They gazed at the rose-trees, fingering the stalks and petals. One of them had attached a white rose to his lapel.

Mrs Lutchman wandered anxiously in and out of the house, examining with distress the trampled strips of lawn and the crushed petals she saw scattered on the rose-beds.

'Try not to stand on the grass too much,' she pleaded. 'It not good for it to have lots of people walking over it.'

The men moved away. 'I don't know what she making a fuss about,' one of them said. 'Is more weed than grass any-way.' Suppressing their laughter, they withdrew to the pave-ment.

Mrs Lutchman bent down and peered closely at the worn patches of grass. 'They wouldn't do it if it was their garden,' she murmured to herself, gathering the strewn petals, which, without knowing why, she took into the kitchen and placed on a saucer.

Mr Khoja moved briskly about, issuing orders. This, in practice, meant telling the less important people that they were in the way and, to the more important, outlining his plans. 'See that nobody drive in front of the hearse,' he warned the drivers. 'Your time to be out in front there will come soon enough, so don't worry. And another thing. Try and keep close together behind it and don't blow your horn too much. Remember it's not a wedding.'

'You can trust we, Mr Khoja,' the more important people replied, flattered that the great man should take them into his confidence.

'Well, you better go and tell the rest of them what I tell you.'

Thus armed, they made the round of the mourners. 'Drive behind the hearse and don't blow your horn too much. Is a funeral, not a wedding you going to.'

'Who is you to be giving we orders?' the recalcitrant would ask.

'That's what Mr Khoja tell me to say. That's who I is. If you don't like what I tell you, go and argue with Mr Khoja, not me.'

'Okay. Okay. Don't get excited.'

The hearse, sleek and shining, its windows hung with thick, mauve curtains, its darkened interior agleam with polished brass ornamentation, was parked in front of the gate. The driver dozed against the steering wheel. Mr Khoja supervised the arrangement of the surplus wreaths on the roof of the hearse.

'Spread them all over. That's right.' He directed the two men provided by the funeral home, whose immaculate, funereal discretion of the night before had been frayed by his rough treatment and indignation when it was discovered that the ice-box had leaked. He stepped back to study the effect. 'That won't do. I don't know what kind of people they send me. Spread them around. Make it look pretty,' he bellowed at them. One of the men cursed softly. 'What? What's that you saying? I hope to God my ears fooling me.'

'Nothing, sir. I was just complaining about the heat.'

'I hope so for your sake.'

The two men looked at each other and went on arranging the wreaths.

'That's a lot better,' Mr Khoja said. 'That's the kind of service I demand.'

Before the procession could depart, a prayer had to be said over the dead man's body. Ramnarace, the pundit, who had come on a motor-cycle, bustled around the coffin making small clucking sounds, presumably designed to convey his sympathy. In fact, he seemed quite happy. It was a long time since he had been called upon to officiate at so important an event.

Mrs Lutchman and her sons, the sisters and Mr and Mrs Khoja stood in a closed circle around the coffin. Ramnarace thumbed through the books he had brought with him. Finally he put them aside and, clasping his hands together, began to chant over the body. Mrs Lutchman cried silently, letting the tears roll unhindered down her cheeks, and Ramnarace, spurred by her tears, recited his prayer with a rising fervour, having long grown accustomed to eliciting no response at all from his clients on these and other occasions. The sisters, unmoved, gazed sternly at the flower-decked body, now and again directing stern glances at the weeping Mrs Lutchman. Mr Khoja's expression was uncompromisingly businesslike.

At length, Ramnarace finished his chant. He gazed at the corpse, then at Mrs Lutchman, with a satisfied smile.

'Only one more thing left to do,' he said, rubbing his hands. 'Your sons must sprinkle some of this water over the body now,' He handed Bhaskar a brass lotah. 'You just have to sprinkle a few drops, son.' Bhaskar sprinkled the water. 'Now hand it to your brother and let him do the same,' Ramnarace directed.

'No.' Romesh backed away, shaking his head.

'He not going to bite you,' Ramnarace said. 'All you got to do is sprinkle a few drops of this water.' Romesh shook his head, pressing himself into the folds of his mother's dress.

'This boy has been playing the fool since yesterday,' Mr Khoja glared at Romesh. 'Sprinkle the damn water!'

'Don't be so harsh with him, Govind. It's his nerves,' Mrs Khoja reminded her husband gently.

'Nerves! He want a good belt across his tail. That will teach him to have nerves.'

Romesh forced his way through the circle and ran out of the room into the yard. Ramnarace, disconsolate, sprinkled a few more drops over the body. 'It's not really all that important,' he said.

The circle broke, except for Mrs Lutchman, who, leaning over the body, removed one of the wreaths and extracted the handkerchief she had placed in the breast pocket of the suit. She smelled it and after applying a fresh dose of perfume, she folded it back carefully into the pocket and replaced the wreath.

Gowra Ramnath, the same to whose house she had fled so many times during the early days of her marriage, came up and put her arm around her shoulders. 'Don't take it so hard, Baby. Whatever happen does happen for the best.'

Mrs Lutchman was overcome by a fresh wave of tears. 'He wasn't such a bad husband at all, you know. When I think of all them things I used to say about him to you, I doesn't know what to do with myself. He wasn't a bad husband at all.' She blew her nose and fiddled with the wreaths.

'What you used to say was the truth. You have nothing to reproach yourself for, Baby. He should have count himself lucky to have a wife like you.'

'You see Romesh?' Mrs Lutchman asked.

'I was comforting him just now. That boy taking it really hard, you know.'

'I just don't understand that child, Gowra . . .'

'Vimla,' Mr Khoja called impatiently from the door, 'you holding us up.'

Mrs Lutchman and Gowra moved away from the coffin. The two men from the funeral home stepped forward and lifted the coffin off the trestles and balancing it with a gingerly discretion, carried it out of the sitting-room to the waiting hearse. Mrs Lutchman followed close behind them. People began getting into their cars. Mrs Lutchman, Bhaskar and Romesh were to go with the Khojas. The neighbours stared from their windows.

Mr Khoja fretted while the two men settled the coffin in the hearse. 'They going to drop it on the road, you wait and see.' He tapped anxiously on the dashboard. This, so far, had not been one of his better funerals.

'You mustn't be so impatient, Govind. These men know what they doing.'

They did not drop the coffin on the road and eventually the two men swung the door of the hearse shut and all was ready. The coffin was visible through the glass at the top of the door and Mrs Lutchman kept her eyes fixed on the shining brown box covered with wreaths which swayed slightly as the hearse moved hesistantly away from the gate. Some of the neighbours waved.

It was a hot, windless afternoon. The procession went slowly through the half-empty streets of the city, gathering speed on the outskirts. They drove for a short time along the Eastern Main Road before turning off onto the Churchill–Roosevelt highway. On either side were fields of rice and water-cress. The peasants, ankle-deep in water, stopped their work to stare at the procession. To the left, the fields dissolved in the distance into the blue of the Northern Range; and, to the right, into the swamps fed by the Caroni River. The wreaths on the roof of the hearse wilted in the heat and one of them slipped over the side and rolled into the ditch running along the side of the road. It was a bad omen and Mrs Lutchman frowned. Theirs was the first car after the hearse and behind them stretched the long line of cars, their roofs and windscreens glinting in the sunlight.

The procession left the highway, branching off into a rough dirt track. Where the track joined the road, there was a grocery, closed for the afternoon. However, some Negro boys were idling in the shade at the front of the shop. They rose when they saw the hearse and ran, jeering, out onto the track. 'Coolie funeral!' they shouted, and going up to the hearse pressed their faces against the glass to have a better look at the coffin. Some of them jumped onto the bonnets of the following cars reduced to a crawl and banged their fists on the metal. 'Coolie funeral!'

The hearse increased its speed and they were soon left behind, but for their cries of merriment, in the gathering clouds of dust. 'You would think they would have more respect for the dead,' Mrs Lutchman said, noting this second bad omen. She kept her eyes fixed on the coffin which, now that the road was bumpy, lurched unsteadily on its platform. Mr Khoja, biting his lower lip, did not answer her.

The track twisted its way through a plantation of coconut trees. Trunks, grey and pock-marked, and curving at a multitude of angles to each other, knitted a crude tracery against the sky. The sunlight, tumbling through the mop of leaves at the summit of each tree, fell across the track in luminous yellow bands ribbed by purple shadow. Further on, the Caroni glimmered through the trunks, and the trees thinned as the procession wound its way towards the bank. The line of cars lessened. Only the hearse and Mr Khoja were permitted to drive right up to the bank. The rest approached on foot, lost in the billowing clouds of dust.

The river, brown and muddy, flowed slowly. Cleared of vegetation, the banks formed an arena of hard, beaten earth, littered with the cold, burnt-out traces of former pyres, now rectangles of grey and black, sheltered from the wind by the trees.

'That's where we cremated Ma.' Mr Khoja pointed at one of the grey and black rectangles and, walking up to it, knelt down and picked up a handful of the ash which he let run through his fingers. The sisters too came up and stared at it, all alike silent and meditative.

Mr Lutchman's pyre had been built at the edge of the arena. The fresh pine timbers had been stacked in a square, one on top of the other, like a meticulously constructed pile of matchsticks. Ramnarace walked round it. 'Is good wood,' he told Mrs Lutchman. 'Give it enough ghee and whoosh!' Ramnarace swept his arms upwards in imitation of the flames he envisaged.

Mr Khoja, dusting the ash of his mother's pyre from his hands, issued fresh instructions to the men from the funeral home. The coffin was taken from the hearse to the pyre onto which the surplus wreaths were also distributed. Only the silver-plated handles of the coffin were visible through the covering blanket of fern and flowers. The mourners, coated with dust, stood in small groups gazing at the pyre with its crown of coffin and wreaths and Ramnarace and Mr Khoja fussing at its base. Doreen stood a long way off talking to Wilkie.

Ramnarace started to pray. Mrs Lutchman, Bhaskar and Romesh standing beside her, bowed her head on her bosom. The mourners took off their hats. Badwatee crossed herself and counted the beads of her chaplet. The prayer was not a long one. Ramnarace signalled to the men from the funeral home and they brought him the tin of ghee which was to set the pyre alight. He spread it evenly around the base, and when all was to his satisfaction, he lit it.

Wavering spirals of smoke fought their way through the layer of pine. The first flames sparked and spread, flooding over the sides of the pyre. A thickening pall of black smoke rose like a curtain hiding the coffin, only to be dispersed by a sudden gust of wind, revealing once again the wreaths and coffin. The wood crackled and exploded. The flames leapt higher, until the pyre itself was finally engulfed. The currents of hot air rising from it danced and set the trees and stretch of river behind it ashimmer.

The heat was intense and Mrs Lutchman walked down to the brink of the river with her sons. From time to time, she turned her head to look at the flames. Slowly, they lost their earlier force. The pyre sagged and crumbled, jettisoning its charred fragments. Eventually, only the interior glowed. The wreaths and coffin had disappeared, buried and lost in the smouldering pyre. The mourners began to drift back to their cars. Mrs Lutchman studied her reflection in the muddy water.

Mr Khoja approached her, jangling his car-keys. 'Come, Vimla. It's time to go back home now. Don't worry. I'll bring you back tomorrow morning.' Mrs Lutchman allowed herself to be led back to the car. Thin lines of smoke were still rising from the pyre. She turned her head to look at it. 'That will take hours yet to burn itself out,' Mr Khoja said. Mrs Lutchman nodded. Ahead of them, they saw the hearse jolting over the rough track. Mr Khoja started the car and they drove back to the house.

The following morning she returned with him. The ashes were warm and digging with her hands, she managed to collect some of her husband's charred bones which she put in a small silver case. This she brought back to the house and locked away in the cabinet among her precious items of tableware.

After this, for two successive nights she had terrible dreams that woke her up in the middle of the night. She consulted Ramnarace.

'He angry with you,' Ramnarace said. 'He want back he bones. You shouldn't have done a thing like that. The dead is very jealous of what is theirs.'

Mrs Lutchman returned and threw the case into the river. Then she went and stood by the cold rectangle of ash, now indistinguishable from the rest, and weeping, she begged his forgiveness. After this, the nightmares stopped. But, whether this was a good or bad omen, she was unable to tell.

Part Two

Chapter One

1

The sisters considered Mrs Lutchman an unfortunate woman. They saw in her someone much weaker than themselves, who had allowed herself not only to be misused by her husband, but, worse still, had actually formed an affection for him. They prided themselves on their knowledge of the world, their control of those bits of it that affected them, and their strength of will. Affection (of the peculiar kind they considered Mrs Lutchman to have) was a conceit that could only corrupt its victim. Therefore, her husband's death was, from their point of view, salutary. It would open new vistas before his wife and initiate her into the practice of those higher, more realistic forms of selfishness of which they were the past masters. They were ready to welcome her with open arms, charitable to the last. But Mrs Lutchman was to disappoint them. She was saved by her relative youth and, more to the point, her husband had lived too long.

The gradual but inexorable disintegration of the clan had for a long time highlighted in Mrs Lutchman's mind the necessity for independence. There was no longer even the Faithful for her to turn to. They had crumbled away. Darling had crossed the line and joined the ranks of the Rebels. Badwatee had become more and more enmeshed in her heretical religious practices and showed little aptitude or taste for the endless plottings hatched by Urmila. Saraswatee, under the influence of Renouka, had gone off on an eccentric tack all of her own and publicly disavowed any interest in the affairs of the clan. Indrani, of course, was as she always had been, mysterious and unapproachable.

Nevertheless, Mrs Lutchman's idea of independence had little in common with that of the majority of the sisters. It was not her own narrow, personal independence that she desired.

From the very beginning of the break-up of the clan she had unconsciously sought comfort in her own home, among her husband and two sons. To this extent, the sisters were correct: Mrs Lutchman was weaker than they. Her life expressed itself in the service of others. She could not live solely for herself. She had been taught from an early age that as a person she was of no intrinsic importance and that her value, such as it was, would lie in loyalty and obedience. It was a lesson enthusiastically imparted by the elder Mrs Khoja and dutifully learnt by her young ward. There was no going back on it. It was to her own immediate family she had turned when that loyalty and obedience had been deprived of its original object. And there it had found a new attachment. This, above all, was what the Khoja sisters had found so distasteful. It was an area of life they had never really experienced and which, as a result, they held in genuine contempt. Their own family life had been strangled too early on and so they had gone in one step (Saraswatee excluded) from loyalty and obedience to sterile, meaningful rebellion.

But, with her husband dead, the whole of Mrs Lutchman's carefully wrought edifice was thrown into jeopardy. His salary had provided their sole means of support and his small pension was hardly sufficient to live on. Bhaskar was just about old enough to go out to work, but Mrs Lutchman would have nothing to do with Mr Khoja's suggestion that he should do so. She was determined that he should complete his education.

It was generally agreed that Mrs Lutchman was being deliberately awkward, 'too big,' as Urmila had put it, 'for she boots.' Mr Khoja in particular was extremely worried. He feared that he might have to subsidise the Lutchmans for a long time to come. It was an appalling thought, and, with this at the back of his mind, he advised her to sell the house and live, at a nominal rent, with one of the sisters. Urmila, who seemed to have the surest commercial touch among the Khojas (she ran a small grocery which was doing very well), declared her willingness to take the Lutchmans in rent-free, provided Mrs Lutchman helped her in the shop and Bhaskar left school and found himself a job. 'Is high time he get all of this doctor nonsense out of he head,' she said. 'I could find him a job as apprentice to a mechanic any time.'

Mr Khoja agreed, and he spent much time and energy trying to persuade Mrs Lutchman of the soundness of the idea. Nevertheless, so that his motives might be above suspicion, at the same time he gave her one hundred dollars. He had become of late very sensitive to charges of miserliness and he took good care to publicize his generosity. Mrs Lutchman accepted the money, but refused both to sell the house and to allow Bhaskar to leave school.

'But how you think you going to live?' Mr Khoja had demanded angrily. He felt cheated.

'I will think of something. Just give me time,' she replied calmly.

'Don't think I going to dole out money to you all the time, you know.'

'I not asking for anybody's charity. You give me this of your own free will. I didn't ask you for it.'

'You will never get a better offer than the one Urmila make you. This is your last chance to decide. Who put this idea into your head about Bhaskar being a doctor in the first place?'

'Is what his father wanted him to be,' Mrs Lutchman said, 'and what the boy himself set his heart on.'

'But you can't become a doctor just by saying you want to be one. As Urmila was saying, it's a foolish thing to put all these modern ideas in the boy's head.'

'Determination can move mountains. I does say prayers every night for him.'

'Prayers won't get you very far without money,' Mr Khoja said bitterly.

'Determination can move mountains. You yourself tell me that once.'

Mr Khoja nodded slowly. His sayings had a way of rebounding on him. 'What about that money I lend you a long time ago when you wanted to open up that little fruit stall? You haven't paid me back as yet. Prayers didn't get you very far then. You think they going to get you anywhere now?'

'I'll pay you back when I get some money.'

'Where you going to get the money? You going to pay me out of what I just give you?'

'That wouldn't be a sensible thing to do.' Mrs Lutchman spoke without a trace of irony. 'I'll pay you when the time come. I'll say my prayers.'

Mr Khoja began to see what he was up against. He had hoped she would return the money. Unfortunately, he had underestimated her peculiar brand of realism and her tenacity. He noted with unhappy surprise this previously undisclosed aspect of her character.

'So, you definitely make up your mind? You not going to sell the house?'

'No. I got to think of the children.'

'But Vimla . . .'

'Bhaskar still have some important exams to take.'

'Oh, I was forgetting he going to be a doctor. Dr B. Lutchman.' Mr Khoja laughed. 'But Vimla, try and see some sense . . .'

'Where there's a will there's a way.'

Mr Khoja threw his hands up in the air and scowled. It was yet another of his favourite aphorisms turned against him. 'Well, don't blame me when you starving. Don't say I didn't try to help you.' He thought regretfully of the hundred dollars he had wasted. 'Money doesn't grow on trees, Vimla. Remember that.'

'I will think of something. Don't worry.'

The house had become for Mrs Lutchman the most concrete symbol of her independence. If that were to go she would have nothing left. She had identified herself completely with it. The roses, the avocado tree, the camera and developing kit which she had secreted in the wardrobe, all of these things were more to her than merely physical objects. They represented her husband's frailties, that part of him on which, without his knowing it, she had lavished much of her tenderness and affection. If instead of frailty there had been strength, then they would not have mattered so much. They would have become objects like any other for which she had no special use. If the camera had taken good pictures, she would not have worried about it; if the avocado tree had been healthier and borne much fruit, she would not have worried about that. But, it was their very failure in her husband's hands which enhanced their value in her eyes. They embodied his struggles and his weaknesses. In a sense, she had, by making them symbols of his failure, animated them, and hence her determination to guard and preserve them, to frustrate the efforts of those who would have her do otherwise. To sell them would be a betrayal and a dishonour.

She extended this attitude to everything, above all to her two sons. There formed in her mind the conviction that they owed it to their father to become a better type of man than he had been. Her ambitions for them ceased to be merely pleasant dreams. From her husband's ashes, she fashioned a new man to whom she could refer all that she did. This was a necessity: she was not daring enough to act entirely on her own initiative. It was by means such as these, then, that Mrs Lutchman succeeded in creating for herself new reasons for living.

She found a buyer for the Morris Minor. The car had worked well and impinged so little on their lives that she parted from it without much regret. The man to whom she sold it, a mechanic who could not afford the fifty dollars she asked for it, offered her forty dollars and a dog as payment for the remainder. Mrs Lutchman accepted. 'It's a genuine sheep-dog that,' the mechanic assured her. 'I sure it don't have another dog like that in the whole of Trinidad.' Mrs Lutchman believed him and she was very proud of the animal. It had the hallmark of quality: its hair was long, covering its eyes. She named it Rover and boasted about its pedigree to the Khojas.

Mr Khoja was sceptical. 'I wouldn't trust what these people tell you, Vimla. A real sheep-dog wouldn't survive two days in the climate we have here.' Shadow II, plump and porcine, lay panting at his feet. Mr Khoja patted him. 'I have never hidden the fact that my dog here is a thoroughbred mongrel. In fact, I would go so far as to say that I'm proud of it. It's the best kind of dog for this climate. You see how thin his hair is?' Shadow II licked feebly at his hands. With the passing years, he and Blackie had come to resemble each other more and more – except that Shadow II was considered a more valuable relic.

Mrs Khoja protested. 'Govind, you know what you saying is not true. Shadow I had a lot of Alsatian in him. The man we buy it from say that he father used to be a police dog. And they, as you know, is pure Alsatian.' Shadow II stared gratefully up at her.

'What Sumintra saying is true,' Mr Khoja informed Mrs Lutchman. 'But I don't like to advertise the fact. Shadow II's grandfather was a police dog.'

'Well, I still say Rover is a sheep-dog,' Mrs Lutchman insisted. 'You should come and see him. His hair does come down all over his eyes.'

'You ever see a sheep-dog, Vimla?'

'I don't see what that have to do with it.'

Mr Khoja knew better than to pursue the point. 'Have it your way, Vimla,' he replied. 'If I ever have some sheep I'll bring them for Rover to look after.' He and Mrs Khoja both laughed.

'You is a really wicked man, Govind,' Mrs Khoja said admiringly.

Mrs Lutchman, however, returned home unrepentant and Rover, greeting her with a happy bark, begged to be fed.

Nevertheless, neither Rover nor the forty dollars the mechanic had paid her could solve Mrs Lutchman's financial problems. Happily, her commercial instinct came to the rescue. Urmila, despite everything, was her source of inspiration. She had taken in some lodgers and shown not only the feasibility but also the profitability of the undertaking. Indeed, Urmila's commercial instinct had gone well beyond this. She had sold her five acres of land (a group of the sisters, fancying themselves cultivators, had pooled their resources and planted sugar-cane. Unfortunately, the project had been losing money since its inception and was on the verge of collapse) and with the money from this and the rent her lodgers paid, she was planning to expand her grocery.

Mrs Lutchman saw in this not merely sound commonsense, but an additional aesthetic merit which was quite independent of elementary profit and loss considerations. She determined to follow in Urmila's footsteps. Lodgers would do as a start.

She worked out plans to divide the largest room in the house where she and her husband had slept into two and to redecorate it. The grocery or its equivalent would come later. She sold her five acres, which she had left idle (Ram refused to countenance her plans for joining the sisters. For this advice she was subsequently grateful) to the farming group of sisters, and set about preparing for the coming of the lodgers.

A thin partition was built dividing the main bedroom into two; she washed the walls a light pink, put up new curtains and bought two second-hand beds. Lodgers were not hard to find. They were chiefly young men from the country districts who had jobs in Port-of-Spain. Mrs Lutchman prided herself on her motherliness. 'I going to treat you as my own sons,' she announced to them on the first day. 'Not as guests. I want all of you to feel really at home here. You must call me Ma.' The lodgers smiled shyly at her and said nothing.

2

In the midst of all these concerns and her regular round of weddings, funerals and visits to the family, a new and unexpected dimension was suddenly added to Mrs Lutchman's life. New neighbours moved in next door. In itself, there was nothing remarkable about this, since that particular house, for no obvious reason, had always harboured a floating population.

Mrs Lutchman would have taken these latest tenants in her stride, but for one thing: Mrs MacKintosh told fortunes. To be more exact, she read tea-leaves. This had emerged, apparently quite casually, in a shouted conversation through the kitchen window, the week after Mrs MacKintosh had moved in. It is likely that Mrs MacKintosh suspected that Mrs Lutchman would prove a most valuable customer. If so, she was right.

'What you does do here in Trinidad?' Mrs Lutchman asked.

'One thing and another,' Mrs MacKintosh had replied evasively. The two women sized each other up.

'You does work here?'

'In a sense.' Mrs MacKintosh laughed. Mrs Lutchman laughed too, wondering what it was that was so funny. 'Sometimes I do a little tea-leaf reading on the side,' Mrs MacKintosh added. 'Just to amuse myself, you know.' Mrs MacKintosh unbuttoned the long sleeve of her blouse and squinted at her wrist. She seemed to be very interested in what she was doing. Mrs Lutchman watched her.

'You does read tea-leaf, eh? I never meet anybody who could do that before.'

Mrs MacKintosh finished the examination of her wrist and buttoned the sleeve. 'All it needs is a little practice,' she said casually. Mrs Lutchman got the impression that she was losing interest in the conversation.

'What else you does read? Cards? Palms?'

'Occasionally. When I'm in the mood. But I prefer to read the leaves. I find them more reliable.'

'So people does say.' Mrs Lutchman had invented that little phrase on the spur of the moment. She knew nothing about tea-leaf reading. In fact, she had never heard of it until now. 'You must read mine one day. Just for a joke,' she hazarded. Mrs Lutchman laughed and this time she knew why.

'I'm not doing anything this afternoon,' Mrs MacKintosh replied, gazing narrowly at Mrs Lutchman. 'So if you want . . .' She started to unbutton the other sleeve.

'That's a good idea. Come over and see me this afternoon.'

The matter was arranged and that afternoon Mrs Lutchman, not a regular tea-drinker, entertained Mrs MacKintosh to her first cup of tea in the sitting-room. She was, she hoped, laying the foundations of a lasting friendship.

Mrs MacKintosh was in her early fifties and almost bald. She had thin, scattered wisps of greyish-white hair which she attempted to spread evenly over the hairless patches of her scalp, a face deeply wrinkled and furrowed by folds of pale, freckled skin, and a pair of blue eyes which, set in a livelier face, might have been described as penetrating, but in hers assumed a vacant, wandering expression: except on those occasions when, pursuing her quarry, they focused into a hard, narrow stare.

She dressed carelessly, with a deliberate, rough outmodishness calculated to lend stature to her professional pretensions and disarm, by the poverty they hinted at, her more suspecting clients. To protect herself from the ravages of the sun, she wore long, shapeless skirts made from a coarse material, thick, woollen stockings and a pair of boots that covered her ankles. For the same reason, all her blouses had long sleeves. At least twice a day, she examined her wrists to see whether or not the area of brown skin had grown larger or smaller.

Mrs Lutchman lived up to her expectations, and in the months that followed they evolved a profitable working relationship. In return for her predictions, to which Mrs Lutchman had rapidly become addicted, Mrs MacKintosh received two pounds of granulated sugar and a jar of skimmed milk every Friday.

Mrs MacKintosh considered herself a specialist. It was her firm belief, and one Mrs Lutchman had come to share, that tea-leaf reading yielded the most reliable results. She did indeed admit to having a certain measure of respect, though guarded and hedged with reservations, for crystal ball gazing. But this particular skill, which she admitted she regretted not having, had been strangled at the source when she lost her crystal ball. It had proved too expensive to replace. Palm reading and dream interpretation she dismissed as nonsense. Mrs Lutchman swallowed these teachings whole and unconsidered, listening with the rapt attention of a disciple to all that Mrs MacKintosh had to say. From these Friday afternoon sessions she eventually was able to piece together her personal history, and the hardship she found there served only to increase her admiration.

Mrs MacKintosh, it appeared, lived a precarious life. She had been born in the slums of Glasgow and had been deserted by her husband two years after they had been married and left to take care of a polio-stricken son and a daughter. The daughter had subsequently married and emigrated to Australia. Mr MacKintosh had fled to Peru – in some versions it was Ecuador, but the basic idea remained the same – where it was rumoured, mainly by Mrs MacKintosh, that he owned vast coffee plantations. He sent her money occasionally, but it was too erratic a source of income for her to depend on it.

Having as a child shown a remarkable flair for guessing games, she had taken up tea-leaf reading to supplement her income. Then her husband, in a fit of repentance, had paid her passage out to Trinidad where he was working at the time. For some months they lived together reasonably happily, before she discovered that he had in the meantime remarried and had a wife and family in South America. She threatened to go to the police (which, as Mrs Lutchman herself was to find out later on, was a favourite resort of hers), and was only mollified by the payment of a substantial sum of money. They had, of course, separated after that. He had returned to Peru (or Ecuador) and she, with the money he had given her, had bought the house where Mrs Lutchman now found her.

Mrs Lutchman's delicate probings revealed that Mrs MacKintosh was still struggling to make ends meet. Buying the house had used up most of the money and with her husband well out of her clutches and safely ensconced somewhere in South America, her situation was little short of desperate. Mrs Lutchman worried about her friend's plight. She feared, however, transferring her own feelings to Mrs MacKintosh, that if she tried to help, Mrs MacKintosh might misconstrue it as 'charity' and the tea-leaf readings be brought to an abrupt halt. That was a risk she was not prepared to take. She made further delicate soundings. She need not have worried. Mrs MacKintosh regarded all that she received not as 'charity', but simply as what was rightfully due to her. Her misfortunes had killed any scruples she might have had. The world, she felt, owed her a living.

Thus had begun the weekly donations of granulated sugar and when Mrs MacKintosh, elaborating on the theme of her hardship, went on to complain with increasing frequency of her son's chronic ill-health, Mrs Lutchman added to her weekly donation the jar of skimmed milk. Her kindnesses did not end there. She introduced her to the Khojas and then, gradually, to the other members of her family. They fell upon her eagerly, all of them proving as keen as Mrs Lutchman to have their fortunes told. So it was that Mrs MacKintosh had established a circuit of admiring addicts whose homes she visited on different days of the week.

What she was paid by them in return for her services, they kept to themselves. Mrs MacKintosh had, oddly enough, imported a new element of discord into the rivalries of the sisters. She was made, by the very nature of her business, privy to all their secret longings and jealousies and they would, each of them, have liked to have her entirely to themselves. As it was, when they were all together, they acted out the absurd pretence of not ever having met, seen or heard of her, half-suspecting one another of having been told their secrets.

Mrs MacKintosh was, apart from this, a pleasant person to have to consult. Her predictions were sufficiently vague and elastic and, what was even better, they were always optimistic. Her clients were inundated under tides of imminent good fortune. 'I see a lot of money coming to you,' she would say. 'From overseas. You see that dollar sign and that pair of wings?' And her client, peering at the mess of tea-leaves, would make a swift mental summary of those people she knew who lived abroad. If the tea-leaves were really propitious, Mrs MacKintosh would elaborate. 'The person who is sending it has an "a" in their name, or it might be an "e". I can't be sure.' The promised money never arrived. 'Sometimes these things take years to come about,' she would explain, unruffled by the dashed hopes of her clients. Thus, faith in Mrs MacKintosh was preserved.

But this unremitting flow of good fortune was not only confined to promises of untold wealth coming from persons unknown living abroad. Sometimes it concerned itself with things nearer at hand, and as time passed, Mrs Lutchman showed herself more interested in the latter. Chief among these were Bhaskar and Romesh. What was presented to her eyes every day was not enough. She needed supernatural assurance that it was all as it should be, that what on the face of things seemed so unpromising might conceal within itself the seeds of a greater good fortune. She needed Mrs MacKintosh as a necessary intermediary between her sons and herself. Thus, they lost their immediacy, fading ghost-like into the tea-leaves. Her first concern was Bhaskar. Every Friday afternoon she would put the same questions.

'You see anything there about Bhaskar?'

Mrs MacKintosh appeared to consider thoughtfully, turning the cup this way and that. 'There is a lot here about him,' she would reply. 'He's a very bright boy. If I judge rightly he's going to come near the top of his class.'

'He going to come first?'

'Well, I can't be sure about that. The tea-leaves are not very clear. You see how jumbled up they are down there?'

Mrs Lutchman glanced briefly at the cup. 'You think somebody going to cheat him?'

Mrs MacKintosh was glad to oblige. 'I wouldn't say that was impossible, judging by the leaves. There might be some dirty work afoot. Somebody with an "e" in their name doesn't like him very much.'

Mrs Lutchman reviewed those people she knew whose name included an "e". It was a formidable list. 'You don't see any other letter in the cup?' she asked.

'Yes. Come to think of it there is another letter here I didn't see the first time. An "i". Does that help you at all?'

Mrs Lutchman's face broadened into a smile. 'I don't know what I would do without you, Mrs MacKintosh. I feel sure is that Mr Rice who does teach him geography. I always thought that the masters at school didn't like Bhaskar. I just don't understand why they have it in for that boy. That Mr Rice never liked Bhaskar, you know.'

'What did you say his name was?' Too great a precision always worried Mrs MacKintosh.

'Mr Rice.'

Mrs MacKintosh scowled. Her blue eyes wandered vacantly over the room. 'Mr Rice, you say.' She twirled the cup. Adding yet a third vowel would have been unrealistic. She decided to risk it, just this once. 'Yes. I see him here. There's going to be a death in his family soon. Somebody with an "o" in their name.'

Unfortunately, Mrs Lutchman did not know the names of any of Mr Rice's relatives. Still, the news that one of them was going to die was satisfying. She brought her hand down heavily on the table. 'That will serve him right for cheating my son.'

Mrs MacKintosh smiled and went on to tell Mrs Lutchman of the large sums of money that she would soon be receiving from overseas.

3

Bhaskar had never been as handsome as his brother. He was plump and dark, with a boxer's blunted face overspread by a flattened nose. He had none of Romesh's easy charm or urges to violent outbursts of temper and outrageous behaviour. Strangers were invariably surprised to learn they were brothers. They had grown up separate and apart. Romesh had stuck to his childish promise after the stone-throwing incident, although he had not been openly hostile to Bhaskar. But this separateness owed as much to Bhaskar's character as it did to Romesh's stubbornness. Nothing, it seemed, could alter that character. It was dour, plodding and humourless, incapable of reacting to its environment, except negatively and reluctantly. It seemed to have been set once and for all. True, it might change its shape but only at the expense of its own distortion. There was in Bhaskar's world no room for novelty or passion.

He never doubted he was going to be a doctor. Bhaskar accepted that as he accepted everything else and conscientiously did the right subjects at school. He made up for his mediocrity by his application, and his reports were tireless in stressing his good behaviour. Mrs Lutchman bought him a desk and a reading light and, when he was approaching his final examination, a bottle of tonic wine.

Bhaskar worked hard for this examination, studying until midnight and getting up at four o'clock each morning and working until dawn. Mrs Lutchman was pleasantly worried.

'You mustn't work too hard, son. You'll get sick.'

'I have a lot of work to do, Ma,' he would reply, flicking

through the pages of his book and frowning. 'There's a lot of notes I got to make still. This biology exam is always a stiff one.'

'I wouldn't worry so much if I was you, son. With the amount of work you does do and my prayers, you bound to pass.' Her face darkened. 'Unless somebody bribe the examiners and they cheat you. Anyway, Mrs MacKintosh say you going to do well.'

'I don't believe in what Mrs MacKintosh say. With all them things she tell you, we should be millionaires by now.' Bhaskar stared seriously at her.

'That kind of thing does take time, son. Mrs MacKintosh never say it going to happen overnight. It might take years for all you know.'

'Well, it taking a damn long time if you ask me. We go be dead by the time all the thing she say happen.'

'You should have faith,' Mrs Lutchman said.

Yet, all the same, Bhaskar was comforted by these predictions. It spurred him on. He made voluminous notes which he copied word by word from his text-books. There was no picking and choosing with Bhaskar. He copied everything, with the result that his notes were no more than replicas of the text. Romesh had pointed this out one day and Bhaskar had lost his temper. Notebook after notebook he filled in this fashion. In others, he made painstaking diagrams of tadpoles, frogs, lizards. He dissected cockroaches with razor blades, picked flowers from the garden and made neat, exquisite drawings in Indian ink of their petals, sepals, stamens and pistils. His room was filled with rows of bottles containing all his specimens which he had carefully distinguished by differently coloured labels.

His room was a hive of industry. Night after night Mrs Lutchman, relaxing in the sitting-room, would hear him pacing the floor, reciting aloud from his notes which he intended to learn by heart. Sometimes he would come to her and ask her to test him. Mrs Lutchman, the notebook open on her lap, corrected his mistakes gently. 'Is an "and" you should say there, son. Not "but".' And Bhaskar, stamping his foot in annoyance, would begin all over again. He learnt his notes, or rather, his text-books, by heart and Mrs Lutchman boasted about the fact to friends and family. They were impressed. Visitors to the house were taken upstairs to his bedroom and there given a guided tour of his specimens and Bhaskar would give impromptu recitals on, say, the dogfish. The visitors would marvel at his remarkable memory and Mrs Lutchman, standing in the doorway, would observe their reactions with shining eyes. Bhaskar, head bowed, listened to his praises being sung.

Unhappily, he did have one weakness: his English. Bhaskar was not literary and the General Paper, in which he would be called upon to write essays on a variety of subjects, worried him. His spelling, in particular, was bad. It seemed to be a congenital deficiency and even the lists of difficult words he had compiled did not really improve matters. Still, Mrs Lutchman tested him patiently every morning after breakfast, shaking her head sadly at his mistakes and telling him not to worry. Nevertheless, Bhaskar despaired. To remedy the situation he took to reading the essays of Bertrand Russell and Charles Dickens' novels. But even this did not help. Bhaskar comforted his mother and himself with the thought that it was by no means the most important part of the examination.

'What they want,' he told her, 'is people who know all about animals and flowers. They don't want you to write pretty pretty English. And, I tell you something else, Ma. I don't want to sound as if I boasting, but is a fact that nobody else could draw as good as me.'

'I know that, son. You don't have to tell me. Everybody who see what you does draw think you is a really great artist. You have a hand for that.'

Mrs MacKintosh lent her support to this view. 'What the examiners want,' she informed Mrs Lutchman, 'is people who can draw and who know about animals. They don't want people who could write.'

'That is exactly what I thought myself,' Mrs Lutchman replied. 'All this writing business is a lot of nonsense.'

'Mind you,' Mrs MacKintosh cautioned, 'it's always an advantage to know how to write.'

'Bhaskar know enough,' Mrs Lutchman said firmly.

Mrs Lutchman relayed the news to her son.

'What did I tell you, Ma? Mrs MacKintosh come from England so she must know what it is they want and don't want.'

Bhaskar passed the examination, but his results were mediocre. Mrs Lutchman cried, but Bhaskar raged not against the examiners, but against Mrs MacKintosh.

'Is she who mislead we,' he stormed. 'Saying they don't care how you does write and spell. I sure that is what bring me down because all the rest was perfect. I didn't make one mistake in the other papers. Not one mistake. Is that damn Mrs MacKintosh.' Bhaskar stared bitterly at the bottles of specimens ranged about the room.

For once, Mrs Lutchman was inclined to agree that (perhaps) Mrs MacKintosh had made a mistake. 'I just don't understand it. Mrs MacKintosh was so sure that you was going to come out top. I just don't understand it.'

'You should stop giving she all that sugar and skimmed milk. That will teach she a lesson for fooling people like that.'

'She was so sure. I certain there must be some other explanation for what happen. Maybe the examiners make a mistake and confuse you for someone else. I've heard of that kind of thing happening. I'll ask Mrs MacKintosh and see what she have to say about the whole thing.'

Mrs MacKintosh had a great deal to say. 'Somebody cheated him,' she explained. 'Not in England though, but over here. Somebody with an "e" in their name.'

'Is that Mr Rice, not so?'

Mrs MacKintosh was cagey. 'It might be. But I wouldn't jump to that conclusion straight away. Don't you know anybody else with an "e" in their name?' she asked with a hint of desperation.

'I know hundreds of people with an "e" in their name if it come to that. But none of them would want to cheat Bhaskar. No. I know for sure is that Mr Rice behind it.'

'But I thought you said he teaches geography.'

'That have nothing to do with it, Mrs MacKintosh. That man had something against my son right from the beginning.

Don't you worry. He would find ways and means to cheat Bhaskar even if he have to kill himself doing it.'

'But why would he want to cheat Sonny Boy?' Mrs MacKintosh tended to use terms of endearment whenever she suspected she was getting out of her depth.

'That's what I want to ask him. It must be jealousy. He think Bhaskar too bright.'

Mrs MacKintosh twirled the cup, squinting at the tea-leaves. 'Funny that I didn't notice this before,' she said. 'Yes. It's very funny that I should have missed that. Look at that.' She passed the tea-cup to Mrs Lutchman. 'Do you see what I see, Mrs Lutchman?'

Mrs Lutchman strained, but in the end she had to confess herself beaten. 'What is it you see there? Like you find some definite proof that is Mr Rice who cheat Bhaskar?'

'Not exactly. The person name also has a "u" in it. And,' she added hastily, 'I mean their surname not their Christian name.'

'A "u" you say.' Mrs Lutchman was astonished. She grabbed the tea-cup from Mrs MacKintosh. She studied it. 'I don't see any "u" there, Mrs MacKintosh.'

'It's difficult to see,' Mrs MacKintosh admitted. 'Sometimes you need a trained eye to see what's there. Otherwise, of course anybody could do this job.' She laughed. 'No. There are things which only the trained eye can see.'

'A trained eye!' Mrs Lutchman was visibly shaken by the news. She returned the cup, crestfallen. 'I must say I don't see a "u" in there.'

'I would be extremely surprised if you did,' Mrs MacKintosh replied calmly. 'But there can be no doubt about it. There's definitely a "u" in the person's name.'

So, it was not Mr Rice after all. 'Maybe they cheat him in England?'

'Maybe. It certainly is possible.' Mrs MacKintosh was quite ready to deny her previous assertions. The further removed the person, the better.

'This is a case for Govind,' Mrs Lutchman said with sudden decision. 'Only he can handle this now.'

Mrs Lutchman went to see him and outlined her suspicions,

taking care to keep Mrs MacKintosh's name well out of the conversation.

Mr Khoja was reluctant to interfere. 'I don't see why somebody way over in England should want to cheat Bhaskar, Vimla. They don't even know him for a start.'

'You never know.' Mrs Lutchman widened her eyes mysteriously and stared at the reflections in the glass bookcases. 'Anyway, you could write a letter to the board in Cambridge and ask what happen. You have nothing to lose by that.'

'Except my reputation.'

'Eh?'

'Nothing. Nothing.' Mr Khoja laughed apologetically. 'You expect me to do you favours, but you never want to do anything I tell you to do.'

'What you tell me to do that I didn't do?'

'You mean to say you forget already?'

'You mean about going to live with Urmila? You know why I can't do a thing like that.'

'So even after all this business, you still think Bhaskar is going to be a doctor?'

'Yes. The boy set his heart on that.'

'Okay. Okay. Let's not start all that up again. But if I do this for you, you must promise to do something for me in return.'

'What?'

'I'll tell you when the time come. You promise?'

'I promise,' Mrs Lutchman answered recklessly.

Mr Khoja wrote to the Examination Board in Cambridge. Their reply was brusque. No, there had been no mistake. Every year they received hundreds of enquiries of this nature, but they always took the greatest care to see that no mistakes were made. There was, they repeated, no mistake.

This letter rankled and Mr Khoja cursed himself and Mrs Lutchman.

'I don't enjoy being insulted,' he told her. 'My reputation must be mud in Cambridge now.'

Mrs Lutchman ignored him. 'Who sign the letter?' she asked.

'What does that have to do with it?'

'I have my reasons. Tell me who it is sign the letter?'

'Montague. J. T. Montague. You satisfied?'

Mrs Lutchman clapped her hands together. 'That's the man. That's the man.'

'What man?'

Mrs Lutchman collected herself. 'Nothing, nothing,' she said hastily. 'I was thinking about something else.'

'Thanks,' Mr Khoja said, folding the letter away into his pocket.

Thus, the mystery was solved. 'Just imagine,' Mrs Lutchman told Mrs MacKintosh, 'that the Chairman of the Board himself decide to cheat him.'

'Nothing you can do about that,' she said.

Despite his poor results and Mr Khoja's official disapproval, Bhaskar applied to several English universities. Mr Rice was among those who gave him recommendations and Mr Khoja, on being pressed, also provided one. He enjoyed composing it, setting forth his theory of education and quoting Rousseau at length. Only in the last paragraph, and that almost as an afterthought, did he mention Bhaskar by name and exhort the authorities to admit him to their 'hallowed halls of learning'.

Mr Khoja's eloquence got Bhaskar nowhere. All his applications were rejected. Day after day, the identically worded letters rolled in, wishing him luck in his applications to other universities and saying how sorry they were not to have taken him. Mr Khoja took it as a personal rebuff and put it all down to the fact that his name was 'mud' in Cambridge. Bhaskar, as such, hardly concerned him. He was much more involved with the fate of his letter of recommendation and had been entertaining glorious dreams of it being hailed as a document of the first importance.

'I just don't understand it,' Mrs Lutchman said.

'Is all Mrs MacKintosh's fault,' Bhaskar wailed at the receipt of each letter of rejection.

Mrs MacKintosh was unperturbed. 'I didn't say they were going to admit Sonny Boy this year. It might be next year or even the year after that. It's almost impossible to say. It's even possible that he might be admitted to a university in a different country altogether.'

'America?'

'Might be. There's certainly an "i" and an "a" in the leaves. Look for yourself and see. Don't take my word for it.'

Mrs Lutchman looked and saw nothing. 'Yes. I see what you mean. Is as clear as daylight down there in the leaves.'

'You are getting a trained eye.' Mrs MacKintosh smiled serenely at her.

As a result of this, Mrs Lutchman advised Bhaskar to apply to American universities. He did. They flooded him with pamphlets.

'They want him real bad,' Mrs Lutchman told Mrs MacKintosh. 'Real bad. You should see how much books and that kind of thing they does keep sending him.'

'There's certainly an "i" and an "a" in the leaves,' Mrs MacKintosh confirmed.

But, despite the flood of pamphlets and Mrs MacKintosh's unflagging assurances, the American universities rejected him. Once again, the identically worded letters rolled in.

'I just don't understand it,' Mrs Lutchman said. 'I see the "i" and "a" myself. It was as clear as daylight at the bottom of the cup.'

'You should stop giving she all that sugar and skimmed milk,' Bhaskar insisted.

Mrs MacKintosh was, as before, unperturbed. 'Maybe it was Russia he should have applied to. There's certainly an "i" and an "a" there. They've got some very good universities in Russia. Why doesn't Sonny Boy apply to one of them?'

Bhaskar applied to Russia. They sent him back a letter written in Russian and many books detailing the success of collective farming. Bhaskar was plunged in gloom.

Mrs Lutchman too was a trifle surprised by the Russian response to her son's application.

'They acting as if the boy want to study farming,' she complained to Mrs MacKintosh.

'Why doesn't he study farming then?' Mrs MacKintosh suggested.

For the first time, Mrs Lutchman's faith in her guide was shaken. It was then that she heard from Mr Khoja (he had refused to write any more letters of recommendation. 'The way things seem to be going, it looks as if it's going to be a full-time job,' he said) that the Indian Government was offering scholarships. She urged Bhaskar to apply. He was reluctant.

'Don't be stupid, boy. Remember what Mrs MacKintosh say. An "i" and an "a" she say.'

'How come we know is not China or Albania or Argentina?'

'Is not Mrs MacKintosh fault if a lot of countries have an "i" and an "a" in their name, son.'

Bhaskar applied.

'He applying for an Indian scholarship,' she told Mrs MacKintosh.

Mrs MacKintosh reacted to the news instantly. 'It's funny you should say that, Mrs Lutchman, but there's a turban in the leaves today. Look and see for yourself. I was always wondering what that little lump in the middle of the cup was. But I didn't want to raise your hopes unnecessarily.'

Mrs Lutchman peered anxiously at the mess of leaves. At first, she saw nothing. Simply a 'little lump', as Mrs MacKintosh had said, but the more she looked at it, the more convinced was she that what she saw at the bottom of the cup was, in fact, a turban.

Mrs MacKintosh was correct. To Mrs Lutchman's secret surprise, Bhaskar's application was successful.

'You is a genius, Mrs MacKintosh.'

'I could have told you it was India a long time ago,' Mrs MacKintosh confessed. 'But I don't like to say things unless I'm really sure.'

Even Bhaskar was prepared to forgive her. Mrs Lutchman was jubilant.

'You still want me not to give she the sugar and skimmed milk?'

Bhaskar blushed and said nothing.

4

Overjoyed, Mrs Lutchman paid hurried visits to all the members of her family with Bhaskar in tow, to deliver the news. She held a thanksgiving prayer at home over which the peripatetic Ramnarace presided. She bought suitcases and trunks, sheets and pillowcases, shirts and trousers, marked them all carefully with his name in Indian ink (she would not let him do it), and spent several days packing.

Her final task was to take him to the Khojas. Mr Khoja, believing himself instrumental in Bhaskar's success, had gone to the lengths of inviting mother and son to a formal lunch. This was unheard of, but part of the reason was Mrs Khoja's acquisition of a set of 'At Home' cards, then quite unknown in Trinidad. However, before unleashing these on her unsuspecting friends, she had decided to play safe and make a trial run on Mrs Lutchman and Bhaskar.

Mrs Lutchman and Bhaskar went to Woodlands two days before Bhaskar was due to leave. They used the steps at the front of the house. Mrs Khoja greeted them at the door.

'How nice of you to come,' she exclaimed in her most polished accent.

Mrs Lutchman was rather taken aback by this greeting. She did not know that Mrs Khoja was practising a 'new' hospitality taught her by her husband.

'You wasn't expecting we today?' Mrs Lutchman glanced nervously around her.

'Of course we was. I mean, of course we were. Do come in and take off your coat.'

'Coat?' Mrs Lutchman looked at Bhaskar, mystified. 'I don't have a coat, Sumintra.'

'Well,' Mrs Khoja giggled helplessly. 'Do come in anyway and have a seat.'

They went inside, shuffling uncomfortably behind Mrs Khoja, their shoes sinking deep into the carpet. Brass ornaments sparkled everywhere. That too was a new thing. Mr Khoja, sitting in his usual place, was reading a book and taking notes. 'Hello, hello,' he said genially, getting up. 'I'm glad you could make it.' He signalled to his wife.

'Do have a seat,' she giggled. She led Mrs Lutchman across the room to an armchair. Mrs Lutchman sat on the edge of the seat. Bhaskar stood beside her, rubbing his hands together.

'What would you like to drink?' Mrs Khoja asked.

Mrs Lutchman, bewildered, gazed, as was her wont, at the reflections in the bookcases.

'Coca-Cola, water,' Mr Khoja prompted.

'A little water wouldn't be too bad.'

'And you, Bhaskar?' Mr Khoja said kindly.

'Coca-Cola?' He looked hesitantly at his mother.

'Then Coca-Cola it will be,' Mr Khoja said.

Mrs Khoja went into the kitchen and returned with glasses of Coca-Cola and iced water. The Khojas watched them drink. Mrs Lutchman sipped at her water as if it were a precious fluid. Bhaskar, wilting under this unrelenting scrutiny, toyed with his glass of Coca-Cola, turning the glass round and round in his hand. When they had finished drinking, Mr Khoja, as a mark of esteem, talked about his ideas on education and his plans for opening a new school.

'You know Doreen James, don't you, Vimla? I believe she was a friend of your husband at one time. You introduced me to her at your place on the night of the wake. She's a most remarkable woman, you know. How did your husband ever get to know her? It's amazing what they found in common. Still. Our ideas on education are remarkably close. She's a great fan of Rousseau. We talk here sometimes into the early hours of the morning.' Mrs Lutchman raised her eyebrows. 'I must say it's truly refreshing to meet such a person.'

Mrs Lutchman perked up. 'You mean she going to help you out in the running of the school?'

'I haven't worked out my plans as yet. That will take at least another two years or so. But I have her in mind as a sort of supervisor. She's a most remarkable woman. Did you know she was writing a book at one time?'

'Yes. I believe Ram was helping she with it.'

Mr Khoja scowled. 'Yes. So I gathered.'

'I haven't seen she for a long time,' Mrs Lutchman said.

'Not since the cremation, in fact. But I thought she was very nice the few times I meet she.'

Mr Khoja shook his head at his wife, another of his signals. She jumped up from her chair. 'Lunch is served. This way.'

She led them to the dining-room. Mrs Lutchman had never been there before. Most of it was taken up by a long rectangular mahogany table, highly polished, and a chandelier. The food, served by the faithful Blackie, did not quite match the surroundings. It was a simple chicken curry and rice, though Mr Khoja was also provided with a tomato and lettuce salad. He kept his democratic instincts in check. During lunch, Mr Khoja talked some more about his revolutionary ideas on education and ended with a homily on ambition.

'There was this boy I used to know – his name is not important – he was at school just before my time and, you know, Bhaskar, ...' Mr Khoja directed his tomato-tipped fork at Bhaskar, '... his family was so poor they couldn't afford electric light. In fact, at one time he left school for a bit to go and earn some money to keep his mother.' Mrs Lutchman fidgeted and stared down at her plate. Mr Khoja leaned back in his chair and digested the opulence of the dining-room, chiefly the crystal chandelier glittering sumptuously from the ceiling. 'His family was so poor,' he went on, pleased by the effect of his words, 'they couldn't afford electric light. Something you and me take for granted. I mean, not only could they not afford electric light, but they couldn't even afford to have oil-lamps. Not one oil-lamp in the whole house. They used to have to go to bed when it got dark. Imagine that if you can. See how you would feel if you had to go to bed just because it get dark.' Mr Khoja scanned his audience. Mrs Lutchman belched appreciatively and Mrs Khoja opened her mouth wide in disbelief. Mr Khoja dabbed his chin with his napkin – he alone had been given one of these – and sipped delicately at his water, as if it were champagne. Bhaskar stared dumbly at him, his fork poised just above his plate. Mr Khoja put down the glass and wagged his head sadly.

'They didn't have candles?' Mrs Khoja asked, gathering up the bits of rice that had fallen on the table-cloth from Bhaskar's fork, and arranging them in a little heap on the side of his plate.

Mr Khoja snorted. 'Candles? What candles?' He returned to the oil-lamps. 'Not one oil-lamp in the whole house,' he repeated. 'And this boy I'm telling you about – well, he's a grown man now, of course – that boy, do you know what he used to do for light? Guess. You just try and guess.'

Mr Khoja said this so challengingly and with such vehemence, that Mrs Lutchman felt obliged to follow Mrs Khoja and open her mouth wide as well. She leaned forward expectantly.

'I'll tell you, since you can't guess. That boy used to catch fireflies and put them in an old jam-bottle.' Mr Khoja, nodding his head, waved his fork at each of his listeners in turn. He lowered his voice. 'And he would study like that.' Mrs Khoja's jaw sagged, but she did not take her eyes off her husband. 'You don't believe me, eh? you think I'm making all that up? But take my word. He would go straight home from school – walking three miles and back every day without shoes, take note – change his clothes, what clothes he had to change, that is, catch a few fireflies in the yard, put them in the jam-bottle, close the bottle, wap!' – Mr Khoja clapped his hands together at this point – 'and take them inside and begin to study. Today, that man is one of the most successful men in this community, a doctor with a big house and a rich wife to boot. And on top of all that, he is one of the nicest men I know. Generous to a fault and honest as the day is long. You couldn't want a better doctor either.'

Mrs Lutchman breathed freely again, but her look of wonderment did not lessen.

'But didn't the fireflies die being locked up in a bottle like that? They couldn't breathe inside of there, I should think.' Mrs Khoja was impressed but not entirely convinced.

Mr Khoja snorted and speared another slice of tomato with his fork. 'You don't kill fireflies as easy as that, Sumintra. Take my word. They are some of the strongest insects on this island. And anyway, even if they did die, all he had to do was go out in the yard and catch some more, not so?'

Mrs Khoja nodded. 'That's true,' she said, and continued to eat her food.

'That's the kind of boy he was,' Mr Khoja added. 'Never stopped trying. He was prepared to give up being a doctor so he could look after his old mother.' Again he looked at Mrs Lutchman who, avoiding his gaze, stared meditatively up at the chandelier.

After lunch, Mr Khoja pressed a wad of five one-dollar bills into Bhaskar's hands and Mrs Khoja gave him her blessings, advising him to boil his water before drinking. Bhaskar, posing on the front steps, had his photograph taken by Mr Khoja. This picture Mrs Lutchman had framed and hung in her sitting-room, where it was stared at by the lodgers and, for a considerable time, was to remain a constant source of pleasure to her.

5

Bhaskar was to go by ship to England and fly from there to India. The night before he left, Mrs Lutchman sat up a long time with him. She fussed with his passport, made sure that all his clothing was properly marked and stuck labels on the suitcases. Bhaskar watched her do these things in silence.

'Well,' Mrs Lutchman said, when she had pasted on the last label, 'I think we all ready now. You must have a good night's sleep. We have a busy day ahead of we tomorrow.'

Bhaskar yawned.

'You should be more excited than that, boy.' Mrs Lutchman slapped him playfully on the shoulder. 'You have a whole new life beginning for you tomorrow and here you is yawning.' She put her arm round him. 'I still have one more thing to give you. I decided to leave that to the last.' She got up and went into her bedroom, returning with a box wrapped in tissue paper.

'You know what this is?'

Bhaskar shook his head.

'I thought you wouldn't.' She laughed and sat down beside him. 'I was keeping this especially for you.' Her face grew serious and her hands rustled gently across the tissue paper. 'I'm sure it's what your father would have wanted me to do.'

Bhaskar stared at her interestedly. 'What is it?'

Mrs Lutchman unwrapped the tissue and showed him the camera. 'That is yours now. You must take good care of it.' She handed it to him. 'It cost over two hundred dollars new, that camera.'

Bhaskar, after turning it round several times in his hands, rested it on the bed. 'Didn't he buy a developing kit as well?'

'Yes. But I want to keep that here with me. Unless you really want it.'

'No, no, Ma. You keep that. I don't think I'll be developing my own pictures.'

'Come. Let me pack it for you.' Mrs Lutchman took the camera from him and packed it in one of the suitcases, sandwiching it carefully between layers of clothing. 'It should be safe there. Try not to knock it about too much.'

'Don't worry, Ma. I'll take good care of it. But . . .' he gazed anxiously at her, '. . . you sure Romesh wouldn't mind your giving it to me?'

'I don't see why he should. You is the eldest. It must go to you.' She kissed him. 'Sleep well, son, and don't worry about Romesh.'

Bhaskar left at midday the following day. Mr and Mrs Khoja were at the docks to see him off. Mrs Lutchman wept profusely when the ship slipped its moorings.

'What you crying for?' Mr Khoja said. 'Just think, he going to come back home a doctor. Dr B. Lutchman. What you always wanted him to be. You should be laughing, not crying.'

'I know,' she replied. 'But all the same, you know, when you spend years bringing up a child, is not an easy thing for a mother to see him leave she. He going to come back a man . . .' The rest of the sentence was lost in her sobs.

Chapter Two

1

With Bhaskar gone, Mrs Lutchman's thoughts settled on her younger son and what she discovered there distressed her beyond measure. He had inherited all of his father's antipathy to Mr Khoja, but whereas she had been able to laugh at her husband's railings, she suspected that Romesh nurtured an implacable, unreasoning hostility of an altogether different kind. Laughter was unable to conjure it away. It was extremely painful for her to discover a Rebel inside her own camp.

Romesh's passion for the cinema knew virtually no limits. At first, this had amused Mrs Lutchman (though never her husband) and she had talked indulgently of it to friends and family. 'I never in my whole life see a boy who like going to the pictures so much. He does come back home and tell me all what happen in the film. You wouldn't believe this, but one time I even catch him making face in the mirror just like one of them film-star.' She waited for his obsession to die a natural death. But, far from dying, as he grew older his fervour seemed only to intensify and by the time Mrs Lutchman realized what was happening, it was too late. The cinema had taken her son away from her.

He went every day, occasionally to as many as three shows, and his favourite boast was the number of times he had managed to see the same film. 'I see *Back to Bataan* seven times in the last six months,' he would announce to his friends, 'and *Shane* five times. Man, I could spend my whole life just going to see them two pictures.' This was no idle boast. Romesh meant it and even his friends were impressed. It did not take long for his notoriety to spread.

Mrs Lutchman watched him slide away from her, powerless to interfere. It was as if his body had been taken over by the soul of another. She was dimly aware that he went to school with decreasing regularity, spending his days away from the house roaming the streets with his friends, waiting for the cinemas to open their doors. He began to smoke. Mrs Lutchman was not unduly surprised. Romesh's decline showed all the classic symptoms. He, on the other hand, did not attempt to hide the fact; on the contrary, he declared his intention to begin smoking quite openly.

'But you know that's a stupid thing to do, boy. It not good for your health,' she had said.

'My health is my own business,' he replied, flourishing a packet of cigarettes. He took one out and lit it, blowing the smoke inexpertly through his nose. 'And another thing. I is not a boy any more. I is a man now. Try and get that into your head.'

'Watch how you speak to me, Romesh. To me you will always be a boy.'

'Well, then you going to have a lot of surprises coming to you.'

Mrs Lutchman shook her head sadly. 'I don't know who it is you take after, son. Is not me and is certainly not your father.'

'I truly grateful for that.' Romesh laughed.

'Why don't you behave like your brother? You think Bhaskar would ever speak to me as you does speak to me?'

'That is another thing I grateful for.'

'All the same, you is my son and no matter how hard you try, you can't change that fact. And so I still say that smoking going to ruin your health.'

'That's my business.'

'Is my business too. I didn't carry you in my belly for nine months and raise you for you to go and harm yourself.'

Romesh shrugged. 'I didn't ask you to do that.'

'You owe me something, nevertheless. Mind, I not asking you to live your life for my sake. I don't want any of my children to ever have to say I force them to do this or that. Your life is your life. Is you who have to live it, not me. But, all the same, as your mother I still have the right to try and give you good advice. That is my right and you can't take that away from me. You or nobody else could take that away from me.'

'I don't see why. You only trying to soften me up with all

your fancy speeches, but if you expect me to come crying on your shoulder. you go have to wait a damn long time. You mark my words.'

'I tell you already to watch how you speak to me, boy. Keep that sort of language for your friends in the gutter.'

'I is not a boy any more. I is a man now. And I won't have you insulting my friends. You hear that? You just keep telling yourself that and we'll get along fine. Just fine.' Romesh rested his hands on his hips and gazed steadily at his mother.

Mrs Lutchman calmed down. Her normal responses, the only ones she knew, were not appropriate to the situation. She was not equipped to deal with this conglomerate shadow of a hundred Hollywood heroes.

'So, you make up your mind to smoke?' she asked softly.

'I glad you finally realize that.'

'And nothing I can say will make you change your mind?'

'Nothing. I is the sort of man who mean what he say. I is no little piss-n-tail like Bhaskar.'

Mrs Lutchman nodded. 'Okay. I try my best to make you see sense. Is not for me to live your life for you. You go ahead and do what you want. You could murder yourself, for all I care.'

'I don't need your permission.'

Mrs Lutchman studied her son. His eyes shifted away from hers. When they returned, they bore a different expression. She got the impression they were no longer seeing her.

'All right, Romesh. All right.'

And so Romesh smoked and Mrs Lutchman, infinitely adaptable, rapidly accommodated herself to the fact. Eventually, she herself began to buy him his weekly supply. Romesh, whose interpretation of his independence was sufficiently flexible, accepted these weekly gifts without demur.

Without bothering to tell her, Romesh stopped going to school altogether. Mrs Lutchman was not aware of this for a long time, since he continued to leave the house as usual every morning, negligently swinging a tattered pile of text-books. It was not until she received a letter from his headmaster that she realized what was happening. She reproached him gently.

'You never tell me you leave school, son.'

'I didn't think you would be interested.'

'And who put that idea into your head, eh? What you think your father would say if he was alive today?'

Romesh shrugged. 'I wouldn't care what he say even if he was alive. I don't pay attention to cowards.'

Mrs Lutchman, suddenly reaching up, slapped him. 'I wouldn't have you speaking of your father like that, you hear! He is not one of your gutter friends. He was twice the man you will ever be. He had more ambition for you than you have for yourself.'

Romesh rubbed his hand meditatively across his cheek and smiled. 'Make sure that's the last time you do something like that, Ma.'

Mrs Lutchman flinched, her anger subsiding into bewilderment. 'So. You learning fast. You threatening your own mother now. What's the matter with you son? Why don't you give yourself a chance, eh? Is that what you call being a man?' She spoke hesitantly, as if the question were addressed not to him but to herself.

'Just make sure that that is the last time you slap me. That is all I have to say.' Romesh had not ceased to explore the tender spot on his cheek.

'That is all you have to say,' Mrs Lutchman repeated in the same perplexed voice. 'That is all you have to say to your mother after eighteen years.' Her eyes roamed his face in search of some clue that might explain and thereby lessen the pain she felt at that moment. She did not find it. 'What you going to do now, then?' she asked.

'Find a job and move out of this house for a start. I can't stand living under the same roof with those people.' He was referring to the lodgers. 'When I find a job I going to get a little room somewhere where I can be by myself. This place is like a blasted hotel.'

'You would be starving if it wasn't for this "blasted hotel".'

'I prefer to starve than go on living like this. If my father had been more of a man ...'

'Leave him out of this, Romesh. What kind of job you have in mind?'

'How do you expect me to know that already? I'll have to wait and see.'

Romesh took his time. For several weeks he did nothing. He left the house early in the morning and spent the entire day lounging on street corners with his friends, returning home late at night. More often than not he had been drinking and on some nights, presumably incapacitated, he did not come back. Mrs Lutchman asked for no explanations and he offered none. The situation was a not entirely unfamiliar one. Once or twice his friends came to the house and Romesh, taking them up to his bedroom, drank there instead.

Their favourite sport at such times was baiting the lodgers. Shy and retiring, they were ideal victims. Romesh waged a ceaseless war against them. In the mornings, he monopolized the bathroom and did not allow them to read the newspaper; at mealtimes, he glowered at them; and he refused point blank to let them use the sitting-room when he was at home. Fortunately, he was hardly ever there, but all the same, the lodgers were cowed and whenever Romesh was present, locked themselves in their bedrooms. Thus, Mrs Lutchman's protestations of motherliness were deprived of their substance.

Rumour drifted back to her that he and Renouka had become extremely good friends and it was at about this time that Romesh stopped living at home. His friendship with Renouka had been particularly distressing for Mrs Lutchman, drawing her, as it inevitably did, into a fresh whirlpool of scandal.

2

Trouble had been brewing in Saraswatee's household for some considerable time. It was an open secret that Rudranath, her husband, squandered most of his salary in support of a mistress, and, having abandoned his previous modernity, had fallen into the habit of beating his wife and daughter regularly. Curiously, his infidelity was allied with this unexpected outburst of puritanism.

Rudranath had reverted to that very Hindu orthodoxy which he had formerly abhorred and which had kept him away from the Khoja catthas and led him to send his daughter to a fashionable Catholic school in Port-of-Spain. Conversion had been sudden and his mistress was blamed. No one had ever set eyes on her (she was supposed to live in a remote village in the south of the island and to have run through as many as four husbands) but gossip painted a detailed and very lurid picture of her character. One thing, however, was certain. Religion did indeed play a very important part in her life. She was given to seeing visions and hearing voices which ordered her to do peculiar things like bathing naked in the sea at full moon and, as one of the sisters had put it, 'taking away other people husband from them.' Whatever the truth of these stories and whatever her powers real or imagined were, the fact remained that Rudranath had been successfully lured away.

Overnight, he had begun to find fault with everything his wife and daughter did. Their celebrations at Christmas were the first thing to attract his wrath. On Christmas Eve, while Renouka and Saraswatee were entertaining their Christian friends to dinner, Rudranath, who had sat silent all through the meal, had got up quite casually from the table and then with a sudden roar of rage, lifted the tree bodily and dashed it against the wall. Then, one by one, he broke off the branches and flung them through the window. Their Christian guests had fled.

His former admiration for Renouka was replaced by an implacable hatred. She, the apple of his eye, was transformed into the source of all evil, hopelessly corrupted by her Catholic education; and Saraswatee was, in his eyes, her mindless tool. The shortness of his wife's dresses (they fell just below the knee), something which he himself had encouraged, now offended him deeply. The sight of her exposed knees drove him into towering, uncontrollable furies, culminating finally in a rampage through the house when he beat her with a tamarind whip and ripped most of her clothes to pieces. He himself went out the following day and bought yards of material to replace the destroyed dresses. He insisted on designing them himself. The dresses were in pale, sober colours, loosely fitting and, most important, covered her ankles. The terror-stricken Saraswatee accepted the new regime without complaint. A period of relative peace and calm followed this outburst. Then, Rudranath was struck by another happy idea. When his friends visited the house, he had Saraswatee parade before them in her unflattering wardrobe.

'No brassiere for she,' he would say, pointing at her sagging bosom. 'None of that new-fangled modern business for she. Come, Saraswatee, let them feel your breasts and see how strong and healthy they is without a brassiere.'

But his friends baulked at the idea. 'We could see well enough from where we is,' they said.

'Is my devil daughter who used to put all them ideas about fashion into she head. I going to fix she one day too. You wait and see. But you must feel Saraswatee breast before you go.' And Saraswatee, half-dazed, would submit herself to a closer scrutiny by her audience, though none of them would ever dare to touch her breasts.

The news of these unusual fashion parades spread and the number of Rudranath's friends multiplied rapidly. Soon, in order to satisfy the growing demand, these fashion parades became a weekly affair. Their success seemed to inspire Rudranath.

'This is only the beginning,' he declared. 'I have a lot of plans in store for she yet. And Renouka too. I going to cut that devil horns one of these days.'

Their appetites whetted, his audience waited impatiently for the promised developments. Rudranath racked his brains. Till then, strangely enough, he had forgotten, or probably stopped noticing, that his wife used thin applications of rouge, lipstick and perfumes. It was left to a 'friend' to discover this inconsistency.

'But I notice that Saraswatee does still smell sweet,' the friend objected.

The audience murmured appreciatively.

'All that lipstick and rouge don't go with the rest,' the friend added.

'You know something?' Rudranath replied, 'You damn right. I going to fix that.'

Rudranath was as good as his word.

'Who do you think you is?' he shrieked at her. 'Who you trying to smell sweet for?'

'Leave she alone, Pa. Don't you think you humiliate she enough already? What you want to do? Drive she mad?'

'I going to fix you soon too, Renouka. I going to cut your horns off and make you parade naked in front of all them men, so they could know what the devil does look like under all them skirt and petticoat and brassiere you does be wearing.' Rudranath laughed. 'That will show you how to play modern with me. Is you who put all these devilish ideas in your mother head.'

'I think you gone mad, Pa. You should go and see a doctor. Maybe is overwork causing you to behave like this and shame we in front of all them people you does bring here.'

Renouka's position in the matter had been ambiguous until now, despite her father's threats. She had inherited his independent spirit, taken his rebellion against the Khojas at its face value, and it was difficult for her to accept this abrupt reversal. His insanity had deprived her of an essential support and seemed to make nonsense of her efforts to escape from the attendant disorder and chaos following hard upon the death of the elder Mrs Khoja. Above all, she had wanted to abstract herself completely from the affairs of the Khojas, to pretend they had never existed.

She had encouraged her mother to be 'independent', to wear her dresses short, to eat beef and pork (Saraswatee had refused to go so far), and to ignore the endless squabbling over the inheritance. Whether rightly or wrongly, Renouka felt that what was happening now was intimately connected with all that she had strived to efface from her mind. She was back where she started. The wheel had turned full circle. Her father's modernity had fed itself on the backwardness of the Khojas, a sign of weakness and not strength. The momentum was bound to fail. Try as she would, even her own rebellion had had as its centre the old Khoja system. Pathetically cherishing her illusions of modernity and independence, she too had continued to orbit about that old world, even after it had ceased to live. Renouka, betrayed by her father and betrayed by herself, gave way to despair.

Rudranath bore down on her, his eyes flashing. 'What you saying to me, girl? Let me hear you say that again, you little devil.'

Renouka dodged her father. 'I say you mad. Mad! Mad! You hear that?' She wanted to weep, but the tears would not come.

Rudranath, head lowered, made a rush at her. Renouka, too agile, jumped aside.

'I going to make you repeat what you just say, you little devil. I going to screw it out of your mouth for you.' Her father dashed past her into the kitchen. He returned, brandishing a large knife, which he was drying on his shirt.

Mother and daughter screamed, scrambling for protection against each other.

'Rud, Rud,' Saraswatee implored. 'I will do anything you want me to do. Look!' She scrubbed vigorously at her lips and cheeks. The lipstick spread in a red smear down her chin.

Rudranath, brushing his hair back with quick, abrupt movements, chortled. 'So, you two little devils frightened of me now, eh!' He felt the edge of the blade. 'Is a sharp little fella I got here. And I going to cut your neck with it just as if you was a chicken. It going to have a lot of blood here today.' The image appeared to please him. He rested the knife against his throat and moved it slowly back and forth. Mother and daughter screamed again, backing away towards the front door and verandah. 'That's right. You run away from me like a chicken and I go catch and feather you like a chicken.' He made plucking movements with his fingers. Rudranath laughed.

Never taking their eyes off him, Renouka and her mother continued their retreat towards the door. Rudranath lumbered heavily in their wake, his eyes darting from one to the other. Then he lunged forward and grabbed the collar of his wife's dress and pulled her roughly towards him. Saraswatee uttered a low howl and clutched at her throat as she saw the knife rising to meet her. Rudranath spun nimbly and catching hold of her arm, flung her back into the room. She fetched up against the kitchen door and crumpled in a heap on the floor, burying her head in the folds of her billowing skirt. 'Is not you I want. Is she. Is she.'

Renouka, mesmerized, had stopped dead in the centre of the room, her eyes fixed on her mother and her mouth hanging open. 'Is not you I want,' Rudranath repeated hoarsely. 'Is this little devil here with the short skirt and red lipstick.' He leaped at her. Renouka, recovering herself, cried out at the top of her voice and, turning sharply, ran through the sitting room out to the verandah. A passer-by stared curiously at her and continued on his way. 'Come back here, you devil in disguise, and let me cut your horns off for you. I going to do for you today. I didn't want a devil for a daughter. Don't think you going to get away from me so easy. I too smart for you.' He chased her down the steps, brandishing the knife above his head. Renouka, choking on her screams, her hair flying behind her, ran through the yard out into the road. Several people had come out from their houses to watch the chase. The road here was a narrow dirt track, deeply rutted and dotted with pools of water. Renouka stumbled in one of the ruts and fell. She kicked off her shoes and gathering up her skirts, crawled panic-stricken through the mud.

Her father, laughing joyfully, was almost upon her, before a group of the spectators, sensing the very real danger, flung themselves at him and threw him to the ground. One of them took the knife and tossed it into the ditch, choked with weeds, running along the side of the track. Rudranath, his arms flailing helplessly, stormed and cursed and begged them to release him so that he could cut her neck 'just like a chicken'. Renouka, seeing her father pinioned, picked herself up and started to run, before she stumbled and fell a second time. This time, she made no attempt to raise herself, but lay there in the pool of water, her dress soaked and mud-stained and clinging to her body.

The villagers were not unduly disturbed by what had happened and the police were not called. They were accustomed to such family disturbances. It was not unusual for someone to go berserk and they knew that at any time it could be one or the other of them whose turn it would be to run amok, perhaps armed with a gun and not a kitchen knife.

Renouka was carried back to the house, but Rudranath, surrounded by a circle of villagers, was not allowed to return until he had calmed down. Renouka did not stay long in the house. She packed a few clothes into a suitcase and prepared to leave. Saraswatee looked on silently.

'Why don't you come with me, Ma? We could find a little room somewhere in Port-of-Spain and I could get a job.'

'You want him to murder me, Renouka? He go come looking for we. And anyway, what would be the point in my going with you? He need somebody to look after him.' Saraswatee spoke without conviction.

'He don't need anybody to look after him. He have he woman, not so?'

'He go murder me if I do that, Renouka. I'll stay with him for a little while longer and we'll see what happen then. Who knows? He might decide to go and live with she for good. I'll come and stay with you then.' Saraswatee was not endowed with that high sense of duty which Mrs Lutchman had possessed to the greatest degree. Despite the feelings of guilt that welled up in her, she was, all the same, sorely tempted to go with her daughter and the only thing that really prevented her was the fear that Rudranath might come to murder her.

Renouka left shortly after, making her way through the yards of the neighbouring houses.

This incident formed the climax of Rudranath's puritanical mania. As a final gesture, he had indeed thrown Saraswatee's cosmetics out of the window, but it was an action lacking in fervour and genuine enthusiasm. The weekly fashion parades stopped and when some of his 'friends' still insisted on turning up, he refused to let them enter the house. About Renouka's departure, he had not a word to say.

Rudranath gave himself up to lethargy and indifference. Nothing seemed to interest him, not even his mistress. She dropped out of his life as mysteriously and as silently as she had first come into it. He performed his daily motions with a mechanical rigidity, that gradually infected his gait, his dress, his facial expression and finally his speech. One morning he refused to leave his bed. His face was heavy and waxen. He lay stretched under the blankets, taut and pallid, gazing bleakly at his wife bent low over him. Rudranath was unable to move his legs or utter a single word. The following day, he was admitted to the Colonial Hospital. They could do nothing for him and a week later he was transferred to the St Ann's Mental Hospital – the Madhouse, as it was more popularly known. Saraswatee, making full use of her unlooked for emancipation, raised the hems of her dresses.

3

Renouka was an enterprising girl. For a few days she stayed with her friend Sona (whose sari she had been so unsuccessful in tying) and her husband. Sona was already a mother of two and expecting her third child. She had grown fat and ugly. It was an unhappy reunion. Their friendship had not fully recovered from the blow dealt it by Mrs Khoja and during the time Renouka stayed there, there were further unpleasant references to it. Matters were complicated by the fact that her husband was not faithful to her. The boy who had stared sadly at his naked feet on the day of his wedding had blossomed into a playboy, and Sona was jealous of Renouka. Her husband was assiduous in pursuit of their guest and Renouka was less discouraging than she might have been. Therefore, it was with grateful relief that they parted company after Renouka had found a job as a receptionist to an Import–Export Company and moved into a room of her own in one of those boarding-houses that infested the area near the Queen's Park Savannah.

Staying in the same house was a commercial traveller, a copper-skinned Negro who toured the country areas in a van and tried to sell refrigerators and other, as he was pleased to describe them, 'luxury household appliances.' He was one of those people so imbued with the spirit of their profession, that the infection spreads to their everyday discourse. The commercial traveller spoke in the language of advertisements. He claimed to know the strengths and weaknesses of his customers 'inside out' and, judging by the success he had in selling them his goods, goods they did not need, this was more than an empty boast.

His van was garishly decorated with advertisements for his wares. These were interspersed with pictures of Negro and Indian women in bikinis, holding transistor radios. For the commercial traveller was a keen student of politics and he felt that the decoration of his van, apart from boosting sales, encouraged nationalist sentiment and was a positive contribution to racial harmony. This may have been no more than a rationalization of an unbridled passion for ornamentation of all kinds, since his room, in many respects, resembled his van. The walls were covered with the pendants of scores of American universities, pictures of naked and half-naked women (white this time) cut from magazines, advertising posters, and the costumes he had worn at successive carnivals.

In this frenetic atmosphere, Renouka sat and listened to his tales of coups, double-dealings, and his analysis of the political situation in the areas he visited. 'Those people only understand one kind of language,' he told her. 'Rum. Just wave a bottle of rum in they face and they go come running to vote for you, just like flies. Is as simple that.' He was, by the same token, a stern critic of Mr Khoja. 'That man is a bloody fool,' he said. 'Going around the place and talking about Rousseau and the noble savage. He don't know the first thing about politics. If Rousseau was a rum drinker, I would understand.'

He was excited to discover that Renouka was a niece of Mr Khoja and endeavoured to water down his previous criticisms. She dissuaded him and instead regaled him with lists, invented and true, of the injustices and crimes he had committed. The commercial traveller was fascinated and flattered to be let into the 'secrets' of the Khoja family. During this time Renouka had allowed herself to be ruled by the frenzy that had been threatening to overwhelm her ever since her father had gone mad. Unable to weep, it was with a kind of delicious, mocking self-hatred that night after night she unburdened herself to this astonished and ingratiating stranger who, having misunderstood, now overrated that he had come to consider his 'good fortune'. He tried his best to look shocked and serious and concerned. He believed that as a result of these nightly confessions Renouka was uniquely tied to him. As he said to his admiring friends, 'I have she under my thumb.'

In this heady atmosphere, their acquaintanceship grew and came to fruition. Among his friends, the word went abroad that the commercial traveller was in love, that he had at last, after years of fruitless philandering, found a woman of dog-like devotion, who appreciated his talents and with whom he could see 'eye to eye' on every topic.

'You must remember who she is,' he would tell them. 'She is no ordinary Indian batee from the country, you know. She is the niece of Govind Khoja himself, a girl with family and money behind she. Man, you should hear the scandal she does tell me. I know everything it have to know the Khojas. What I know, can't be licked and can't be beat.'

Contrary to the impression conversations like these might create, the commercial traveller was not primarily interested in Renouka's alleged fortune. What he savoured was the fact that she was an Indian girl ('and no ordinary BATEE either') and a relation, however minor, of a large and important family. He had stormed a barrier he always believed to be impregnable and his friends treated him as they would an adventurer who had explored hitherto unknown lands.

They questioned him closely, chiefly about her sexual abilities.

'Fine, fine,' the commercial traveller would reply guardedly, smiling shyly. 'But I can't tell you everything we does do together. I mean, you wouldn't really expect a man like me to betray all the trust she put in me, eh?'

His friends clearly expected him to, and the commercial traveller, after his initial reticence whose real import had fooled no one, obliged. He gave them detailed minute by minute descriptions of their meetings. They listened, absorbed and intrigued. In the end, all that remained of Renouka in their mind's eye were the visions of a naked brown body tutored in all the arts of love.

Renouka did not contradict these stories. She went about quite openly with the commercial traveller, occasionally accompanying him on his trips into the countryside.

'She does be jealous about what I does do when I not with she. She like a real tigress when it come to love. She want me to spend all my time with she. Is as if she can't breathe when I not with she.' His friends were awe-struck at the ascendancy he commanded over this girl. His voice acquired a special liquid, sensual quality when he pronounced 'she'. He never referred to her by name. 'She' implied all that he intended, an unerring indication of dependence and total sexual possession. The commercial traveller had never been so happy.

Romesh was a regular visitor. Renouka had met him one day in the Queen's Park Savannah and brought him back to her lodgings. The commercial traveller was very much to his taste and Romesh lent his whole-hearted support to his affair with Renouka. The commercial traveller was delighted. Then, his jealousy was aroused. He saw that Renouka had fallen on Romesh with the same zeal with which she had fallen on him, and indeed appeared to prefer him. Romesh's temper matched hers and he introduced her to the delights of the rum bottle. He did not resist Renouka's advances. The commercial traveller stood aside, disgusted, envious and indignant.

'Cousins,' he would exclaim. 'You is cousins.'

'So what?' Renouka would reply. 'You have nothing to complain about. You does still have your fun.'

'Anyway, what wrong with the three of we living together?' Romesh asked. 'We is all good friends around here. Share and share alike.'

'But you is cousins. Cousins!'

Yet, despite his very real indignation, the commercial traveller could not bring himself to break with Renouka. Her body had gradually imposed its own tyranny, and he realized the fragility of his 'influence' over her. Renouka was little more than a bird of passage and the threat of departure increased the pleasure she gave him. Consequently, he believed he was in love and, not wishing to take any unnecessary risks, the three of them settled down to a disputed peace.

'Too much talk and joke does lead to you know what,' Romesh would say to Renouka. It was their favourite joke and the commercial traveller could never understand.

4

The family fell on the scandal with relish. Mrs Khoja, in particular, was incensed to the point of unreason. 'I don't blame Romesh all that much,' she said. 'He was always a nervous boy and I feel sure is Renouka who put him up to that. Let God kill me on the spot, if I didn't always say that girl would come to no good and now we all know for a fact that she is a whore. I could have tell you she was going to turn out like that when she was only a baby. They should have hang she right there and then. I myself would have help knot the rope. So help me God, if I had the chance I would do it now. I would hang she until she dead as a stone. Remember that day she went and cut she hair without asking for Saraswatee permission? They shouldn't have beat she then. They should have hang she.' Thus Mrs Khoja and more in the same vein.

At the beginning, Saraswatee received a measure of sympathy. A liaison with a Negro was something on which the Khojas could all agree. A liaison with a cousin left them delightedly aghast. For a short while, it was almost like old times. They shook their heads at each other and said, 'We was right to make them eat separate. Think of how much more thing like that would have happen if we didn't put we foot down.'

'To me,' Urmila replied, 'it look as if we didn't put we foot down hard enough.'

Having to this extent justified themselves, the sisters were happy, and Saraswatee was even mildly fêted. But, it was not long before Saraswatee forfeited this sympathy. Far from disapproving of her daughter, she seemed to condone her behaviour. She visited the culprits in their lodgings near the Queen's Park Savannah and, what was much worse, taking advantage of her husband's absence, allowed Renouka and the commercial traveller to stay in her house. The credit, including even that which had automatically accrued to her from Rudranath's illness, she squandered by her recklessness. It was replaced by tirades against her shamelessness and the frequently expressed hope, piously formulated, that Rudranath might never recover and live on to be a burden to her for the rest of her life. This, the sisters unanimously agreed, was the only punishment appropriate to the magnitude of her sins. Mrs Khoja suggested that mother and daughter be hanged together from the same tree. Mrs Lutchman was silently appalled and she alone took no part in the recriminations levelled against Saraswatee.

Attention, however, soon shifted from these scandalous proceedings, and the malice of the Rebels found fresh food on which to feed itself; for it was at this juncture that Mr Khoja decided to put himself up for election to the Legislative Council.

Chapter Three

1

It had taken Mr Khoja many years to decide that the time was 'ripe' enough to 'carry his ideas to the people'. Being well ahead of the times, as he had confided to his disciples, he was afraid of the ignorant misunderstanding his doctrines and dismissing him as a fool. In the event, it turned out that his doctrines hardly mattered. The people came not to be taught but to see and to laugh, since, from the very start of the campaign, it was his personal reputation, not his revolutionary theory of education, that he was forced to defend.

What had influenced him to come forward now were considerations not entirely political in nature. Indeed, Mr Khoja's political ambitions had been, at heart, purely speculative, an idle preoccupation to which his status as head of the clan entitled him. It formed an essential part of what he liked to call his 'charisma', not meant to be tested in action, but designed to function in a carefully controlled environment: among family, friends and disciples. Anything going beyond these was liable to miscalculation, open to the threat of failure in which the symmetry of his world would be destroyed.

He realized that even at the end of those many years of 'waiting' the people were no more ready for his ideas than they had been at the beginning. He never expected they would be. However, what weighed much more heavily with Mr Khoja was the situation in the family, and it was this, ultimately, that determined him to cast aside his caution, emerge from the safety of the darkened sitting-room and plunge into the world of flesh and blood politics.

His loss of status as the universally recognized head of the clan rankled. It had meant nearly everything to him, supporting as it did the mass of his pretensions. He relished the ritual it entailed and the automatic respect it brought him. Mr Khoja had led, within his theologically formalized world, a centripetal existence, in which people and events gravitated towards and came to rest round about him, as to their natural God-given centre. He had been, in all that transpired in that cosy, self-contained world, the Unmoved Mover. And Mr Khoja was, first and foremost, a child of habit, accustomed and adapted to move in those channels, rigid and predetermined, carved out for him by circumstances. Deprived of his authority at the head of the family, he was like a fish out of water, breathing the noxious air of rebellion and insult. Unhappily, in the years since his mother's death, this is exactly what had happened. Thus, since he was to be debarred henceforth from playing the guru to his own family, he would be guru to the people at large. The purveyor of an incomprehensible doctrine on education could not be challenged or called to account: the masses could only listen, be mystified and obey. So, at any rate, Mr Khoja believed.

Refusing to join any of the already established political parties, Mr Khoja did the next best thing. He formed his own. It was called the People's Socialist Movement. To a large extent, the party existed only in Mr Khoja's mind, despite the elaborate constitution he had worked out for it. Apart from his own theories on education, set out at length in a pamphlet written by himself, the party had little to say about other social issues. 'Education is at the root of all our troubles,' he wrote in his preamble and steadfastly refused to discuss anything else. However, the lack of a comprehensive programme was merely part of the trouble (and not a very important part either, since the rival parties had little to say about anything). More serious was the shortage of funds and consequently candidates. Mr Khoja refused to donate more than a thousand dollars. 'I'm no fool,' he told his wife, 'to go and throw away thousands of dollars just like that.' All the persuasions of the disciples were in vain. 'Collect from the people,' Mr Khoja advised them. 'The People's Socialist Party' (Mr Khoja tended to forget the name of his party) 'is a party of the people, for the people, by the people. What do you think the word "Socialist" means? It is up to the people to support us and provide the funds we need. Back to the people!'

This, in fact, was all that emerged from the disciples' pleading: the slogan 'Back to the People!' was officially adopted by the P.S.M. at a congress held at the house in Woodlands. Eventually, the people rallied to the cause in the guise of Mr Cardoso who had grown extremely rich on the cocoa trade. But even this was only just enough to save the party from bankruptcy. In the end, the People's Socialist Movement could only afford to sponsor three candidates, Mr Khoja himself and two of the leading disciples.

The main threat to the existence of the party came, apart from its rivals who did not regard it with any seriousness, from the clique of Rebel sisters headed by Urmila. No sooner had they heard of its formation than they immediately started to campaign, quite openly, for Jagdev, the candidate of the People's Democratic Movement. This was tantamount to an official declaration of war. To date, the dissensions within the clan had been allowed to simmer just below the surface. The proprieties, however reluctantly, had been observed, and although rumours of a rift were not lacking, they had been deprived of substance.

Now, it had been made public property, the meat of common gossip, and the line of battle was, for the first time, clearly and unambiguously drawn. Rumours about the inheritance spread, and Indrani was once again made the focus of indignation. Delegation after delegation of the Rebels went to visit her at her house in the country and returned with harrowing tales of her poverty, her physical decrepitude and the state of permanent embitteredness in which she now lived as a result of her brother's ('She own brother!') greed and hard-heartedness. Mrs MacKintosh, who had been giving comfort indiscriminately to both sides, was having a field day.

2

Some weeks before the election, Mr Khoja summoned Mrs Lutchman to the house in Woodlands. The gate was locked and bolted. Mrs Lutchman jangled the bell and waited. The grimy feet of the mechanic who lived next door, protruded from under the hulk of a battered car. Mrs Khoja came slowly down the front steps to meet her, smoothing down her oiled hair which shone in the bright sunlight. She had grown fatter recently and the first wrinkles had appeared on her forehead. The conflict was taking its toll on her too. Mrs Lutchman watched her, her eyes devoid of their accustomed lustre.

Shadow II growled miserably at his mistress's heels. Mrs Khoja opened the gate and stepped out on to the pavement. Shielding her eyes from the sun, she looked slowly up and down the street, as if to make sure no enemy spy were lurking in the vicinity, waiting for an opportunity like this to break into the house. Mrs Lutchman squeezed past Shadow II and went inside and Mrs Khoja, satisfied that there were no suspicious persons hanging about, shut and bolted the gate with the same jailer-like cautiousness.

'You can't take enough care these days,' she said, leading Mrs Lutchman through the door on the ground floor. 'You know they even writing letters to Govind saying that they going to shoot him before the election.'

'Who writing them?' Mrs Lutchman asked in a mechanical tone of voice. She stared at the table-tennis board, up-ended against one of the pillars. It was coated with a thick layer of dust.

Mrs Khoja shrugged her shoulders. 'I don't think that too difficult to guess, Baby. Even if they didn't write it themselves, I sure it was they behind it.' She spoke softly, pronouncing 'they' with a slight hiss. 'You wouldn't believe,' she went on, 'the kinds of thing they saying about Govind. I mean it does even embarass me to talk about some of the things they does keep saying about we. In one of the letters they even say they going to poison the dog. Imagine that. As if Shadow II could do them anything.'

Mrs Lutchman glanced at Shadow II who was panting labouredly in their wake. She said nothing.

Blackie was sitting on the steps of the 'servant's room' fanning herself with a newspaper. Shadow II, barking weakly, left them and, staggering across the yard to her, collapsed panting at her feet. Mrs Lutchman and Mrs Khoja climbed the shuddering flight of steps, past the shuttered, 'temporary' kitchen, and entered the silence of the inner sanctum with its familiar odour of Huntley and Palmer biscuits. A poster was nailed to the kitchen door. There was a photograph of an unsmiling, austere Mr Khoja. Above the photograph it said simply, 'Vote for G. Khoja' and below it was printed the slogan of the People's Socialist Movement, 'Back to the People!'

'You like it?' Mrs Khoja asked.

Mrs Lutchman was disappointed. She would have preferred something more flamboyant. On the other hand, Mr Khoja thought that its simplicity indicated a profound integrity. 'It real nice,' she replied. 'Is a good photo they take of him.'

'Govind just working on one of his speeches. I'll go and see if he ready to see you.' Mrs Khoja left her and went into the sitting-room.

Mrs Lutchman could hear them whispering together, but she could not catch the words. She walked over to the window. Blackie was stroking Shadow II and cooing softly into his ear, which kept flapping up and down in swift, jerky movements. Lines of washing screened the neighbouring houses. The yard next door was littered with discarded iron-mongery, chiefly motor-car fenders and batteries. A radio, incising the stillness, played loudly.

'You could come in now, Baby.' Mrs Khoja pushed her head through the curtain and beckoned her inside.

Mr Khoja, sunk in his favourite chair, was surrounded by piles of books and scattered papers. A tall reading lamp, the only light in the room – the windows were closed and the curtains drawn – fenced in the chair within a circle of yellow light. A book with many pages lay open on his lap. He had taken off his glasses and, eyes closed, thrown his head back against the chair. Mrs Lutchman felt her way carefully between the pieces of massive furniture, accustoming herself to the gloom. She noticed a new acquisition, a piano, thrust smugly in a corner of the room. There was a sheet of music on the lid. Mrs Khoja, following closely behind her giggled softly.

'I learning to play the piano. A man does come to teach me twice a week.'

'I was wondering who was the musician. It hard to learn?'

'He think I have a talent for it. The other day he was saying that soon I go be have to teaching him.'

'You never know what you will turn out to be good at,' Mrs Lutchman said seriously. 'Life is a funny business.'

Mr Khoja had not yet acknowledged her presence. He had remained in the same position, his eyes still shut and apparently asleep.

'I thought I hear him talking to you just now,' Mrs Lutchman said.

Mrs Khoja gazed at her reproachfully. 'All this business taking a lot out of him,' she murmured. 'He does fall asleep just like that.' Mrs Khoja snapped her fingers. 'Every meeting he hold they does come by the busload just to heckle and give him a hard time. That Jagdev don't have a conscience at all. He does pay them to do that.'

Mrs Lutchman clucked mournfully. 'That man should have been in jail years now,' she said.

'To tell you the truth, Baby, I sorry he ever enter this election business in the first place.' She sighed. 'But if you is a man like Govind and you got a social conscience, you got to go through with it, whether people like it or not.' The phrase, 'a social conscience', she had picked up from her husband and Mrs Lutchman, who had never heard of such a thing before, agreed.

'You could see it on his face,' she said. 'Look at how thin his cheeks getting and he losing his hair too. Look at that bald patch he getting right in the middle of he head. I remember when he was a child he used to have thick, thick hair, just like I have now. You must feed him up good, Sumintra. Give him a lot of milk and tonic wine. Build him up. That will work wonders with him. Or, if he don't like that, you could always try a little bush tea.'

Mr Khoja shifted restlessly on the chair and half-opened his eyes, as if he were emerging from a deep slumber. His gaze swept over the glass-fronted bookcases before coming to rest, tiredly, on the mess of books and papers scattered round his chair. He rubbed his eyes, blinking into the outer darkness.

'Rousseau, Rousseau,' he murmured, glancing at the book on his lap.

Mrs Lutchman fidgeted, waiting for him to acknowledge her presence. She coughed. Mrs Khoja put a finger to her lips. 'Ssh.'

'Ah, Vimla. You are here.' Rousing himself, Mr Khoja sat up, pretending he had only just seen her. 'Sorry to keep you waiting. I was having a little nap. I keep falling asleep these days. You been here long?' His eyes strove to convey innocence.

'Only a few minutes.'

'Rousseau is giving me a great deal of trouble,' he confided.

'Who?' Mrs Lutchman came closer and squinted at the book.

'A French philosopher. Or *philosophe*, if you prefer that. A remarkable man. I believe I have mentioned him to you before.' Mr Khoja's tone seemed to imply he was talking about a personal acquaintance. 'If he were alive today he would have been one of the founder members of the People's Socialist Congress.'

'People's Socialist Movement,' Mrs Khoja corrected him gently.

Mr Khoja shrugged his shoulders. 'He might even have been Chairman,' he went on, unperturbed. 'I would gladly have stepped down to make room for the Genevan.'

Mrs Lutchman said nothing. She was amazed by this display of generosity. 'If only Ram could hear him now,' she thought to herself.

Mr Khoja closed the book, marking his place with a pencil. He laughed. 'I don't know why I'm worrying and tiring myself over all this for. The people don't care to listen to my message and anyway, certain parties, whose names I needn't mention, are sure to see to it that I lose this election. No matter how many thousands of votes I get. The vested interests are scared stiff of what I would do.'

'You shouldn't speak like that, Govind. Don't let the vested interests get you down. You are doing what you have to do. What God, as you yourself was telling me, intended you to do here on this earth. Is not everybody who have to bear the burden of a social conscience like you.' Mrs Khoja smiled radiantly at her husband.

'It's never easy for a man like you,' Mrs Lutchman added. She was tempted to weave a 'social conscience' into her words of praise, but suspecting that it might not be prudent, she dismissed the idea. Instead, she said, 'And I know for sure you not going to lose the election anyway.'

'And who tell you that, Vimla?' Mr Khoja had a pretty shrewd idea of the source of Mrs Lutchman's confidence. Nevertheless, he was interested. It was possible that she might have other reasons, for instance a dream, for saying what she had said Mr Khoja shared with his family a furtive belief in omens of all kinds. In his case, it was used to strengthen his conviction of divine appointment.

Mrs Lutchman evaded the question. 'Nobody tell me that. I feel it in my bones you going to win.'

'Govind always doubting his own abilities,' Mrs Khoja said. 'It's the worst habit he have. Modesty will be his undoing one of these days.'

Mr Khoja leaned back in his chair. He enjoyed hearing himself discussed in this way. It was from the sum total of impressions such as these (that is, the reflection of himself in the opinions of other adoring people) that he was able to piece together an idea of what he was or, more accurately, what he imagined himself to be. They formed the basis of his self-esteem and, therefore, needed constantly to be replenished; more so than ever in these latter days. He listened to the two women talk, his eyes closed and his clasped palms sheathing his nose. Mrs Lutchman reiterated her belief that he was going to win the election 'hands down' and Mrs Khoja, in between these effusions, elaborated on the theme of her husband's virtues. Eventually, Mr Khoja was moved to make a small protest.

'I feel sure that it's that old woman – what's her name? Oh yes, I remember now, Mrs MacIntyre . . .'

'MacKintosh,' Mrs Khoja corrected him.

Mr Khoja glanced sourly at his wife. 'Ah, yes. Mrs MacKintosh. I feel sure, Vimla, that it's your friend Mrs MacKintosh who put all those ideas into your head.' He grinned at Mrs Lutchman.

The suggestion embarassed her sufficiently for her to lie. 'Mrs MacKintosh have nothing at all to do with this,' she replied. 'I don't see her all that often anyway and I don't think that she even know you running in the election.'

The Khojas, of course, were not unacquainted with Mrs MacKintosh. She visited them, as Mrs Lutchman knew, on Wednesdays when Mr Khoja invariably had his teacup read, though like Mrs Lutchman, 'only as a joke'.

Still, the capacity for self-deception among the Khojas being what it was, both parties quickly persuaded themselves that there were no contradictions in what had been said.

'Yes, I suppose you are right,' Mr Khoja said. 'If she didn't know I was running in the election, she couldn't have told you that.'

'Exactly,' Mrs Lutchman nodded.

'Exactly,' Mrs Khoja echoed.

The atmosphere lightened considerably after this and they resumed their discussion of the election.

'Sumintra was telling me that they writing letters threatening to kill you before the election.'

Mr Khoja smiled. 'That's all they good for. I know lots of people – I could name them for you if I want except that I don't go in for smear politics – who would be really pleased if they could get rid of me. Assassinate me.'

There was a moment's silence while his two listeners savoured and explored the melodramatic possibilities of the situation. Assassination. They toyed with the vision of a crazed gunman and Mr Khoja, in a pool of blood, lying prostrate at his feet.

'Just like Gandhi,' Mrs Khoja said.

'That's just what I wanted to say, Sumintra. They have it in for him just like they had it in for the Mahatma. No difference at all.' Mrs Lutchman gazed grief-stricken at Mr Khoja.

'But some people don't need guns to kill a man,' Mrs Khoja continued. 'They could do it with they tongue alone. You hear the latest thing they saying about Govind?'

'Sumintra, Baby have her own worries to think about.' Mr Khoja tried to restrain his wife from elaborating. It was not often that he showed such concern for others.

'Let me talk, Govind. She bound to hear it sooner or later and she may as well hear it from we first. That will show you have nothing to hide.' She turned to Mrs Lutchman. 'They saying he have another woman. Imagine. A man like Govind. You know the woman yourself.'

Mrs Lutchman stared at her open-mouthed. 'Don't tell me that . . .'

'Exactly. You hit the nail on the head. They saying Miss James is his woman. You should hear how Urmila running she mouth all over the place and the kind of lies she telling about how they planning to run away . . .'

'That's enough, Sumintra!' Mr Khoja shouted at her. 'Vimla is not interested in hearing about all that rubbish. I wish that was all I had to contend with.' He turned to Mrs Lutchman. 'That's why I ask you to come and see me today. You remember the promise you make me?'

'What promise?' Mrs Lutchman was dazed by what she had just heard, though even she was aware (without having to formulate it in so many words) that Mr Khoja was too innocent to concoct such an escapade. He had neither the aptitude nor the imagination for it.

'You mean to say you forget already?'

'No. No. I was thinking of something else.' Images of an assassinated Mr Khoja alternated in her mind with the less credible image of an unfaithful Mr Khoja. She dismissed the latter thought and looked at him attentively.

'You are always thinking of something else when I speak to you. You don't have to do what I ask. Say no if you want to. I'm accustomed by now to that kind of treatment from my family. But what with Romesh and Renouka . . . .' The Khojas, husband and wife, gazed accusingly at her.

'What it is you want me to do for you?' Her voice was pained. 'You know that I not like the rest of them. I'll go and do what you want me to do without thinking twice.'

'I don't want you to say later on that I force you, that I went and make you do something against your will. Say no if you want to.' Mr Khoja polished his glasses.

'You know I not like the rest of them,' Mrs Lutchman repeated.

'It's something I would do myself if I had the time. But all these speeches . . .' His hands fluttered over the sheets of paper covered with his large, ornate scrawl. 'I want you to go and see Indrani for me,' he said at last, 'and find out if she's really been saying all those things about me. About Miss James I can't do anything. If people stupid enough to believe that, well ... but Indrani is different. I know we didn't get on when we were children together, but I'll be surprised if she really holds a grudge against me.' Mr Khoja spoke with an increasing lack of conviction. 'Certainly not to that extent,' he added as an afterthought. 'After all, it was I who give her that extra five acres of land. You would expect her to be grateful for that.'

'I sure she grateful for what you give she,' Mrs Lutchman said.

'I wouldn't bet on that, Baby.' Mrs Khoja stared grimly at her. Her eyes had not lost their earlier hint of accusation.

'I want you to explain to her that I don't hold anything against her. I'm prepared to forgive and forget. Also, you could tell her it would be nice if she could come here and spend a few days with us. She could stay in the back room.' A look of commiseration stole over his face. 'She must get very lonely in the country living out there all by herself. And for another thing,' he continued off-handedly, 'If she decide to spend a few days here with us, it would put a stop to all that gossip floating about the place.'

It was impossible to resist. Mrs Lutchman consented to act as go-between and two days later, bearing gifts with her (an old sari which Mrs Khoja had discarded and some chipped glasses and cups which she had also discarded) she made the pilgrimage to the decaying house in the country.

3

For several years now, in fact since the death of the elder Mrs Khoja, Indrani had not stirred from the house in the country. She attended neither weddings nor funerals, visited no one and went out of her way to discourage visits from any of her relatives. Eventually, it had come to be accepted that Indrani was the true heir of the Khoja mystique, the fated receptacle and keeper of all that mass of antique Khoja hagiography a lore, thus receiving from afar the ghostly obeisances of the clan.

The more sentimental might make the journey to the old house in the hope of refreshing themselves. But this was a futile longing, a mirage that could only end in distress and disappointment. For Indrani, in her self-imposed exile, had become a symbol not of vitality, but of death and decay. The pilgrim was glad to leave and immerse himself once again in the struggles and dissensions tearing apart the body of the clan. Nevertheless, Indrani's detachment did serve a useful purpose. She was the empty vessel into which the Rebels could pour all their jealousies and discontents. What she felt about this, no one either knew or cared.

Indrani had taken her passivity to the extreme limits. Her conversation was, for the most part, minimal. She would stare wide-eyed and dispassionate at her uncomfortable visitor, listening to all that he might have to say and yet displaying not a flicker of interest. Now and again she would twirl one of her bracelets languidly around her wrist or, perhaps, smooth the folds of her dress. Her eyes, however, never strayed from the face of the speaker and seemed to follow, with minutest attention, the agitated movements of his features.

She had let the house crumble about her. The woodwork had rotted away in many places, and when it rained heavily, the roof leaked. Several of the windows on the upper floor had been broken and not repaired and the floorboards creaked and moved underfoot. Neglect showed itself everywhere. The corrugated iron fence leaned at a crazy angle and some of the sheets had given away completely. The yard to the back of the house had been virtually abandoned. There was a thick carpet of tangled weed and, in season, the pervasive stench of the uncollected, rotting mangoes that had fallen from the two mango trees, allegedly planted by the elder Mr Khoja. The mangoes were eaten with reverence during the lifetime of the elder Khojas. Now, however, they were allowed to rot, though with a hardly diminished reverence. The children from the neighbourhood invaded and took what they could. This roused Indrani to a pitch of fury and she would chase them away, flailing out wildly with a broomstick and vowing vengeance on their families. Another relic of old times was the large copper basin used for collecting rainwater. This was rusted over and gradually decomposing. There was a shallow pool of fetid water at the bottom in which the mosquitoes hatched their eggs. A cloud of them hovered perpetually about the basin, the 'copper' as it used to be called, skimming swiftly in a whirring mass across the stagnant pool.

Yet, amid the general air of dilapidation, Indrani maintained, in those parts of the house she inhabited, a scrupulous though arid cleanliness. It was a closed world, in which all that was meant to happen had already happened. Everything had long ago been assigned its place and there was no room now for change or improvement. To do so would have been a desecration. An inexorable decay was the sole law Indrani recognized. It was the ultimate passivity to which she had surrendered and Indrani, living at the heart of it, had no need for the company or the solace provided by the living.

She did, however, perform one curiously positive act during these years of incarceration. At some point, she had taken under her wing an ageing Indian peasant, a decrepit old man of about seventy, whom everyone called Sadhu. What his real name was, no one knew. He was not of the district and his connection with Indrani remained an unresolved mystery.

Certainly, her motive for this adoption was not philanthropic; at any rate, Sadhu's style of life belied such a suggestion. He lived in a tiny cubby-hole (formerly a broom cupboard) on the ground floor. Here, he slept on a collection of rags which Indrani had made up for him as a mattress. On the floor next to his bed were the scattered instruments of his existence. Chief among these was a flour bag, its red emblem faded into indecipherability and tied at the top with a bit of string. He used it as a pillow. Like everything else about Sadhu, what this bag contained was a mystery. He never opened it. It was assumed to be filled with his clothes, but Sadhu always wore the same ragged dhoti and torn vest grey with age, so that it was impossible to be really sure. Indrani had provided him with a condensed milk tin which he used as a cup and a battered enamel plate. These items composed the sum total of his furniture.

Sadhu did next to no work. Occasionally, he swept and cleaned the kitchen, but this was a spasmodic gesture of usefulness which he seemed to feel incumbent upon him. Most of his time he spent wandering through the house (he was not allowed upstairs), his hands tucked into the waist of his dhoti, or sitting crouched in the shadow of the fence at the front of the house, endlessly chewing and gazing with dull, bleary eyes at the passing cars.

Although Indrani cooked for him, they took their meals separately, he crouched in his cubby hole, she in her bedroom upstairs. They hardly ever uttered a single word to each other. At dusk, Sadhu retired to his cubby-hole for the night, where he lit a candle and lay awake for a long time on his bedding of rags, smoking a long, thin-stemmed pipe and staring up at the ceiling.

4

Sadhu greeted Mrs Lutchman with a crooked, indecisive grin, cowering further back into the shadow of the fence. Members of the family always frightened him and most of them took advantage of the fact. Mrs Lutchman, however, waved pleassantly at him.

'Eh Sadhu!'

Sadhu grinned.

'Taking a little fresh air I see, old man. Indrani home?'

Sadhu nodded, relieved to know that the encounter was going to be a harmless one. 'Inside,' he croaked, pointing a withered brown arm at the house.

Mrs Lutchman thanked him. 'Take care of yourself then, old man.' She pushed open the gate, which had almost entirely detached itself from its hinges, and walked slowly into the yard. On either side it was walled in by taller buildings which, in the afternoon, threw deep dark shadows. A luxuriant vine had spread a rich jungle of leaves and twisted stems up the side of one of the houses. The yard, as a result, was cool and shady, with a pleasant smell of vegetation.

Mrs Lutchman paused at the doorway. 'Anybody home?' She listened for an answer, her voice echoing hollowly among the rafters. There was no reply. She went inside, gazing with interest around her. The pounded earth floor had been recently sprinkled and swept and she could still see the marks left by the broom. The air here was dry and musty. She explored further and peeped into the kitchen, the door of which swung idly open. That too, like the rest of this part of the house, seemed to have fallen into disuse. A row of navy blue enamel cups with white rims hung from nails knocked into the wooden wall above the stove. The pots and pans were lined neatly along the shelves of an open cupboard. She went up and unhooked one of the enamel cups and put it to her lips. She shook her head, smiled, and replaced it on its hook.

Leaving the kitchen and feeling more and more of a fugitive, she walked through the rest of the house to the back yard. She could go no further because of the bush. A cloud of mosquitoes dipped and dived over the rusting copper basin. 'Shame, shame,' she said, retracing her steps, her mind alive with images of other days.

She paused for a moment outside the door to what used to be called the threshing room. On an impulse, she pushed it open and went inside. The rice mill was still there, though the fan belt had long since frayed and broken. Even now, there was a faint, lingering odour of rice. It was very dark, despite the open door. She sighed and went out, closing the door softly behind her. She called again.

'Anybody home?'

This time there was an answer. 'Who is that calling?' The voice, dry and dusty as the house itself, seemed to come from very far away.

'It's Baby, Indrani.'

Indrani was silent for a time. Mrs Lutchman waited. At length, the answer came. 'I upstairs. In Ma old room.' She sounded weary, resigned to this latest in a series of intrusions.

Mrs Lutchman climbed the flight of wooden steps. Its relative solidity surprised her after all she had just seen. Indrani was having her afternoon rest. Her head was swathed in a white bandage, rather like the ones the elder Mrs Khoja used to wear for her 'headaches'. She lay flat on her back, her arms stretched taut and and lying parallel to her body.

When Mrs Lutchman came into the room, she raised her head an inch or so off the pillow, and signalled impatiently she should close the door behind her; this though she was already in the process of swinging it shut. The room, at the end of a long gallery skirting the east-facing side of the house, was the largest in the house. It overlooked the yard at the back and had a view, across the neighbouring roof-tops, of sugar-cane fields.

The windows were fitted with tiny squares of coloured glass, red, green, blue and yellow, which Mrs Khoja had had fitted when her eyesight had first begun to fail her, in order, so she had said, to rest her eyes. The result was a murky gloom of indeterminate colour, except when the sun shone directly into the room. Then, there was a kaleidoscopic patchwork on the walls and ceiling. Now, however, with the door closed and the sun shining elsewhere, the murky gloom prevailed.

The centre of the room was occupied by a big brass bedstead, companion to the one Mr Khoja had been given, though less glittering and ornate than his. Its only decoration was a simple fringe of pink tassels round the top and a bulging roof of blue satin drained of its sheen. The brass had not been polished for a long time and in some places was already turning green.

The bed echoed the bleached, lustreless appearance that characterized the room as a whole: the unvarnished wood, gone grey with age, of the floor and walls, the thin, cream-coloured strips of lace curtain, the frayed rug at the side of the bed. Framed pictures decorated the walls. There was a sepia photograph of the elder Khojas, taken in a studio against a background of sailing ships in full sail; another of their son as a child with long, plaited hair; drawings of Indian gods and goddesses; and hidden in one of the darker corners, an unframed likeness of the Virgin Mary, the sole, surviving souvenir of the elder Mrs Khoja's eclecticism.

Indrani sank back on the pillows, her face almost invisible in the gloom.

'Like you have a headache, Indrani?' Mrs Lutchman peered through the gloom at her.

'It's my eyes. They giving me a lot of trouble these days.

The light does hurt them real bad sometimes.' Her voice crept through the darkness, frail and aimless, directed as much at the four walls as at her visitor.

'You should take some aspirin. I find they does work wonders in no time at all.' The efficacy of Mrs Lutchman's remedies (and she had a remedy for everything) never varied. They all worked 'wonders'.

'I don't like swallowing tablet. They does choke me.'

'I remember Ma used to have the same complaint,' Mrs Lutchman sympathized. 'Maybe what you need is a good purge. I find that does work wonders when everything else fail me.'

'I had enough purge when I was a child,' Indrani said tiredly.

The Khojas were noted for their purges. The elder Mrs Khoja had made it one of her rituals, and insisted that her children and dependants be purged at least once a month. The penalty for omission was a beating. There were exemptions however – for her son and herself.

Indrani, wriggling gingerly, sat up and reached for a jug of water that lay on a table beside the bed. It was too far away. Her arms went limp and flopped on her lap. 'You want to pour me out some water, Baby?' Indrani flailed her arms helplessly and collapsed back into the pillows.

Mrs Lutchman poured and handed her a glass of water. 'Here. Don't tire yourself.'

Indrani took a minute sip and returned the glass. 'The heat does parch my throat out dry like a husk. Thank you.' She dried her lips with the sleeve of her dress. This was yet another of her mother's complaints that Indrani seemed to have inherited. Mrs Lutchman drank the rest of the water herself and refilled the glass. 'Reach for that box under the bed for me, please, Baby.' Indrani indicated a spot near the head of the bed. Mrs Lutchman lifted the edge of the counterpane and drew out from under the bed the box of medicines, Indrani's constant, inseparable companion. She offered to open it for her. A lock, a recent refinement, had been attached to the lid.

'No. No. I'll do it. Is a difficult lock to open. Only I know how it does open.' Indrani's voice was suddenly stronger, more authoritative. Mrs Lutchman handed over the box obediently. Indrani felt in her bosom for the key and with a steady hand opened the lock and replaced the key in her bosom. 'This is a really tricky lock,' she repeated. 'I make Sadhu buy it just because of that.' The medicines were stacked as neatly as they had always been. She took out from among them some sweets wrapped in brown cellophane. She popped one of them into her mouth and began sucking on it gently. Very carefully, she arranged the bag of sweets in the box and clicked the lock into place with the same steady hand. However, immediately she had completed this operation, Indrani relapsed into her former weakened condition. She extended a shaking arm towards Mrs Lutchman and begged her, in a wavering voice, to put the box back where she had found it.

'What's that you sucking?' Mrs Lutchman asked.

'Cough drop. They very soothing for the throat.' Indrani sucked contentedly at her sweet.

Mrs Lutchman was disappointed. She had expected it to be something more exotic. She felt that cough drops lacked the grandeur of either bush-tea or aspirins. 'Sumintra give me some things to give you,' she said, after a while. 'It's just a sari and some cup and glass.' Mrs Lutchman showed her the parcels. Indrani's mouth drooped. She glanced dully at the parcels and rested them on the bed. 'You want me to open them for you?'

Indrani, absorbed in sucking her sweet, did not answer. Instead, her eyes wandered vacantly over the room, displaying the aimlessness of the blind. Mrs Lutchman, discomfited, approached the bed. 'Govind was asking after you the other day,' she began. Indrani's eyes focused. She stared intently at Mrs Lutchman, but still she said nothing. 'He wanted me to ask you ...' Mrs Lutchman stumbled in her search for the right words. Indrani rolled the sweet from one side of her mouth to the other. Mrs Lutchman listened to it knocking against her teeth. 'You must have hear,' she started afresh, looking around her in confusion, 'all this talk and gossip that been going round the place about Govind.' Indrani nodded. 'Urmila and the rest of them ...'

'Urmila come to see me the other day,' Indrani interrupted,

her voice muffled by the sweet. 'She was telling me that Govind take up with some woman or the other.'

'That's another of they lies,' Mrs Lutchman replied passionately, abandoning her previous hesitation. She sat down on the edge of the bed.

Indrani gazed at her calmly. 'Well, with all that going on these days – don't think I haven't hear about Romesh and Renouka and all that side of the business. I does hear everything that happen – is not easy to tell who lying and who telling the truth. You all as bad as one another. Just imagine Renouka going about the place with that nigger! What do you think Ma and Pa would have say if they was alive today?' Her sweet having been sufficiently ground down, she crunched on it.

'I not trying to excuse my son,' Mrs Lutchman said softly. 'Nothing could excuse what he doing. But is Govind I come to talk about. You know he would never do a thing like that. I know the woman myself. I meet she hundreds of times. She and Govind planning a school together. That's all. That is why they does see each other so much. All the rest you hear from Urmila and Shantee is lies. Lies! Govind would never do a thing like that. He have higher things to think about.'

'I don't know about having higher things to think about,' Indrani said, 'but I must say, all the same, that what Urmila and Shantee tell me really surprise me. I myself can't see Govind doing a thing like that. But, as I was saying, with all that happening these days, you never know who to believe or not to believe.' Indrani spoke with relish, fully aware of her power.

'Well it not true,' Mrs Lutchman said hotly. 'I know for a fact is not true.'

'How you know that?'

'I just got to look beyond my nose to know it not true.'

'But Urmila and Shantee swear to me it was true. After all, it was they who tell me about Renouka and that nigger. They didn't lie about that.' Indrani smiled sanctimoniously into the gloom.

'Well it not true. I know for a fact Govind would never do a thing like that. He not that sort of person. He's a deep philosopher. People like him don't run away from they wives.' Indeed, the more Mrs Lutchman thought about it, the more fantastic the accusation seemed to her. She began to understand the type of man he was. It had put him in perspective. No. Govind would never be capable of doing a thing like that. His talents lay elsewhere. She was comforted by these reflections and said, 'But is not all that nonsense I come to talk to you about.'

'The last time Urmila come here she wanted me to sign some paper or the other,' Indrani went on in an undertone, as if she were speaking to herself.

'Paper?' Mrs Lutchman was alarmed. 'What kind of paper she wanted you to sign?'

'Something about the land and jewels I believe it was.' Indrani spoke carelessly, smoothing the folds of the sheet. 'She want me to testify in court.'

Mrs Lutchman gazed at her in astonishment. 'Court! And you sign the paper?'

Indrani threw her hands up in the air. 'Me sign any paper? I is an old, sick woman. I don't have much longer in this world. Sometimes I does feel as if my spirit travelling already. So what I have to do with court and that kind of thing? You tell me. I can't tell you how week after week somebody does come here to harass me. I is an old woman. A sick woman. And yet not a week does pass without one of you coming down here to disturb my peace. For a long time I keep myself quiet and listen to what the rest of you have to say. Listen till I give myself a headache. Take what happen last week, for instance, when Urmila come to see me. I didn't say a word. Not one word. You could ask Sadhu. He was there at the time. I just sit there in the kitchen and listen. It was after that I take to my bed. But now I going to speak my mind and you could tell everybody what I say. I don't want to have nothing to do with who get what and who didn't get what. That was Ma business and Ma business alone. What she do with the land and jewels is no concern of mine. The way things going I does feel it would have been better for she to throw everything in the sea.'

'That's exactly what I does say myself,' Mrs Lutchman said.

'Let me finish speak. You could say what you want after I

done.' Indrani held up her hands for silence. She paused and took several deep breaths. Then, adjusting the pillows around her, she sat up. 'I going to tell you one more thing and you could tell it to Govind since he send you here as his messenger.'

'Nobody send me here as they messenger,' Mrs Lutchman protested. 'I make up my own mind to come.'

'Let me speak. You could say all what you have to say when I finish.' Indrani held up her hand as before. 'I don't care which person messenger you is. That is your business. But what I want you to tell Govind when you see him is this. You could tell him I don't want any of that land he give me. If you must know, it not good for anything. The soil hardly rich enough to grow a blade of grass. What Ma herself choose to give me I happy with. That is mine and when I dead all of that is going to be his. I don't have any children to pass it on to and, anyway, he is the eldest. But I never ask for his land. If he want, he could take it all back tomorrow. Don't forget to tell him that for me. Urmila and the rest of you could do and say what you want. You could drag the Khoja name through the mud as much as you want. The whole set of you behaving as if you without name, pride or ambition. I glad Ma and Pa dead so they didn't have to live through all of this. But Ma know about it. And Pa too. Don't think that just because they gone to another world they don't know what happening in this one. They does speak to me in my dreams about it sometimes. Last night they come crying to me and shaking they head. "Indrani! Indrani! What these people, we own flesh and blood, doing to we name? What they doing to we name?" That is what they does come saying to me night after night.'

Mrs Lutchman watched her with large, frightened eyes. Indrani, exhausted by her speech, fell back among the pillows and closed her eyes. Mrs Lutchman got up and strolled around the room, looking distractedly at the pictures on the walls. She stopped at the foot of the bed.

'All of we not like that, Indrani,' she said gently. 'Is only Urmila who behaving really bad. Like the Devil take possession of she. She is the ringleader. The rest of them wouldn't be behaving like they doing if she hadn't gone and put all those ideas in their head.'

Indrani shifted restlessly on the sheets, but she did not open her eyes. Her lips moved endlessly up and down as her mother's had done. The resemblance, at that moment, was striking.

Mrs Lutchman recalled the real purpose of her mission, suddenly so unimportant. Still, she had given her word. 'Govind want you to come and spend a few days with him in Woodlands,' she said timidly. 'It must get very lonely for you living out here all by yourself in the country.'

'I not lonely. Who say I lonely? I like living by myself. Anyway, if it come to that, I have Sadhu to keep me company.' Mrs Lutchman waited for her to go on. Indrani's face was now almost invisible in the thickening gloom. 'Govind still have the drum?' she asked suddenly, opening her eyes and searching in the twilight for Mrs Lutchman.

She was taken aback by the abruptness of the question and it took her some time to understand what Indrani meant. 'What drum is that?'

'You mean to say you forget about that already? I talking about the drum that Pa bring over with him from India. What other drum it have to talk about? I think that drum should be here in this house. Not in Woodlands.'

'When you go to Woodlands you could ask him about it.'

'What my going to Woodlands have to do with all this? I talking about the drum. It belong in this house. This is its rightful place. I had a dream about it the other night. They was very angry. I never see them so angry before. They say, "What happen to we drum, Indrani? What happen to we drum?"' Indrani might have been talking in her sleep.

'You not going to Woodlands?'

'What you take me for, Baby? I too old and sick to travel so far. Anyway, Woodlands don't have anything for me to want to go there. My time for gallivanting about the place was finished a long time ago. A long time ago.' The light in the room darkened suddenly. It was late. 'Yes,' Indrani went on, 'that's another thing I want you to tell him for me. Tell him to send the drum here for me to keep. Tell him I had a dream about it and they was very angry. Very angry. The drum belong here, not in Woodlands.' Indrani continued to repeat this phrase with a kind of delirious insistence. Mrs Lutchman listened to her. It was now totally black in the room. Gradually, Indrani ceased her murmurings. She seemed to have fallen asleep. The silence in this room at the back of the old house was oppressive. A profound melancholy gripped Mrs Lutchman, a wordless grief. She thought anxiously of home. Rover had to be fed. She tiptoed up to the bed and peered intently into Indrani's face to see if she had really fallen asleep.

'Don't forget to tell Govind,' Indrani whispered. 'The drum belong here, not in Woodland. Tell him I had a dream which say so.'

'I must be going now, Indrani. It getting late and I still have to cook food.'

Indrani held out her hand. Mrs Lutchman searched for it in the darkness and kissed it. 'Don't forget,' she whispered again. 'Tell him I had a dream.'

'No, I won't forget. I will tell him when I see him.'

She tiptoed slowly out of the room and closed the door gently after her. For a moment, she paused outside the door and listened. There was no sound inside the bedroom. She went downstairs and walked quickly through the darkened house.

Sadhu was still crouched under the fence, smoking his pipe. He got up when he saw Mrs Lutchman coming.

'Like you does spend the whole day out here, old man!' She laughed. Sadhu grinned stupidly at her.

'I was just going to make my tea and go to sleep,' he apologized. Visitors interrupted the rhythm of his life. He hobbled into the yard and drew the sagging gate after him. Mrs Lutchman watched him disappear through the blackness of the doorway and hurried off to the bus station.

Chapter Four

1

Mr Khoja listened in silence to Mrs Lutchman's report of her visit. She had decided not to tell them everything Indrani had said, omitting the bit about 'dragging the Khoja name through the mud' and the information vouchsafed to Indrani in her dreams. This she did to protect Mr Khoja's sensibilities from unnecessary outrage. It would have been hurtful for him to hear that he had been bypassed and that these communications from the dead, which he would naturally have regarded as one of the prerogatives of his status, had been granted to so mean an individual as his sister.

He was, after a fashion, quite pleased to hear that Indrani intended to return the useless five acres of land he had given her out of 'the goodness of his heart'. He disliked seeing his possessions whittled away and he had tended to recall his act of generosity with a sort of melancholy resignation. Nevertheless, Indrani's independence of spirit rankled and, in the end, outweighed this unexpected reprieve. Mrs Khoja, not hampered by these subtleties, was unable to hide her disappointment and disgust.

'People just don't have any gratitude these days,' she complained, assuming that accusing look and tone in her voice with which Mrs Lutchman was already familiar. 'You give them an inch and they want to take a mile.' She had succeeded in convincing herself that Indrani had returned the land only because of her greed for more; and, of course, to 'spite' them. 'I wonder who she think she is. People just never satisfy with what they have.'

'And she want the drum on top of all of that,' Mr Khoja mused, hoping to add a little fuel to the flames of his wife's wrath.

'Exactly. That is exactly what I mean. Not satisfy with what you give she, she want to take everything you have away from you.' Mrs Khoja seized happily on this detail of the drum which she had forgotten. 'That woman getting too big for she boots, if you ask me. Imagine she saying that the drum really belong with she. Soon she go be saying that this whole house and all it have in it belong with she too. I just can't believe my ears any more.'

Mrs Lutchman feeling that her silence might betoken a measure of agreement with Mrs Khoja, said, 'Is only the drum she ask for. Nothing else.'

Mrs Khoja pounced on her. 'Only the drum! Only the drum! That is what she would like me and you to believe. But she can't pull the wool so easy over my eyes. Not my eyes!' She laughed. 'No. Is more than the drum Miss Indrani want from we. She want this whole house. She feel just because she spend a little of she time – as if nobody else wouldn't have do the same! – looking after Govind mother, she have a right to everything. That is what she feel. You take my word.' She turned to her husband, leaving Mrs Lutchman to stare at the reflections in the bookcases. 'Is your father who give we that drum,' she said to him. 'Because you was the eldest child and only son. Some people really bold-face. It might have been different if you had a brother.'

Mr Khoja was silently thankful that he had not been blessed with a brother. That would have added too great a complication to his life. However, he agreed with his wife.

Mrs Khoja danced in virtuous glee around the room. She pranced up to her husband. 'And mark you,' she went on, 'on top of all that, she too proud to come and stay with we in Woodlands.' Then she darted across to Mrs Lutchman standing bemused in the centre of the room. 'And why, I ask you? What it is she have to be so proud of? I want you to tell me that!'

Mr Khoja intervened. 'Calm yourself, Sumintra. Remember the doctor tell you not to get too excited.' He turned to Mrs Lutchman. 'It's her nerves, you know. She's a high-strung, sensitive woman.'

'I want you to tell me why she too proud to come and spend

a few days here with we in Woodlands,' Mrs Khoja persisted, ignoring the appeals of her husband. 'You just give me one good reason why.'

'She say she too sick to travel,' Mrs Lutchman said.

'Sick! She too sick to travel! What next I ask you?' Mrs Khoja performed another of her little dances. She believed that illness of any kind was one of the prerogatives of high status and that illness among those she considered her social inferiors was a usurpation of that privilege. (Blackie, for example, had never been officially allowed a day's sick-leave. Fortunately for her, she had been blessed with a robust constitution. She was expected to live without incident and, when the time came, to die quietly and without any unseemly fuss.) 'What kind of sickness she say she have?' Mrs Khoja demanded.

'She say she eyes giving she trouble.'

'Huh! You hear the latest one, Govind? Rheumatism and diabetes too low-class for she. She say is she eyes giving she trouble.' Eye troubles were, in Mrs Khoja's opinion, an infirmity visited only on the most select people. They both laughed, though Mr Khoja did so with less conviction than his wife. The Enlightenment had left its traces on his outlook.

'She like the sari I send for she?'

'She thought it was very nice. And she like the pattern a lot too.'

This mollified Mrs Khoja slightly. 'I should think so! And what about the cups and glasses? She like those too? Or wasn't they expensive enough for she?'

'She thought they was nice as well. She tell me to thank you. It was exactly what she needed.'

'I surprise she didn't send them back. What you say, Govind? A real little picker and chooser eh!' Mrs Khoja giggled happily. Indrani's acceptance of her gifts had reestablished some, at any rate, of the proprieties of the superior-inferior relationship.

Mr Khoja had, while all this was going on, been flicking through the pages of his volume of Rousseau and making notes with a pencil in the margin. Mrs Lutchman, seeking to divert Mrs Khoja's attention away from Indrani, said, 'Like you making up another speech on that French philosopher you was telling me about the other day?'

Mr Khoja closed the book. 'Who? Jean Jacques Rousseau? I'm glad to see you are getting some benefit from my company, Vimla.' Mr Khoja laughed. 'But I'm not writing another speech. Jean Jacques is too good for the common people. To be frank with you, I'm getting a little disillusioned with the common people. They don't seem to have much interest in my message. What I'm doing now is for my own benefit really. These philosophes – Diderot also is to be admired – are an endless mine of inspiration for me. And Sumintra too,' he added, hoping to placate his wife. 'She knows all about the social contract these days.'

'Don't fill Baby head with all that stuff, Govind. You can't expect she to understand what it is you saying just off the bat like that.' Mrs Khoja gazed proudly at Mrs Lutchman. Her intellectual snobbery surprised even her husband. He adopted a more modest approach.

'Anyway, there is no point in my writing speeches since I'm sure to lose the election no matter what I do.' Mr Khoja was in sore need of another orgy of praise.

'You musn't say things like that,' Mrs Lutchman comforted him. 'The race is still to run. That is the main thing. Not what other people who jealous of you say and think.' Mrs Lutchman smiled contentedly at him. 'I'll let you into a little secret,' she said. 'You shouldn't have any doubts after that.' Mr Khoja perked up. 'Remember I was telling you a while back that I had it from a good source you was going to win the election?'

Mr Khoja pretended he had forgotten. 'I don't remember such things, Vimla. But tell me all the same.'

'Mrs MacKintosh see a "o" and a "a" in the leaves as clear as daylight one afternoon. I see it myself.'

Mr Khoja feigned scepticism. 'Did she indeed? I must say though I don't believe in that kind of hocus-pocus.'

'Is not hocus-pocus,' Mrs Lutchman replied stoutly. 'Almost everything Mrs MacKintosh tell me come true. She see a "o" and a "a" in the leaves as clear as daylight.'

'How do you know it doesn't mean I am going to lose?'
'I know,' Mrs Lutchman insisted stubbornly.
Mr Khoja smiled and returned, greatly soothed, to his book.

2

Mr Khoja's contentment was short-lived. He was a man who had fallen into the habit of pinning nearly all his faith on portents, natural and supernatural. His sense of divine mission had never been supported by rational considerations. Publicly, he scoffed at superstition, as was natural to a 'child of the Enlightenment', as he liked to describe himself to the more gullible, adoring disciples. Privately, however, he had his horoscope cast by an astrologer in India who advertised his skills in the *Trinidad Chronicle*, took careful note of his dreams and was depressed by the sight of a black cat crossing his path. Also, in his darker moments, he had been cheered by Doreen's unflagging enthusiasm and admiration. 'You,' she had declared, 'are a phenomenon! A phenomenon!'

Then, without warning, the portents took a sudden turn for the worse. The first blow was Shadow II's abrupt departure from this world. Blackie had found him, quite dead, on the steps of the servants' room, the flies walking with impunity over his yawning mouth. Mr Khoja refused to believe that it was simply the result of old age. In his world, things were never as simple as that. He was convinced that everything that happened contained a secret message which had to be deciphered and interpreted. Thus, Shadow II's death was the work of malign influences brought into play by his enemies, a sign of divine displeasure. The second blow was a nightmare he had had of what was undoubtedly the devil (Mr Khoja's dreams tended to have a theological bias) knocking at his bedroom window and begging, in the sweetest tones, to be granted entry into the darkened sitting-room. The third, and perhaps the most telling, had been contained in yet another of those anonymous, threatening letters which he now received nearly every day. In it, the full scope of Mrs MacKintosh's deceptions and duplicities had been brought to light. This revelation had snatched his last grain of comfort away from him.

Now he realized that she varied her predictions to suit the tastes and interests of her clients. The writer had supplied him with detailed evidence. Mr Khoja felt bewildered and ashamed of his credulity. Even Doreen's effusions were of no help. Mrs Khoja tried to soothe his wounded pride. She too inhabited a peculiar and extremely devious world.

'Maybe she was telling you the truth and lying to them,' she consoled him. 'You must admit that kind of thing does happen.'

Mr Khoja groaned. 'It's all Vimla's fault,' he said. 'It was she who introduced that damn woman to us.'

'I always tell you not to listen to your family. None of them have your good at heart. Still, you never know. Maybe it's you and not them who will have the last laugh. After all, we used to pay Mrs MacKintosh very well.'

Mr Khoja was not convinced. 'The next time that woman, that ... that confidence trickster dare to show her face here, don't allow her to set one foot past the gate, you hear. Set the dog on her, if you have to.' Then he remembered that Shadow II had died. And Mr Khoja hid his face in his hands. 'I feel like reporting her to the police.'

'Why don't you do that then? They might deport she back to Scotland.'

'I will only look like a fool if I do that. Jagdev wouldn't lose the opportunity to make a laughing-stock out of me. Oh! I have drained the cup of bitterness to the very bottom. Rousseau! Rousseau!'

3

But Mr Khoja was wrong. He had not drained his cup of bitterness to the very bottom.

It was Romesh who first suggested to Renouka and the commercial traveller that they should campaign actively for Jagdev. The commercial traveller's van would be extremely useful. It was well known in the constituency and Jagdev would be only too delighted to have yet more Khojas rallying to his cause. Also, he paid his campaigners well. The idea appealed to Renouka instantly and her relationship with the commercial traveller took a turn for the better. His vanity touched by the suggestion that he could play a part in bringing down the house of Khoja and by Renouka's overtures of affection, he agreed. Terms of payment having been worked out with Jagdev, he attached a loudspeaker to his van and covered the bikini-clad women with posters urging the electorate to vote for Jagdev. From then on, the conspirators toured the constituency playing loud Indian music and distributing sweets and leaflets to the village children. They, more than anyone, wrecked Mr Khoja's hopes. It was an unrelievedly scurrilous campaign and they made no attempt to disguise the fact that they were relations of Mr Khoja. They made innuendoes about his marriage, referred to his treatment of Indrani and accused him of wanting further to 'line his own pocket by robbing poor people like you'. Thus, Mr Khoja's integrity (his answer to Jagdev's flamboyance) was brought squarely into question; and as he was not a particularly good public speaker and, what was worse, terrified of exposing himself to hecklers, he had no means of defending himself.

The situation placed the Rebels in a quandary. They could not bring themselves to support Mr Khoja, nor yet remain neutral in the contest. The opportunity for public disobedience was too good to miss. They compromised. Jagdev was rejected in favour of the third candidate Narayan. That he was certain to lose was an inconvenience they were prepared to accept.

4

Mr Khoja's constituency lay in the sugar-cane belt and, the area being predominantly Indian, all three parties fighting the seat had nominated Indians in the hope of confusing the electorate. This they succeeded in doing admirably and the only effect of the campaign, apart from the damage it wreaked on Mr Khoja's reputation, was the series of ephemeral slogans touted by the supporters of the rival candidates.

Electioneering was a not too difficult business. It was confined largely to tours of the area in vans equipped with powerful loudspeakers, blaring forth the slogans of the candidates interspersed with popular songs. The candidates themselves made only rare personal appearances, the bulk of the work being done by their agents and younger supporters.

Jagdev was, undoubtedly, the most professional of the candidates. Officially, he was in disgrace; 'the maverick', as the *Trinidad Chronicle* described him, 'of the Chamber.' Two years previously he had resigned from the Legislative Council after charges of corruption which, despite the fact that they were never proved, were sufficiently damning. Not that Jagdev had cared. He enjoyed handing in his resignation and the notoriety it subsequently brought him. This had vastly increased his standing and he was now almost certain of winning the coming election.

Certainly, on the ground of flamboyance alone (and that was the only thing that really mattered) he deserved to do so. He adopted the American style of electioneering with great success. He was the first to have a 'motorcade': an organized parade of cars through the straggling villages. Jagdev had ridden at the back of an open American car, garlanded with flowers, one of his arms entwined around a beautiful girl, while with the other he waved a bottle of rum at the crowds lining the road. It was a noisy affair, an exuberant display of camaraderie, and it had gone down well. This had effectively sealed the fate of the other candidates.

However, it had not prevented them from following up with feebler versions of their own. Mr Khoja, in a final despairing assault on the electorate a week before the election, had organized a more sedate motorcade. He too rode at the back of an open American car garlanded with flowers, but, determined not to be a slavish imitator of Jagdev, there was no beautiful girl and no bottle of rum. Instead, Mrs Khoja, dressed in one of her gorgeous saris, sat smiling nervously beside him, while her husband waved a volume of Rousseau at the crowds lining the road.

This was not what they had come to see and the motorcade was not a success. If anything, Mr Khoja's reputation plunged even lower as a result of it. The crowds jeered, a few bottles were broken under the wheels of the car and when someone hurled a stone that almost shattered the wind-shield, Mr Khoja decided he had had enough of electioneering. He had the roof hauled up and ordering the driver to detach the car from the motorcade as discreetly as he could, drove back to Woodlands. He vowed never again to expose himself to the scorn of an undeserving electorate. Mrs Khoja advised him, on threat of assassination, to remain at home until the end of the election. Mr Khoja was easily persuaded. Not trusting his agent (he suspected desertion on every side) he asked Mrs Lutchman to be present at the counting of the votes and to make sure that no mischief was done that might further prejudice his chances. 'It's a small enough favour to ask in the circumstances,' he said to her. 'I'm not holding you accountable for your son's actions. But . . .'

Mrs Lutchman jumped at the offer to be of service. Here surely was one way of redeeming herself. The one obvious sacrifice, to break with Mrs MacKintosh, she had not the strength of will to do. She had tried several times to call her friend to account, but at the last moment, confronted by those vacant blue eyes, her courage invariably failed her. The loss of Mrs MacKintosh's services was a prospect too distressing to contemplate. It would have created a gap in her life that nothing could possibly fill. Her weakness doubled her already acute feelings of guilt.

The day before the election Romesh came to the house to collect some of his clothes. It was the first time she had set eyes on him for nearly a month. He was drunk.

'I praying to God,' he told her, 'that that man not only lose the election, but that he lose his damn deposit as well.'

'But what it is you have against him so, son? What it is he do to you that you having to behave like this? You realize what all this doing to me?'

Romesh stared stubbornly at the floor. 'He does treat all of we like dog. And not only people like me. But you as well. You really think that you and he is friends? You think he like you, eh? Well, let me tell you something. He only using you, as he would like to use all of we if he had the chance. In his eyes, you and the rest of we is expendable. We don't count for nothing. We is all dog to him. Well, those days finish for good, you hear. He going to get what's coming to him.' Romesh smiled a leisurely smile. 'I myself have been working out a few more plans.'

'What kind of plans?' Mrs Lutchman asked apprehensively. 'You don't think you do enough damage already?'

'It have a lot more damage to do.' Romesh giggled. 'You'll see when the time come. Don't worry your head about all that as yet. All stool pigeons deserve what they get.'

Mrs Lutchman shook her head. 'Is Renouka putting all them ideas in your head, son?'

'Don't exert yourself about who putting ideas in my head, Ma.' Romesh lowered his voice and stuck his hands inside his trouser pockets. 'Don't exert yourself about that.' A great joy shone in his eyes. 'You hear about him getting stoned?'

Mrs Lutchman nodded. 'Was that your work too then?'

'I wish it was. But I wasn't there that day. Mind you, if I had the chance I myself would have stone him. I would have stone him dead.'

'I don't understand you at all, son. As your father used to say, you seeing too much film and taking it for real life. But don't think just because you behaving like a star-boy you could stop me from going to help out your mamoo in his moment of need.'

'Who's stopping you, Ma?' Romesh held out his arms towards his mother, an impressively lazy gesture. 'Who's stopping you?' He lit a cigarette and dropped the match on the floor. Mrs Lutchman bent down to pick it up. Romesh watched her, his eyes narrowing into a Hollywood smirk. 'What's that old witch got to say about the election?'

'You mean Mrs MacKintosh?'

Romesh nodded. He blew a perfect smoke ring that hovered like a halo above his head.

Mrs Lutchman brightened. 'She say Govind going to win.' It was the only weapon she could use against her son and, for the moment, she pushed to the back of her mind the darker side of the story. 'It was as clear as daylight in the leaves,' she went on hurriedly. 'She see a "o" and a "a". I see it myself.'

Romesh doubled up with laughter.

'What you laughing at so? All I say was ...'

'A real old witch,' Romesh spluttered. 'So she see an "o" and "a" at the bottom of the cup, eh?'

'Yes. I don't see . . .'

'And you see it as well, eh?'

'Yes. But I . . .'

'Don't exert yourself, Ma. Don't exert yourself.' And, still laughing, Romesh left the room. Mrs Lutchman listened to him cackling as he slammed the front door.

5

A carnival atmosphere prevailed on the night of the election. Groups of youths wandered about the streets shouting and singing. Many of them were drunk, and, encouraged by the example of Jagdev, shook bottles of rum in the faces of the passers-by. Mrs Lutchman, buoyed up by her official status, pushed her way through the throng which had gathered on the steps of the 'Community Centre', where the votes were to be counted.

The Community Centre was a one-storeyed concrete building with unwashed walls, the sole boon conferred by the Government on a constituency that had proved impervious to all its efforts. Apart from its use on election nights, it provided a venue for stray lecturers on Hindu mysticism and other equally exotic subjects. It had reached the height of its glory when another stray, an itinerant English princess, had stopped there on a tour of the countryside.

The building had been cleared of its sparse furnishings and three long tables had been arranged parallel to one another. The returning officers had already taken up their stations when Mrs Lutchman arrived. In front of each one stood a square brown box. Policemen stood at discreet intervals around the room. A reporter from Radio Trinidad tripped busily about in a tangle of cord and wires. Photographers from the *Trinidad Chronicle* stood at the ready with cameras and rolls of film. They fussed endlessly with their cameras. Outside, the cries of the crowd rose and fell away. Mrs Lutchman, uncertain as to her true function, took up what she considered a strategic position in a corner of the room, and stared hawkishly at everybody.

The Chief Returning Officer came up to her. 'Who tell you you could come in here?' he demanded.

Her nostrils fluttered scornfully. 'I don't think you know who you talking to, my good man.'

'If you don't tell me who you is, I'll have to throw you out of here.' The Chief Returning Officer spoke in a deliberately loud voice and the reporters, scenting trouble, hurried across to them.

'What happening?' the man from Radio Trinidad asked the Chief Returning Officer. He ignored the question and repeated his warning to Mrs Lutchman in an even louder voice. She opened her handbag and showed him a card Mr Khoja had given her.

'That satisfy you?'

'You should have shown me this in the first place, Madam.'

The reporters peeped over his shoulder, trying to get a glimpse of the card. The Chief Returning Officer pushed them away. He chuckled.

'I don't think your brother stand much of a chance, Mrs Lutchman, if you want me to be frank with you.'

Mrs Lutchman drew herself up to her full height. 'Nobody ask you for your opinion, my good man. He will only lose if people like you decide to cheat him of his rightful place.'

The Chief Returning Officer laughed. 'I don't have no need to cheat him. He do all the work for we already.' He grew more serious. 'In any case, you shouldn't insult the dignity of my office. I'm strictly impartial, I assure you.' He walked away, tall and dignified. One of the photographers pushed himself forward.

'I thought I recognized you, my dear Mrs Lutchman. I haven't seen you since your late husband's funeral. Much water has flown under the bridge since then, as they say.'

Mrs Lutchman studied the photographer's face and shook her head perplexedly. He was wearing a pair of dark glasses and, strangely, a yachting cap.

'Don't you recognize me? I've grown a lot thinner lately. Wilkinson is the name, Ma'am. Wilkinson, late of the Department of Education and best known to his friends as Wilkie.' Wilkie took off his dark glasses with a flourish and grinned happily at Mrs Lutchman.

She was not pleased to see Wilkie. His manner reminded her of the Christmas Eve dinner party. It was a memory that had never ceased to pain her. Wilkie had quite obviously regained all his old ebullience. She held out a limp hand. Wilkie pumped it enthusiastically.

'Yes, my dear Mrs Lutchman. Much water has flown under the proverbial bridge since I last saw you. For a start, the man you see before you is no longer a bachelor. In fact, he's the father of a small boy.'

'I'm very happy to hear that, Mr Wilkinson.'

'Yes. Old Wilkie finally got trapped. Even now some of the boys still can't believe it.'

Mrs Lutchman scowled.

'Yes,' Wilkie went on, 'and not too long after that I left the Ministry and got a plum job on the *Chronicle*.' He tapped the camera hung round his neck fondly. 'I owe it all to this, you will be glad to hear. I entered a little photography competition the *Chronicle* was running at one time. They was searching for new talent. I had the good fortune to take away the first prize. Maybe you saw the picture? A beautiful sunset scene entitled "Every Cloud Has a Silver Lining"?'

Mrs Lutchman congratulated him weakly. 'You must excuse me, Mr Wilkinson, but I don't read the papers much these days.'

'Ah! What a pity. But fortunately I think I have a copy of it with me. I always carry it around with me as a good-luck charm on all my assignments.' He searched in the breast pocket of his jacket and brought out a crumpled brown envelope. One of the reporters from the *Trinidad Chronicle* nudged the man standing next to him. They laughed softly. Wilkie held the photograph close to Mrs Lutchman's face. 'You like it?'

'It very nice, Mr Wilkinson. You is a talented man.'

Wilkie was self-effacing. 'Not really, Mrs Lutchman. You do me too much justice. It was all luck, though when I tell the boys that they don't believe me. You can't succeed in this life without a little luck, is what I always say. You could ask the boys if those very words are not always on the tip of old Wilkie's tongue.'

Mrs Lutchman stared distractedly around the room. The reporters had taken out their notebooks and were biting the tips of their pencils meditatively. One of them pushed his way forward, the same who had laughed at Wilkie.

'What chance do you think your brother has tonight?' he asked.

Wilkie decided to come to her rescue. 'Frankie, leave the woman in peace. How you expect she to answer that question?'

'Don't bother, Mr Wilkinson. I'll answer him.' Mrs Lutchman, turning to face the questioner, replied as if to a challenge. 'I think he stand a very good chance.' Her eyes widened. 'If people don't cheat him that is,' she added as a further challenge. The reporters were interested. They crowded closer round her. Wilkie's camera flashed.

'Don't worry, Mrs Lutchman. I'm not taking a picture of you. I was only trying it out. Fellas! Fellas! Leave the woman in peace.'

Frankie cursed. 'Why don't you go and show your damn picture to somebody else, eh? Why you have to stay here and bother we?'

'You think they going to cheat him?' another reporter asked, scribbling in his notebook.

'I wouldn't be surprised. They have had it in for him a long time now.' The reporters scribbled.

'Who exactly are you referring to?'

'Don't answer him, Mrs Lutchman. That will get you into a lot of trouble.'

'Why don't you take your camera and go from here? Nobody talking to you.'

'My brother have more to offer the country than any of the other candidates. He is an honest man, more than you can say for most of them.'

'Who exactly?'

'That is none of your business.'

'What about all this scandal about the family inheritance we've been hearing so much about recently, Mrs Lutchman?' Frankie asked with a show of the greatest respect.

'That is none of your business,' she replied angrily.

'Is it true,' Frankie persisted, 'that Mr Khoja's marriage is on the rocks?'

'I leave that for the scandalmongers to decide,' Mrs Lutchman said and turned away from him, refusing to answer any more questions. Wilkie's camera flashed again. He was consoling himself.

At that moment, the Chief Returning Officer announced the first results. The reporters left her and dashed across the room. Mr Khoja was trailing badly. A grim expression settled over Mrs Lutchman's face. She could discover no one cheating outright. The Radio Trinidad reporter spoke urgently at intervals into his microphone. Mrs Lutchman's gloom deepened. Outside, the crowd was growing and responding to each new bit of information with blood-curdling cries of delight. The rumour filtered through that Jagdev had arrived. Wilkie dashed outside, his camera blazing. Mrs Lutchman could hear Jagdev addressing the crowd. The third candidate, like Mr Khoja, had thought it wiser to stay away.

There were not many more votes to be counted and still Mr Khoja had not managed to scrape together a sufficient number to save his deposit. Mrs Lutchman walked across to a window and looked out at the crowd. Jagdev, garlanded and waving a bottle of rum, had been lifted shoulder-high. The results flowed on, relayed to the crowd through a loudspeaker: S. Jagdev, 3,252; R. Narayan, 624; G. Khoja, 223. Mrs Lutchman stopped listening.

The Chief Returning Officer, waving a sheet of paper, called for silence. He spoke into a microphone, booming out the final result. The crowd roared and a wave swept against the door. Wilkie, the camera swinging from his neck, came running up to Mrs Lutchman. 'He lose his deposit,' he said sadly. 'Still, two hundred and twenty-three people vote for him. It could have been worse.'

'They should have a recount,' Mrs Lutchman said.

'No chance of that, Mrs Lutchman. It was a clear-cut result. An absolute majority for Jagdev.'

'They cheat him, Mr Wilkinson.'

'You shouldn't say things like that, Mrs Lutchman. If any of them people outside hear you say that, they might beat you up on the spot. Take care.' And with these words of advice, Wilkie hurried off to take more photographs of the victorious candidate.

'Speech! Speech!' The cry was taken up by the crowd. The doors were opened and Jagdev was borne in, swigging from the bottle of rum, on the shoulders of his supporters. 'Speech! Speech!' The Radio Trinidad reporter thrust a microphone near his lips. Jagdev, swaying drunkenly, did not seem to realize what was happening. He grabbed the microphone and slurred into it. 'Thank you, my many friends. Thank you for your ...' He drank some more rum, wiping his lips with the back of his hand, and then forgetting once more where he was, nodded sleepily. The microphone fell from his hand. There was much applause. Jagdev was living up to their expectations. The Radio Trinidad reporter, trying hard to disguise his annoyance, handed back the microphone. 'Speech! Speech!' the crowd cried. Jagdev opened his eyes. 'Thank you, my many friends, for your support. I want you all to go home now, eat your roti and curry and drink some more rum for me.' Again the microphone slipped and fell from his hand. The crowd swept around him. Jagdev stared sleepily at them and took another sip from his bottle. He closed his eyes and this time appeared without doubt to have fallen asleep.

Mrs Lutchman watched all this from her corner. Wilkie was still busy taking photographs. She left the room as discreetly as possible, going out through a back entrance. She was convinced that a majority of the ballot boxes had been 'thrown into the river'; this despite the fact there was no river in the immediate vicinity. The culprit too had acquired a face and name. In her mind, but for the corruption of the Chief Returning Officer Mr Khoja would have won easily. Highly indignant, she set out for Woodlands to make her report.

6

The Khojas had adapted themselves to a state of siege. They had stocked food sufficient to last them a week and disconnected the telephone. Also, they went as little as possible to the front of the house, not wishing to attract unnecessary attention. Mrs Khoja had ministered assiduously to this state of insecurity, feeding into her husband's nightmare her belief that there were plans afoot to assassinate him. Mr Khoja welcomed this threat. It consoled him for many of his recent disappointments and thus they both basked cheerfully in the shadow of the assassin's gun.

On the night of the election they had spent a quiet evening listening to the results as they came in on the radio. Mrs Khoja tended her dolls, undressing and cleaning them with a damp towel, a ritual she carried out once a month. Mr Khoja, wearing a pair of blue silk pyjamas bought by his wife as a birthday present, lay sprawled on the bed reading a Hindu devotional text. He had, for the moment, become disenchanted with Rousseau. He had acquired the habit of making notes in the margins of his books and now as he read, he pencilled in remarks like: 'how true!', 'perceptive!', and 'note!'. This last was the most frequent, but to what end these things had to be noted remained obscure as much to himself as to his wife.

'You shouldn't read with the book so close to your face, Govind,' Mrs Khoja said, looking up from the doll's dress she was mending. 'That way you bound to spoil your eyes.'

'My eyes can't be any worse than they are already, Sumintra,' Mr Khoja replied. He wrote something in the margin of the book. 'Listen to this and tell me what you think. "Only he who knows the truly small can know the truly great".' Mr Khoja took off his glasses and cleaned them on his sleeve.

'Is a very profound thing it saying.' She held up the doll's dress for him to see. 'Is a real pretty dress, don't you think?'

Mr Khoja glanced briefly at the dress. 'Yes. It very nice.' He returned to his book. The radio played softly, news of the election interspersed with dance music. 'Switch it off, Sumintra. I can't stand that announcer's voice.'

Mrs Khoja switched off the radio. She was glad to do so. The news was unrelievedly bad. All three candidates of the People's Socialist Movement were taking a heavy beating.

'Why don't you open a window?' Mr Khoja asked, suddenly irritable. 'It getting very hot in here.' He wiped the nape of his neck.

'It too dangerous, Govind. You can't tell what people will do.'

All the windows in the room had been closed as a precaution against a stray bullet fired from the rooftops. Mrs Khoja had thought of every contingency.

'Okay.' Mr Khoja was reluctant to give up his cherished illusion. He nodded and buried his head in his book.

There was a rattle at the gate. The bell jangled faintly. Husband and wife stared at each other questioningly.

'Better to ignore it,' Mrs Khoja advised. She continued sewing and Mr Khoja made more notes in the margins of the book. The gate rattled again, this time with more insistence. Someone, a man, shouted their name.

'You better go and see who it is, Sumintra. Maybe somebody give Vimla a lift back home.'

'But it too early for she to come back, Govind.'

Vague shouts drifted up from the street, but they could not catch what was being shouted.

'It sound as if is a man and a woman down there,' Mrs Khoja said. She laid the doll's dress aside. Mr Khoja rested the book on his stomach, drumming with his fingers on the cover.

'Open the window and take a peep,' he suggested.

'Like you gone mad or something, Govind? One shot is all it need.'

Again the gate rattled. It was now being shaken violently. There was more shouting from the street, the higher sound of a woman's voice separating itself from the hoarse laughter of a man.

'I think you better go and take a look,' Mr Khoja insisted. He was hoping that it might be someone with unexpected good news.

Mrs Khoja went to examine herself in the mirror. She combed a stray lock of hair into place and arranged the dolls in their accustomed positions on the dresser. She walked through the darkened sitting-room and out to the verandah, pausing at the top of the front steps. She stared at the two figures standing on the pavement. They had taken care to position themselves well away from the glow of the street lamp. Their shouts rose when they saw her and one of them, the man, came up and rattled the gate vigorously. The bell swayed ineffectually back and forth with a hollow rattle.

'Who is it?' she called.

'We have a message for you,' the man answered. The girl laughed.

Mrs Khoja craned her neck forward, squinting into the darkness. 'What kind of message you have for me?'

'The message not for you. It for your husband.'

The girl giggled.

'If is only a message you have for we, why you laughing so much for then? Come nearer the light so I could see who you is.'

'We not laughing at you. We laughing at something else,' the man shouted back. But he did not come any closer to the light.

'Tell me what the message is and I'll tell my husband. I don't want to disturb him. He resting in bed.'

'I can't do that,' the man replied. 'I have orders to deliver it to your husband in person. Is an important message. Something about the election,' he added for good measure.

Mr Khoja had crept up softly to the edge of the verandah, sheltering behind the sitting-room door. 'Ask who it is give them the message,' he whispered.

Mrs Khoja started. She had not known he was there. 'Tell me who it is give you the message first,' she said.

The two figures held a conference. The man came up to the gate, carefully avoiding the circle of light thrown by the street lamp. 'Is Mrs Lutchman who give me the message.'

'Well, why didn't you say so in the first place?' Mrs Khoja demanded angrily. She was disappointed. 'You was making enough noise to wake up the whole street. You should have better manners than that.'

'Sorry. Sorry.'

'It too late to be sorry now after you wake everybody up.' She went slowly down the steps, lifting the edge of her sari. 'Who is that you bring with you?'

'Just a friend.'

Mrs Khoja unlocked the gate. The man, who had been standing with his head bent so that Mrs Khoja could not see his face, suddenly leapt forward and pushed hard against it, forcing Mrs Khoja back. She uttered a little shriek of alarm. 'Watch what it is you doing, boy. You nearly make me fall in the flower-bed.' The man pushed harder still.

'You could fall where you want. I don't care. To hell with you.'

Mrs Khoja, struggling to retain her balance, caught a glimpse of her assailant's face for the first time. 'Romesh! Govind! Is Romesh, Baby son.' She smelled the rum, strong and sweetly pungent, on his breath. Mrs Khoja retreated, astonished, into the bed of flowers. The girl came running up out of the shadows and added her efforts.

'Govind! Govind! Call the police. They gone mad, I tell you. They gone mad.'

Mr Khoja showed himself at the top of the steps. 'What's happening down there? What the hell do you two hooligans think you are doing to my wife? You don't think being traitors is enough?'

The girl pursued Mrs Khoja into the flower-bed.

'They trampling all we nice plants, Govind,' Mrs Khoja wailed. 'Call the police.'

The girl pulled roughly at Mrs Khoja's sari. 'Hello, Mamee. You recognize me? I come for you to teach me how to tie sari.' She thrust her gloating face close to Mrs Khoja. She too had been drinking.

'Renouka!' Mrs Khoja tried to get hold of the hand tugging at her sari. 'What it is you doing to me, girl? You gone mad?' Mrs Khoja's voice dropped to a whisper. They might have been talking confidentially.

'Yes. That's right. I gone mad. Insane.' She tugged at the sari.

'Hooligans! Traitors!' Mr Khoja shouted. 'Leave this house this instant or you'll be sorry.'

'You does really tie saris well, not so, Mamee? Well, I learning too, you hear. I learning real fast.'

Mrs Khoja whimpered. 'Govind! All we beautiful flowers.'

Mr Khoja started to come down the steps. 'I'm going to call the police this instant and have you hooligans carted off to jail. What about you, Romesh? Being a traitor wasn't enough? Jagdev didn't pay you enough to stab me in the back? I hope you know your behaviour driving your mother into the grave.'

'You stay where you is!' Romesh bellowed. 'And you better not put my mother name in your mouth if you know what's good for you. Is not me who driving she into the grave, is you. Is you who driving she and the rest of we into the grave.'

The neighbours watched from their windows. Some of them were laughing. Their laughter distracted Mr Khoja. He continued to descend the steps, though more slowly. 'Don't forget I have a telephone here.'

Romesh laughed. He shut and bolted the gate. 'The police will have a lot of climbing to do when they come,' he said.

Mr Khoja had stopped when he saw Romesh bolting the gate. Romesh rushed up the steps towards him. 'You take care of she, Renouka, and I'll take care of him.'

Renouka and Mrs Khoja staggered silently over the bed of flowers, as if anxious to efface their presence.

Mr Khoja, planting his feet well apart, prepared to meet the assault. It was just then that he remembered the telephone had been disconnected. He wavered. In a moment, Romesh was upon him, his arm locked around his neck. Mr Khoja struggled to free himself. 'You're just drunk,' he said. 'And there's nothing worse than a drunk, cowardly traitor. Only a coward would do what you are doing here tonight.' His voice was thick.

'Say that again.'

'I say you are a drunken coward.'

Romesh slapped him.

'Say that again.'

'I say you are a drunken coward and that you will only end by driving your mother to her grave.'

Romesh slapped him even harder.

'No, Govind. Don't provoke him,' Mrs Khoja wailed. 'He'll murder we if you provoke him.' She gathered her torn, ruffled sari about her shoulders and started stumbling slowly up the steps. Renouka leaned against the gate, breathing heavily and watching her.

Romesh tightened his grip around Mr Khoja's neck. 'You not going to call me coward again? I thought you was a hero. Like you frighten to spoil your nice blue pyjamas?'

'You're a ...'

Romesh raised his hand.

'Govind!' Mrs Khoja wailed, now reduced to almost crawling up the steps, the border of her sari dragging behind her. 'I begging you. Don't provoke him. He'll murder we here tonight if you do that.'

Mr Khoja sunk his head into Romesh's sleeve and said no more.

'He's an old man, Rom. You is young and healthy. Don't do that to him, for God's sake. I begging you.'

'Sumintra!'

Mrs Khoja paid no attention to her husband. She crawled up to Romesh, the only person to whom she had ever allowed equality of disease, and hugged the folds of his trousers. He looked down at her, grovelling and weeping at his feet. Romesh smiled his Hollywood smile.

'Think of your mother, Rom. And the memory of your dead father. Don't shame them and yourself, I beg you.'

'Since when you care about my mother and father so much?'

Renouka, still leaning against the gate, stared dispassionately at the group on the steps, biting at her fingernails.

'You stifling him, Rom. Let him go. He won't harm you. I will make him promise that he won't harm you. I will tell him is your nerves. He's an old man. He not as strong as he used to be.' Mrs Khoja caressed the folds of Romesh's trousers.

'Sumintra!'

'Let him go, Rom. He won't do you any harm. I'll make him promise. You wait and see.' Mrs Khoja left Romesh and crawled across the step to her husband. Romesh tightened his grip. Mr Khoja groaned. 'It's only his nerves, Govind. Promise that you won't do him any harm, and he'll let you go. You'll see.'

Mr Khoja groaned again.

'Promise him, Govind.'

'I promise.'

'Repeat it,' Romesh ordered. 'I want to hear you repeat it.'

'I promise.'

Romesh let him go.

'You see, Govind, I tell you he would let you go. He is a good boy really. It's only his nerves.'

Mr Khoja felt his neck. Mrs Khoja struggled to her feet. Renouka continued to lean against the gate, watching them.

'We've come to pay you a little visit,' Romesh said, lighting a cigarette and flinging the still burning match into the verandah. 'I hope you don't mind we using the front steps, but as guests we thought ...' Romesh laughed. 'Renouka and I thought we would like to see the old place again.' He stuck his hands into his trouser pockets and gazed casually about him. The Khojas were silent. 'You not going to show we around?'

Mrs Khoja grasped her husband's arm. 'No harm in showing them, Govind.'

'There is nothing for them to see here.' Mr Khoja replied firmly.

Romesh flexed his fingers. 'Like you want me to teach you another lesson? This time I promise ...' His long fingers waved spider-like in the darkness.

'Govind. Show them. I beg you.'

'For your sake I'll do it,' he said. 'But only for your sake, Sumintra,' He returned Romesh's stare. 'This way then.' He climbed the remaining steps to the verandah.

'Come on, Renouka. We're about to be given a guided tour.'

They waited for Renouka to join them, before embarking on their guided tour.

Mr Khoja switched on all the lights in the sitting-room. 'Well, what would you like to see?' he asked. 'That thing above your head is called the ceiling, what you see below your feet is called the floor and those funny-looking things along the walls are called books. You might have heard of them before.'

'He's a real smart guy, isn't he, Renouka?' Romesh flicked some ash on the carpet. Renouka seemed embarrassed. 'But not smart enough!' And, with an abrupt kick, Romesh shattered the glass of one of the bookcases. Mrs Khoja screamed and tottered against her husband.

'Don't worry, Sumintra. Is only a few pieces of glass. And, after all, you got to make allowances for the boy's nerves.'

Mrs Khoja began to cry. The fragments of glass lay scattered across the carpet.

'What's this thing here called, smart guy?' Romesh pointed at the wall.

'Don't provoke him, Govind.'

'Good.' Romesh ground his cigarette into the carpet. 'You does learn quick.' He strolled easily about the room. He stopped near the piano. 'So, you is a musician as well.' He brought his fist down heavily on the keyboard. The sound resounded through the room, shaking the myriad brass ornaments. 'It need a lot of money to furnish a place like this.' He picked up an ornamental dagger which Mr Khoja sometimes used to open his letters.

'Romesh!' Renouka ran up to him.

'Don't worry your head, Renouka. I not going to stab him. Not tonight anyway.' He laughed loudly and unnaturally. Even for Romesh the cinematic aspects of the situation were proving too much.

'I think we better go home now,' Renouka said.

'You go if you want. I still have a few things I want to discuss with smart guy here.' He pushed her away and picked up a brass paperweight. 'Nice and heavy. What you does use it for?'

Mr Khoja watched him, his face expressionless.

Romesh rolled the paperweight about in his palm. 'You does read all them books you have here?' Romesh asked. 'Once I used to know a guy who used to read a lot. Just like you, in fact.'

Mr Khoja said nothing.

'Perhaps this might loosen your tongue for you.' He hurled the paperweight. There was a sound of glass exploding. Shattered fragments sailed in the air. Mrs Khoja screamed and cowered against her husband.

'Don't worry, Sumintra. It's only glass.'

'Only glass! Only glass! I go teach you to say is only glass.' Romesh's face contorted in a sudden fit of rage. He ran along the line of bookcases, kicking and breaking the glass as he went, succumbing when he reached the last to a bout of hysterical laughter. 'Only glass! That go teach you to try and make a fool of me and say is only glass.'

Mrs Khoja uttered a long, low howl. She had begun to tremble.

'If you don't have any respect for me and the house, at least have some for her,' Mr Khoja said quietly. 'Like you, her nerves are not too strong.'

'What's in there?' Romesh had pretended not to hear.

'Only our bedroom. There's nothing in there to interest you.'

'That's for me to decide.' Romesh kicked the door open. He walked inside and looked around. The Khojas followed him. Renouka went out to the verandah and sat down on the front steps.

Mrs Khoja went up to him and rested an arm lightly on his shoulder. 'You can see for yourself, Rom, that it have nothing here to offend you. Only we bed and clothes and things like that. Nothing at all to offend you.' Her trembling intensified.

'What's that?'

'Is only a prayer, Rom.'

Romesh ripped it off the wall. He began to read it aloud. 'The Lord is My Shepherd ... what kind of prayer is this, eh? I thought the both of you was such good Hindus, always telling the rest of we what is right and what is wrong and preaching to everybody. You is the biggest set of hypocrites I ever meet in my whole life.'

'All god is one God, Rom. Is the spirit, not the form that matter.' She knelt down beside him and hugged his knees.

'Sumintra! Get up!' Mr Khoja strode across to her and dragged her forcibly away from Romesh. 'What kind of behaviour is that?'

Mrs Khoja did not resist her husband, but she continued all the same to moan softly. 'All god is one God, Rom. Is the spirit not the form that matter.' Her eyes swivelled, white and bloodless, in their sockets.

'Is smart guy putting all that nonsense in your head? Watch me.' Mrs Khoja raised her head. Romesh tore the card once, then again, and scattered the pieces on the floor. Mrs Khoja watched him as a child might a magician performing some conjuring feat. He walked over to the dresser. 'And what is all this we have here, eh? Dolls! I thought only children used to play with dolls.' He picked up one of them.

'Don't break them, Rom.' Mrs Khoja fought to release herself from her husband's grasp. 'If you do that is as if you killing my own children.'

'Sumintra! You don't know what you saying.' Mr Khoja glared at his wife, but she seemed not to understand. She dragged herself away from him and collapsed once more at Romesh's feet.

'So they like your own children, eh? I always thought you was mad. Now I know for sure.' He twisted one of the doll's arms. It broke and fell into his hand.

'No! No! Rom.' Mrs Khoja uttered a piercing scream. 'I begging you, Rom. You murdering them. You have blood on your hands now.' She sank on the floor sobbing.

'Sumintra!'

'Watch!'

Again Mrs Khoja looked up from the floor, obedient and submissive. Romesh broke off the other hand. She gazed up at him. 'No, Rom. You don't understand and I was so sure you would understand.'

Romesh swept the remaining dolls off the dresser. They clattered to the floor. Mrs Khoja reached for one of them and cradled it.

A police siren wailed at the end of the street. Romesh dashed to a window and opened it. The siren came nearer, floating indecisively near the house. It stopped. A crowd of people had already gathered outside the gate. Romesh stepped back from the window and closed it.

'You safe now,' Romesh said.

It was Blackie's hour of glory. She it was who, using the spare key entrusted to her, had slipped quietly out of the house and informed the police of the happenings upstairs. It was the most positive act she had performed in her entire life.

Chapter Five

1

Romesh was sent to jail for six months. Mrs Lutchman wept in court when the sentence was passed. Romesh, however, consistent to the last, displayed neither emotion nor repentance. His Hollywood gangster smirk never left his face. He relished the situation, pleading guilty and making no attempt to excuse his behaviour or defend himself.

He had permitted himself only one outburst. This had occurred when Mr Khoja suggested to the magistrate that he take into account, as a mitigating circumstance, the fact that Romesh had been, as he put it, 'under the influence of a well-known local beverage', and thus not totally responsible for his actions. Romesh had tried to shout him down, saying that he did not 'want or need' any of his 'damn favours'. Mr Khoja, who throughout had behaved with impeccable gallantry, smiled and advised the magistrate not to attach too much importance to the 'passions of this misguided youth', quoting an appropriate passage from *Emïle*. Romesh had had to be forcibly restrained by two policemen.

Mrs Lutchman had sat at the back of the court, gazing dully at her son. In her own way, she too had conducted herself as calmly and dispassionately as he. She was inured to Romesh. As she looked at him standing there, handsome and cinematically arrogant, his hair neatly parted and smarmed down, his hands thrust into his trouser pockets, she had constantly to remind herself that this youth was indeed her son. Sometimes she felt that what was happening there, in that court-room, had little to do with her. The young man in the dock was a ghost, a purely physical replica of the true son she carried still-born within her. The magistrate, the lawyers, the reporters and photographers, were all like actors in a nightmare; reminiscent of those that had plagued her for two successive nights after she had collected her husband's charred bones from the burnt-out pyre. They had only ceased after she had returned and thrown the silver case into the river. So too, she was now consigning another relic, her son, to a different life in which he would have even less need of her. It was yet another act of dispossession. Her presence there was a ritual observance and her tears, when the sentence was passed, were meant not for the young man visible to her eyes, but for that other son who had failed to see the light of day.

2

Renouka, like Mrs Lutchman, sat at the back of the court-room next to her mother. Saraswatee was the only person present who wept continuously while the case was being heard, constantly brushing her tears away and sniffling into her handkerchief. Renouka, for much of the time, kept her eyes fixed on the floor, now and again letting them roam over the ceiling. Only at rare intervals did she lift her head and allow her gaze to rest momentarily on the suited, strutting figures juggling with papers at the front of the court-room. At these times, she studied them with a dry-eyed apathy for a few seconds before allowing her head to droop again.

The police had not arrested her. She had been spared by Mr Khoja in a sudden outburst of magnanimity. He had informed them of her attempts to restrain Romesh and added that she had been acting entirely under his influence. Previously, she would have found his generosity galling. She knew that, properly speaking, it was not generosity at all that had led Mr Khoja to plead for her. It was, rather, a manifestation of his power. He was playing a game, neither more nor less. But on the night of the election, after she had fought with Mrs Khoja in the flower-bed, her despair had lost its raging, self-destructive force. She was no longer capable of the grand gesture of refusal. She had sat in silence at the top of the steps while Mr Khoja argued at length with the police. In the place of that fury had come an overpowering sense of futility and with it, weariness. Renouka had run out of steam. She was no longer capable of rage.

Though not suffering from 'nerves' to the same extent as Romesh, Renouka was more intelligent than he was and she knew, unlike him, that her theme had been played out. She was, up to a point, herself again. On the other hand, Romesh was still imprisoned in the meshes of his Hollywood fantasy. She remembered him shouting at her as the police took him to the car, 'Stool pigeon'. She watched him now staring insolently at the magistrate and Mr Khoja, but she felt too hollow and drained to summon up any of her reserves of pity.

The commercial traveller sat on the bench behind her, a fixed, inane grin on his face, watching Romesh perform. He gave the impression of enjoying the spectacle. This was deceptive. From time to time, a pensive scowl spread over his face as he looked at the curve of Renouka's neck. They had quarrelled, and Renouka, two days after the election, had left her lodgings and returned home to live with her mother. The commercial traveller had gone several times to the house and, falling on his knees, begged her to return to him. She refused. He became threatening. 'I will tell everybody all them things you used to tell me. You can't get away from me that easily. It not so easy to rub out what happen, you know. If I was really smart I would have give you a baby.' Renouka was not moved. 'You can say anything you want,' she replied. 'And even if you had given me a baby it wouldn't have made any difference.' 'Suppose,' the commercial traveller said, 'I tell everybody about the way you and Romesh used to carry on. What you go do then?' Renouka laughed. 'They know about that already.' The commercial traveller was distraught. He began to cry. That too made no difference. After that, he had lost control of himself altogether. 'You is nothing but a coolie girl,' he shouted at her, 'and I do everything with you that I ever wanted to do. I only sorry I didn't give you a baby.' Renouka was amused. The commercial traveller saw that all was lost. What would he tell his friends? So it was he sat there in the court-room nursing his own private tragedy and gazing alternately at Romesh and Renouka, the twin causes of his troubles.

On the very last bench, the members of Romesh's gang of drinking companions had ranged themselves, all of them chewing gum and studying their hero with a slightly fearful admiration. Many of Romesh's more cinematic remarks had been uttered simply for their benefit and they had shown their appreciation by applause and hooting; that is, until the magistrate had threatened to arrest them for contempt of court. They were prepared to follow their leader, but not to jail. The warning had had the desired effect. Thus, even they had set a limit to their fantasy.

When sentence was passed, Romesh was escorted out of the court-room handcuffed to a policeman. Mrs Lutchman stood on the pavement outside the court and waved a white handkerchief at her son as he was driven away to prison.

3

The trial was a boon to Mr Khoja. There were photographs of him in the *Trinidad Chronicle* collecting the bits of broken glass and standing in the trampled flower bed with Mrs Khoja. However, no mention was made of the broken dolls. His speeches to the court were reported in full. It was the miracle he had been hoping for. Mr Khoja emerged as a man of considerable 'moral stature' (so the newspaper described it), prepared to forgive and forget the wrongs done to him. His political stock rose in proportion and it was predicted that before long he would be enjoying his 'rightful place in the counsels that shape the destiny of the country' (again the phrase used by the *Trinidad Chronicle*).

The Rebels were furious. They had been outmanoeuvred at the last moment and wracked their brains to find some way to recoup their losses. Nothing presented itself. Mr Khoja had even made a convert – Saraswatee. She had attempted to overwhelm him with her gratitude for sparing Renouka, but he had refused her kisses and her tears. 'Save them for your husband,' he advised her. 'He need them a lot more than me.' Nevertheless, she baked a cake for him and bought him a tin of Huntley and Palmers biscuits.

The Rebels' most important and effective weapon, the inheritance, had been taken away from them. At the height of their campaign on behalf of Indrani, they had forced Mr Khoja to act circumspectly and, on the whole, they had been successful. He had lived frugally and done nothing extravagant. Now, however, with his slanderers silent, he was freed of these restraints. He had shown up his critics and the money was now his to do what he liked with.

And Mr Khoja knew what he wanted to do with the money. He wanted to build a new and very big house with a proper library to store his books. Over the years, he had grown increasingly dissatisfied with the house in Woodlands. For a start, there was the area itself. When they had first moved in, it was quiet and respectable, a suburb of doctors and lawyers, American cars and well-dressed children. But commerce had invaded and with it came noise and an entirely different class of people, like the neighbours next door, a family of motor mechanics. The doctors and lawyers moved out with their American cars and well-dressed children and in their place came the motor mechanics (the area was infested with them) the small shopkeepers and their badly dressed children. These migrants depressed the man of the people. They gave the place a bad name.

Then, there was the house itself, unprepossessing and old-fashioned. The size of things was an important factor in Mr Khoja's life. It infected his view of the world and the things he found in it. Put briefly, the bigger anything was, the better it was bound to be. Function and circumstance were unimportant and secondary considerations. This attitude he extended to all his possessions, except of course his clothes and, to a lesser extent, his wife.

Thus, Mr Khoja never bought a book under two hundred pages long if he could help it. The volumes lining his shelves were thick and massive; his car was the biggest on the market; and so were the gas-stove and refrigerator, the plates, cups and saucers, the dining-room table, the chairs and the piano. He had furnished his house on a monumental scale and among these vast objects he and his wife moved like pygmies.

'What's the point,' he asked his wife, 'of putting in new glass in these bookcases?'

'You can't leave them expose to all the dust and dirt, Govind. They go spoil in no time at all.'

'I will tell you something, Sumintra. What we need is a library. A real library. An air-conditioned library. That will keep the dust away.'

Mrs Khoja made a valiant attempt to think clearly and say something constructive. 'Where you going to build it?' she replied. 'Downstairs? But you know that if you touch one plank in this place the whole house go fall down.'

'Who say I going to build it in this place?' Mr Khoja smiled a faraway smile. He held his wife's hand. 'No, Sumintra. You misunderstand me.' He patted her wrists. 'I've got something quite different in mind. I'm thinking of building a big new house in Tropic Vale with a library filled up with books, shelves reaching right up to the ceiling. And a thick, thick carpet on the floor ...'

'What colour?'

Mr Khoja thought for a bit. 'How about green? A deep green? I think you would like that. Yes, a thick green carpet in the library. And in the sitting-room and dining-room we'll have a red carpet like the one we have now, only better and more expensive. And we'll buy the biggest crystal chandelier you could find in Trinidad and have that in the sitting-room and we'll have lots of real mahogany tables which Blackie will have to polish every day.'

Mrs Khoja squeaked delightedly. 'A crystal chandelier. A real crystal chandelier.' She squeezed her husband's hands. 'I always wanted one of those. And we must have tiles, Govind. We could even tile the sitting-room if you want.' She gazed up imploringly at her husband. Tiles were for Mrs Khoja, as for the sisters, the very epitome of luxury and modernity. Urmila had recently tiled every room in her house.

Mr Khoja laughed and patted her wrists again. 'Not in the sitting-room.' His wife's face fell. 'What about the thick red carpet we are going to have there? Like you've forgotten that.'

'Yes,' she said mournfully. 'I was forgetting about the carpet. But we could still tile the kitchen and the bathroom and the verandah, not so?'

'The bathrooms, you mean. Not bathroom. Yes. We'll have tiles all there,' Mr Khoja replied with a trace of sadness in his voice. 'We'll have tiles wherever you want them, except in the sitting-room. Is that a bargain?'

'That's a bargain, Govind.' Mrs Khoja shivered with delight. 'That's a bargain.'

'You will like living in Tropic Vale,' he said, speaking to her as if she were a child. 'The air there will be very good for your health.'

Tropic Vale was a new housing estate situated a few miles west of Port-of-Spain, near the sea. The land had been bought up by an enterprising firm of real estate agents and divided up into plots of an acre each. They had landscaped it, built a criss-cross of narrow roads planted with palm trees and hibiscus, installed water and electricity, and advertised in the *Trinidad Chronicle*. 'A chance to build your own paradise.' The response was even better than they had expected. The rich, anxious to build their own paradise, flocked by the score to buy the plots of land now going at exorbitant prices, and built extensive rambling houses with swimming-pools. Of the latter, some were heart-shaped, some kidney-shaped, and some round. One eccentric built himself a rectangular pool, only to find himself instantly damned throughout Tropic Vale as being completely devoid of any imagination. In the event, he made up for it by installing cracked storm lanterns, which did not work, on his gate-posts.

When Mr Khoja took his wife to see the plot of land he had bought, she said ecstatically, 'Is just like those pitcures of America you does see in magazines.'

'That's right,' her husband replied uneasily, secretly overawed by the splendid displays of originality and opulence he could see scattered about. 'But we not going to be like the rest of them,' he added. 'I'm going to build an old-fashioned two storeyed house. Still, I'll tell you one thing, Sumintra.'

'What?'

Mr Khoja surveyed the scene. The wind coming in from the sea ruffled his few remaining strands of hair. 'I'll tell you one thing,' he repeated. 'Our house is going to be bigger than the rest of them put together. You mark my words.'

Mrs Khoja nodded. It was a consoling thought.

4

When Romesh was released from prison, he did not return home. Instead, one of the gang came armed with instructions to collect everything from the house that belonged to him. There was not a great deal, only a few shirts and pairs of trousers and his shaving apparatus. Mrs Lutchman packed them all into a box which she tied up with a piece of string and handed over. She had been tempted to include *Treasure Island* but had looked all over the house and not been able to find it.

'You sure that is all you have for him?' The young man gazed suspiciously at her, then at the box.

'You think I would try and keep what rightfully belong to him? I is not a thief, you know. I is his mother.'

'Nobody saying you is a thief, Queenie.' It was Romesh who had conferred this title on her, which subsequently had been universally adopted by his friends. 'You might just have forget one or two things.' He stared insolently at her.

'I would be grateful to you if you didn't call me Queenie, young man. I old enough to be your grandmother. My name is Mrs Lutchman. My son didn't leave much of his things here with me. You know as well as me that in the last few months or so he hardly spend any of his time home with me.'

'I know. I know,' the young man said.

'Unless,' Mrs Lutchman added, 'he want the book his father buy for him one Christmas. It call *Treasure Island*. But like it get lost. If when I find it . . .'

The young man laughed loudly. 'No. No. You could keep that. I sure he wouldn't want that.' He shook his head, grinning at her. '*Treasure Island*. I must remember that one. Romesh never let out he was such a big reader.'

Mrs Lutchman dried her face with the sleeve of her blouse. 'He never read it.' She stared distractedly at the stains patterning the front of her dress. 'You know where it is he going to stay?' she asked softly, her head still bent and staring at her dress.

'I wish I knew myself,' the young man answered. ' "Rumesh" is the most unpredictable person I know. Even I didn't know he was going to beat up that house. What a guy! A truly great guy, one of the originals. I don't think you ever really appreciated his talents.'

'That kind of talent hard for a mother to appreciate.' She looked up from her dress and gazed searchingly at the young man's face. It seemed to her prematurely aged, to be superimposed on a dulled youthfulness. A kind of uneasy compromise between maturity and immaturity had settled over it. The cheeks, though yet unwrinkled, were hollow and sunken, and the skin stretched over the bone appeared almost translucent. It could have been a rubbery mask drawn over to hide the real face underneath. His eyes, bloodshot and lifeless, avoided her scrutiny. 'Look ...' she began, then seemed to change her mind. 'Tell him to take care of himself,' she said finally.

'I'll give him the message,' the young man promised. He paused, then to Mrs Lutchman's surprise repeated more gently, 'I'll give him your message Mrs Lutchman.'

'Just one more thing,' she said, encouraged by this. 'I don't think is too much to ask. Is only a small favour.'

The young man was embarrassed. His expression hardened. 'What it is you want me to do for you now?'

'If ...' Again she turned away and studied the front of her dress. Her mouth contracted. 'If anything happen to him, if he fall sick or something like that, you'll let me know?'

The young man was relieved. 'Sure I'll let you know, Mrs Lutchman. But, as I was saying, if I was you I wouldn't worry about Romesh. He know how to take care of himself. He's a big man now. Prison is no joke.'

'Yes. I know he is a big man now,' she repeated after him, 'but even big men does fall sick sometimes. You must give me your promise all the same.'

The young man rested his hand across his heart. 'I promise,' he said.

He kept his promise. About a month later he was back to tell her that Romesh had left the island. He had gone to New York. Mrs Lutchman took the news calmly. Her questions were purely factual.

'How did he get the money?' she asked.

'I think he borrow some and work for the rest. He was working in a gas station down Mucurapo for a bit. He can work very hard when he want to, your son.'

This aspect of Romesh's character surprised Mrs Lutchman, but, though pride stirred fitfully in her breast, she said nothing about it. 'I wonder who it is lend him the money. He couldn't have get all that much working in a gas station.'

The young man shrugged his shoulders. 'Who cares who lent him the money? Romesh is a popular guy. Some people I know would die just to do him a favour.'

Mrs Lutchman was astonished when, some weeks later, he sent her a postcard from New York with a picture of the Empire State Building on the front. The card said very little, though, again to Mrs Lutchman's surprise, he did apologize for not telling her of his departure. But, he wrote, he had had no desire to 'make a fuss' and 'embarrass her.' After that, she never heard from him again. She carefully put the postcard among those other treasures – the developing kit, the crushed rose petals she had gathered from the garden on the day of her husband's funeral, the jewellery she never wore – all of them reminders of what might have been but which, due perhaps to some indelible quirk in nature, had been denied their proper expression.

She continued to receive the occasional bit of news from the young man with whom Romesh corresponded regularly. One afternoon he came to the house in a flurry of excitement, waving a letter in the air. Mrs Lutchman was in the back yard bent over the washing tub. Rover, his hair long and matted, lay panting under the avocado tree.

'Great news! Great news!' he shouted. Rover lumbered up to him in a friendly way and licked at his trousers. The young man kicked him away.

'You shouldn't kick him like that,' Mrs Lutchman said angrily. 'He wasn't going to bite you.' Rover rubbed himself against her skirt. She patted him. She gazed at the thin pieces of paper flying through the air. She could just see the untidy, slanting scrawl. 'What happen?' she asked, a look of alarm spreading over her face. She stared at the fluttering pieces of paper.

'Your son is a married man now. He got married last week.'

'Married?'

'That's right. Last week it happen. Is a rich girl too. Let me see.' He steadied the bits of paper and squinted at the writing. Mrs Lutchman, coming up, tiptoed in an attempt to peep over his shoulder. The young man shifted so that she should not see. She walked slowly back to the tub and picking up a piece of her washing began to wring it. 'Ah yes. Here it is. He get married to a Puerto Rican girl.'

'A Puerto Rican?'

'That's right. A little coloured girl. A Negro in fact. Just like me.' The young man seemed very proud. 'That boy was true to the last,' he said. 'Christ! What a guy! What a guy! One of the originals.'

Mrs Lutchman pegged the washing out on the line, carrying the clips in her mouth.

'That will call for a little celebration tonight,' the young man continued. 'What you say to that?'

Mrs Lutchman mumbled something through the clips.

'What you saying?'

She shook her head to signify that it was not important. The young man came across and clapped her on the shoulder. 'So long then, Mrs Lutchman, I must go and spread the news now.'

The family was duly scandalized. Mr Khoja, in a fit of absentmindedness, gave her twenty dollars and immediately afterwards wondered why he had done such a foolish thing. Mrs Khoja said, 'But they does speak Spanish in Puerto Rico, not so, Baby?' Mrs Lutchman did not know and Mr Khoja had to confirm the fact. 'But I never know Romesh could speak Spanish. Still, he was always a bright boy. I suppose that's why he does suffer from nerves.' Mrs Lutchman was silent. This aspect of the matter appeared not to worry her all that much.

The young man never came again. Mrs Lutchman assumed that he too, encouraged by Romesh's example, had set off for New York to find himself a Puerto Rican heiress. Her sole source of information now was Mrs MacKintosh. From her, Mrs Lutchman learned that Romesh was healthy, happy, rich and entirely successful in all that he undertook. He was dogged, Mrs MacKintosh confirmed, by good fortune.

'It's there in the leaves,' she said. 'Just look at that ring and if that is not a dollar sign I'll eat my hat.'

And Mrs Lutchman, bending over and staring hard at the mess of leaves, saw nothing. 'Yes,' she would reply. 'I see the ring and dollar sign clear as daylight at the bottom of the cup.'

Romesh's capture of the Puerto Rican heiress did not impress the sisters. She was forced to listen to their self-righteous caterwaulings. She did so in silence.

'If you had paid attention to we at the beginning,' they said, 'all this confusion wouldn't have happen and you would have had no cause to come crying to we now.'

Mrs Lutchman had not gone 'crying' to them. They had come to her. Nevertheless, she made no protest.

'But no. You wouldn't listen to we. You had to be obstinate and listen to your own mind, following what your worthless husband say and not heeding our words. You see where all that get you? You wouldn't make Bhaskar find a job and you wouldn't go and live with Urmila. No. That was too much for you to do. Your son had to be a doctor.'

'And he going to be a doctor,' Mrs Lutchman replied.

'He not a doctor yet. Bear that in mind. He still have two or three years to go and a lot could happen in that time. And even if he come back a doctor, who say he going to make much of you in your old age? Education does make children ungrateful. You was too obstinate, Baby, and now you paying the price. What a man sow he have to reap. Your crying won't do you any good now. It too late for that. Just hope that Bhaskar don't turn out as ungrateful as his brother. Don't think just because he studying to be a doctor the same thing can't happen. Just hope and pray. That's all that's left to you.'

They offered her no solace for her loss. Looking at their ageing, wrinkled faces, she could detect no trace of genuine sympathy or pity. Of such things, it seemed, they were incapable. They were washed out. The aridity of those lives communicated itself so strongly to her at that moment, that instinctively, she recoiled and shied away from their sterile preachings in fear and disgust.

5

It was a time for departure. Not long after Romesh had married, Renouka too departed the island. She was emigrating to Canada intending to work there as a domestic servant. She came to bid Mrs Lutchman good-bye.

'So, like you too leaving we for good, Renouka?'

'You shouldn't say things like that, Mousie. You making it sound as if I going away to die or something.' She smiled at Mrs Lutchman. 'It might only be for a few years, you never know. I mightn't like the place at all.'

Mrs Lutchman did not contradict her. 'And what going to happen to your mother?'

'I hoping to send for she after I see what the place is like.'

'And your father?'

Renouka lowered her eyes. 'That is another question altogether, Mousie. I would have liked him to come with us but I don't think he would like it over there. Anyway, what would be the point? He not good for anything after what happen.'

Rudranath had left the St Ann's Mental Hospital. He lived apart from his family (exactly where no one knew). He had not returned to his old job. Instead, Rudranath drove a taxi. Mrs Lutchman had travelled with him once or twice, but he was silent and uncommunicative. He seemed not to know who she was. Her overtures had been repulsed with looks of blank incomprehension and he received her fare as he would that of any other passenger. This had startled her, but in time she grew accustomed to the sight of his car picking up and letting off passengers on the Tragarete Road into Port-of-Spain. However, her unease was such that she no longer flagged him down. Rudranath, for his part, seemed neither to notice nor to care.

Mrs Lutchman looked at Renouka and nodded. 'Maybe you right,' she said. She kissed her on the cheek and wished her luck. Not many weeks afterwards, Saraswatee followed her daughter out to the prairies of Saskatchewan, and Rudranath, unperturbed and probably unaware, continued to ply his taxi along the Tragarete Road.

Some time later, Mrs Lutchman found the copy of *Treasure*

Island she had been searching for. It lay in a box containing old shoes and discarded clothing. On impulse, she wrote neatly across the inside front cover in large, laboriously constructed lettering, 'Romesh Lutchman, left Trinidad June 1955. Married in New York August 5th.' She closed the book and hid it among her other treasures. The record was complete.

Chapter Six

1

Bhaskar had been away for four years. He wrote regularly. From the accounts he gave he appeared to be making good progress and had already passed a couple of major examinations. He sent his mother pictures of himself and his friends, taken with the camera.

'What a lot of weight he is putting on,' she would exclaim delightedly to the lodgers, comparing it with the photograph in the sitting-room taken by Mr Khoja on the day of the farewell lunch. And she would add, 'But then he was much too thin as a boy.' The lodgers listened patiently at breakfast and dinner to her rhapsodizing on the days she received the letters. 'You know,' she would tell them, 'once that boy set his mind on something, nothing in the world could make him change. He would stick to it through thick and thin. You think he wanted to be a policeman or fireman when he was small? No sir. Nothing like that. From the time he was five years old he used to say to me, "Ma, I going to be a doctor when I get big." Those were his exact words. Cross my heart.'

The lodgers would murmur appreciatively. They had begun to dislike Bhaskar. Mrs Lutchman bought an album in which she arranged in chronological order all the photographs Bhaskar sent her and this too she exhibited at regular intervals, not only to the lodgers but to the Khojas and Mrs MacKintosh.

Mrs MacKintosh, naturally, provided her with the information Bhaskar's letters did not supply. She assured Mrs Lutchman that he was the most brilliant student in his year and that his professors were extremely fond of him. The most frequent 'sign' in the tea-leaves was what Mrs MacKintosh was fond of describing as 'long, thin fingers'.

'I wonder what that mean?' Mrs Lutchman would ask,

knowing well what the answer would be, but longing to hear the sacred words fall from Mrs MacKintosh's own lips.

Mrs MacKintosh never failed her. 'That, my dear Mrs Lutchman, can only mean one thing.' Her blue eyes wandered vacantly over the room. 'Yes. That can only mean one thing. He is going to be a famous surgeon. That sign means he has delicate fingers. There can be no doubt about that. You can take my word for it.'

'A famous surgeon,' Mrs Lutchman repeated dreamily. 'A famous surgeon.' She would lift her eyes to the framed photograph of the plumpish young man, standing at the top of a flight of steps, his cheeks folded into a strange smile.

Thus comforted and reassured, she waited with a full, secure confidence for the return of her son. She imagined it all. Dr B. Lutchman, no longer a mythical but a real person, with an air-conditioned office in the city and an impressive house, perhaps in Tropic Vale. There in minutest detail was the neat white tunic, the black bag and the stethoscope dangling from the neck. 'You must take these tablets three times a day without fail,' she imagined him saying. 'After meals. Not before.' She wondered what sort of woman he would marry, and Mrs Lutchman took a silent vow that, whoever she might be, she would treat her nicely. They would be friends and no doubt, just as she had gone to the house in the country, her daughter-in-law would come to this house to bear her children. And her grandchildren: what would they be like? Would they resemble Ram? She puzzled over their names and characters and pictured herself scolding them and advising them to follow in their father's footsteps. 'He is the best surgeon on the island,' she would say. 'Watch what he does do and try and copy him.' At night, she dreamt of hospitals and operating theatres and long, thin fingers wielding the scalpels. In such a manner did Mrs Lutchman wait for her son.

2

She occupied her days by looking after the lodgers and Rover. Rover had not proved quite the dog she had led herself and others to expect. Admittedly, his hair could not have been much longer. It almost covered his eyes and hung in clotted strands from his back and legs. But Rover was less than eighteen inches tall, hardly big enough to impress anyone, neither friend nor foe.

Nevertheless, undaunted by this, Mrs Lutchman spread rumours about his viciousness and ferocity. To lend stature to these claims, she nailed a sign on the front gate that read, 'Beware of the Dog', painted in large black letters. This fooled no one. Rover's meekness was almost legendary. It was a well-known fact that he only barked at strangers from behind the safety of the closed gate. The moment they entered the yard, he either licked joyfully at them or, tucking his tail between his legs, retreated with an ineffectual snarl into the house. Rover had only one victim to his credit and that, not a thief but a lodger. Mrs Lutchman, despite her protestations of sorrow, was proud of this exploit. As she said afterwards, 'You just put one foot wrong and he on top of you in no time at all. That dog wouldn't let you get away with a thing.' This was cold comfort to the bitten lodger, who thereafter developed an undying hatred for the animal.

To encourage his ferocity, Mrs Lutchman stopped feeding him rice and curries and gave him instead Dr Ballard's dog food. The advertisement had promised her a bouncy, healthy animal. For two weeks Rover lapped it up and Mrs Lutchman, in a burst of optimism, bought a whole case of the stuff which she obtained at a discount. That was overdoing it. Rover's taste for Dr Ballard's declined as rapidly as it had arisen. Chunks of the ground-up meat lay uneaten on his plate. Mrs Lutchman tried to tempt him with different flavours and even went so far as to change the brand of dog-food. It made no difference. Rover began to wither away, looking less and less like that bouncy animal shown on the label. Tins of useless Dr Ballard's lined the cupboard in the kitchen and Rover staggered lethargically through the house to collapse under the kitchen table and gaze up at her with sad, yearning eyes. The bitten lodger was overjoyed. Mrs Lutchman surrendered. She plied him with rice, curries and stews and, slowly, Rover returned to life. His tail began to wag again and his eyes regained their sparkle. Disgusted, Mrs Lutchman gave away the surplus tins of Dr Ballard's to Mrs MacKintosh. She was rather taken aback by this gift.

'But you know I don't have a dog, Mrs Lutchman.'

'You could find some use for it, I sure.'

Mrs MacKintosh frowned, but in the end she accepted it. What she did with them, Mrs Lutchman never discovered.

On race days, Mrs Lutchman went to the Queen's Park Savannah to see the horses run. Spreading a blanket on the grass in the shade of one of the tall trees, she would watch the horses canter from the paddock to the starting gate. Leaning her back against the tree trunk, her legs stretched straight out before her on the blanket, Mrs Lutchman made her predictions for the race.

She had her definite favourites among the jockeys and an equally definite distaste for others. Her favourite was a jockey called 'Mice' Poolool. She followed his progress eagerly, rejoicing in his triumphs, despairing in his defeats. As was her habit in so many other regions of her life, her interpretation of what happened when his horse failed to find a place in the first four was devious.

Mrs Lutchman could never bring herself to believe that he had been straightforwardly outmanoeuvred. 'I sure they squeeze him against the rail in the back straight,' she would say to herself, scanning the list of horses and jockeys provided by the newspaper which was an indispensable item on these outings. 'They have it in for that man, I tell you. They want to break his leg. They is a lot of crooks the pack of them.'

Thus, in Mrs Lutchman's mind, the 'back straight' assumed a notoriety that no amount of reasoning could correct. What happened there lay at the root of all Mice Poolool's failures. It was the source of all misfortune and evil. 'Mark my words,' she would tell the lodgers, 'they going to kill that man in the back straight one of these days. Jealousy don't know no bounds.'

At the end of each race meeting, she made a note of his position in the final placings of the jockeys. Luckily for her, Mice Poolool was one of the better jockeys and always finished well up in the ratings. She would nod her head in satisfaction. Virtue had ultimately, and despite all the nefarious dealings in the back straight, triumphed. Only after the last race of the day had been run would Mrs Lutchman stroll leisurely back to the house, recounting to herself the events of the day and compiling a catalogue of the defeats and triumphs of her hero. These she would retail over dinner for the benefit of the lodgers.

Apart from looking after the lodgers and Rover, visits to the family, trips to the Queen's Park Savannah on race days, the regular round of weddings and funerals and feuding with the neighbours about the breadfruit tree, Mrs Lutchman discovered a further diversion in the beggars who, for some unknown reason, had taken to roaming the district on Saturday mornings. They came to the house, men and women, in groups of three or four. Mrs Lutchman would stand by the front gate, her dark face creased by a benevolent smile, doling out the pennies from her handbag and admonishing them not to spend it on drink. Bowing and scraping, they in return would shower blessings on her and her family and promise not to misuse what she had given. One of them had offered to read her palm, but, faithful as ever to the precepts of Mrs MacKintosh, she refused. 'It's not reliable,' she explained. Once every month, she brought them into the kitchen and fed them. One old man in particular she had cause to remember. He was tall and thin, with long straggling white hair and a thick beard. He refused to eat the food because it did not have any meat in it. As he was leaving, he picked one of the larger avocados off the tree. Mrs Lutchman was so astonished by this piece of boldness that she said nothing. After that, she never saw him again.

Religion had gradually come to play a bigger role in her life. She attended pujas at least twice a week. The opportunity for doing this came from a newly formed body, the Hindu League. It raised funds from bazaars, raffles and, most important, donations from wealthy Hindus. Mr Khoja was one of its leading lights. Wracked by internal dissensions (at the inaugural meeting there were already threats by some people to break away and form a rival group), it somehow managed to survive the rivalries and clashing interests and, to the general astonishment, actually succeeded in buying an acre of land bordering the Churchill-Roosevelt Highway a few miles out of Port-of-Spain.

Here it was planned to build a 'cultural centre'. For the moment, however, nothing could be done. The Rebels had seized upon the League as a convenient weapon in their war against Mr Khoja and several of its founder patrons (Mr Cardoso, Catholic though he was, had once again rallied to the cause and donated a thousand dollars. He was made an honorary member), chief among them Mr Khoja, had withdrawn their support. Jagdev, seizing his opportunity, had had himself elected Chairman of the League and there were rumours of a move afoot to have him declared Chairman for life. Prominent among those responsible for this sad state of affairs was Urmila. Jagdev had long forgiven her her desertion at the time of the election and their friendship had become increasingly intimate. There was even talk that they might marry. She had been elected Secretary of the League, a post she relished. Week after week she flooded its members with notices of 'important meetings' which never took place and intriguing ideas for fund-raising drives, like fashion shows and concerts, which also never took place. It was not long before Urmila emerged as the true boss of the League and Jagdev, whose interest in the 'cultural centre' was nominal anyway, faded into the background, little more than a figurehead to the energetic, ambitious Urmila.

Mrs Lutchman remained aloof from the politics of the League. True, she deplored Urmila's schemings and mismanagement, but she never said so aloud. The election had killed her taste for such things. Lacking a home, the League held its pujas in the homes of the richer members. Mrs Lutchman attended these pujas regularly and at the end of each one, dropped a shilling into the collection-box handed round by one of Urmila's minions. This money disappeared without trace.

There was another unlikely advantage to be gained in going to these pujas. Rover adored the prasad she brought back home with her. He would wait patiently at the front gate for her return and leap upon her in an attempt to get at the little paper bag. At first, thinking it sacrilegious, she refused to let him have it. But Rover's disappointment was so great that finally she consulted the ubiquitous Ramnarace, one of the League's panel of pundits.

'Nothing wrong with that,' he told her. 'Anyway, the prasad not all that good either. It almost uneatable if you ask me.'

That was true. The prasad was stiff, floury and tasteless. As in everything else the League put its hand to, it had, through lack of money, to be done on the cheap. Even Mrs Lutchman, despite her religious fervour and her disapproval of Ramnarace's frank opinion, was forced to admit that she was unable to bring herself to eat it. Thus, she was secretly relieved to discover that it was perfectly permissible to give it to Rover. And Rover loved the prasad. It was no passing fancy like his flirtation with Dr Ballard's. He fell upon it with a joy that never diminished and Mrs Lutchman, to please him, began bringing home two bags instead of one.

'You is a real little Hindu,' she would say, watching his tail wag as he buried his head in the paper bag. 'A real little Hindu.'

At Christmas time, Mrs Lutchman brought the artificial tree out of its wrapping and set it up, as her husband had done, in the sitting-room. She decorated it with the help of the lodgers. The lights bubbled and threw weird shadows across the ceiling and walls; and, as a special treat, she bought a bottle of Gilbey's wine which she shared with the lodgers.

3

It was not long after Mrs Lutchman had celebrated Bhaskar's fourth Christmas away from home that his letters ceased to arrive. For a month, there had been nothing. The lodgers tried to comfort her. 'Maybe they get lost in the post. Don't worry. I sure you will be hearing from him soon.'

'You really think they get lost in the post?'

'I sure that's what happen.'

Mrs MacKintosh studied the tea leaves with extra care. The long, thin fingers had disappeared and in their place came nothing. But she too was optimistic. 'It's possible Sonny Boy has a little illness. Still, I don't think it's anything to worry about. It might be no more than a little fever. You'll be hearing soon. Don't worry.'

Another two weeks passed. The lodgers were less assured in their explanations and they stopped concocting their elaborate tales of lost letters that had turned up years afterwards. Even Mrs MacKintosh allowed a frown to cross her face. 'It's very funny,' she said. 'I was so sure you would have heard from him by now.' This was the first time she had confessed herself at fault. Mrs Lutchman was frantic. She forgot her good resolutions.

'That boy must have taken up with some woman or the other and gone and forget his mother. Is some no good woman who leading him astray. Fever don't take so long to get cured.'

The lodgers and Mrs MacKintosh were silent. Mrs Lutchman went to the Indian Commissioner's office, but they could tell her nothing. 'The Indian postal service is very good,' they informed her. 'Letters hardly ever get lost.' She broke down and cried. They promised to make inquiries, but nothing was done. She wrote letters endlessly to her son at the usual address and finally received a reply from one of his friends saying that Bhaskar had had to discontinue his studies because of illness. But the letter did not say what the illness was. Again she sat down and wrote her large, laborious scrawl to the professors, to her son, to the Indian Ministry of Education. And after weeks a reply filtered through. Mr Lutchman had had a nervous breakdown and was in a hospital where he was receiving suitable medical treatment. They apologized for the delay and confusion, explaining that they had thought it wiser not to alarm her unnecessarily.

Mrs Lutchman was beside herself. She had no clear idea what a nervous breakdown was. It conjured up before her visions of the lunatic asylum at St Ann's. She had been there once to see Rudranath. She pictured to herself the neat lawns and beds of brightly coloured flowers, the carefully planted trees, all of which conspired, ultimately, to emphasize the distress it sought to disguise. Her dreams were filled with images of the men and women incarcerated there, lost to life and the world. The sight of Rudranath's taxi along the Tragarete Road, redoubled her frenzy. Was her son to be one of these? She gazed distraught at the photograph of the young man standing at the top of a flight of steps. Was he to end his days being taken for walks in the late afternoon across those well-tended lawns? She knew so little and was forced to appeal as a last resort to Mr Khoja.

She had not told him or the other members of the family what was happening. For a long time she could not bring herself to make that terrible admission. Now, however, it was too late. Mr Khoja's intervention was effective. He wrote to the university, in his best authoritarian manner, and got a reply immediately. Mr Lutchman was well enough to travel and they had decided to send him home. There was no question of his being able to continue his studies. Mrs Lutchman took the news surprisingly well. The certainty of this one thing – his return – comforted her. She began to prepare his room for him.

4

Bhaskar's arrival was uneventful. There was no crowd of relations waiting to greet him on the dock, such as awaited the coming home of the most obscure relative who, by that simple act, was transformed, for a few days at least, into a figure of interest, to be listened to with respect. Only his mother and Mr Khoja were there to meet him. Mr Khoja, dressed as if for the office (he liked to give the impression that he had an office), was at his kindest and most sympathetic, fussing around Mrs Lutchman. He was one of those people who, if they flower at all, do so only in the midst of tragedy.

Mrs Lutchman sat quietly on one of the cane-backed chairs in the lounge, staring at the posters of blue, tropical seas and white sand beaches on which bikini-clad American women reclined under gay umbrellas. 'Visit the sunny Caribbean, home of the steel-band, the limbo, the calypso, and dance the night away in one of our modern, luxuriously appointed hotels.' Mrs Lutchman swept her eyes along the row of similarly worded posters, lining the walls of the lounge. She was wearing an unadorned white dress reaching to her ankles and at every slight movement, the gold bracelets on her wrist jangled. Her expression was difficult to decipher. A casual observer would not have known whether she was sad or happy.

Several people, recognizing Mr Khoja, came up and chatted with him. At other times, he wandered off by himself for extended periods and returned with news of the ship's progress. It was already over an hour late. Mrs Lutchman smiled at each new communication and her bracelets jangled. The lounge filled up with people, waiting to welcome returning sons and daughters, eager to sample their attractive foreign accents. 'Hello Ma. Hello Pa.' 'Eh! But look at him,' they would say, 'talking like a real Englishman.' Mrs Lutchman ignored their presence and continued to sit quietly and gaze at the posters.

There was a general stir and rise in the hum of conversation. Mrs Lutchman turned her head involuntarily and saw, beyond the jig-saw of cranes and masts in the harbour, a long, grey ship sliding slowly towards her, smoke pouring from its funnels. Mr Khoja bent and whispered in her ear. She rose from the chair, and, smoothing down the creases in her dress, pushed her way through the crowded lounge and out onto the dock. She watched the gradual approach of the ship. Within minutes, it was close enough for her to distinguish the lines of passengers leaning over the deck rails. Mr Khoja stood beside her, fingering his car-keys and smiling benignly at the groups of chattering people around him.

Mrs Lutchman's gaze wandered away from the approaching ship, to the narrow stretch of water separating it from the pier, then back again to the ship where she could now see the faces of some of the passengers leaning over the deck rails. Many of them were waving handkerchiefs and blowing kisses to those on shore. She turned once more to look at the water and at the throng of happy, expectant faces pressed round her. Mr Khoja tapped her lightly on the shoulder and, extending his arm, pointed at the ship. She followed the line indicated and saw her son, peering down not at her but at Mr Khoja and the crowd on the dock. Mr Khoja jerked his thumb vigorously in Mrs Lutchman's direction and at last Bhaskar swivelled his head slowly and smiled at her. He wore glasses, a new thing, and a drab, ill-fitting suit. But his mother, her back to the boat, did not see. She was facing the row of warehouses, crying. Mr

Khoja swung her round gently, and, drying her tears, she smiled and fluttered her handkerchief. Bhaskar waved back.

The sides of the ship bumped lightly against the dock. There was a scurry of passengers away from the rails. When Mrs Lutchman looked again, Bhaskar had disappeared. The gangway was lowered and the long line of returning students filed slowly down it, carrying suitcases and impressively professional briefcases. Bhaskar was one of the last to appear. He struggled down to his mother and Mr Khoja waiting at the foot of the gangway. He shook Mr Khoja's hand and, dropping the suitcase he was carrying, hugged his mother.

'The camera, son,' she asked softly, 'you still have it?'

Bhaskar released her. Mr Khoja laughed softly. 'Here is your son who has been away from you all these years and that is all you could think of to ask him!'

Mrs Lutchman seemed not to hear. 'The camera, son,' she repeated. 'You still have it?'

'I lose it just before I left,' Bhaskar said.

'You lose it?' She stared at him, wide-eyed, disbelieving. Bhaskar nodded. He took up his suitcase and walked quickly towards the Customs shed.

Chapter Seven

1

The visitors appeared in the days that followed. They arrived with a processional solemnity and talked in whispers to Mrs Lutchman, gazing at the same time with a funereal concern upon Bhaskar, with whom they tried to avoid having any direct conversation. He was not communicative and his silences, which they suspected were deliberate, implied an unfriendliness and hostility which made even the most polite enquiry after his health seem an infringement of his privacy. In addition, there was something the matter with his eyes: they gave the impression of being independent of the rest of him. No one could say precisely what was odd about them, but their suggestion of a life other than the inert one he presented to them was inescapable. He did answer the questions addressed directly to him, but with a curt brevity and pointedness in itself off-putting and made doubly so by that strange quality of his eyes which seemed to be saying that they neither knew nor cared who all these people were or what their questions meant. This was sufficiently unpleasant for most of them never to come back.

Mrs Lutchman too had been ill at ease during the first few days. He had stolidly refused to tell her any more about the camera and how it came to be lost; her other questions he answered with a monosyllabic reluctance and never once did he himself venture to reveal any new information. More often than not, he would merely look at her in his peculiar way and not answer at all, but after a week she had got used to this and it did not bother her unduly. Bhaskar showed no desire to go out and ignored even the newspaper. He tried to avoid any unnecessary human contact, spending most of the day in his bedroom with the door locked, as far as his mother could tell, doing nothing. His presence in the house had a bad effect on the lodgers, those undoubtedly heroic but ill-starred figures. As they had done at the height of Romesh's campaign against them, they were absent more often and took to having breakfast and dinner served in their rooms.

Mrs Lutchman contributed, albeit unwittingly, to this state of insecurity. Afraid of what Bhaskar might do if he were disturbed, she warned them to be quiet, and there were times when, though they were all in the house, the only sounds would be the rattle of pots and pans in the kitchen. Nevertheless, Mrs Lutchman was not an entirely unrealistic woman; she was not so blinded by concern for her son that she forgot the effect this constraint might have on the well-being of her charges. Yet again, her reputation for motherliness was being undermined through no fault of her own and the lodgers were, after all, her main source of income. Should they suddenly see fit to leave, she would be left stranded and would, without a doubt, have to sell the house and live off the charity of one of her relatives. She made an unsuccessful attempt to have the mere pittance of her husband's pension raised. The situation was desperate. It had occurred to her that Bhaskar might be able to teach and it was with this in mind that she decided to go to Tropic Vale and see Mr Khoja.

2

Mr Khoja had found himself becoming, much to his dislike, the patron saint of Mrs Lutchman. If nothing else, it was financially unprofitable. Nevertheless, it flattered him to think that here was one person who saw him as a man of limitless power, to whom all doors opened automatically and for whom all problems were as no problems. Therein lay his weakness. His increasing political notoriety only strengthened these beliefs and it was obvious to Mrs Lutchman that he alone could extricate her from her present predicament.

The house Mr Khoja had built in Tropic Vale was, as he had promised his wife, large and old-fashioned. It was aggressively so. There were few concessions to modernity. It was a square, two-storeyed building, surrounded by a high concrete fence. This fence had given the greatest offence to his fellow residents and they had gone to the lengths of signing a petition demanding that he demolish it. They claimed, with considerable justice, that it was a hideous blot on the landscape and 'wrecked the unity of the environment'. Mr Khoja, however, had resisted all their efforts. 'That wall is staying there,' he told them, 'whether it wrecks the unity of the environment or not. You will only demolish it over my dead body.' The wall stayed, but Mr Khoja's peace of mind was severely shaken. There were very few people in Tropic Vale who deigned to talk to him. Even conducted tours of his air-conditioned library with its fine stock of books and thick green carpet failed to make them change their minds.

He received Mrs Lutchman kindly, in what he called his 'study', an adjunct off the library. Its only furniture was an impressive mahogany desk and two chairs, a big, upholstered one for himself and a smaller, plain wooden one, which he offered to Mrs Lutchman. Yet, despite these trappings of power, Mr Khoja's apprehension was marked. After the initial exchange of pleasantries, Mrs Lutchman launched into the attack.

'I was thinking about Bhaskar. I don't think it good for him to be home by himself all day. What you say?'

'How do you mean, Vimla?' Mr Khoja replied guardedly.

'Well, for one thing, it not healthy for him to be inside the house all day long. He need more fresh air for a start.'

'He could go for walks. There is nothing to stop him doing that. The Savannah not all that far away. He could get all the exercise and fresh air he want there.' Mr Khoja thought he had parried successfully, but he was visibly worried. He was by now well enough acquainted with Mrs Lutchman's dexterity in such matters.

'He is not that kind of boy. Anyway, people go think he crazy if he start walking all over the Savannah by himself. You know yourself how stupid these local people is. No. What I think he really need is something to occupy his mind with.' She shot one of her sharper glances at him.

'Well, if it's mental exercise you think he need and not bodily exercise, I could lend him some of my books to read, though you know I don't like doing that.' It was a sacrifice he was willing to make. He was glad to be let off so lightly. But Mrs Lutchman had deceived him.

'That would be nice,' she said. 'I sure Bhaskar would like that – he used to read a lot when he was a boy. Bertram Russell and people like that.'

'Bertrand.'

'Eh?'

'The man's name is Bertrand Russell. Not Bertram Russell. You shouldn't go about the place changing a man's name just like that.' Mr Khoja gazed severely at her.

'Yes, all right. Bertrand Russell. He used to read a lot of that.'

'Actually,' Mr Khoja said suddenly, getting up from his chair and walking across to the door. 'I have an even better idea. Before I lend him any of my books, he might like to read something that I myself write not too long ago. Wait here.' He went out of the study. There being no reflections for her to stare at, Mrs Lutchman gazed contemplatively into space, fixing her eyes on a point just above where Mr Khoja's head would have been. Mr Khoja returned with a pamphlet printed on pink paper and brandished it before Mrs Lutchman. She read the title: 'Education as Creative Endeavour: A Speech delivered by G. Khoja on the anniversary of the death of Jean Jacques Rousseau, to the Curepe Women's Institute.' He glanced fondly at it and read a few lines of it under his breath, juggling his head in admiration. 'Bhasker could read this and tell me what he think. It's a summary of my ideas in the education field.'

Mrs Lutchman accepted the pamphlet without enthusiasm. 'I'll give it to him,' she said. She folded the pamphlet and put it in her handbag. 'But I still think the best thing for him would be a job. That will take his mind off things.'

Mr Khoja had sat down again, his palms sheathing his nose. Mrs Lutchman gazed at the point just above his head. 'Job?' Mr Khoja's animation disappeared abruptly.

'Yes. Say a little teaching, for instance. Say he read what you write, then before you know it he go be carrying out your ideas.'

It struck Mr Khoja that he was being blackmailed. 'This is

no joke, Vimla. That speech is about serious matters.' Mr Khoja frowned testily.

'I know it's a serious matter. That's exactly why I want you to get Bhaskar a teaching job so he could put your ideas into practice.'

The logic was, in its own peculiar way, impeccable and Mr Khoja wondered whether Mrs Lutchman was even cleverer than he had given her credit for. An outright refusal was out of the question. He played for time.

'But Vimla, my ideas need special conditions before you can put them into practice. They need ...'

'You got to start some time,' Mrs Lutchman said. 'In time you will have your own school but for the time ...'

'How do you know I can get him a job?'

'Well, you are an important man. You know all kinds of people and what you say does carry weight. Everybody know that. Is only your modesty that does prevent you from seeing it.'

It would have taken a much greater man than Mr Khoja to deny these pleasant things. He compromised. 'But that doesn't mean I can get him a job.' He laughed in a way that suggested that this was precisely what it meant. 'And I'm not that important either. I just do what I have to do ...'

'What God intended you to do,' Mrs Lutchman helped him on.

Mr Khoja scowled. 'And you think God intended me to find a job for Bhaskar?'

Mrs Lutchman stared at the point above his head.

'Anyway, what could he teach if it comes to that?'

Mrs Lutchman thought for a moment. 'How about a little biology?' she suggested, in much the same manner as if she were offering a guest pepper-sauce. 'You should have seen all them butterfly he used to catch when he was a boy. And nobody could have drawn better than he.'

'He was studying to be a doctor after all,' Mr Khoja mused. 'Well, I'll try and see what I can do for him, Vimla. Mind you, I don't promise anything. Even I can't move mountains.' He smiled regretfully at her.

Mrs Lutchman was quick to appreciate his caution. She was

anxious to soothe. 'At bottom it's all in God's hands,' she said.

'True. True. You musn't forget to give Bhaskar the speech. You must tell me what he think about it.'

'I won't forget.' She seemed almost gay.

Mrs Lutchman returned home with a lighter heart, and Mr Khoja, against his better judgement, began to make enquiries.

3

Mrs MacKintosh had taken to seeing things again since Mrs Lutchman had told her about the teaching job. It emerged that the long, slim fingers she had been seeing in the cups (and now she saw them in greater abundance than ever) had nothing at all to do with operating theatres and surgeons, but denoted pieces of chalk.

'Sometimes it is very difficult to know exactly what these things mean, Mrs Lutchman. If I had all the facts at my disposal I could have told you that a long time ago.'

'You mean to say that you would have know he was going to be a teacher all along?'

'Without a shadow of a doubt, my dear Mrs Lutchman. Without a shadow of a doubt. Still, as the saying goes, it's better late than never.'

'Right,' Mrs Lutchman said. 'Truer word was never spoken.'

4

When Mrs Lutchman heard from Mr Khoja that there was a vacancy for a biology master in Queen's College, her initial feeling of delight soon gave way to anxiety and misgivings about the whole affair. She had never fully considered what Bhaskar's reaction might be. She had not consulted him about it and now she was afraid he would be angry. The possibility of violence always lurked at the back of her mind. However, she had not failed to notice the changes that had occurred in her son's behaviour since his return. Gone were the prolonged silences and unnatural torpor that had upset her so much at first. In their place had come a mocking irony which he extended not only to other people (prominent among them Mr Khoja) but to himself as well. Release from the terrors of ambition had liberated Bhaskar; if only negatively. He laughed at the absurdities of his youth: the disastrous swimming expeditions with his father, the long nights of fruitless study eked out with bottles of tonic wine, the forays into Bertrand Russell and Charles Dickens. His sarcasm spared nothing. This hurt Mrs Lutchman.

He had, to her surprise, actually read the pamphlet Mr Khoja had given her. It was dedicated to Rousseau, in whose company 'the author' claimed to have spent many a happy hour. It was, as Mr Khoja had said, a summary of his ideas. The style was overblown and garrulous. In it, Mr Khoja wrote that the teacher must consider himself 'a man with a mission'. He must be pure of heart, for only then could he interpret the great teachings of Mother Nature. Above all, he must not be stirred by thoughts of financial remuneration. Mr Khoja laid great stress on this last aspect of the matter. He went on to decry the American influence with its emphasis on 'material well-being and gadgetry' which led its disciples to neglect 'those truths that spring directly from the heart of man and are corroborated by the Great Book of Nature.' Furthermore, that he, 'the author', with a full and humble awareness of his limitations, had made it his life's work to remedy the situation and at great personal expense to himself had decided to found a school 'sometime in the near future.' At this point he had grown lyrical. 'This school will be set in the heart of Nature. Its roof will be the sky and its four walls the surrounding hills; for a bed there will be the soft, green grass and for food, the fruit of the land. The teacher will stroll about the grounds with his little flock of students, naming the fruits and flowers and insects they should chance upon in their wanderings and explaining to them all the wonderful mysteries that lie hidden in the great breast of Nature. They will be taught to read and write in the shade of orange and mango groves and sleep at night with the sky as their star-spangled blanket ...' Thus it went on in similar vein to the end of the lecture. Bhaskar noticed at the end, in small print, a tribute to D. James for 'her unflagging encouragement and sympathy during the darkest hours.'

'Who is this D. James?' he asked his mother.

'Doreen James. You must remember she. She was your father friend.'

Bhaskar laughed loudly.

'What so funny? Don't tell me you too believe all them rumours that was going around one time.'

'What rumours?'

Mrs Lutchman told him and Bhaskar laughed even louder.

'You don't like what your mamoo write?'

'It don't have anything to like or not like in it. It don't make any sense to me. But I must be stupid, that's all.'

'You shouldn't run yourself down like that, son.'

'Who say I running myself down? Is all right for old Khoja to waste his time on things like that. He don't have nothing better to do. But I don't see why he want to have other people waste their time reading it. He and his blasted school. He's been planning that for years now, since before I leave home.'

Remembering this hostile reception, Mrs Lutchman delayed her news. Several times she had been on the verge of mentioning it but had lost courage on seeing the mocking expression that appeared to have taken permanent hold of his face. She regretted having shown him the pamphlet. It had only made her task harder. But their financial situation was precarious and each day lost lessened Bhaskar's chances of getting the job. She steeled herself. 'After all, he can't murder me, his own mother,' she said to herself.

5

It was Saturday and the lodgers had gone home for the weekend. Bhaskar sat slumped on a chair in the sitting-room having his tea and looking out through the open doors at the street. Mrs Lutchman was cleaning the bowl-shaped lightshade which she had unhooked from the ceiling and was now polishing with a cloth. A mound of charred insects lay on a sheet of crumpled newspaper. The sun poured into the room, throwing into sharper relief the patina of dust on the chairs and tables. There was a light breeze and the curtains bellied gently away from the windows. The sitting-room's hard, wooden unattractiveness seemed always to become harder and more wooden at this time of day.

Bhaskar finished his tea and rested the cup on the floor. His attention was caught by the photograph on the wall. He scowled and turned to look again at the street where a steady stream of people were hurrying to the cinema on the corner, just beginning its afternoon show. Mrs Lutchman hoisted a chair on to the dining table and drew herself up, grunting and puffing.

'Pass me the shade, Bhaskar.' She was balanced precariously on the chair and trembled slightly as she took the shade and juggled with the tiny brass chains. 'You better keep the chair steady for me, son.' She laughed nervously. Bhaskar grasped the legs of the chair. Mrs Lutchman steadied herself and cursed softly as the slender chains slipped repeatedly out of their clasps.

'I told you you should have let me do it, Ma. One day you going to fall from up there and kill yourself.'

'I not going to fall. I have a lot of practice putting this on. I wouldn't trust anybody else with it, except your father.'

'I don't know why you don't get another lightshade. This one so ugly and troublesome.'

At last the bowl clicked into place. Mrs Lutchman heaved a sigh of relief and lowered herself to the table. She looked at the shade. 'I think is a very nice shade,' she said.

'But look at all the insects that does die in it, Ma.'

'That will teach them to put their nose in what is not their business.' She slid to the floor. 'Is your father who buy that shade, you know. He choose it specially. And it wasn't all that cheap either.'

Bhaskar smiled sourly. He walked across to the front door and looked out. The house opposite was in shadow and there were some children playing on the pavement near it. From where he stood, he could see the Savannah at the end of the street, criss-crossed by strolling couples. The hills were hidden in haze. At the other end of the street a fight was in progress outside one of the entrances to the cinema and a crowd, including two policeman, had gathered to watch it. Bhaskar returned to his chair and picked up his empty tea-cup. 'Any more tea?'

'I'll make some more for you, son.' Mrs Lutchman gathered up the dead insects and went into the kitchen. There was a rattle of pots and pans. Mrs Lutchman sang. The kettle whistled and she returned with a steaming pot of tea. She waddled across the room and rested it beside him.

'I want you to tell me something, son.' She pretended to be fiddling with the lid of the tea-pot.

'What is it now?' Bhaskar stirred his tea slowly.

'First you must promise not to get angry and secondly you must promise to be truthful.' She stood up.

A flicker of irritation swept across his face. 'What?'

'It's about the lodgers.' Mrs Lutchman had decided to approach her subject indirectly.

'What about them?' Bhaskar compressed his lips.

'Well ... I don't want you to misunderstand me, but sometimes I does get the feeling you don't like them being here.'

'I never said so. What make you think a thing like that?' Bhaskar stared innocently at her. He drained his cup and set it down carefully on the saucer.

'It's not so much what you say or don't say. It's the way you does act when they here. You does make them feel very uncomfortable.'

'They tell you that?'

'They haven't told me a word. It's what I see with my own eyes I talking about.' She gazed anxiously at him, hoping she had made her meaning clear and not offended him. 'You see,' she said reproachfully, 'you losing your temper with me already.'

'I not losing my temper,' Bhaskar said quietly. He poured himself some more tea. 'What you want me to do? Love and much them up?'

Mrs Lutchman shook her head sadly. 'They is we main source of income, you know. You can't go treating them like dirt.'

'So that's what you was getting at.' Bhaskar laughed.

Mrs Lutchman, in her turn, feigned innocence. 'The money

don't bother me at all,' she said. 'Is your own good I thinking about. Maybe the lodgers does annoy you because them is the only people you does see. I think it would be a good idea if you could get out of the house a little more and see some different people. If you go on like this you might ruin ... damage your health. I sure it not good for you to be coop up inside here all day. You could get some kind of job, for instance, not so much for the money but for your own sake.'

'What kind of job you think I could get, Ma? Sweeping the street? Who in their right mind would want to employ a man like me?'

'I tell you before you mustn't run yourself down like that, Bhaskar. There is lots of jobs you could get if you only try.' She avoided looking at him. 'Just the other day, for instance, your mamoo was telling me about a vacancy in Queen's for a biology master. All you would have to do to get that job is to put pen to paper.'

'You ask him to get me a job?' There was an edge to Bhaskar's voice.

'No, no,' Mrs Lutchman replied hastily. 'It was nothing like that. How you get an idea like that into your head? He just happen to mention it in passing.'

'He happen to mention it in passing, eh!' Bhaskar scowled. He was silent for a time. Finally, he said, 'Who tell him, or you for that matter, that I could teach?' He laughed. 'Imagine me teaching! What is it you say they have a vacancy for?'

'Biology.'

'Biology! Imagine me teaching biology. I would do better as one of their specimens.'

'Be sensible, son. You could make a very good teacher if only you put your mind to it.' She felt braver now. He had shown no sign of becoming violent.

Bhaskar smiled scornfully. 'You sounding just like him when he was telling us that story about some damn friend of his who used to catch fireflies and put them in a bottle. You remember that? I sure he make that story up himself to frighten me. It was a load of rubbish.'

'You shouldn't speak of your mamoo like that, Bhaskar.

Even if it wasn't true – and I must say, I never meet the man he was talking about – it was still a very uplifting story. Anyway, your mamoo doesn't lie.'

'Who say? But maybe you right. I don't think he bright enough for that.'

Mrs Lutchman dried her hands on the front of her dress and walked across to the front door. 'Take this job for my sake, if not for yours. I wouldn't suggest anything that I didn't think was good for you.' She looked appealingly at him. He gazed steadily at her for a few seconds.

'All right, Ma. For your sake,' he said resignedly. 'But don't hold me responsible for what might happen?'

'What could happen?'

Bhaskar shrugged. 'Anything.'

'But you going to try for the job?'

'Yes, yes.'

Mrs Lutchman brightened. 'I knew you would see sense. The college not all that far from here either. Just a short walk across the Savannah and you there. Think of all the good that fresh air will do you. You'll lose weight in no time. And you mustn't forget that it have a lot of money in teaching these days.'

'I thought you say the money didn't matter.'

She laughed. 'Well, it always good to have a little extra, not so?' She was cheerful now. Her enterprise had been crowned with success. 'I'll go and let your mamoo know straight away that you interested in the job.'

'But I thought you say he only mention it in passing. That don't mean you have to go and see him.'

Mrs Lutchman regretted her indiscretion. 'He know the headmaster very well. That's why. I believe is Govind who get him the job in the first place.' Mrs Lutchman knew nothing of the sort, but the lie had come effortlessly.

'As far as I can see it don't have one person in this world for who your Govind didn't do a favour at one time or the other. Even Christ must owe him something. I suppose when he dead he going to go and have a little chat with him as well about getting into heaven.'

'You shouldn't speak like that, Bhaskar. I don't see anything wrong with pulling a few string. That's the way the world does work these days.'

'And Heaven by the look of things.'

'You never know,' Mrs Lutchman said mysteriously.

'Suppose I say I don't want him to put in a word for me? Suppose I say I don't want his help? What then?'

'That's a stupid way to look at it, Bhaskar. He could help you.'

'I don't want him or anybody else pulling strings for me.'

'For my sake, Bhaskar. I don't see why you have to be so obstinate about such a little thing.'

'Okay, Ma.' He frowned. 'For your sake. But only for your sake.'

'That's the way, son. You wait and see. You will like the job very much. You must let Mrs MacKintosh read your tea-cup one of these days.'

'Keep Mrs MacKintosh as far away from me as you can,' Bhaskar said quietly.

Mrs Lutchman was struck by another consideration which might have a considerable influence on the success of her plans. 'When Govind ask me what you think about the pamphlet, what you want me to tell him?'

Bhaskar considered. 'Tell him I think is a load of rubbish.'

Mrs Lutchman giggled. 'How you expect me to tell him that?'

Bhaskar shrugged his shoulders. 'You could tell him anything you want,' he said.

6

'And what does he think about the speech?' was the first thing Mr Khoja asked when Mrs Lutchman went to Tropic Vale.

'He thought it had some very good ideas in it. In fact, he couldn't stop talking about it.'

'What bit did he like the best?'

'Oh, he himself tell me he couldn't make up his mind. He thought everything in it was good. Everything,' she stressed.

'Did he like the bit about the sermons in stones?'

'Yes. He thought that was especially good. There was not one single thing he didn't like in the whole speech.'

'That was a quote from the Bard himself. I thought it fitted in very well.'

'The Bard himself! Well! Well!'

'And what about the bit about the sky as a roof and using the hills for walls? Did he like that too?'

Mrs Lutchman was becoming desperate. 'He liked that too. I tell you, Bhaskar like everything you write. He think you is a great writer.'

'I'll let you into a secret then, Vimla.'

Mrs Lutchman was apprehensive. 'What? Something about the job?'

Mr Khoja seemed not to understand what she was talking about. 'I've just begun to write my autobiography.' If such a thing was possible, Mr Khoja blushed.

Mrs Lutchman did not know what an autobiography was. She nodded repeatedly and opening her eyes wide, gazed earnestly at him. 'Your autobiography. That sound nice!'

'And I even have a title for it already. You know what I going to call it?'

Mrs Lutchman shook her head.

'I'm going to call it, *The Confessions of Govind Khoja, Philosopher of Education.* Like the *Confessions* of Rousseau, you know. What you think about that?'

'That sound really nice. But what about the job for Bhaskar?'

The dream went out of Mr Khoja's eyes and voice. He came to with a start. He seemed put out and annoyed. 'Don't worry. I'll see to everything,' he promised. 'And keep what I just tell you to yourself, okay? I can't have publishers breathing down my neck. Don't even tell Bhaskar. I want it to be a surprise.' Mr Khoja was beginning to regret his rashness.

'You mean about the book? About the *Confessions of* ...'

'Yes, yes.' He bid her good-bye with a slightly pained look. 'I must learn to keep my mouth shut,' he told himself.

7

Mr Khoja arranged an interview and Bhaskar put on his ill-fitting suit and presented himself. A week later a letter arrived informing him he had got the job. Mrs Lutchman was overjoyed.

'I tell you they would take you. Mrs MacKintosh predict that. I bet you they thanking they lucky stars they find someone like you to teach there.'

'I know,' Bhaskar replied. 'They might even make me headmaster after a month or so.'

'You could never tell what they would do,' Mrs Lutchman answered seriously.

Bhaskar looked at his mother. 'What kind of world you does live in, Ma?' He shook his head at her. 'Don't tell me Mrs MacKintosh has been shooting her mouth off again. What she seeing this time? B.A. gowns and that kind of thing?'

'I think you being very unfair to she, Bhaskar.'

Mr Khoja was a little surprised and disappointed by Bhaskar's success. He had been vaguely hoping that Bhaskar would make such a bad impression that, influence or no, he would be refused the job. To this end, he had watered down his praise and even expressed to Mr Wall, the headmaster, a few unsolicited reservations. Unhappily for him, he had underestimated his powers of persuasion and Bhaskar's success worried him.

8

Right from the start it was apparent that Bhaskar's career as a teacher was doomed to be short-lived. His appearance was the first thing to tell against him: the drab, ill-fitting suit, the shirts with frayed collars and cuffs, the unfashionably wide ties, the socks sagging at the ankles; and not least, the rounded glasses through which he stared at his students with that vacant, abstracted gaze his mother knew so well, his eyes living a life all of their own. For the school seemed to have had a bad effect on Bhaskar. It brought back the memories of his childhood too strongly and his mocking sarcasm had proved insufficient protection. So, he had reverted.

Bhaskar could command no authority and the classes he took quickly degenerated into a free for all. The boys sang and shouted, threw sticks of chalk at him, and, on occasion, fought with each other. Bhaskar stood on the rostrum and read, his voice drowned by the noise, the notes he had written many years ago for his examination. Fortunately, the text-books had been changed and his technique of note-taking was never brought to light.

He could no longer draw. His hand, when he took up the chalk, shook dreadfully and as he wrote, the chalk scraped and whined along the surface of the blackboard, breaking several times in the process. What emerged was entirely incomprehensible. A jumble of indeterminate squiggles supposed to represent flowers and insects and birds staggered in precarious lines and poses up and down the length of the blackboard. He labelled many things wrongly and the boys flung themselves about the classroom and misled him at every turn. Yet, he did not appear to be embarrassed. When he had been corrected, he would rub out what he had written and carefully write in the new word, saying, 'Yes. That's right.'

His spelling was, as it had always been, atrocious. The boys would shout at him, 'Another "s", Lutchman.' 'Crutchman, you forgot the "p".' The waves of laughter rose and fell. His most common nickname was 'Rafeeq', so called after a recently hanged criminal. This soon ousted the others. 'Rafeeq', after a fashion, became his established name. The boys referred to him thus even when there was no intention of being funny.

They listened for his pronunciation and there again Bhaskar did not disappoint them. 'De torax of insecks,' he wheezed painfully, pointing with his ruler at a mass of confused squiggles. A favourite trick was, as the class progressed, to push their desks closer and closer until he was hemmed in on all sides, a prisoner on his tiny rostrum. He would beg them to give him a 'breathing space'. Then they would push their desks as far away from him as was possible to the back of the class, so that he would have to shout across a large unoccupied area.

'Bring your desks closer, boys,' he would appeal to them. And once again he would be hemmed in from all sides and pressed against the blackboard. When the class was finished, they did not wait for him to go out, but rushed in a mass through the door, pushing him roughly aside. Bhaskar would retreat to the rostrum where, studying his incomprehensible diagrams, he would tap his ruler against his chalk-stained palms and let them pass.

He made friends with no one, neither among the masters nor the students. Yet, as if to further punish himself, he lingered on in the school grounds long after the final bell had gone, watching the cricketers practise in the nets. He would stand by himself, lost in the shadow of a tall samaan tree, his hands buried deep in the pockets of his trousers, staring unblinkingly at them. He left only after they had finished their practice and walked slowly home in the gathering darkness.

The climax of his teaching career occurred during his eighth week at the school. It was an extremely hot, dry afternoon in the middle of the week and the class was dull and unusually quiet. A low hum, like the sound of many voices intoning a prayer, floated down the long corridor from the neighbouring classrooms. Bhaskar had his back to the class, drawing one of his peculiar diagrams. The class listened to the scrape of the chalk across the blackboard and watched the jerky up and down movements of Bhaskar's arm and the spreading stains of sweat on the back of his shirt and under his armpits.

Bhaskar, his diagram completed, turned to face the class. He stared over their heads and addressed the maps on the blackboard facing him.

'I have drawn for you sketches of the digestive systems of the cow and the dawg.' He studied the squiggles on the blackboard and frowned. He hesitated and then with greater resolution said, 'I wish to draw your attention to certain crucial differences between the digestive system of a typical carnivore, in this case the dawg, and a herbivore, the cow, as I have drawn for you. I'll just label them so that you won't get confused.' He wrote in large, block letters above one of the squiggles, 'DOG', and walked heavily across the rostrum to the other side of the blackboard. The chalk scraped. The class sank into a deeper somnolence.

'Oh Jesus Christ no!' one of the boys at the front of the class suddenly whispered. There was a stir of interest accompanied by more shouts. The uproar spread. 'Rafeeq! Rafeeq!' Boys leapt on to desks and danced on the seats while others banged lids and whistled and hooted. Some of them even fell about on the floor.

Bhaskar had written 'CAW' above the remaining squiggle.

He blinked at them from the rostrum and tapped his ruler against his palms. He turned slowly and rubbed the 'a' out with his finger and inserted an 'O'. Somebody began to clap. It was picked up and the applause spread.

Bhaskar trembled visibly, passing his tongue repeatedly over his lips. He took off his glasses, wiped them, and put them on again. Then, without another word, he stepped down from the rostrum and walked quickly out of the classroom. His teaching career had come to an end.

9

Bhaskar walked slowly across the Queen's Park Savannah. The sun was at its hottest. The Savannah was empty save for himself and, far ahead, the small figure of a man limping slowly across it in the direction of the racecourse. A lake of shadow lay across the grass, its edges retreating before a wave of light sweeping across towards him from the direction of the racecourse. The Northern Range, brown and dry, dozed in the sun. The man disappeared behind the Grandstand. Bhaskar laughed out loud. The mocking expression had taken hold of his face again.

When Bhaskar arrived back home his mother was having tea with Mrs MacKintosh. Mrs Lutchman looked at him curiously but said nothing. Mrs MacKintosh smiled broadly.

'Ah, Sonny Boy. Home early today, I see. That gives me a chance to read your cup for you and let you know all the good things coming your way.' She drew a chair for him.

Mrs Lutchman looked worriedly at her son. 'I don't think Bhaskar . . .'

'It's all right, Ma.' Bhaskar smiled. 'I would like to hear what Mrs MacKintosh have to say.'

His mother gazed gratefully at him. Bhaskar sat down and she poured him some tea.

'You are not giving him enough tea-leaves,' Mrs MacKintosh objected.

'Yes, yes. You right.'

Mrs Lutchman scraped the bottom of the tea pot and doled out two teaspoonsful of leaves into Bhaskar's cup. 'That will do, Mrs MacKintosh?'

Mrs MacKintosh, wearing a satisfied grin, nodded. 'That's fine, Mrs Lutchman.'

'Now drink the tea, Bhaskar. Remember it's not the taste that counts.' Mrs Lutchman, well-versed in the ritual, directed operations. When Bhaskar had nearly drained the cup, she held out her hand and restrained him. 'Stop! Now you must pass the cup right round your lips so that the leaves will spread evenly. Yes. That's right.' She patted him encouragingly. 'Good. Now turn it upside down and drain it on your saucer for a bit and then give it to Mrs MacKintosh.' Bhaskar turned the cup upside-down on his saucer and let it drain. This lasted about five minutes, during which time Mrs MacKintosh chatted genially about her triumphs and drank two cups of tea with amazing rapidity.

'You know, Mrs Lutchman, Veronica just wouldn't believe me when I told her she was going to receive a letter from overseas with important news in it. She just laughed. But two days later she got this letter from America which said that her brother had broken his legs in a motor-car accident. She rang up straight away to let me know.'

'People like that don't deserve anything,' Mrs Lutchman said.

'What can one do about such people, my dear Mrs Lutchman? When she rang me up I didn't say a word. I don't like people to think that I'm boasting. In my line of work you've got to be very careful of what you say. All I said was, "that's really surprising, Veronica", and my son and I nearly killed ourselves laughing afterwards.' Mrs MacKintosh grinned happily. 'Sonny Boy's cup looks as if it's sufficiently drained now.'

Mrs Lutchman became serious and Mrs MacKintosh beamed at Bhaskar as a dentist might just before he started drilling. She picked up the cup and examined it.

'Very interesting. This is very interesting indeed. You're a lucky man, Sonny Boy. Born, as the saying goes, with a golden spoon in your mouth.'

Bhaskar raised his eyebrows.

Mrs MacKintosh turned the cup round slowly. 'Ah yes. That's a little clearer. You've got some money coming to you. Have you bought a sweepstake? No? Is anybody owing you money? No? Well, that makes it even more interesting.'

'How much money?' Bhaskar asked.

'Ssh, son.' His mother looked disapprovingly at him. She knew that Mrs MacKintosh hated to be asked such specific questions. She said it disturbed her concentration.

'I just want a rough estimate,' Bhaskar insisted. 'Then I could plan. Since I sure of getting this money . . .'

'I can't say how much, Sonny Boy. The leaves are a bit confused at the bottom of the cup. But some money is coming to you all the same.'

'Maybe it's my salary.'

'Bhaskar!' Mrs Lutchman was horrified. She looked apologetically at Mrs MacKintosh.

'That's all right, Mrs Lutchman. Sonny Boy has a sense of humour, just in fact like my friend Veronica.' Mrs MacKintosh glowered at him. 'But he's going to get some money all the same. The leaves never lie. No doubt about that. Now let's see what else there is.' Mrs MacKintosh bit her lower lip pensively. 'Do you know anybody with an "e" in their name, Sonny Boy?'

'I wonder who that could be,' Mrs Lutchman said.

'Quite a few people, Ma.'

Mrs MacKintosh stared at him with her wandering blue eyes. There was no friendliness there. 'Yes. I see. Well you are going to meet one of them. Let's see. What else? Ah! You're going to get a letter, a very important letter, from overseas. Yes. There's the bird's wings as plain as can be. See?' She showed the bird's wings not to Bhaskar but to Mrs Lutchman, pointing at a mess of tea-leaves. Mrs Lutchman saw nothing.

'Is as clear as daylight down there,' she confirmed.

'Can I see?' Bhaskar held out his hand.

'That would be quite useless,' Mrs MacKintosh replied, snatching the cup away from Mrs Lutchman. 'You need a trained eye to see these things.'

'And Ma has a trained eye?'

'She does indeed, Sonny Boy. Sometimes she sees things which even I have difficulty in seeing. Isn't that so, Mrs Lutchman?'

Mrs Lutchman blushed and stared modestly down in front of her.

Bhaskar withdrew his outstretched hand. Mrs MacKintosh gave the cup a general scrutiny. 'Yes, Sonny Boy. Those bird's wings mean you are going to receive an airmail letter. Things are looking up for you in more ways than one. You see that line there that looks like a finger?' Again she showed the cup to Mrs Lutchman. Mrs Lutchman nodded. 'That is a stick of chalk. That means you're going to climb high in your present profession. And the anchor next to it is a sign of stability and prosperity. I must say this is one of the best cups I've ever seen. So many good things are coming to you, Sonny Boy. It's been a privilege.' Mrs MacKintosh was too overcome to go on, and putting the cup down, closed her eyes. As for Mrs Lutchman, she could hardly contain herself. Bhaskar picked up the cup and looked at it. When Mrs MacKintosh had left, he said to his mother, 'I didn't see any anchor or bird's wings in the cup.'

'That's because you don't have a trained eye,' she replied joyfully.

10

It was only after dinner when his mother was sweeping the kitchen he suddenly said, 'I've left the job, Ma.'

'What's that you say?' She leaned on the broom.

'I said I've given up the job.' Bhaskar raised his voice. 'I walked out this afternoon.'

'You trying to fool me, eh son?'

'No, Ma. I'm not trying to fool you. It's true. That's why I came home so early.'

Mrs Lutchman went on sweeping, though more slowly. 'But what happen? I thought everything was going so well.'

'That's because you don't see what's in front of your eyes. You prefer to listen to Mrs MacKintosh.'

'But what happen, Bhaskar?'

'I find it too tiring.'

'Tiring? But it's only just round the corner.'

'It's not only that. But on top of all that I'm no Rousseau.'

'What Rousseau have to do with it?'

'I wasn't cut out to be a teacher.'

'Who say that?' she asked sharply.

Bhaskar shrugged his shoulders.

'Why don't you go and tell your mamoo? He's the only man to shut them up.'

'I don't see what he have to do with it.'

Mrs Lutchman straightened herself. 'You don't want to go on teaching?'

'No.'

'But what it is get into you all of a sudden?'

'Whatever it is, get into me a long time ago. It didn't only happen today.'

Mrs Lutchman stared at him, her eyes black and very moist. She began to sweep again. 'It's really funny, don't you think? There was Mrs MacKintosh just saying how things was looking up for you. And now this foolish thing gone and happen. I just don't understand it.'

Bhaskar laughed. 'Like her friend Veronica.'

'Who?'

Bhaskar waved his arms angrily. 'Mrs MacKintosh is a fraud. All she want is your milk and sugar. I say that years ago.'

'You mustn't speak like that about the poor woman, Bhaskar. You don't know what a hard life she had. And think of all them things she say that come true.'

'Tell me one thing she say that come true.'

'Well, if you want to look at it in that way ...'

'But what other way it have to look at it, Ma? I don't understand you at all.'

'These things does take time, Bhaskar. She never say it was going to happen now. You need to pray to God and be patient. Like me.' She abandoned her pretence of sweeping and, leaning on the broom, gazed thoughtfully at him.

Chapter Eight

1

The commercial instinct had for long lain dormant in Mrs Lutchman's breast, but now it erupted anew, its former vigour undiminished and greatly refreshed from its slumbers. She recalled what Mrs MacKintosh had said about the long, thin fingers. Surely the bird's wings she had seen must also be capable of bearing another interpretation. If there were no air-mail letters in the offing (and none had arrived), they could mean only one other thing. Mrs Lutchman was not her friend's star pupil for nothing.

'Have you ever thought of keeping chickens?' she asked Bhaskar one day.

'Chickens?' Bhaskar was puzzled. 'I don't know anything about chickens.'

'It don't have much to know, take my word. Listen to me. The only trouble with chickens is the smell and it easy to solve that. You just have to buy a hose – they not so expensive as you think – and hose all the mess away. We have a lot of space out in the back and we could keep a lot of chickens there. You should see how much people going in for it these days. Respectable people too, mind you. Take Dr Metivier for instance . . .'

'Who's Dr Metivier?'

'The man who used to look after Rudranath,' Mrs Lutchman replied impatiently. 'Listen to me. He buy this piece of land up in Chaguanas and before you could blink he have all these thousands of chickens in coops with electric light and that kind of thing. I couldn't believe my eyes when I see it the other day. And hundreds of people does drive up in their cars every day to buy them. You should see them lining up there every Saturday morning. Take my word. It have a lot of money in chicken these days.'

His mother's enthusiasm did not alter Bhaskar's expression. Nevertheless, Mrs Lutchman had spoken truly. Chicken farms had mushroomed on the island. Almost everyone who owned land or could afford to buy some was going in for it, and Mrs Lutchman was convinced that it had brought them untold riches overnight. She painted a lavish, lyrical picture to Bhaskar.

The failure rate was high, since the chickens seemed subject to all kinds of fatal diseases and this, combined with bad management, had forced several devotees of the business into bankruptcy. But Mrs Lutchman, an optimist at heart, chose to forget this gloomier side of the story. Images of rows of electrically lit chicken coops, fitted with neat strips of shining wire and filled with healthy brown birds, flitted across her mind. She saw herself sitting on a box, tending the scales on Saturday mornings, weighing the birds and giving change and chatting with the crowds of customers. She was inspired. A vision of order and prosperity rose before her and this she did her best to transmit to Bhaskar. Mrs Lutchman in full spate could not be denied and Bhaskar succumbed.

In a moment she had forgotten Bhaskar the teacher and replaced him with another Bhaskar, even more fitted to her taste: Bhaskar, the prince of chicken farmers. She talked for a long time about the most suitable wood and wire for the coops, how many chickens they should have to begin with, who would do the building and who their prospective customers would be. Bhaskar intervened with an occasional question and when his mother had exhausted herself, he went up to his room to 'think it over'.

The next day they went out shopping together and ordered the wire and wood for the coops and bought a hose. 'We could use it in the garden too,' she explained. Mrs Lutchman also decided that they must have a sign made and toyed with the idea of a name for their enterprise.

'What do you think about "Esperanza" for a name?' she suggested timidly.

Bhaskar was not encouraging. 'I don't see what you want a name for. We are not Dr Metivier, you know.'

'I used to have a little provision stall when you was still a baby. I had called that "Esperanza". It was a really nice stall painted green and red.'

'And what happened to that?'

Mrs Lutchman's eyes hardened. Her nostrils twitched. 'It would have been a success if it wasn't for the damn police. They say I was blocking the pavement. A load of old lies. I am sure somebody bribe them to do that. If your father was alive he would have tell you.'

'And you had lots of customers before the police move you?'

Mrs Lutchman was evasive. 'Well, business was a little slow, as it was bound to be at the start. But it was picking up, mind you. If it wasn't for the damn police we would have been rolling in money now.'

Bhaskar smiled. 'I don't think it would be such a good idea to call it "Esperanza" then, Ma.'

'You might be right, son. You never can tell how much bad luck it might bring.'

Thus they abandoned 'Esperanza' as a possible title and after Bhaskar had rejected the 'Riviera' and 'Grand Canyon', the alternatives put forward by his mother, she lost heart and settled for 'Chickens for Sale. Apply Within'. She enlisted the help of the lodgers and within a week they set to work clearing the yard and building the coops.

The coops were assembled in the back yard, in a paved area about fifteen foot square. The concrete had been laid by the previous tenants and had developed long lines of cracks in which colonies of weeds, chiefly that imported into the neighbourhood by Mr Lutchman, had established themselves and formed meandering patterns of untidy green growth. Mrs Lutchman had these filled in and a drain dug to lead the excrement away. The coops were successfully screened from the house at the back by the high brick fence with the bits of broken bottle stuck along the top, the handiwork of her husband. She gazed at the glinting slivers of bottle chosen with such care by him and remembering her husband's words, she laughed. It seemed to her that it was his actual voice she was hearing. 'That is to stop your man from climbing in during the night and giving you another child.'

'What is it you laughing at, Ma?'

Mrs Lutchman gazed at her son with sparkling eyes. 'Now it's you who asking me what I laughing at.'

Bhaskar did his share of the work without complaint. He supervised the lodgers in the construction of the coops and had shown a certain flair for carpentry. The coops fulfilled Mrs Lutchman's expectations. They all had three tiers and were fitted with neat rows of shining wire. However, there were no electric lights.

Eventually, the hundred chicks which Mrs Lutchman had ordered arrived and after a few weeks she was able to nail the sign to the front gate, above that other one which said, 'Beware of the Dog'. They were open for business.

2

To Bhaskar's secret surprise, people did actually come to buy chickens. They were mostly people who lived on the street and some members of the family. The Khojas were particularly good customers. They bought three chickens a week. Mrs Lutchman gave Bhaskar an old biscuit tin with a faded label, to keep 'change' in.

Bhaskar insisted on handling every aspect of the business himself, to his mother's great disappointment. She felt cheated. He cleaned and washed the coops, looked after the eggs, killed the chickens when his customers asked him to do so and pored over the accounts before he went to bed. The lodgers would see him from their bedroom windows, dressed in denim trousers and a white jersey, hosing the coops in the late afternoon, peeping shortsightedly at the dark mass of chickens and sometimes taking one out and examining it carefully. He was afraid they would contract some disease.

Unfortunately, the 'trouble' with keeping chickens which Mrs Lutchman had mentioned as its only drawback led eventually to tragedy. It was the one thing her visions of order and prosperity had neglected to take fully into account. Mrs MacKintosh began to drop hints about the smell and the flies. She had good reason to complain. Despite Bhaskar's daily efforts with the hose, the warm, cloying smell of not only the excrement, but the chickens themselves, persisted, clinging like a vaporous blanket to the coops and spreading to the neighbouring yards. Mrs Lutchman bought disinfectant, but that did not help. In fact, it only worsened matters, the odour of the disinfectant blending with the odour of the coops to produce a compound that had somehow succeeded in combining the worst of both worlds. Mrs MacKintosh's hints became less gentle and more pointed. This, however, was not all. The houseflies had descended on the house in hordes. They were everywhere. Mrs Lutchman tried fly-spray, but they multiplied faster than she could kill them off and in the end, having come to the sad conclusion that they thrived on the insecticides she used, she gave it up as a bad job.

Mrs Lutchman listened sympathetically to Mrs MacKintosh's complaints, although she could not help feeling, as she confided to Bhaskar (who was not at all concerned about the flies and the smell) that she was being 'a little unreasonable'. In an attempt to win her over, she offered her a free chicken every week and plied her with double the regular amount of skimmed milk and sugar, hoping gratitude would mute and finally still any further criticism. Unhappily, though Mrs MacKintosh accepted these extra gifts, she was not to be fobbed off so easily.

There was a growing coolness between the two women. Mrs MacKintosh did not go so far as to stop her Friday visits, but her manner on these occasions was more formal and restrained. She interpreted the tea-leaves with less than her usual zest. The promises of large sums of money from overseas fell off considerably and even the number of identifiable vowels was affected. Mrs MacKintosh had decided on a go-slow. She spent much of the time brushing the flies, existent and non-existent, away from her face and screwing up her face at the smells drifting in from the coops. Nevertheless, the break, when it did come, surprised and hurt Mrs Lutchman.

They were seated at their usual places at the dining table in the sitting-room. Mrs MacKintosh turned the cup morosely between her fingers and stared dully at the tea-leaves. Mrs Lutchman sat uncomfortably forward on her chair, acutely conscious of the flies buzzing and diving around the table. The joy of having her teacup read had long vanished. Instead, it had become a trial of strength, a weekly confrontation to which both parties felt compelled to submit themselves.

'Yes. You are going to meet someone with an "a" in their name. Or it might be an "e", I can't tell,' Mrs MacKintosh said without interest, shaking her fist at a fly which had settled on the rim of the cup. The fly circled and came back. Mrs Lutchman banged the table. She had not even tried to think who this person might be. The times had altered radically.

'My son can't stand the flies any more,' Mrs MacKintosh said. 'They are everywhere in the house.' She gazed over the rim of the teacup at Mrs Lutchman. 'You know they spread disease, don't you, Mrs Lutchman?' Her blue eyes, losing their vacant look, focused into a hard, uncompromising stare. 'Just think what would happen if one of us should get yellow fever. A killer disease.'

'You don't get yellow fever from fly, Mrs MacKintosh. You does only get that from mosquito. The yellow fever mosquito, and we don't have yellow fever mosquito here.'

'Well, if it's not yellow fever, it's sure to be something else. I have lived long enough in the tropics to know that there is a deadly disease waiting round every corner. If it's not yellow fever, it's sure to be something else. Flies spread disease. You should know that, Mrs Lutchman.' Mrs MacKintosh spoke with the quiet authority of conviction.

'A fly never kill anybody,' Mrs Lutchman muttered banging the table again.

'They do,' Mrs MacKintosh insisted. 'They kill thousands of Europeans like me every year in Africa. It's called the white man's grave. Thousands die there every year. Maybe it's different for you being brought up in the tropics. But you must know that flies live in rubbish heaps. They breed in them.' She unbuttoned her cuffs and stared for a moment at her wrist.

'I don't have no rubbish heap here, Mrs MacKintosh. We does try and keep the yard very clean. Like you never see Bhaskar hosing it down every afternoon?'

'That hardly makes any difference. It only spreads it around. It's the chickens they like. And that smell, Mrs Lutchman. How can you stand it? Imagine having to live and sleep with that.

I don't know how you manage it. You must be able to do something about it. Surely.'

'It don't smell all that strong. In a few more weeks you wouldn't even notice it. Take my word.'

'I don't take your word, my dear Mrs Lutchman. I positively refuse to take your word. I don't see how the people living on this street could stand it. But I suppose that most of them must have grown up in filth anyway. For all I know, they might even like it. But I'll tell you something, my dear Mrs Lutchman. In Glasgow you won't be allowed to do what you do here. It's against the law. They would prosecute you.' Mrs MacKintosh twirled the cup.

'This is not Glasgow.'

'You are telling me. You can certainly say that again.' Mrs MacKintosh waved a fly away.

'If you keep chickens you must expect them to collect a few flies,' Mrs Lutchman said stubbornly.

'A few!' Mrs MacKintosh cackled. 'The place is positively swarming with them and you talk about a few flies! You must have a sense of humour, my dear Mrs Lutchman. Just like Sonny Boy. People shouldn't be allowed to keep chickens in towns. It's unsanitary. I'll go and report it to the police. They must have something about it in their books.'

'You not in Scotland now, you know, Mrs MacKintosh.'

'I wish to God I was. At least people are civilized out there.'

'Look here, Mrs MacKintosh, I'm not going to sit here and be insulted in my own house, you hear,' Mrs Lutchman raised her voice.

Mrs MacKintosh jumped up from her chair. 'It won't be the last you hear of this, Mrs Lutchman. I'm going to go to the police right now and report you.' She searched in her handbag for the sugar and skimmed milk and, finding them, tossed the parcels on the table. 'And you could take back your bribes as well. I don't need them. I used to accept it only out of kindness to you, because I thought if I refused it would hurt your feelings. But now I see that you don't have any feelings to hurt.' Mrs MacKintosh stormed out of the house, slamming the front door after her. Mrs Lutchman, her head propped on her hands, stared at the rejected parcels. Then, with a sigh, she gathered them up and took them into the kitchen.

Mrs MacKintosh complained to the police as she had promised. The following day a constable came and made a cursory examination of the coops. He was good-humoured. He scribbled a few comments in a notebook and privately assured Mrs Lutchman that she would not be prosecuted. 'She's a little mad,' he said. 'Don't worry.'

The police having failed her, Mrs MacKintosh fell back on open abuse. Pretending to be speaking to her son, she would shout insults at Mrs Lutchman through the kitchen window. 'I can't stand this filth any more, Peter. Smell that. The people who can put up with that must be pigs. They must be pigs.' And she would close her kitchen window with a crash.

Thus it was that a friendship of long standing came to an end. Mrs Lutchman felt her loss keenly, though she did not dare say so to Bhaskar, who had received the news of the rupture with glee. Several times she was tempted to go and plead with Mrs MacKintosh. But then she would remember all the terrible things Mrs MacKintosh had said to her and her pride would reassert itself and prevent her from going. What rankled most was the way she had flung the sugar and skimmed milk on the table. That had made nonsense of the tender sympathies she had cherished towards her.

Mrs MacKintosh, as a final act of vengeance, had tried to rally the neighbours about her and persuade them to buy their chickens elsewhere. She visited them all in turn, offered to read their fortunes free of charge and told them the story of her life. It was a failure. The neighbours did not share her concern and one by one she abused them. Her anger amused them and it had, furthermore, the distinct advantage of bringing the chicken farm to their attention. Sales rocketed.

The other blot in Mrs Lutchman's life was Bhaskar. He worked long hours in the coops with a joyless obstinacy which seemed to her to deliberately deny itself any pleasure and which none of her cajolings could alter. He exhausted himself looking after the chickens and keeping the accounts in order; but the profits, the actual fruit of their enterprise, made no impression on him. He reserved only a small amount for himself. The rest he gave to her.

'But what you driving yourself so for?' she asked.

'Since when a little work is driving myself?'

'Well, a lot of what you does do don't seem necessary to me. Is as if you punishing yourself half the time.'

'Your trouble is, Ma, that you have too many theories.'

'Theory! Only educated people have time for that. I talking about what I see with my own eyes.'

'Look Ma, I'm doing the work, not so?'

'Nobody saying you not doing the work, son, but . . .'

'And it making money, not so?'

'Yes, yes, Bhaskar. But it's not that . . .'

'What is it then?'

'Is the way you don't do anything with the money you does make. You don't buy yourself no nice clothes, you don't go out, you don't want to see anybody . . .'

'I don't see how I does spend my time is any concern of yours, Ma. If I don't want to buy nice clothes and dress myself up like a clown, that is my business.'

'Okay, Bhaskar. Have it your way. I does interfere too much, I know.'

3

The chicken farm continued to prosper, although the number of chickens had increased only slightly. This was due, however, merely to lack of space and Mrs Lutchman, who had not given up her dreams of expansion, discussed the possibilities with Bhaskar.

'We could rent a couple of acres of land from your mamoo. He doesn't use everything he have and I sure he wouldn't mind. He will be getting a good rent for it.'

Bhaskar was not enthusiastic. 'What's the point of that, Ma? Who going to look after it? You think the two of us could do it alone?'

Mrs Lutchman's entrepreneurial spirit rebelled against her son's lack of commercial vision. 'What you talking about, Bhaskar? Who say anything about we doing it on we own?

What I have in mind is something like what Dr Metivier do in Chaguanas. Big, big coops with thousands of chickens and electric lights. The electric light does make them grow faster, you know. And we'll have to hire people to look after if for we and you'll have a nice air-conditioned office and a station-wagon ...'

'What are you talking about, Ma? Like you sleepwalking or something?' Bhaskar took off his glasses and polished them. 'I don't know where you does get all them grand ideas from. That kind of thing need brains and money. Where will we get the money from?'

'The Government giving grants to people. We bound to get one.'

'You'll need more than what they will give you. That's for people who have money already. Where you will get the rest from?'

'I could always ask your mamoo.'

Bhaskar laughed. 'Yes. You really sleepwalking, otherwise you wouldn't say a thing like that. Anyway, what's the point? What's wrong with what we have now? Tell me.'

'I just thought you might like to expand,' she responded meekly, avoiding his scrutiny.

'Expand! That's just a word to you. I bet you you don't have the slightest idea what it will really mean. Once and for all, Ma, get this straight. I don't want to expand. I don't want to. You understand that?'

'Yes, Bhaskar. You don't have to shout at me. I understand.' She gazed sadly at him. 'It was just an idea I had. That's all.'

Mrs Lutchman, her ardour dampened, began to think of other possible lines of activity for herself. Bhaskar stubbornly refused to let her help in the running of the business and with expansion now out of the question, its attraction for her had lessened considerably. There was little for her to do except work in the garden, cook, and look after the lodgers and Rover. This could hardly satisfy her. The success of the farm had nurtured a belief in her commercial prowess amounting to infallibility (after all, the chickens had been her idea), so that Bhaskar's refusal to countenance her plans for expansion was doubly frustrating. It was at this juncture that Mr Khoja intervened with an offer she could only describe as heaven-inspired.

4

Living in Tropic Vale had had a sobering effect on Mr Khoja. Surrounded by an opulence and a mode of life he was unable to emulate, he had become less sure of himself. The gods, he felt, had deserted him yet again and he needed more than ever to have his praises sung. This had led him to commit indiscretions, like telling Mrs Lutchman about the plans for his autobiography and seeking the praises of Bhaskar for his pamphlet. Only with Doreen, who was unstinting in her praise, and his wife, did he feel truly at ease. Naturally, the portents were bad. His nightmares had returned in force. At least two or three times a week he dreamt he was being chased by a black horse down the flowered lanes of Tropic Vale and that his path of retreat had been blocked by a high, unassailable wall. At this point he usually woke up in a cold sweat. Then Blackie, like Shadow II, had died suddenly. The dog's was the only affection she had ever known and she had languished after his death. They had found her one morning in her little room, sitting, as if asleep, on a chair, a rolled up newspaper in her lap, her head resting on the flowered screen. 'She gone to join Shadow II,' Mrs Khoja said, assuming that, in the next world, there was a special reserve for faithful dogs and servants. These were premonitions of disaster and, to add to his troubles, sceptical voices joined the chorus asking when, if ever, he would build his long overdue school.

Gradually, the idea had dawned on Mr Khoja that his school could be at one and the same time a philanthropic institution and a money-making venture. He discussed it with his wife.

'I don't see why I shouldn't treat the damn thing as a business, Sumintra. It going to take thousands of dollars, you know. We just can't let all that money go down the drain.'

Mrs Khoja nodded lifelessly. She had aged, and in the process become much fatter. Her pale skine shone with the liberal dosages of olive oil she applied to it. She had been told it was better than coconut oil. Mrs Khoja had no wish to smell like the lower orders. Her hair showed prominent streaks of grey. The family dispute had undermined her more than she would have cared to admit and she had never completely recovered from the invasion on the night of the election. She had not bothered to repair the dolls Romesh had broken and, though they lined her dresser as before, she no longer sewed them new dresses or cleaned them. They remained as they were, gathering dust, their mutilated arms hanging limply, their dresses torn and faded. She would not throw them away, despite her husband's pleas. 'They sick and old just like me,' she said. 'You can't expect them to be young and pretty forever.'

She listened now in silence to her husband trying hard to justify himself.

'All the people I approached as possible teachers,' he was saying, 'far from seeing what a privilege and honour I was doing them, asking them to take charge of young minds free of charge, all they could think about was the salary. And you should hear the salaries they want. Hundreds of dollars a month they were asking me for. What do you expect me to do? I can't sit back and watch all my money go floating down the drain.'

Mrs Khoja glanced down at the gold bracelets hugging her fleshy arms. 'Why don't you give up the idea, Govind? You could go into another kind of business.'

'I wish I could, to tell you the truth. This thing is hanging like a ton of lead around my neck. But tell me all the same what kind of business you had in mind?'

'Chicken farming?' She looked helplessly at him.

'No, Sumintra. But that's not for me. It have too many of those around the place now. Every dog and cat seems to be keeping chickens these days. And you mustn't forget that I've already committed myself publicly to building this damn school. I can't go back on my word and open a chicken farm instead. People will laugh at me. Just think of what Urmila and Jagdev will say when they hear about it. No. It's got to be something involving children. There's no getting away from that.'

'That's true. I wasn't thinking of it that way.'

They gazed disconsolately at each other.

'There's nothing for it but to charge school fees. It's against my principles, mind you, but I just can't afford to throw away thousands of dollars like that. Oh Rousseau! Rousseau! Rejoice that you didn't have to live in such a mercenary age.' The Child of the Enlightenment stared wearily up at the crystal chandelier that hung shimmering above their heads. 'It will have to be a high-class school and, in return for good school fees, high-class teaching. Who knows? We might even make a profit out of it?'

The result of all this was that Rousseau was virtually abandoned and instead, Mr Khoja went into the education business. For a start, he could not have his school in the country, in the heart of Nature itself. The reason for this was simple. All the rich people, the only ones who could afford to pay the fees he was asking, lived in the town. They would not send their children away to a school in the country.

Therefore he bought a large wooden house near the centre of the city and this he converted into the Endeavour Infants' School. Nature, in any but its most barren and uninspiring forms, was totally lacking. The Endeavour Infants' School did not even have a proper school yard, squeezed as it was between a tailoring establishment and a firm that sold electrical equipment. Mr Khoja comforted himself with the reflection that this was only an interim arrangement. 'People are not ready for my ideas as yet,' he told the education correspondent of the *Trinidad Chronicle*, 'I've got to introduce my ideas bit by bit.' Nobody believed him. Mocking cartoons appeared in the newspaper and Mr Khoja's political star, which till then had been rising, went into a new decline.

Still, he pressed on, trying to make up for his patent betrayal of Rousseau in other ways. He ordered the latest in desks and blackboards and, having read a book on child psychology recommended by Doreen, painted the classrooms in bright colours and bought a variety of 'constructional' toys. He appointed Doreen 'supervisor' and hired four teachers, all of them young men from the country districts. This was done not from any desire to infuse a strain of nature into the Endeavour

Infants' School, but simply because they were prepared to accept smaller salaries.

An important feature of the school was supposed to be its standard of hygiene – the rooms were sprinkled with disinfectant every morning – and the compulsory vegetarian lunches. Mr Khoja looked round for a 'matron' who would supervise this domestic aspect of the affair. Unfortunately, like the teachers, the candidates he interviewed for the job all demanded regular salaries. Then it was Mr Khoja remembered Mrs Lutchman. He went to see her.

'You must admit I have done you many favours in my time,' he said to her.

'Yes. I don't deny that.'

'And you must admit that I've never asked any of you in return.'

'What about the time you send me to see Indrani?'

'That was a long time ago, Vimla, and if I remember rightly I didn't force you to do it. You decided of your own free will. You can't deny that.' Mr Khoja looked accusingly at her.

'I don't deny that.'

'Well, now I want you to do me a favour.'

'What?'

Mr Khoja outlined his plan. In return for looking after the domestic arrangements of the school, he would pay her the minimal salary of ten dollars a week. 'I'm losing money myself,' he said. 'But I feel it my duty to run this school.'

Mrs Lutchman jumped at the offer. All was now ready and Mr Khoja advertised the school in the *Trinidad Chronicle*. 'A new and progressive school for one hundred pupils, designed with the latest ideas on psychology and hygiene in mind and supervised by Miss D. James, author and expert in anthropology.'

The school did not open with its full complement of pupils. This was disappointing, but it did not seem to discourage Mr Khoja unduly. 'They will come, you wait and see,' he comforted his wife. 'They will come with their tongues hanging out of their mouths.' Secretly, however, he was worried. His nightmares had not left him and night after night he was chased by the black horse through the lanes of Tropic Vale.

Mrs Lutchman settled into her new job with ease and enthusiasm. She got on beautifully with Doreen. 'Isn't it fun, Mrs Lutchman, to be in charge of a school like this? Isn't it absolutely heavenly? I've always had a tremendous interest in the education of children.' Mrs Lutchman threw herself heart and soul into the affairs of the Endeavour Infants' School. She left early in the morning, spending the entire day away from the house and returning late in the evening when she would give Bhaskar a full report of the day's events. He sat at the table in the kitchen, his accounts book spread open before him, chin propped on his hands, listening to her patiently, if a little ironically.

'So Doreen James thinks it's fun, eh?'

'You should see how she does be bustling about the place,' Mrs Lutchman replied.

'I have a feeling old Khoja don't know what he has let himself in for by putting that woman in charge.'

'What you mean, son?'

'Nothing. Nothing. So it's all fun, eh!' He laughed out loud. Mrs Lutchman, stifling her own doubts, watched him and pretended to be mystified.

Absorbed in the school and its affairs, she was altogether happier. Her life had acquired a full and interesting rhythm, though Bhaskar sometimes wondered whether his mother really appreciated the fact that she was working in a school. His misgivings were not without foundation. Mrs Lutchman talked solely in terms of business: profit and loss margins and how much Mr Khoja could expect to make if he got the full complement of pupils. It is possible she would not have liked it as much if she had not come to the happy (and not unrealistic) conclusion that it was really another kind of farm, or, better still, considering her duties, a restaurant, albeit for children.

5

It was in the south of the island that chickens first began to die. The disease spread north, leaving in its wake ruined farms and businessmen. The Government was concerned and offered compensation to the larger establishments. When Bhaskar's chickens died, he was not given any compensation, his enterprise being on too small a scale. He did not complain. He put the dead chickens in boxes and left them on the pavement to be taken away. When the last of the chickens had gone, he washed and cleaned the coops with his usual thoroughness and made some additional notes in the accounts book. All of this he did mechanically and efficiently, betraying no signs of regret or sorrow at what had happened.

At first, Mrs Lutchman was inclined to think that no great harm had been done. For her, the problem resolved itself simply and naturally: Bhaskar would buy some more chickens and carry on as before. Epidemics, such as this one, were an accepted risk. But Bhaskar had reverted to silence and inaction and responded to all her blandishments with that peculiar, abstracted gaze which had frightened her so much formerly and which, on occasion, could still affect her powerfully. Not long before the disastrous epidemic, he had built an 'office', in fact little more than a wooden shed, next to the coops and here it was he now sat all day, sometimes even having his meals there.

Mrs Lutchman knocked gently at the door of the shed. She had just returned from the school and her shoes and the lower half of her dress had an even covering of pale dust. There was no reply and she pushed the door open and went in. It was very dark inside the shed, which still had the acrid smell of new wood. The floor was littered with old shavings. Bhaskar sat hunched in a corner on one of the chairs he had brought there from the kitchen, leaning against his worktable. He was wearing his usual white jersey and denim trousers. The sky, framed by the open door, was reflected in his glasses. He did not look up when she entered. For some time, she watched him without speaking. At last she said, 'Son, but what's the matter with you?'

Bhaskar raised his head, but not to look at her. He stared through the open door at the empty chicken coops.

'It's not the end of the world, you know, Bhaskar. You can always start it up again. What you think all them other people doing? Yours wasn't the only chickens to die. Try and remember that.'

'What would be the point of doing that, Ma? You mean to say what happen wasn't enough for you?' Bhaskar was still staring at the empty chicken coops.

'"What's the point! What's the point!" You always asking what's the point about everything I does say to you.' Mrs Lutchman, mimicking his tone, stood facing him, arms akimbo and slightly belligerent.

'I don't want to, Ma. That's the "point". I don't care what the hell other people doing. That is their business, not mine.' Bhaskar, shifting in his chair, kicked at the shavings on the floor.

'What do you mean you "don't want to"?' She mimicked him again and smiled. She felt that all he needed was a little cheering up. 'You say the same thing when you give up the job at Queen's.'

'We not talking about that,' Bhaskar said sharply. 'We are talking about the chickens, so let's stick to that. I said I don't want to go on with them. I can't say it any plainer than that, unless you want me to spell it out for you.' Stressing each word, he looked his mother full in the face. She stopped smiling. The sky glittered brightly in his glasses. It was impossible to tell what was going on behind them.

'You need more light in here,' she said. 'You can't stay in here like this all the time. It's not good for your eyes.' Mrs Lutchman enjoyed inventing these vignettes of medical folklore. They comforted her. Bhaskar remained where he was and Mrs Lutchman, sighing, put on the electric light which was extended from the kitchen by a long cord. She studied the confusion in the room. 'But I don't understand, Bhaskar. You had a good little business here. All you have to do is get some more chickens and after a few months everything will be like it was before.'

'I don't want it to be like it was before.'

'What, you mean you want to have a different business?' Mrs Lutchman clutched desperately at this straw.

'For God's sake, Ma! Can't you leave me alone? Do you always have to be pestering me with something or the other? What the hell do I have to do with another kind of business? What you want me to do this time? Grow rice in the garden?'

He got up abruptly from the chair and went and stood near the door.

'I don't want you to grow rice.' She spoke softly. 'I'm sorry, Bhaskar. I didn't mean to . . . It was just that . . .'

Bhaskar pressed his fingers against the doorposts. The sky was darkening rapidly. He closed the door and came back to his chair. 'It's I who should be sorry, Ma. I didn't mean to shout at you.'

Mrs Lutchman began to cry. 'I really is a stupid old woman, eh? Behaving like this. Pestering you.'

'Look Ma,' Bhaskar went on, adopting a gentler, more apologetic tone and choosing his words carefully, 'it have nothing to do with the chickens. I know it's a pity they die and I had to close down the business, but that was bound to happen one way or another. You couldn't expect me to go on keeping chickens for the rest of my life. The only thing is that it happen now rather than later. But this was bound to happen. It have nothing to do with chickens at all.'

Mrs Lutchman dried her eyes and gazed at him perplexedly.

'You see, Ma . . .' Bhaskar frowned, squeezing his cheeks. 'You must see that I don't enjoy keeping chickens. I wouldn't even if I had a station-wagon and an air-conditioned office. I just did it because you were so . . . that's not true.' He stopped and spread his fingers out on the worktable. 'That's not true,' he repeated. 'It wasn't because of you that I did it.' He seemed to be talking to himself. His mother watched him, afraid to interrupt. 'Well, you know what I trying to say. In a way, it was a kind of joke, a joke I was playing on myself. Only the joke was beginning to get a bit stale, if you understand.'

'I don't understand what it is you trying to say, Bhaskar. What was a joke?'

'The whole thing, Ma. The whole thing was a joke.'

Mrs Lutchman nodded. She half-understood what her son was trying to tell her. They were both silent. After a while, she said, 'Well, what you want to do now then?'

'Do? Do. Do.' He savoured the word as if it were some strange, exotic thing. 'What do I want to do? More like what do I want to have done to me. Another joke perhaps.' He laughed. Then, becoming serious, he said, 'Nothing, Ma. I don't want to do anything.'

'Perhaps your mamoo could find you another job.'

'No, Ma. Mind you, that would be the best joke of all, if he offer me a job in that school. But I don't feel up to being one of his fireflies.'

'Fireflies?'

'It's not important, Ma. Don't worry.'

'Do you want your food in here?' she asked wearily.

'No. I'll go and have it in the kitchen.'

He left the shed and walked across the yard to the kitchen. Mrs Lutchman lingered in the shed. She sat on the chair and ran her finger over the shining red cover of the accounts book. She opened it and saw the columns of figures with comments pencilled in at the side in Bhaskar's untidy script. She shut the book, turned off the light, and followed him into the kitchen.

6

Mrs Lutchman lay awake a long time that night. It was unusually hot and stifling, without a breath of wind. She got out of bed and opened all the windows in the room and, leaning out, she inhaled deeply. The stillness outside, focusing her thoughts even more, was depressing. She returned to bed and throwing her blanket aside, tossed uselessly on the sheets. The large, scalloped leaves of the breadfruit tree next door were visible through the windows. On the street, several dogs were growling and barking at each other and she could hear them rustling and searching among the dustbins on the pavement. A bout of snarling and fighting would end in a high-pitched yelp of pain followed by silence, then renewed rustling and another fight. Mrs Lutchman tossed restlessly.

Bhaskar was her chief, but not her only source of worry. The school too had run into difficulties. During the months that she had been working there, she had succeeded in completely identifying herself with it. She had guarded its fortunes closely, jealous even of Mr Khoja's presence, until finally her selfless devotion had made her an invaluable asset to him. But Mr Khoja had managed things badly (Mrs Lutchman would never admit this) and the school was not making a profit. Indeed, it was operating at a small but perceptible loss. The pupils never materialized in the numbers he had predicted and, as an inducement, he reduced the fees. This had, however, made only a marginal difference. There had already been one strike over the inadequate salaries he paid his teachers and another was threatened. Doreen James had proved herself a palpably inefficient 'supervisor' (Mr Khoja would never admit this). Most of her time she spent telling Mrs Lutchman what 'fun' being in charge of the Endeavour Infants' School was, and having an affair with one of the teachers, ten years younger than herself.

She poured out her heart to Mrs Lutchman. 'He wants me to marry him. What do you think I should do?'

'But you old enough to be his mother,' Mrs Lutchman had replied, perhaps a trifle harshly.

Doreen winced. 'That's what I keep telling him,' she said, putting a brave face on it, 'but he wouldn't listen.'

'You should be more firm with him then.'

'Oh, I do try. Really I do. But he's a mad, mad boy.'

And so it had gone on day after day.

It had never occurred to Mr Khoja that his troubles had arisen, partly at any rate, because he had been too niggardly. Mrs Lutchman could have told him that. 'What you need to do,' she had said to him, 'is to expand.'

'Expand where?' he replied, glancing at the tailoring establishment and the electrical shop.

No, on the contrary, Mr Khoja believed that he had spent too much, that he had been extravagantly generous, and so he decided to make economies. He simplified the already simple vegetarian lunches which the school provided and eventually, he abandoned them. He replaced none of the broken toys. After these reforms, the number of pupils decreased yet further and Mr Khoja found himself, as a result of his economies, in deeper trouble than ever.

Mrs Lutchman tossed and turned. The dogs, having exhausted the nearby dustbins, had moved down the street and their growls were muffled and distant. Only towards morning, when the sky had begun to lighten, did she fall asleep.

7

Bhaskar's depression worsened. For days on end he did not leave the house, but sat in the shed leafing through the pages of the accounts book. He was silent and for the most part totally uncommunicative. Although he hardly ate anything, he began to grow fatter. Mrs Lutchman, at a loss as to what she should do, said nothing. He began to smoke and within a week had graduated to well over twenty cigarettes a day. Mrs Lutchman gazed at the puffed face and the eyes with the peculiar expression. Looking at him a wave of desolation swept over her.

'You want to see a doctor?'

Bhaskar shrugged his shoulders. Mrs Lutchman interpreted his silence as consent. She made inquiries and Bhaskar was admitted as an outpatient at the St Ann's Mental Home, under the care of Dr Metivier, the same whose chicken farm had so inspired her. Bhaskar was given a variety of attractively coloured pills and, as years before his room was lined with the bottles containing his biological specimens, so now he arranged his bottles of pills along the shelves. The parallel did not escape him. 'It's what certain people, like Urmila and the rest of them, might call poetic justice,' he said to his mother.

Two of the lodgers, alarmed by the turn of events, handed in their notice. Mrs Lutchman, panic-stricken, tried to persuade them to change their minds.

'But what it is get into the both of you so suddenly?' she cried. 'I was like a mother to you. I used to treat you like my own sons.'

'Is nothing to do with you, Mrs Lutchman . . .'

'Call me Ma.'

The lodgers were embarrassed.

'Is nothing to do with you,' they repeated. 'But we feel that Bhaskar don't really like we.'

'Who say Bhaskar don't like you? Come with me now and ask him.'

They shook their heads. 'We don't have to do that. We know.'

'But how you could do this to me?'

'We don't mean any harm by you, Mrs Lutchman. Believe we.'

Mrs Lutchman, holding her head in her hands, moaned softly. 'How the two of you could do this to me? How you could do this to me?'

The lodgers looked at each other. However, their minds were made up. They left the house the following week.

8

One disaster seemed to spawn others. Mr Khoja announced the closure of the Endeavour Infants' School. The threatened strike had occurred and, for him, this was the last straw. He sent carefully worded letters to the parents of his pupils, lamenting the state of modern society, which he blamed for the failure of the school.

Bhaskar was in bed when Mrs Lutchman returned home at lunchtime on the last day. He was sitting up smoking a cigarette. He looked up quizzically at her when she entered the room. Mrs Lutchman asked how he was and then sat heavily on the edge of the bed and stared at the floor. The branches of the breadfruit tree scraped against the roof. She listened to it orchestrating her despair. Their financial situation was critical. She had not told him the school was going to be closed, though he was aware of its difficulties. This she had done less from the desire to save him worry than to allay her own apprehensions.

To the end, and despite all the evidence to the contrary, she had hoped the disaster would be averted and that what she had always regarded as the ultimate calamity would not befall her. But, disregarding her prayers, it had befallen her and now it was out of the question for them to go on living as they had been doing. The cost of Bhaskar's medicines alone was sufficient reason. The house would have to be sold and she and Bhaskar would have to seek the charity of friend or family. Her friend Gowra had already offered to let them come and live with her in Coalmine. Mrs Lutchman had laughed at the idea. 'We not ready to do that yet,' she had said. 'But, don't worry, I will let you know when the day come for that.' The day had come. So much then for her independence: it was yet another relic to add to her store of souvenirs. Mrs Lutchman was quiet for a long time before she spoke.

'Your mamoo has closed down the school, Bhaskar.'

Bhaskar grinned puffily. 'Not enough money in Mother Nature, eh?'

Mrs Lutchman was offended. 'You know he wasn't in it for the money, son. He was doing a service to the public.' Bhaskar lit another cigarette. She lowered her voice. 'I don't know what we going to do now, Bhaskar.'

Bhaskar jiggled his toes and smiled dreamily at his mother. 'I don't see what the problem is, Ma. We have to become serfs. No problem at all. To become a serf is the easiest thing in the world. So I don't see what it is you worrying about. Think of all the people who are dying for you to become a serf. There's Gowra and Urmila for a start.'

'Serfs, son? What's serfs?'

'Slaves, Ma. Serfs and slaves are one and the same thing. Almost.'

Mrs Lutchman, startled by the word 'slave', especially by the viciousness with which he had uttered it, jumped. 'You don't know what it is you saying, Bhaskar.'

'Don't fool yourself, Ma.' He flicked the ash from his cigarette into his cupped palm and blew it away.

'That's what people does call self-pity.'

'You ever notice, Ma, that the only people who does talk about self-pity are those who don't have nothing to worry about? I bet you old Khoja busy pitying himself right at this moment. Why don't you go and tell him what you just tell me?' Again he flicked the ash into his palm and blew it away.

'Don't blow your cigarette like that, son. You will dirty the counterpane.' She got up and dusted it. It was the pink counterpane her husband had bought on impulse that rainy Christmas Eve.

'Sometimes I does envy Romesh,' Bhaskar said.

Mrs Lutchman gave him another of her frightened looks.

'That show you don't know what it is you saying, son. If we is slaves then Romesh was just as much a slave as the rest of we. You think a free man would have tried to behave like them film star? You think a free man would have treat his own mother the way he treat me? What it have to envy in that? What it have to envy in all that suffering he bring to me? Just because he gone away from here, that don't mean he any better or happier than the rest of we, you know. And I for one is nobody slave. People does only become slaves when they make themselves one.'

Bhaskar watched her, astonished. 'You becoming a real philosopher in your old age. Bertrand Russell better watch out.' He laughed. 'Remember how you wanted me to have an air-conditioned office and a station-wagon?'

'And you would have had all those things if you had put your mind to it.'

Bhaskar flung his cigarette violently out of the window. 'Like you will never learn? Where you get all your stubbornness from?'

'But is you who bring the subject up, Bhaskar. Not me. I was only telling you what I think.'

'I'll tell you what I think, Ma. When I die you must put me out in a box on the pavement and let the rubbish van take me away. That will be fitting, don't you think? You might get old Khoja to write me an epitaph. He would enjoy doing that. "A man who gave his life in the noble cause of poultry." I sure he will think up something.'

'How could you say things like that to me, son? I didn't come here to talk about all that nonsense. I come here to talk about what we going to do now. Give me your help and advice for a change.'

'I give you my help and advice already.'

'You mean you not going to help me?'

Bhaskar lit another cigarette. 'I want you to have the privilege, the honour, of carrying out the last free act in your life. It's up to you to decide whose slave you want to be.'

'I say already that is only you who can make yourself a slave, Bhaskar. Nobody else. Mind you, I not saying that is a nice thing to live off somebody else charity. But we not going to be paupers. I will still have your father's pension and the money I'll get from the sale of the house. And if the worst come to the worst, I could always open up a little vegetable stall like I used to have before. That way, who will we be a burden to?'

Bhaskar, however, was not listening. He was gazing at the bottles of pills ranged along the shelves in the room.

Mrs Lutchman walked slowly to the door.

'Oh, by the way, Ma,' Bhaskar called after her, 'I have some news for you too.'

Mrs Lutchman came back to the side of the bed.

'Dr Metivier think that the best thing for me to do would be to go to England and get treatment there.' Bhaskar twiddled his toes. 'What you feel about that?'

She gazed at him. The set expression on her face did not alter. 'He's a doctor so I suppose he know best,' she said. She moved away from the bed.

'They don't have the facilities here,' Bhaskar added.

Mrs Lutchman, her back turned to him, nodded.

'But is not definite.' His voice was almost apologetic.

'Well, let's think about that when the time come then.'

She went quickly out of the room, her face averted, and closed the door softly after her.

9

Mrs Lutchman exercised her 'privilege'. She advertised the house and arranged for Bhaskar and herself to live with Gowra and her family in Coalmine. Urmila was deeply offended. No sooner had she divined Mrs Lutchman's plight following the failure of the chicken farm and the closure of the school than she came to see her.

'My offer is still open,' she said. 'It take you a long time to learn, but it never too late.'

Mrs Lutchman thanked her for her kindness and generosity, but she refused.

'Obstinacy is going to be the death of you one day, Baby,' she replied angrily. 'You see where it get you to? I don't know who to blame more, you or your no-good husband.'

'I would have you know, Urmila, that Ram was a very good husband to me.'

'What about that woman he used to have? You call that being good to you?'

'That is our business, Urmila. I'm the best judge of that, not you or anybody else.'

' "Our business". But hear she talk! Since when you getting so modern? "Our business." Huh!'

'Our business'. Mrs Lutchman had not realized she had used the phrase. She had never permitted herself such an intimacy, certainly not in the presence of the sisters. It was like a first declaration of love.

'Yes,' she repeated slowly. 'That was our business. Our business.'

Urmila, outraged, left the house convinced that Mrs Lutchman was beyond redemption.

Gowra ran a small shop which it was agreed that Mrs Lutchman would look after. Part of the money from the sale of the house would be set aside for paying Bhaskar's passage to England, should the need arise. She sold most of the furniture which it would have been impractical to take with them. She insisted, however, on keeping the wardrobe and the cabinet. The bowl-shaped lightshade from the sitting-room she also decided to take with her, and if it had been at all possible, she would doubtless have transported the avocado tree with her. The remaining lodger was given notice and she cried when he left. She felt she had never been given a proper chance to be a mother to them all. Circumstances had decreed that it should be otherwise.

A buyer was eventually found for the house, but she did not get as much for it as she had anticipated. 'Look,' she told the man, 'it near the Savannah. Two minutes' walk and you there.'

The buyer shook his head. 'And what about them gambling clubs and the cinema at the end of the street? Like you forget about those!'

'But look here,' she insisted, 'you getting a ready-made garden and a zabocca tree for nothing.'

'I wouldn't call that a garden,' the buyer said. 'I been noticing how much weed it have and is a funny kind of weed too, if you ask me.'

'That, my good man, is not a kind of weed. With care, you could make a really nice lawn out of that. You should see how pretty it does look when it have a lot of space to grow on.'

The buyer laughed out loud. 'Who fool you?'

Mrs Lutchman pursued the matter no further. She was, on the whole, not displeased with what she had got. As she told Bhaskar, 'I should count myself lucky for getting anything at all the way things are these days.'

'And what way are things these days, Ma?'

'Tight, son. Things are tight all round.'

Bhaskar grinned mockingly at her and lit a cigarette.

10

The removal van came late one afternoon. Mrs Lutchman stood on the pavement and supervised the packing. Mrs Mac-Kintosh, rocking on her verandah, stared coldly at her. Rover, who had not been in a car before, gave her a great deal of trouble and in the end they had to put him in a box. He whined piteously. When the house had been emptied, Mrs Lutchman took a final turn round the yard and bade farewell to the avocado tree and the roses. The sun lit up the stolid, rectangular front of the house. It was a bit more cracked and weathered than when they had first come, but all in all it had survived the years well. Her ambition to repaint it white had never been realized. She lingered for a moment by the front gate and pictured her husband as he was on the day he had died, a straw hat set rakishly over his head; his dark face staring up at her and trying to dissuade her from leaving him alone; and before him, on the ground, stalks of anthurium lilies and a pair of shears. Mrs Lutchman bowed her head, then walked quickly out of the yard and climbed into the van.

Chapter Nine

1

Coalmine lay in the heart of the sugar-cane country. The name of the town (in so far as it could be classified as anything other than a settlement) was misleading. There were no coal-mines in the area and, as far as anyone knew, there never had been.

Gowra Ramnath was in her early fifties, good-looking in a full-lipped way, with an originally very pale complexion, but reddened by the sun. As a result, she was nicknamed 'Cherry' by some of her friends. Like all Indian women of an earlier generation, she had been married young to a man of her parents' choosing. She had successfully given birth to seven children, six boys and a girl, in almost as many years. But then, unlike the Indian women of an earlier generation, she had rebelled after the seventh and refused to have any more.

The boys, tall and slim, had taken after their mother in complexion and good looks. The two eldest had already married and lived in San Fernando. The girl, to her mother's distress, was dark and ill-featured and Gowra, having a near pathological hatred of physical ugliness, had tended to treat her badly. It was an odd obsession in an otherwise tolerant woman, and though it had brought her much uneasiness and soul-searching, she was unable to rid herself of her prejudice. In her assessment of people, the soul invariably took second place to the body. She had liked Mrs Lutchman because, from the very beginning, she had been attracted by her fine nose. Like Mr Lutchman in the early days of his marriage, when Gowra thought of her friend, she tried to think only of her fine nose. Despite her unattractiveness, her daughter Sonya had become pregnant and was driven out of the house at Gowra's insistence. It was not moral outrage that caused her to do this; at least, it was not a conventional moral outrage. Ugliness, Gowra felt, barred its possessor from the enjoyments of the senses and thus her daughter's attempt to gratify her desires offended her. However, she had relented and Sonya now lived in the house with her child, though in the process she had become little more than bootblack to her brothers.

The Ramnaths were not exceptional people. Mr Ramnath worked, like his neighbours, on the sugar estate, drank heavily and, when the opportunity presented itself, beat or, more accurately, fought with his wife. Gowra's submission was a product of her husband's fancy. It was a well-known fact in Coalmine that there were occasions when she belaboured him, usually when he was drunk and unable to reply, for Ravi was a big, muscular man.

Ravi Ramnath was well over six feet tall, with a swarthy complexion and a crudely constructed face. He dressed invariably in khaki trousers and khaki shirts, held together by a broad leather belt. The impression of animal strength was reinforced by a pair of heavy, mudstained boots. Despite the impression of violence and brute strength he exuded, Ravi was a curiously patient man. At the end of her child-bearing period, his wife had had a succession of lovers, men in no way different from him, and done presumably out of an innate love for adventure. True enough, Ravi beat her, but without any real sense of conviction. It was what Coalmine expected of him and Ravi, conformist at heart, obliged. He never once threatened to disown her. As they grew older, he beat her less often and instead drank more heavily, while Gowra let longer periods pass between her affairs. The compromise worked well.

Although Mrs Lutchman and Gowra were about the same age, in their relations with each other Gowra had always assumed the role of senior partner. She had disliked Mr Lutchman intensely. 'He's underhand, I tell you, Baby. You could see it in his eyes and the way his mouth does always hang open.' She had said this constantly during the early days of their marriage and Mrs Lutchman did not contradict her. In the following years, she had kept a watchful eye on developments in the Lutchman household and vehemently condemned Mr Lutchman's liaison with Doreen. She had liked Romesh very much; 'more than my own children even,' as she had once told Mrs Lutchman, and was in the habit of finding excuses for his worst behaviour. 'If that boy come and live with me, he wouldn't give half the trouble he does give you,' she said, perhaps with some truth. Even now, when he had not been heard of for many years, she continued to refer to him with regret and affection.

She did not feel the same way towards Bhaskar. His ugliness told against him and, in addition to this, she had found him cold and unresponsive: he did not have the necessary sensuality which was a prerequisite for her liking anyone. He was 'Baby's son' and that was the only reason why she took any notice of him.

Gowra had invited them to live with her not because she needed any help in running the shop – it was small and Sonya could have done that adequately; not because of any sympathy for Bhaskar's misfortunes – she was convinced that everything had sprung from some ineradicable flaw in his character; but simply because she was distressed by 'Baby's bad luck' and, aware of her love for commerce, felt that pretending to work in the shop would 'take her mind off her worries'.

2

Coalmine was for the most part strung out along either side of a main road which cut its way through the sugar-cane fields. Where the Ramnaths lived, however, there were houses only on one side of the road. There were fields to the back and front of the house. When the Lutchmans arrived, the canes were nearly ready to be cut and all around was a green, leafy sea through which the wind crept day and night. Across the road from the Ramnaths, the fields were protected by a wire fence, grown brown and rusty with age and broken in places. Its purpose was to protect the canes from passing motorists. Not far beyond the fence, the fields were interrupted by a deep ravine which carried water only during the rainy season. For the rest of the year, its bed was dry and sandy and scattered with stones smoothed into strange shapes by the water. Sometimes people came there specially to collect these stones. It was

Coalmine's sole tourist attraction. Behind the house, the fields stretched away across a flat, unbroken plain to engulf the Usine whose chimneys showed clearly in the distance. The entire area was overhung by the sweetish, dusty smell of the countryside.

The Ramnaths' house was built entirely of wood and stood on pillars about twelve feet off the ground, designed to protect it from the flood waters that occasionally came sweeping across the fields from the ravine in the rainy season. Part of the area enclosed by the pillars was occupied by the shop. Here, the pounded earth floor had been covered over with boards. The shop sold chiefly rice and vegetables, but, as an added attraction, there were also bottles of Sunny Fizz soft drinks displayed on the shelves, together with jars of sweets. The rice, whose dry, musty smell was all-pervasive, was stored in huge bins standing under the counter. Much of the space behind and to the front of this counter was taken up with jute bags filled with a variety of vegetables: cabbages, yams, tomatoes and potatoes. There was also an impressive weighing scale of tarnished copper, calculated to appeal to Mrs Lutchman's commercial and aesthetic instincts.

Behind the partition separating the shop from the rest of this area, several hammocks had been slung from the beams of the ceiling. It was here that the family relaxed. There were many chickens and ducks running freely in the yard which was baked hard and yellow by the heat. An outhouse at the back served as a lavatory.

The family lived upstairs where there were four large, airy bedrooms, a sparsely furnished sitting-room and a primitive kitchen. Mrs Lutchman and Bhaskar shared the bedroom which overlooked the fields at the back of the house. It had been divided into two by a flimsy partition. The boys slept two to a room on narrow bunks. Sonya was banished to the sitting-room floor where she slept with her child.

3

From the first, Bhaskar kept very much to himself, but Mrs Lutchman immediately busied herself looking after the shop.

The commerical possibilities were limited but, as she told Bhaskar, she did not want Gowra and her family to think that she had come there to live as a 'parasite' off their charity and Bhaskar, being in one of his sullen moods, had replied that he could not think of any other way to describe it. Mrs Lutchman had shaken her head at him and hurried off downstairs to the shop.

Gowra took hardly any notice of Bhaskar. He retreated to his room as if he were under siege. However, he did not find being there entirely unpleasant. He derived some comfort from his self-imposed isolation and liked his room, his 'cell' as he was fond of describing it, with its bare boards swept clean every morning by Sonya. The furniture, as in the rest of the house, was minimal. There was a narrow bed along one wall, a dresser on which there was always a jug of water and two glasses patterned in red and green, and a vase of faded paper flowers.

Bhaskar gradually came to know Sonya better. She swept his room every morning and made the bed. After a while, perhaps as a result of their growing familiarity, she began bringing her child with her, a girl; and Bhaskar, taking the child on his knee, would play unenthusiastically with her while Sonya cleaned and tidied. Sonya, leaning the broom against her hip, would look at them and laugh. The child, just over a year old, was called Sita. One morning, Sonya brought him a cup of tea. Bhaskar was surprised and embarrassed. He had never really talked to Sonya before this, but now he felt that her kindness obliged him to do so.

'How old is the child, Sonya?' He was dangling Sita from his knees.

'She will be fourteen months soon, God be praised.'

Bhaskar examined the child's face. It was extremely dirty and he wondered vaguely why God should be praised. He looked at Sonya and saw that Sita did not resemble her a great deal. She would be much prettier than her mother. He tried to picture the unknown father and imagined a watery, handsome youth, trousers held up by a paper-thin belt and falling low on the waist. He recoiled from the image. His revulsion was not founded on any concern for Sonya. It was simply the image his fancy had created that repelled him and aroused a hostility bordering almost on hatred. He shuddered and shook himself.

'Do you see the father much, Sonya?' 'The father.' He had used it without thinking. It occurred to Bhaskar that it must rob the act of any saving dignity it might have had, and he regretted having said it. Still, it was suitably biological and he comforted himself with the reflection that Sonya must be accustomed to it and would not mind.

'Yes. From time to time, you know. He doesn't live around here any more now. He have a job in Port-of-Spain. Things get too hot for him here.' Sonya giggled. 'But he does still send the child a little money.' 'The child.' Sonya never referred to Sita by name. Bhaskar smiled. He began to feel more at ease with her.

'That's very good of him,' he replied seriously, staring up at Sonya's face.

She laughed. 'You wouldn't say so if you know all the rigmarole we had to go through to squeeze them few dollars out of him. You have no idea how much Pa had to threaten to beat him up before he agree to give the child money.'

'Did you love him?' Bhaskar swung Sita gently to and fro. She was screaming with delight.

Sonya's face went blank. The question seemed to astonish her. Then she laughed loudly, slapping her thighs.

'I suppose he was good-looking, then?' Bhaskar persisted.

Sonya considered. 'Yes. He wasn't bad. Yes. I would say he was good-looking. He had a lot of other girls running after him, you know. I wasn't the only one he give a child to.'

She was apparently proud of the fact, and, in a way, it did absolve her of a certain absurdity. There is always some comfort to be gained from numbers. It was the closest she ever came to justifying what had happened.

'Did you run after him or did he run after you?'

Sonya shrugged her shoulders. 'I never really stop to consider that,' she said.

'Would you have liked to marry him?'

Again the blank expression, but this time only fleeting. She shrugged her shoulders. 'Why should he want to marry me, eh? A lot of the other girls was better-looking than me. He just had to snap his fingers and hundreds of them would have gone running to him.'

Bhaskar was looking at her intently. He stopped swinging Sita and let her down gently on the floor. 'So you have no regrets?'

Sonya smiled. 'Regrets? You think I have time for regrets?' And she picked up her broom and started to sweep again.

Bhaskar, reviewing their conversation, did not find it hard to understand that the unprepossessing Sonya should have been so effortlessly seduced and Sonya herself betrayed no signs of shame or remorse or questioning wonder. 'After all, I kept chickens for a while,' he said. 'At bottom, that isn't very different from Sonya having a child.' He stared at Sita grubbing about on the floor in the wake of Sonya's broom. The pity he had begun to feel for the child suddenly vanished. He understood that it was just another way of pitying himself. Sonya herself was not a deserving case. She could hardly be described as a fallen woman: she had nowhere to fall from. Therein lay her strength. Degradation, insult, injury, had no meaning when applied to Sonya. She was susceptible only to the pain and pleasures of the body. If they were to become friends, she would treat him much as she treated the stones and the trees and the act that had led to this child with the dirty face: without judgement, without the thought that it could have been otherwise. In other words, Sonya had no ambitions. She was the most extreme fatalist Bhaskar had ever known.

They began going for walks together in the afternoon, climbing over the rotting wire fence and following the narrow track through the cane-fields down to the ravine where they sat on outcrops of rock and drew patterns in the sand with their toes. Sometimes they competed to see who could find the most strangely shaped stone and Bhaskar built up a collection of these in his bedroom. Their conversations were about trivial things: the height or name of a particular tree, how deep the water in the ravine was during the rainy season and whether or not it was likely to flood the fields. Sonya looked forward to these floods and confessed to Bhaskar that now and again she prayed for them to come. 'I would like to row all over the place in a boat,' she said. 'I would really enjoy that.' 'And suppose the house gets washed away, what would you do then?' Bhaskar replied. Sonya went into peals of childish laughter when he asked her this and said that she probably would enjoy that too. They spent at least an hour there each afternoon talking of such things, Sonya going into peals of laughter at all that Bhaskar said whether funny or not, while he dug his toes deeper and deeper into the sand and gazed at her with a kind of never-ending astonishment. They had become friends.

4

The sugar-cane fields were fired preparatory to reaping. The flames leapt above and within the mass of green leaves which hid the slender purple stalks. Charred fragments that travelled for miles floated light as wisps in the air, settling on the roads and in the yards of the houses. The sweetish country smell became tinged with the aroma of burnt charcoal and vegetation.

It was a busy time of year when the estate workers earned large sums of money, drank less (that would come later), leaving home early in the morning and returning later than usual in the evening on their bicycles. When the firing was finished, the workers, men and women, moved on to the fields where the burnt stalks, shorn of their leaves, stood curving up from the banked beds of earth, waiting to be cut down and loaded onto the lorries and carts to be taken to the factories.

Ravi was no exception. He was sterner and more taciturn and even his wife treated him with greater deference. That year the crop was going to be a good one and there was more work than normal to be done. Ravi worked extremely hard, helped by his sons. When he wheeled his bicycle into the yard late in the evening, Gowra rushed to prepare him a cup of tea and silently served him his food which she had kept warm and ready. He walked ponderously into the kitchen, his heavy black boots creaking and coated with mud, the sleeves of his khaki shirt rolled above his elbows, and washed his hands long and thoughtfully in the kitchen sink. He would take his seat at the table with an equally thoughtful deliberation. He ate slowly and grimly, chewing hard on his food and staring moodily out at the darkness, ignoring his wife who stood, one arm resting lightly on the back of his chair, watching him eat in respectful silence. The family, warned to keep away from him, retired downstairs to the hammocks.

Mrs Lutchman, anxious not to give cause for complaint, stayed in her room after she had closed the shop for the day. From her window, she followed all the activity in the fields. She watched the burning of the canes, and, when it was near enough, heard the roar and crackle of the flames through the undergrowth. She saw the furrows, first with the burnt canes standing up starkly out of the ground, like ruined pillars, and then the reapers invading with their machetes, cutting expertly at the stalks. The cut stalks were loaded onto trucks and carts which jolted across the fields to the lanes leading to the factory. Finally, the fields dark and deserted with a covering of black leaves and abandoned stalks; and, in the distance, the rattle of the railway taking the produce of other fields, perhaps to different factories.

She was impressed and a little frightened by the change in Ravi, though she knew that this man, at present so austere and sober, would, in a few weeks' time when his work was done, be once more transformed into that drunken, brawling individual who returned home only after the rum-shops had closed and fought with his wife. When the work was done, Mrs Lutchman watched the transformation and listened, alarmed, to the shouts and obscenities he and his wife flung at each other. Sometimes he was so drunk he could not climb the front steps and was forced to sleep all night in one of the hammocks downstairs. These changes in Ravi indicated as accurately as the coming of the rain the passage of the alternating seasons. It was something Mrs Lutchman would have to learn to live with.

5

During all this time Bhaskar had continued his weekly visits to Dr Metivier. He had never again mentioned the possibility of his going to England for 'further treatment'; and Mrs Lutchman, on her part, had pushed it to the back of her mind. She had watched with a mixture of anxiety and hope her son's growing intimacy with Sonya. Anxiety because she disapproved of his friendship with such a woman, hope because in her company he seemed so much more at ease and happy. With her capacity for seeing only what she chose to see, Mrs Lutchman dwelt on the latter, and eventually she came to forget the larger threat altogether.

Therefore, when Bhaskar calmly announced to her that Dr Metivier had definitely decided that it would be best for him to go to England, she behaved as though she had heard of it for the first time.

'But you shouldn't spring a thing like this on me so sudden, son.'

'What you mean "spring a thing like this on you so sudden?" I tell you about it months ago. Months ago!'

'You had say it wasn't definite.'

'At the time it wasn't. But is definite now. They have all the facilities over there.'

'But St Anns is a big place. They didn't have to send Rudranath to England and he was a lot worse than you.'

Bhaskar's eyes darkened. 'I don't see why you have to drag Rudranath into all this. I telling you what Dr Metivier say – what he say to me just a few hours ago. You feel you know better than Dr Metivier what good for me?'

'I is your mother. I sure to know a few things he don't know. It wasn't he who bring you up when you was small.'

Bhaskar clenched his fists. 'So, you know more than Dr Metivier? You trying to tell me he don't know his job? In that case you should write a letter of complaint to the Department of Health. Once they read what you say he would be out of that job in no time at all.'

'Don't get angry with me, Bhaskar. I was only wanting to find out.'

'Find out what?' he demanded harshly.

She shook her head. 'It don't matter. I'm sure he know what's best for you. And so, you definitely going?'

'Yes.'

'I suppose,' Mrs Lutchman said, lowering her eyes, and smoothing down the front of her dress, 'if they have all the facilities, as you say, and if he think a change of scene will do your health good, you will have to go. We better see about booking you a passage and that kind of thing. The money from the house should be more than enough to pay for that. When you have to go?'

'In about six weeks or so. There's no hurry.' Bhaskar avoided looking at his mother.

'And how you want to travel? By boat or plane?'

'Boat. I like travelling by boat.' He thought of Sonya.

'I never been on a boat in my life.' She raised her eyes. 'I always used to say to myself that if I had the money that is one thing I would like to do. Go to India, Benaras, and bathe in the Ganges. Your grandfather used to tell we about that when I was still a child. I does see so much people leaving but I never had cause to leave and go anywhere myself.' She laughed. 'But, time passing me by now and I getting too old to be thinking about such things. Anyway, I have a feeling that I is the sort of person who might get seasick, so what would be the point, eh?'

6

The news of Bhaskar's departure saddened Sonya. They sat in the ravine, digging their toes into the sand and throwing pebbles at a stump on the opposite bank. That evening she did not laugh, not even at his jokes.

'Is a surprising thing,' Sonya murmured, looking pensively at a stone she had picked up, 'I never thought of you leaving here. I used to think you had come to stay for good. Like your mother.'

'Come here to stay for good! You almost make it sound like a death sentence.'

'Your mother taking it well?'

'My mother could take everything,' Bhaskar said, without a trace of irony in his voice. He flung a pebble with all his strength at the stump. The pebble hit the stump. 'See if you can do that,' he challenged.

'I not as strong as you,' Sonya replied. Her voice was muffled. He looked curiously at Sonya and saw that she was crying.

7

The time for Bhaskar's departure was fast approaching and Mrs Lutchman decided to have a farewell puja for him. She would have liked to have done it on the grand Khoja scale but she did not have the necessary money and anyway there were many people, including some members of the family, who would not have come. Still, she dutifully sent them all invitations.

A small tent was built to the side of the house and chairs hired from a local firm. This last was not strictly speaking necessary since the Ramnaths possessed numerous benches, but it gave Mrs Lutchman that sense of occasion which she felt was lacking. She thought how mean everything looked when compared to the great constructions of the Khojas. There would be no one arriving several days beforehand (Ravi had expressly forbidden this) and no singing in a temporary, steaming kitchen. They would come early in the morning, well-dressed and without their children, sit quietly and watch the ceremony and leave after lunch. It was with a heavy heart that she went about the preparations.

The house had been cleaned thoroughly and even Sita looked sparkling. Ravi and Gowra had remained very much in the background and Mrs Lutchman, upset by their indifference, suspected that they disapproved of her having the puja there. The boys, apart from the youngest, had decided not to be present and Mrs Lutchman interpreted this as yet another slight. It was she and Sonya who had done most of the work.

The window was open in Bhaskar's room and a cool breeze, circulating gently, ruffled the curtains. The moon, almost full, hung low in the cloudless sky and shed a blue light on the empty fields. Mrs Lutchman was sitting on the bed. Beside her were the two neat, white rolls of cotton she had bought to give to the pundit. Bhaskar leaned against the windowsill, his back to his mother. He was smoking a cigarette and the blue smoke curled about the room, chased by the wind.

His passage had been booked for the following week and his

old trunks were piled along one side of the room. The torn and tattered labels of a previous journey plastered to the lids had not been removed. The ink had faded, but it was still just possible to read: 'Bhaskar Lutchman, Bombay, India. State-room 220'.

'Well, son, you getting everything in order?'

Bhaskar turned to face her. He had insisted on doing the packing himself this time. 'I think so, Ma. I still have a lot of time.'

She gazed at the trunks. They were all coated by a thin layer of dust. 'Eh boy! But you haven't even dusted them properly,' she said softly, and with a sad laugh got up and began to dust them.

'Sit down, Ma. Don't worry. I can do that myself. You must be tired.'

Mrs Lutchman, ignoring him, finished the dusting, and straightening her back, sighed.

'How long do you think you will have to stay there?' She was sitting on the bed again, holding a copy of the *Ramayan* open on her lap.

'It depends on what these people say and have to do. I don't know. Perhaps I might even settle there.'

'Settle there?' She attempted to feign surprise.

'Yes. Why not?' He spoke as if the idea had occurred to him for the first time. They were playing a game with each other. 'Maybe I could even get married.'

'Get married?' Again she attempted to feign surprise. The possible significance of those walks to the ravine had not been lost on her. Sonya was not the bride she would have chosen for her son.

'What so surprising about that? I've got to settle down some time.'

'But who would you get married to, son?'

Bhaskar winked at her. 'Sonya.'

Mrs Lutchman was less prepared for the announcement than she had thought. For a brief moment she lost her composure. She could not tell whether or not he was being serious. 'Sonya!' she echoed. 'But there will be a scandal, Bhaskar.'

'I don't see why there should be a scandal, Ma. She's a big

woman. I'm a big man. We get on well together. Why should there be a scandal?' He said this with an outward show of patience, much as he might have done if he were delivering a lecture. But the hint of mockery in his voice together with his efforts to be falsely reasonable, irritated her.

'So you don't see why there should be a scandal? And you call yourself a big man? What do you think your father would say if he was to hear you talking like that?' She looked at him. 'I suppose this is another of your "jokes" like you was telling me about that time when the chickens die and you didn't want to start up the business again?' She went up to the window and glanced bitterly at the blue darkness outside. Her powerlessness had reached its limit. She could only talk uselessly now and grapple with the shadows of all her desecrated ambitions which she felt crowding in upon her. It was to the shadows that she addressed herself now. 'She has a child, Bhaskar. A bastard child! She don't even have your education. Why you want to destroy yourself for? And me. I is not a selfish woman. I don't want to tell you how to live your life. That is one thing my children could never accuse me of. But I have never lived for myself either. I wasn't made to live like that. And what are you leaving me now? What will I have when you go away from me in a week or so? What?'

'What do you want me to tell you, Ma? That you was an unfortunate woman? And what about me? I was your unfortunate son. It's better for me to go away from you, don't you see? I'm a kind of corpse, as dead to you as Pa and Romesh is. You mustn't let my breathing in and out fool you. You must face up to the facts some time. We are all dead to you. As you say, you wasn't made to live for yourself. But then you wasn't made to live for the dead either. It's much better for me to go and leave you. You are a much stronger person than the rest of us put together. A much stronger person.' Bhaskar spoke almost in a whisper. 'I have to go, Ma. You must see that. Remember how you had to throw Pa bones back in the river because it was giving you nightmares? Well, my living here with you is another kind of nightmare. Let me go and the nightmare will stop. I tell you, Ma, it's the best way. The only way.'

'Sonya could only drag you down to her level, son. Don't go away from me.' She turned away from the window suddenly and threw herself at him, hugging and kissing him, the tears streaming freely down her cheeks. 'Oh Bhaskar! My son. Don't go from me. It's not even your child. Not my grandchild!' The anger had gone from her voice. Mrs Lutchman rested her head on her son's shoulder. She was pleading, cajoling. It was not the child she wanted to talk about, or Sonya, or their marriage for that matter. She could not say what it was she wished to talk about. Mrs Lutchman felt no personal hatred for Sonya and did not blame her for what was happening. She was too intelligent to do that. For her, she felt nothing, not even pity. What she felt now was not entirely new to her. She had experienced the same thing that night at the Khoja cattha when the sisters had danced and sung and Mr Khoja had played the drum. Later she had lain in the darkness beside her two sons, gripped by a wordless grief. Then, she had been fortunate enough to find a solution in her own home and family. Now, groping, there seemed to be nothing. Her eyes roamed over the labels on the trunks.

'What do you think Ravi and Gowra will do when they hear about it?'

'What can they do? Murder us? I wouldn't put that past Ravi and, if it come to that, then that's the end of it, not so?'

'Not for all of us, Bhaskar. Is not the end for all of us.'

Bhaskar had sprawled himself, half-on, half-off the bed. He jiggled his toes.

'How you intending to get married?'

'In the Registry Office.'

'I suppose that's the best thing in the circumstances.' She needlessly rearranged the rolls of cotton lying beside her.

'You will go over there together, I suppose?'

'If Ravi and Gowra give her the money. It's the least they could do.'

His mother nodded. There appeared to be nothing else to say on the subject. 'Tomorrow's not going to be like the old times, eh Bhaskar?'

Bhaskar looked at his toes. 'Different times, you know, Ma.'

His flippancy was painful, but she let it pass. 'Still, it used to be so nice, don't you think? You would be too small to remember how we used to go to the old house in the country, but Woodlands was nearly the same thing, except that Ma wasn't too well then. You remember how all the family and everybody else used to gather at your mamoo house. And all your mousies singing in the kitchen, and the children playing cricket on the pavement.' Her eyes shone as she spoke.

Bhaskar finished the examination of his toes. 'And old Khoja,' he said, 'playing God upstairs.' He softened, seeing the expression on his mother's face. 'I don't mean it like that, Ma. I was only being foolish. It's a pity that things not like that any more. In a way, it's a great pity.' He touched her shoulders lightly.

Mrs Lutchman gazed gratefully at him. 'Well, I mustn't keep you up any more. We've got to get up early tomorrow and you must have a good sleep tonight.' She kissed him. 'I'll wake you in the morning.' The moon had drifted away from the window, but the breeze continued to blow and the curtains moved soundlessly.

8

It was still dark when Mrs Lutchman awoke. She did not get out of bed immediately, but lay there staring up at the ceiling. A cock crowed from just below the window and another answered it from the yard next door. Mrs Lutchman huddled under her blanket and listened. The breeze had died away during the night, but it was cool in the room so early in the morning. Her eyes gradually grew accustomed to the darkness and she could make out the black bulge of the wardrobe, the shape of a chair with her clothes draped over it, the cabinet and a dresser, like Bhaskar's, with a jug of water and two glasses. However, there were no paper flowers. On one of the walls, there was a picture of the god Shiva trapped in the contortions of his dance; but whether of creation or destruction she was unable to tell.

She got out of bed reluctantly and went into Bhaskar's part of the room. He was sound asleep and breathing heavily. She could see that one of his feet had shaken itself free of the blanket. Mrs Lutchman glided hesitantly over his indeterminate form, but did not wake him.

She had seen her successive dreams, at bottom one dream, wither and dissolve. She reviewed the stages of that failure: a marriage so many of whose happinesses she had had to invent for herself and which, so it seemed to her, had ended on the brink of success; a son virtually dead to her; the house that had had to be sold; and now Bhaskar, failed doctor, teacher and chicken farmer, on the point of leaving her and sealing that departure with a worthless marriage to a worthless girl. Today, she must perform her final act of dispossession. All that was left to her, apart from the few sticks of furniture she had brought with her, was the dog; and even he had run away twice, trying unsuccessfully to make his way back to the house near the Queen's Park Savannah. She would be ending her days a remote and curious figure, lost in the house of the Ramnaths.

The sky had begun to lighten and the clouds on the horizon flushed pink. Mrs Lutchman roused herself and tapped Bhaskar on the shoulder.

'Son, son. Get up. It's time,' she bent and whispered in his ear.

Bhaskar turned over and grunted. He opened his eyes and stared at her sleepily, almost without recognition. 'What's the time?'

'It must be nearly six now.'

'I won't be long.' He closed his eyes again, licking his lips.

She slipped silently out of the room and went to wash and get dressed. Sonya was still asleep with Sita curled close against her stomach. Mrs Lutchman shook her gently and told her to get up.

The sky had lightened considerably by the time Bhaskar got out of bed. He leaned out of the window and looked at the pale, tinted clouds and at the dark, wet fields. He shivered a little and waited for Sonya to bring him his cup of tea.

9

Mrs Lutchman busied herself downstairs. Together with Sonya, she dismantled the hammocks, arranged the chairs and benches, cut flowers and draped them round the images on the puja mound and washed the banana leaves on which the guests were to be fed. Gowra appeared and helped to make the prasad, a skill which Mrs Lutchman did not possess. The smells of cooking penetrated the house: burnt sugar and flour for the prasad and after that the mingled aromas of boiling rice, curried vegetables and dahl.

The guests began to arrive at ten o'clock. Ramnarace made an early appearance, arriving – flamboyantly attired in bright green overalls and a crash helmet – on a motor-cycle which he drove into the yard with needless violence. He came in carrying large, brown volumes of the Hindu scriptures together with an assortment of other smaller books piled on top of these (Ramnarace was prepared for any religious contingency). They had been strapped to the pillion of his motor-cycle and one of them had almost had its cover blown away. He dumped the books carelessly on one of the benches and slipped smoothly out of his overalls to reveal an immaculate and impressive grey suit.

He was a thin, spare man whose undeniably ascetic appearance (as his detractors said, probably his sole qualification to be a pundit) was enhanced by a cultivated soft-spokenness and a pair of round, rimless glasses which he wore perched affectedly low on his nose. But, physique and manner apart, he did not behave in any way that was noticeably holy, and it was a source of constant wonder and speculation how he had managed to acquire his religious skills. There had been some scandal about his marriage and to counteract rumours of his infidelity he now lived ostentatiously alone. His wife had left him. Unfortunately, this had failed to quell the gossip that circulated about him and his reputation as a womanizer persisted. Happily, these slanders did have one positive advantage. Ramnarace was a cheap pundit. Doubtless, painfully aware how slender his claims to the religious life were, he made few demands on his customers, content to receive two instead of four rolls of cotton, and thus he was in constant demand by poorer Hindus.

Mrs Lutchman bustled up to meet him as he stood casting a professional eye on the arrangements made for the morning's business. She clasped her hands prayerfully before him and Ramnarace, returning the greeting, asked if everything was in order. Satisfied that everything was as it ought to be, he disappeared upstairs and went to sleep.

Only about half the people Mrs Lutchman had invited came. Though by nature an optimist, she had not expected it to be otherwise and her preparations reflected this. If everyone had turned up there would not have been enough chairs and food. Those who had come were mostly women, dressed in their best clothes, heavily perfumed, powdered and jewelled. Urmila was there in all her Sunday finery, determined to prove her forgiving nature. She was now the richest among the sisters. Her grocery had expanded into a supermarket and she had built a new house with tiles everywhere. It was rumoured that she was supported by Jagdev. She sat next to Shantee, looking round defiantly at the other guests. Shantee had for some time been running a small shop, but that did not appear to be getting off the ground. She had willingly attached herself to Urmila, whom she had come to regard as her patron. They went everywhere together. Badwatee sat apart from them, though she too was looking defiantly around her, though for different reasons. After years of flirtation, she had been received into the Roman Catholic Church. She sat next to Darling, who, ailing and wracked by diabetes, lived with her off the meagre income they gained from their lands. Indrani, of course, had not come.

The guests sat fanning themselves, waiting to be served, with gestures and looks that implied they had many more important things to do after this and were impatient to be off and rejoin the mainstream of their concerns. Mrs Lutchman, sensing this, became hasty and flustered.

The Khojas, as was their custom, were among the last to arrive. Mr Khoja, as a mark of his status, was allowed to park in the yard. His presence there resulted from the feeling that it was right and proper to patronize his former employee. He had the casual, relaxed air of the man who, though busily engaged in grappling with the turmoils of the world, had given himself a holiday. This was deceptive. Mr Khoja's political ambitions lay in ruins after the failure of the Endeavour Infants' School, although he had not given up without a struggle. After the closure of the school, his passion for educational reform had been decidedly lukewarm. Instead, he had chosen to concentrate on the housing problem, but Mr Khoja's heart was not in it and it was generally agreed that his views were, on the whole, orthodox and uninspired. Then that too had been quietly dropped and Mr Khoja, at the age of sixty, had found himself without a vocation. Even his autobiography failed to inspire him. Like Doreen, he discovered that he 'couldn't write', and the ten pages or so he had actually written lay gathering dust in his study. To make matters worse, he had recently developed a kidney complaint.

In marked contrast to his wife, he had grown much thinner and his saffron complexion had deepened. Mrs Khoja, fat and sickly, with a childish, open-mouthed smile, was wearing a gloriously red sari bordered in gold. She, on the other hand, had discovered a new reason for living. Her husband's kidney complaint had come to her as a godsend. It had given her something to care for and talk about.

When they arrived, the sisters studied them with undisguised hostility. Urmila jangled her bracelets and her nose twitched, and Shantee and Darling followed up with feebler versions of their contempt. Badwatee, the heretic, stared stolidly at the ground. Thus there was only Mrs Lutchman left to pounce in and devour the great man.

Mrs Khoja giggled uncomfortably at the sisters. 'His kidneys . . .' she began, then stuttered and fell silent when she recognized the immutable hostility written on those faces. She turned to Mrs Lutchman. 'Let we go to the kitchen, Baby, and see what the women are doing.' Mrs Lutchman led the way. There were no 'women' in the kitchen and her presence there flattered and gratified Mrs Lutchman.

Ravi, awed by Mr Khoja, wore a gaberdine suit many sizes too small for him, with matching two-toned shoes, a combination he reserved for occasions like these. He shuffled up to Mr Khoja, who had positioned himself modestly in one of the back rows of chairs, and uttered a few reverential words. Mr Khoja was friendly though condescending, and Ravi was delighted.

Ramnarace reappeared, clad in a dhoti and bare to the waist, with a silver chain hanging round his neck. He was followed by Bhaskar, also dressed in a dhoti, and Mrs Lutchman wearing a new dress she had bought. Ramnarace managed to look remarkably severe, Bhaskar uninterested and Mrs Lutchman mournful. The three participants grouped themselves round the puja mound. The talking in the room died away and Ramnarace in an unsteady, quavering voice proceeded to chant from one of the books.

The puja went on a long time. The voice of the pundit droned on and one or two people fell asleep, waking at intervals with a start when Ramnarace blew the conch horn and rang the bells. A group of children from the neighbouring houses, attracted by the noise, stood on the grassy verge at the side of the road and watched. Bhaskar did not understand what was happening. He executed Ramnarace's directives mechanically, following sleepily the delicate movements of the pundit's hands as he picked up one object or another and indicated what he should do. Mrs Lutchman, alert and bright-eyed, knew what had to be done and did not wait to be told. Sometimes she anticipated Ramnarace and this annoyed him. Bhaskar saw how genuine and devout her profession of faith was. Occasionally, she caught his eye and smiled. He gazed at her hands, the worn, sun-blackened fingers pressed closely against each other, then at her hair, which she wore loose and which showed the first streaks of grey. Now and then, she would close her eyes and her face would be distorted in an effort of prayer and concentration.

His attention roamed from the chanting Ramnarace and contemplation of his mother and settled on Mr Khoja, who had closed his eyes and thrown his head back. Bhaskar smiled. The conch horn was blown and the bell rung at intervals. There was no wind and the odour of burning incense was overpowering. A young child whimpered and its mother in a low, angry whisper tried to silence it, without success. Feet shuffled restlessly and there were frequent bouts of coughing.

At last it was over. Garlands of red and yellow flowers hung round the necks of mother and son and the guests, rising, stretched themselves and, talking loudly, drifted off to the long tables laid with banana leaves. The women did not wait for the men to eat first. That too was a thing of the past.

10

After he had eaten, Bhaskar chatted with the guests. They gave him the names of people they knew in London and their addresses. Bhaskar, pretending to be delighted, wrote them down on scraps of paper. He went up to the Khojas. He watched Mrs Khoja's fingers scrape the yellow grains of rice and dahl between the ribs of the banana leaf.

She looked up at him. 'When you leaving?'

'Next week, mamee.'

Mrs Khoja scrutinized his stomach. 'You must take good care of your kidneys, boy. They is the most precious part of your body. You mustn't let them catch cold in England. God only give you two kidneys to last you through the whole of your life. Take care.'

Bhaskar promised to take care of his kidneys. Mrs Khoja shook her head disapprovingly. 'Apart from the danger to your kidneys,' she went on, 'you should know your place is here with your mother, boy. She not getting any younger, you know. You shouldn't be leaving she all by sheself.' Mrs Khoja scraped away at the food with her fingers, a picture of contentment.

Bhaskar, frowning, turned to Mr Khoja. 'I forget to ever thank you for that pamphlet you give me to read, Mamoo. You are a first-rate writer.'

Mr Khoja's eyes darkened. 'It's nothing, nothing,' he said hastily, glancing at his wife.

'But I really enjoyed it. Didn't Ma tell you? All that thing about Rousseau and Nature. It was very inspiring.'

'Yes, yes. All that's in the past now. It was too pure a vision for these modern times.'

'I will never forget that story you told me about the fireflies either. Is that doctor still alive?'

'Doctor? What doctor?' Mr Khoja toyed unhappily with his food.

'The doctor who when he was a boy had to catch fireflies because his parents were so poor.'

'Oh! That doctor! I haven't seen him for a long time,' Mr Khoja replied vaguely.

'I always wanted to meet him.'

'Who?'

'The doctor.'

'If you weren't going away to England I would have introduced him to you.'

'You shouldn't talk so much, Govind. You know it's not good for your kidneys. You should know about that, Bhaskar. You was going to be a doctor.'

'I didn't get as far as the kidneys,' Bhaskar said good-naturedly.

'Yes,' Mr Khoja sighed, in response to some inner prompting. 'I'm setting down all that in my autobiography.'

Urmila, who was sitting behind them, snorted and whispered malevolently to Shantee.

'Your autobiography, Mamoo?'

'Yes. My Confessions. I'm writing my Confessions.' Mr Khoja could scarcely conceal his distress.

'It's going to be all about your ideas on education, I suppose?' Bhaskar prompted him.

'Only partly. There's going to be a lot about the housing problem in it as well.'

'I didn't know Rousseau talked about that.'

'Not directly,' Mr Khoja admitted. 'It's going to take me a long time to finish though. My kidneys, you know.'

'Yes. You must be very careful.'

'I've been telling him the same thing for these past months,' Mrs Khoja said. 'But he wouldn't believe me.'

Bhaskar laughed and moved on.

'I thought you didn't want anyone to know you was writing your autobiography,' Mrs Khoja said reproachfully, when Bhaskar was out of earshot.

Mr Khoja sighed. He seemed weary. 'I don't want all these people to think I'm a fool, Sumintra. They must know that Govind Khoja is still a force to be reckoned with on this island. I don't want to give anybody the impression that I'm a beaten man.'

'Well, the main thing, as I see it, is to take care of your kidneys. I'm sure all this writing you want to do not good for it.'

'Yes. You right, Sumintra. I wasn't taking the state of my kidneys into account. I must take great care,' he said.

11

After they had eaten, the guests began taking their leave of Mrs Lutchman and Bhaskar. Bhaskar smiled agreeably with everyone including Urmila, who shook his hands coldly and nodded 'significantly' at Mrs Lutchman. He promised to write to them all. Mr Khoja jangled his car-keys affably and said he would send him a copy of his book when it was published. Mrs Khoja kissed him on the cheek. Ramnarace was among the last to leave. He wagged, for reasons best known to himself, a warning finger at Bhaskar and left, as he had come, with the same needless violence, disappearing down the road in a flash of green.

And so they had all gone and the house was quiet again.

Ravi took off his suit and reverted to his khaki uniform and boots. He was rude and ill-tempered and after quarrelling with Gowra went to the rum-shop. Mrs Lutchman changed from her new dress into her working clothes and, with Sonya's help, began clearing away the debris. There were bits of food and soiled banana leaves everywhere. Chairs and tables had been scattered in the yard and under the house and the flies had descended in hordes.

Mrs Lutchman called in those of the children who were still standing on the road and gave them what remained of the food. The prasad, however, she kept for Rover. She gathered the chairs together, cleaned and folded them and stacked them against the pillars. She cleaned and scoured the tables and threw the banana leaves into an overgrown ditch at the back of the house. The sticks of incense continued to burn on the puja mound, though more feebly. She gazed at the mound and at the brass images of the gods and goddesses, the bright flowers which she had placed on them earlier that morning now limp and faded.

It was quiet and extremely hot. Bhaskar had gone to sleep. Ravi was out getting drunk and Gowra, during these last days so unfriendly, had disappeared. The day had continued windless and there was not a cloud in the sky. How flat and withered everything seemed at that moment: the fields with the young sugar-cane, the blue sky, the spotless yard which Sonya had sprinkled and swept.

'Rover!'

Rover came bounding up to her, and snatched the parcel of prasad she was holding up teasingly before him. She gazed at him as, with his tail wagging, he buried his head in the paper parcel.

'What a little Hindu you is,' she said. 'A real Hindu dog.'

12

Bhaskar and Sonya were married the day before they left for England. Ravi had taken the news badly and there had been a violent quarrel in which he abused both Mrs Lutchman and Bhaskar. As for Sonya, he slapped and kicked her and vowed to murder her. But after this outburst he had gone away and got drunk, remaining like that for days. Gowra, though no less displeased than her husband, controlled her temper better. She felt she 'owed it to Baby', comforting herself with the further reflection that if Sonya was to have a husband, it was appropriate that she should marry someone like Bhaskar, a man probably as ugly as she was.

'One mouth less to feed,' she told Ravi, when he had sobered up. His bout of dissipation had lowered his resistance and, conceding the truth of this, he reluctantly gave his permission and, even more reluctantly, agreed to pay the passage (third-class) of Sonya and her child to England.

Bhaskar and Sonya got married in the Registry Office in Port-of-Spain. Mrs Lutchman was there and so was Gowra.

Ravi had decided to stay away. 'I don't know what I might decide to do at the last minute,' he said.

The next day, Mrs Lutchman made that journey to the docks, already so familiar to her, and sat in the reception room gazing at the gay posters of tropical beaches. Bhaskar insisted that she leave before the boat sailed and so, some minutes before he embarked, she kissed them both goodbye and left.

13

With Sonya gone, Mrs Lutchman was given full charge of the shop. Twenty years before, she would have thrilled to the prospect that it opened before her. Regretfully, she understood that it had come twenty years too late. Mrs Lutchman had lost her taste for commerce and longed now for nothing.

The shop was closed during the afternoons, business being virtually non-existent then, and Mrs Lutchman, her offers of help about the house refused, retired to her room. She was grateful for the solitude it gave her. She enjoyed sitting at the window, hung with cheap lace curtains that fluttered constantly in the breeze blowing in from over the cane-fields. Protected from the noise of the traffic on the road running past the front of the house, the room was quiet and, sitting at the window, she would look out at the chimneys of the factory, listening to the faraway sounds of tractors and men's voices and the rumble of the trains on the railway that lay hidden somewhere among the fields.